MATCH UP

EDITED BY

LEE CHILD

SPHERE

First published in the United States in 2017 by Simon & Schuster
First published in Great Britain in 2017 by Sphere

1 3 5 7 9 10 8 6 4 2

Printed and bound in Great Britain by Clays Ltd, St Ives plc

Papers used by Sphere are from well-managed forests
and other responsible sources.

Sphere
An imprint of
Little, Brown Book Group
Carmelite House
50 Victoria Embankment
London EC4Y 0DY

An Hachette UK Company
www.hachette.co.uk

www.littlebrown.co.uk

MATCH UP

ALSO BY THE INTERNATIONAL THRILLER WRITERS

Face Off

For the members of International Thriller Writers

CONTENTS

INTRODUCTION

NORMALLY, I'M NOT MUCH OF A JOINER. BUT BACK IN 2005, WHEN I was asked to be part of a fledging group of writers who were forming a new association, I immediately said yes. It was called International Thriller Writers (ITW), and the whole idea intrigued me. Finally, an organization devoted entirely to the thriller genre. I signed up, becoming a founding member. I was so onboard I accepted a position on the first board of directors, then, a few years after that, served as copresident. I have to say, I've enjoyed every minute of my involvement. So when I was asked to be the editor of this anthology, I jumped at the chance.

Everything about ITW is different. Its motto is a warning to itself. *When we imitate we fail.* One of the organization's greatest innovations was the elimination of dues to its members. Full membership (available to working thriller writers) has long been free. To support itself, ITW publishes anthologies. It began with *Thriller* (2006), edited by James Patterson, the first collection of thriller short stories ever, now regarded as one of the largest-selling anthologies of all time. *Thriller 2* came in 2009, edited by Clive Cussler, then *Love Is Murder* in 2012, edited by Sandra Brown. In between those was a young-adult volume *Fear* (2010), spearheaded by R. L. Stine. ITW also made a name for itself in audio with *The Chopin*

Manuscript (2007), edited by Jeffery Deaver, which won the Best Audio of the Year, and *The Copper Bracelet* released in 2009.

Then came *Face Off*.

The pairing of branded writers, along with their iconic characters, in the same story. Twenty-three contributors, eleven adventures. Published in 2014, *Face Off* became a *New York Times* bestseller. The idea was so popular that we try it again with eleven new pairs of branded writers, together with their iconic characters.

Only this time it's male versus female.

A match up.

And what fun.

The following pages are filled with some wonderfully unique tales. Once-in-a-lifetime pairings. Where else would Steve Berry's Cotton Malone enter the magical world of Diana Gabaldon? Or my character, Jack Reacher, square off with Kathy Reich's incomparable Temperance Brennan? Then there's Lisa Scottoline's feisty Philadelphia lawyer, Bennie Rosato's, chance encounter with Nelson DeMille's former-NYPD homicide detective, John Corey.

Eleven unique tales.

All a joy to read.

Each is preceded by an intro where I detail the process the team went through in melding their different characters. Many of the teams had never met each other before. None had ever written together. This is truly a novel experience—for both the writers and the readers. At the end are bios on the contributors, a chance for you to learn more about these amazingly talented individuals.

So settle in.

And enjoy.

Match Up.

Lee Child
June 2017

SANDRA BROWN AND C. J. BOX

S ANDRA BROWN BEGAN WRITING IN 1981. BEFORE THAT SHE worked as a model and in television, including weathercasting and feature reporting on the nationally syndicated program *PM Magazine*. And though she's published over seventy novels, with over eighty million copies in print worldwide, she admits to one handicap.

She's short story challenged.

"It's just not something I've written a whole lot of," she says.

Luckily, C. J. Box does not suffer from that affliction, which made him the perfect partner for Sandra. Chuck is a Wyoming native and has worked as a ranch hand, surveyor, fishing guide, and small-town newspaper reporter, and he's even owned an international tourism marketing firm. He has over twenty novels to his credit, and short stories are not unfamiliar. He also has a character, Joe Pickett, so the idea was to connect Sandra's Lee Coburn with Pickett. By a stroke of great luck, at the end of Sandra's 2011 novel *Lethal,* Coburn ended up in, of all places, Jackson Hole, Wyoming.

Which is Joe Pickett country.

Talk about fate.

Everything just got easier after that.

Together, Sandra and Chuck plotted the story. Then Chuck wrote the first draft and sent it to Sandra for an edit and rewrite. They went back and forth, until both were pleased with the outcome. Chuck's comment summed it all up.

"Sandra was a dream to work with it."

You're going to like this unexpected encounter between two of the most rugged protagonists out there today. Both harken back to another time, and the story's title poses an interesting question.

Honor & . . .

HONOR & . . .

WHEN JOE PICKETT SET OUT THAT MORNING, HE HADN'T ANTICI-pated coming face-to-face with a killing machine.

It was an unseasonably warm late-September day. As a favor to another game warden, Joe was scouting the western slope of the Gros Ventre Range above Jackson Hole, deep in the black timber.

When he heard the staccato series of high snapping sounds in the distance, he reined his gelding Rojo to a stop and leaned forward in the saddle to listen with his head turned slightly to the southeast, the direction from which he thought the sounds had come.

For a time all Joe heard were Rojo's snuffles and snorts as he caught his breath after their hard climb. Then, two heavy booms rolled through the trees at ground level, and Joe realized that what had started out as a routine day had turned potentially dangerous—for three reasons.

First, the sounds weren't natural. It was a popular misconception that the mountain forests were silent because there were few people in them. Fact was, the wilderness was a riot of noise. Elk, moose, and grizzly and black bears broke through tree limbs and sometimes knocked over dead trees, not so much walking through the brush as crashing through it. Add to their racket chattering squirrels, shrieking hawks, and wolves and coyotes howling at a pitch that seemed designed to curdle human blood, and the mountains became damned noisy.

But there was a natural rhythm to the cacophony.

What Joe had heard intruded on that natural rhythm in a way that set his senses on high alert.

Second, the source of the sounds was curious. He was nearly sure he'd heard a flurry of semiautomatic gunshots from multiple weapons fired at once, followed by a pause. Then came the two heavy, high-caliber shots.

It didn't compute.

He was well schooled on the firing sequences of hunters after big game. True sportsmen prided themselves on expending as few bullets as possible. It was about the hunt, and accuracy, not raking an animal with gunfire that would spoil the meat. Besides that, the opening of elk season on this particular mountain range was a week away.

Last, the area was remote and without roads. Down in the valley were thousands of rental cabins, camping sites, and hotels, all easily accessible. But it took an effort to get up here, this high in the mountains, and no one would go to the trouble without good reason.

The lawman in him wondered what that reason could be.

Of course, he could just leave it alone. This wasn't even his district. The only reason he was in Teton County was because the local game warden, Bill Long, had asked him to help check on remote elk hunting camps because he couldn't get to all of them before opening day.

Joe was granting the favor, partially in order to give his family—wife, Marybeth, and teenage daughters, Sheridan, Lucy, and April—a mini-vacation. Gauging by the number of shopping bags that were piling up in the corner of their hotel room, Joe figured he would lose money on the deal rather than make a little extra, but there were so few perks for his family in his line of work that if he could treat them to a few days in Jackson Hole, he was happy to do it.

He could report hearing the distant gunfire to Bill Long, who might even know who was responsible for it and have a logical explanation.

Or maybe not.

But Bill definitely wouldn't want him to wade into a potentially dangerous situation on an unfamiliar mountain without backup or local support. So maybe he should—

Pow-whop.

Dammit.

Another heavy shot.

And it came with the abrupt, brutal, closed-in point-blank sound of a bullet hitting flesh, which carried a completely different sound than a miss.

It was a game changer.

He turned his horse toward the southeast, did a mental inventory of his shotgun in its saddle scabbard and handgun in its holster, clicked his tongue, and said, "Let's go, Rojo."

He could smell the camp before he could see it. Clinging to the brush and evergreen boughs was the stale odor of grease from cooking fires mixed with the sweat of dirty men.

That, and the smell of gunpowder.

It was the smell of a hundred elk camps Joe had entered over the years.

Without warning Rojo snorted and balked. The horse detected something ahead that Joe hadn't noticed.

He urged him on.

Entering a wilderness campsite for the first time was always fraught with tension. Small, bonded groups enjoyed getting away from it all. Inside the camp were guns, alcohol, and as often as not, clouds of testosterone. The last thing hunters wanted to see was a representative of the Game and Fish Department asking them questions and checking licenses and permits. And the last thing Joe wanted to do was surprise them or appear threatening, because he was always outnumbered and outgunned.

It was part of the job.

"Hello, there," he called out. "Just your friendly neighborhood game warden here."

There was no response, although Joe thought he heard footfalls through the brush on the far side of the camp. Someone running away?

"Hello?" he called out again.

Rojo walked forward, taking halting steps. Joe sat tall in the saddle and didn't look down as he untied a leather string that secured the butt of his shotgun in its scabbard. He hoped he wouldn't have to pull it out.

He pushed through the trees into a rough clearing and took it in all at once. Four dirty wall tents, stumps where trees had been cut down, camp chairs for sitting, a large blackened fire ring that was still smoldering, and trash strewn everywhere. It was a crude and dirty camp, he thought, something out of the Gold Rush days or built by mountain men just before the winter roared in. He decided he didn't much like the people in the camp. They had little respect for the wilderness and practiced poor camp hygiene.

Walls of trees surrounded the clearing. Beyond them the mountains rose vertically in three directions to their treeless summits. Granite outcroppings pierced through the trees like knuckles, a few of them topped with massive eagle nests. Just inside the tree line were a small mountain of coolers and cartons of canned food. A yellow Gadsden DON'T TREAD ON ME flag with a coiled rattlesnake hung from a crooked flagpole made of a bark-stripped lodgepole pine. On the far side of the clearing was the framing and half walls of a large log building still under construction. The walls were no more than four feet high. It looked like a crude open shoebox. Hand tools—axes, saws—leaned against the outside of the structure.

What appeared to be a bundle of dirty clothing was lying half in, half out of the open framed door of the log building. Only when he rode closer did he realize it was the body of a bearded man with wide-open eyes and a bullet hole in the center of his forehead.

The body was twitching in what might be death throes, and the smell of gunpowder hung bitter in the still air.

The fatal wound was that recent—the kill shot Joe had heard.

He tried to keep his heart from racing by placing his right hand over his breast pocket and pressing.

It didn't help.

He cleared the shotgun from the scabbard before dismounting and walked Rojo across the opening to tie the gelding up to a dead tree. Rojo was understandably spooked and he wanted his horse to stay put. Before calling in the incident to dispatch on the handheld radio or the satellite phone—both of which he'd left back in his saddlebag on the horse—Joe wanted to check on the condition of the victim in the doorway.

He took a deep breath and raised his gaze up above the treetops as he walked across the clearing toward the fallen man. The hair on the back of his neck was standing up. He could see no movement on the mountainsides or even an eaglet poking its head up in one of the nests. But he had the feeling—and it was only a feeling—that he was being observed from above.

Maybe whoever had shot the man and run off had come back?

He leaned his shotgun against the log wall and squatted next to the gunshot victim. He was grateful to be low and out of sight, on the other side of the building.

He reached out and pressed his fingertips to the man's dirty neck. No pulse. The victim was indeed dead now and completely still. His gray eyes were staring but unseeing, and a single black trail of blood from the bullet hole had congealed on his face next to his nose. Joe wanted to close the man's eyes but not badly enough to touch him again.

The dead man stank as if he'd been wearing the same clothes—greasy jeans, heavy boots, layers of undershirts, shirts, and Dickies denim jacket—for weeks. His skin was ashen and his beard was long and unkempt. He studied the body and noticed the glint of a steel rifle muzzle protruding an inch from beneath the man's shoulder. Obviously, he'd fallen on top of his weapon and it was pinned beneath him.

The muzzle was equipped with a tubular conical guard. A military feature used to reduce the flash of a shot, not an accessory needed by hunters. Just like the camp didn't look or feel like a typical elk camp, the victim didn't appear to have been an ordinary hunter.

Joe had never run across hunters who erected log buildings or raised flags.

What was going on here?

He knew he shouldn't move the body before he photographed it or before a Teton County forensics tech arrived. He couldn't determine if the man had been murdered while standing in the doorway and collapsed on his rifle, or some other scenario. And he wondered if the rifle pinned below the body had been the one he'd heard firing multiple times before the three heavy booms. It certainly looked like the kind of military-style black rifle chambered-in .223 that would make the snapping sound he'd heard.

Maybe, he thought, he'd been mistaken about the number of guns firing prior to the heavy booms. Maybe the dead man had fired his rifle as fast as he could pull the trigger and the shots had echoed around on top of one another until it sounded like multiple shooters.

But who was the victim shooting at?

And who had put a bullet hole through his head?

As he grasped the log wall to push himself back to his feet, Rojo suddenly snorted and reared behind him. He wheeled around to see his horse pull back in sudden fright and with enough momentum to pull the dead tree it was tied to on top of him. The trunk largely missed Rojo but several spindly branches raked the horse's haunches as it fell. Rojo, white-eyed with terror, bolted across the clearing in the direction from which they'd come.

"Stop," Joe yelled.

He watched helplessly as his horse—stirrups flapping on the sides and reins dancing in the air behind its mane—vanished into the northern wall of trees. He took a few steps toward where Rojo had gone, but pulled up short. He'd never run down his gelding. He could only hope that the horse wouldn't go far and that he could catch him later.

That's when he felt a presence on his left, an anomaly set against the dark of the trees.

He turned.

A man had emerged from the timber.

He stood silent and still, but his cold, Nordic eyes were locked on Joe. He was tall and lean and despite his stillness seemed tightly coiled. He wore jeans, cowboy boots, and a light jacket that had seen some wear.

Instantly, Joe knew that this guy wasn't a tourist. Nor was he a stranger to the mountain West. In his right fist was a large squared-off semiauto, a M1911 Colt .45. It looked like a weapon large enough to have punched the big hole in the dead man's forehead.

Joe was grateful the gun was pointed down because he knew it could be leveled and aimed at him much faster than he could retrieve his shotgun from where it was propped against the log wall of the unfinished building. And judging by how the man stood with his feet set, one slightly behind the other, and his shoulders squared, he had no question at all who would kill whom if it came to a gunfight.

He nodded his hat brim to where Rojo had disappeared. "See what you did there."

The man shrugged. "A game warden should have a better-trained horse."

Now that hurt.

•◆•

LEE COBURN DIDN'T LIKE IT THAT THE UNIFORMED MAN WAS STAND-ing there beside the guy he'd killed. He knew what it looked like, and he didn't want to take the time to explain himself or what had happened.

The game warden, this skunk at the party, wore a red shirt with a pronghorn antelope patch on the shoulder, faded Wranglers, outfitter boots, and a stained gray Stetson. He was lean and of medium height and build, with silver staining his short sideburns. He'd seen the game warden glance toward the shotgun he'd left against the log wall, but no effort had been made to lunge for it. Nor had the guy reached for the handgun on his hip.

"I'm a Wyoming game warden. Name's Joe Pickett. I'm afraid I need to ask you to drop your weapon and follow me into town so we can get this sorted out."

He could hardly believe his ears. "Really?"

Pickett didn't flinch. "Really."

He sucked a deep breath and expelled it slowly. "This isn't your fight. You have no idea what's going on here and you don't need to know. I suggest that you remove your handgun and drop it at your feet. Leave your shotgun where it is. Then I'll let you turn around and walk right out of here." He chinned toward the north. "I think your horse ran that way."

Pickett slowly put his hands on his hips and squinted one eye at Co-burn. "I let a guy take my weapons once. It didn't go well."

"Drop the pistol."

The game warden continued to squint and seemed to be thinking, which was starting to annoy him.

Pickett said, "I'm going to lower my handgun to the ground. I'm no good with it anyway. Then I'm going to walk over there to you and place you under arrest."

Coburn snorted and looked around as if trying to see if he was the subject of a practical joke. "You're out of your depth here, game warden. When I give you the chance to walk away, you should take it."

"Why?" Pickett asked, easing his handgun out of his holster with two fingers and lowering it to the ground.

"I told you," he said, with mounting impatience. "This isn't your fight."

"Seems like the fight's over." Pickett gestured to the dead man in the cabin doorway, then stood up and took a step toward Coburn.

"You're not really going to do this, are you?" he asked. "Try and arrest me? Did you notice I'm holding a gun?"

"Everybody in Wyoming has a gun," Pickett said, though he didn't seem so sure of himself now.

Coburn kept his .45 pointed down but thumbed the hammer back with a sharp click so Pickett was sure to hear it.

But the man kept advancing.

What was wrong with him?

That's when he noticed the long thick cylinder attached to the game warden's belt. Bear spray. Pickett wanted to get close enough to hit him with a full cloud. That stuff was ten times more effective than the pepper spray used by street cops.

He raised his weapon. "Not another step."

Pickett hesitated, eyes locked on Coburn and the big round O of the muzzle.

That's when the ground exploded between them, throwing fist-sized chunks of black earth straight into the air. The chatter of at least two semiautomatic rifles was delayed a half second because of the distance.

Pickett jumped back as if stung, flinging himself to his belly, shielding his head with his hands. The game warden rolled to his left as a flurry of bullets bit into the ground where he'd just been.

Coburn dropped to his haunches and raised his .45. He swept the mountainside above the trees, moving his front sights from outcropping to outcropping. He was sure the gunfire had come from up there, but he couldn't see anyone. Behind him, bullets smacked into tree trunks. Pine needles rained down on his head and shoulders, and slivers of dislodged bark stung the back of his neck. He looked up to see Pickett on his hands and knees, launching himself toward the cover of the half-completed building.

Coburn shimmied to his left behind a two-foot-diameter tree trunk that had been recently felled. He squatted behind it for a moment, then came out over the top with his hands extended and the .45 held tight. He aimed at a suppressed muzzle flash far up the mountainside in a fissure in the outcropping and fired twice. He knew he hadn't hit anyone, but the return fire would at least make the shooter retreat for a moment. He used the time to throw himself over the tree trunk and run toward the shelter as well.

He caught up with Pickett, who tripped over an exposed root just as his hat was shot off his head. Coburn reached down and yanked the game warden to his feet. But rather than run straight to the structure, the idiot turned and retrieved his hat from the ground, snatching it as bullets kicked up chunks of earth on both sides of him.

Coburn leaped over the corpse in the doorway and rolled across the dirt floor of the building until he was tight against the far wall. He heard Pickett behind him. Both men pressed their cheeks against the rough log wall while the shooter, or shooters, continued to fire.

He felt the impact of bullets thumping into the outside of the wall, but the logs were sturdy enough that they stopped the rounds.

That was good.

But they were pinned down, and the shooters had the high ground, able to see clearly below, which included three-quarters of the structure floor itself.

"Are you hit?" he asked Pickett over his shoulder.

"I don't think so."

"Did you remember to grab your pistol on the way in?"

"Wouldn't have done any good anyway. But I got my shotgun."

"There's that," Coburn said. "So we have my .45 and your shotgun against long-distance rifles and guys with hundreds of rounds of ammunition."

"How many of them are there?"

"At least two. Maybe all three."

"Three?"

He grunted a yes, contemplating rising to full height and aiming carefully at the muzzle flashes he'd seen earlier. Maybe he could take one of them out and improve their odds.

But the gunfire had stopped.

The shooters seemed to have realized it was a waste of ammo to fire at targets behind a log wall.

"Do you mind telling me what's going on here?" Pickett asked.

"Later. Right now, I think they're trying to come up with their next move."

He spun on his heels and looked east toward the doorway and the dead man. The one direction where the mountains didn't rise above the trees.

"At least they can't get above us from behind," he said. "But they'll see us if we venture more than five feet away from this wall, so stay put."

"I wasn't planning on going anywhere," Pickett said, sounding annoyed. "And when this is over, I'm still going to arrest you for murder."

He sighed.

The man was a bulldog. The worst kind.

"Look," he said, "you can do whatever you want once we get out of here. But right now we've got a little time while they reload and regroup. I need you to call this in and get some backup here. I know the Teton County sheriff has access to a chopper. I can give you the exact coordinates."

"That would be fine if I had a radio or a phone."

He turned angrily. "What kind of law enforcement officer doesn't have a radio or a phone?"

"The kind whose horse was spooked by a lunatic who suddenly appeared from the trees. Everything was in my saddlebags, including my cell phone. You don't have a phone?"

"I did but it's . . . gone."

Pickett frowned.

"What part don't you understand? It's no longer in my possession."

"Did you drop it?"

He swore under his breath. "I gave it to them, and they took the battery out."

"And you thought *I* was a chump."

He felt a flash of anger and considered decking the guy.

But first things first.

"How well do you know these mountains?" he asked.

"Not well at all. This isn't my district. I'm doing a guy a favor."

"Fucking great. I'm stuck here with a game warden who doesn't even know where he is."

"Story of my life," Pickett said with a shrug. "By the way, thanks for helping me up out there when we were running for the cabin."

He nodded.

"What's your name, anyway?"

"Coburn."

"Just Coburn?"

"As far as you're concerned."

"Just Coburn? One name, like Cher or Beyoncé?"

"Lee Coburn, damn it."

"Can you spell it so I get it right on the arrest warrant?"

"Capital F-u-c-k Capital O-f-f."

He briefly considered smacking the game warden on his precious hat with the butt of his .45. Maybe that would keep him quiet for a while. But he needed Pickett to keep an eye on the north while he handled the east, west, and south where the shooters surely were.

"I'll just call you Coburn," Pickett said.

• ◆ •

FOR THE NEXT HOUR, JOE SAT WITH HIS BACK TO THE WALL AND HIS shotgun across his knees, wishing the day had gone in an entirely different direction. He scanned the trees he could see over the top of the walls, hoping the shooters weren't creeping closer to them.

He also kept an eye on the north side of the clearing, hoping against hope that Rojo would wander out of the woods. He hoped his horse was okay. In addition to the shooters perched in the rocks above their position, the timber was populated by the grizzly bears, mountain lions, and other predators who would consider Rojo meat on the hooves.

He checked his watch.

Two in the afternoon.

Marybeth would expect him back by dark, but not before. So unless they could get word somehow to the Teton County sheriff, for the next five hours no one would know he was in trouble or even think to send someone up to look for him. Today, he recalled, the plan for his family was to buy tickets for the alpine slide on Snow King Mountain. Lucy was quite excited about that.

Next to him Coburn sat, watchful, still, lethal. When he moved at all, he raised up just high enough to look over the top of the wall. Each time he did the shooters retaliated by firing shots, which Joe figured was what Coburn wanted. When they fired, he could spot them.

After the last volley, Coburn had aimed and squeezed off a shot. He said he was pretty sure he'd hit his target that time, but he couldn't guarantee it. Which meant there were two shooters left, or two shooters and a wounded shooter. All had high-powered rifles. The odds were still against him and his unlikely ally.

"One of these times when you pop up like a Whac-A-Mole, they're going to blow your head off," he said to Coburn.

"Like a what?"

"A Whac-A-Mole."

Coburn's face remained a blank.

"You know. The kids' game."

Coburn looked down at the pistol in his hand, hefting it. "Never was much of a kid. Didn't play many games." Then he raised his gaze back to Joe and said with derision, "Sure as hell not one called whack a . . . whatever."

Joe tucked that observation away to think about later. "So you're just going to keep letting them take potshots, until you get off a lucky one?"

Coburn glared at him. "Do you have a better plan?"

"Nope."

"Then please shut up."

Joe thought about the canister of bear spray attached to his belt. He could still blast Coburn, disarm him, and bind him up with flex-cuffs. But to what end? Would he then stand up and explain to the shooters in the mountains that everything was okay? That they could put down their arms and surrender peacefully?

Coburn was rude and likely a murderer.

But he possessed one redeeming quality.

He was on this side of the wall.

•◆•

COBURN WAS AWARE OF THE GAME WARDEN WATCHING HIM AS HE reloaded.

Pickett said, "Coburn, before this is over, I'm fairly certain that things are going to get western between you and me."

"I told you this isn't your fight. Do I have to say it again?"

"My family's in Jackson. I'd kinda like to see them again."

Coburn again considered bringing his gun down hard on the crown of that Stetson. He could use some peace and quiet to deal with the situation at hand. He'd never been one to accommodate weakness. It wasn't that he had no empathy or understanding for men not hardwired for action. But in a firefight, and he'd been in many, slow thinkers resulted in the deaths of not only themselves but other brave men too. In this situation, he had two options.

Fight or flight.

But he doubted the shooters would even extend to him the second option.

"If nothing else," Pickett said, "you need to tell me what's going on. It's not every day I start out checking elk camps and end up getting shot at with a psycho next to me."

He snickered. "I've been called a lot of names. But psycho is a first."

"Then prove to me you're not. From where I sit, I see a dead guy with a bullet through his forehead and two or three other guys trying to kill us. It's hard to come up with any other conclusion."

He took that as a challenge. "So what do you think happened here?"

Pickett took a long time to answer, which was a little maddening. "I've seen a lot of strange things up in these mountains. Here in the Gros Ventres, or in my own mountains, the Bighorns. Sometimes these woods look to people like the last best place for them to wash up, when they can't fit in anywhere else. I've run across end-of-times survivalists, sheepherders dealing meth, environmental terrorists, and landowners who run their ranches like tin-pot tyrants.

"When I look around here," Pickett said, gesturing toward the camp beyond the walls, "I see the beginning of something that blew up while in progress. My guess is you and your buddies decided to pick the most remote part of these mountains to set up a little headquarters. For what I don't know. But you figured, like so many do, that you'd be far enough away from civilization that you could do what you pleased, whatever that is.

"So you gathered up your best weapons and tools and got up here somehow and started building your stockade. Then there was a falling-out. That's not surprising, given your foul disposition and the fact that the dead guy in the door obviously carried around a black rifle. So the disagreement, whatever it was about, escalated beyond control. You shot that guy over there, and the rest of the crew headed for the hills. You were going after them when they got the sense to go to high ground and turn on you. That's when I showed up."

He slowly shook his head. "That's what this looks like to you?"

"Yup. Or something like it."

"I'm FBI."

Pickett raised his eyebrows with doubt. "You don't expect me to believe that."

He dug out his wallet badge from his jacket and showed the game warden his credentials.

"I'm undercover."

"Undercover for what?" Pickett asked.

He took a deep breath, then quickly rose up and checked the perimeter to make sure the shooters weren't sneaking up on them. Assured they weren't, he lowered back down and said, "I'm based in Jackson when I'm not on assignment. It's a good place to get my bearings back and recuperate."

"Recuperate?"

He didn't address that. "A few days ago I got a call from my boss, a guy named Hamilton. Real asshole."

"Bureaucrat?"

"As I said. Anyhow, he told me that four really bad actors—white supremacists who call themselves One Nation—escaped from a raid on their compound in West Virginia last month. I've known One Nation was on the bureau's radar for a long time, but I wasn't involved with the case."

"What's their mission?"

"To incite a race war by gunning down white cops in largely black neighborhoods. These rednecks knew that if that happened, the local cops would likely overreact and trouble would spread. They put their whole manifesto on the Internet like so many of these mouth breathers do, but no one really thought they'd follow through. But they did. A couple of cops got shot in South Philly. And all hell broke loose. Riots, vandalism, looting, people on both sides killed, including some grade-school kids. I'm sure you saw it on the news."

Pickett nodded.

"So the bureau raided the One Nation compound outside Wheeling. They arrested a dozen guys and a couple of women, but the four men in leadership got away. No one knew where they went, or whether they'd split up or stayed together. But one of the group in custody said one of the four guys had some familiarity with Wyoming, because he'd been elk hunting out here. Specifically, Jackson Hole. So my boss asked me to poke around, without alarming the locals."

"And you did," Pickett said.

He nodded. "I needed a distraction, so I jumped all over it. It took me a few days before I found a clerk at a hardware store who told me about two guys who fit the description buying up ammo and heavy-duty hand tools. He said they had West Virginia accents and one of them had a long beard like those yokels from *Duck Dynasty*."

"Our man in the doorway," Pickett said.

"I started making forays into the mountains. I didn't think I'd actually run into them. It was really more an accident than intentional. I walked into their camp this morning, before I realized who they were."

"That's when you gave them your phone?"

"It wasn't like that," he said, annoyed. "I told them I wanted to join up. I told them everything I thought they'd want to hear about the country going to shit and the way to finally fix it. They liked what I was saying, but they didn't greet me with open arms. I could tell they were thinking about it, though. If nothing else, they needed help with the building before winter rolled in. These guys aren't exactly geniuses when it comes to construction, as you can tell."

"Most criminals I've dealt with are just idiots," Pickett said.

"I've known many who were fuckin' smart. But these guys are idiots, with a cause. And even though they were friendly at first, they started getting suspicious. To prove I wasn't a threat, I gave them my phone when they asked for it. I wasn't worried because I'd deleted everything on it."

Pickett nodded. "Go on."

"It all went pear shaped when a fat guy with a WHITE PRIDE sweatshirt and a skinny guy who looked like he'd just walked off the set of *Deliverance* decided they'd pat me down to see if I was packing. I was, of course. I started backing off, but that didn't sit well with Duck Dynasty over there, and the next thing I knew he was locking and loading his rifle and aiming it at me. I ran for the trees as the three others went for their weapons. I was able to throw myself into the shelter of a big root-pan, when they all opened up. It sounded like D-Day."

"I heard it," Pickett said.

"Finally, when they paused to reload, I was able to take out Duck Dynasty. That caused the others to strike out on foot. I chased them for a while and then decided it made more sense to see if I could find my phone and call it in. Unfortunately, that's when you showed up."

Pickett raised his hands in a *what-are-you-gonna-do?* gesture.

"But now that I've had time to think about it, I think I have a plan to take these guys on," Coburn said.

"Oh, really? This should be interesting."

He pretended not to notice Pickett's skeptical tone. "I keep them engaged until dusk, like I've been doing. That way, they're on the defensive and they won't have the wherewithal to overrun us. Then, you'll replace me. I'll give you my .45 so they'll think I'm still the one firing."

"Then what?"

"You'll do what I've been doing. Playing the . . . what was it?"

"Whac-A-Mole."

"Right. Popping up every fifteen to twenty minutes to take a shot at them. Keep them guessing when you'll appear and where you'll shoot."

"Meanwhile?" Pickett asked.

"I'll use your cover fire to run out of this building. I'll take your shotgun and get up into the trees and outflank them. Then I'll take them out one by one. They'll be dead before they know what hit them."

Pickett seemed to remain doubtful.

"The best thing you can do to the enemy is keep him off balance," he said. "Given the odds, they won't expect me to take it to them."

Pickett grinned. "I've got a buddy named Nate Romanowski. We butt heads from time to time. I think he'd approve of your plan. But I'm not sure I do."

"You have a better one?" Coburn asked with some heat.

"I'm thinking."

"That gives me absolutely no confidence."

Pickett continued to ruminate. Why did it take this guy so long to form a thought? A glacier could have thawed by the time the game warden said, "So you've been hiking around these mountains all by yourself for weeks until you found these guys?"

"That's what I said."

"Must be running from something yourself."

His hackles rose. Pickett might be slow, but he sure as hell wasn't thick. "That's none of your goddamn business."

"What are you recuperating from?"

He didn't respond.

"You said you were recuperating. What from?"

"What's that got to do with anything?"

"Just wondering. Concussion? Chickenpox? Ingrown toenail?"

He gnawed the inside of his cheek and finally said, "Gunshot."

Then he sprang to his feet and ran along the wall toward the corner of the building, his .45 at the ready. The burly white supremacist in the filthy WHITE PRIDE hoodie had just cleared the trees to the south and was working his way toward the unfinished lodge. The man carried a Ruger Mini-14 rifle with a thirty-round magazine.

"Drop it," Coburn shouted.

WHITE PRIDE raised the rifle.

He fired and hit him center mass. WHITE PRIDE flopped straight back and landed on his butt, still.

"Two down," he coldly said.

He heard a bang, then something hit him with the force of a mule kick and threw him flat on his back.

He couldn't move his upper body.

But his grip on his .45 never wavered.

Pickett rushed over and dragged him along the ground to the log wall.

•—◆—•

PICKETT WAS SURPRISED BY HOW HEAVY COBURN WAS. HE WAS DEAD weight, but still alive. Proof of that was the litany of profanity that poured out as he propped the agent against the wall.

"Son of a bitch, that hurts," Coburn hissed through gritted teeth.

"Where are you hit?"

"Chest."

Not good. A high-velocity round through the chest could be fatal. He reached up and peeled back Coburn's jacket. The bullet had struck just below the clavicle, closer to the shoulder than heart. It looked like a through shot because there was blood coming out from both sides. He'd seen the damage gunshots could do to big-game animals and had become inured to the sight of them. But when a human being was hit, that was different, even if it was a man he had no reason to like.

"I don't think anything vital was hit," he said. "I'm not sure it even broke any bones."

"It hurts like hell."

"You bleeding out is a worry, though."

Coburn grunted.

Joe didn't have access to the first aid kit. That was with Rojo and his saddlebag. "I'm going to use your shirt to bind it up. Lean forward so I can get your jacket off."

Coburn took a deep breath and bent forward. Joe could only imagine how much it hurt to do that. He eased the arms free, pulled Coburn's jacket over his head, then removed the bloodstained shoulder holster. Not taking the time to unbutton Coburn's shirt, he ripped it open and the buttons popped off.

He couldn't help but notice the scar on Coburn's belly. Pink, puckered, recent. "Is that where you were shot?"

"No, I cut myself shaving."

At least that wonderful personality seemed unaffected. Coburn's arms were muscled and rippling with veins. A barbed-wire tattoo banded the left biceps, while the right displayed the words HONOR &.

The second word was missing.

"Honor and what?" he asked, as he fashioned a sling out of Coburn's shirt that went over the left shoulder, under the right armpit, and across the chest. He hoped it would stanch the bleeding on both the entry and exit wounds. "Honor and duty? Honor and sacrifice? Or couldn't you make up your mind?"

Coburn mumbled something incomprehensible.

"Hang on," he said, "I'm going to cinch this tight and tie it off. It's gonna hurt."

Coburn gave a quick nod, the go-ahead, and Joe took that as his cue to pull the shirt as tight as he could and knot it. Coburn didn't cry out, his jawbone locked tight.

He checked his handiwork.

The shirt was taut, but blood was still seeping through. Best he could hope for was that it would slow down the bleeding.

"I don't suppose you can raise your right arm," he asked.

Coburn winced as he tried, but his right hand and the .45 it held stayed in his lap.

"Didn't think so."

"I can shoot with my left."

Empty boast? Hard to say. But he transferred the pistol to Coburn's left hand.

"Just sit here. No more Whac-A-Mole for you."

"We need to keep an eye out."

"I'm not sticking my head up like you did."

"This completely screws up my plan."

"With all due respect, it was a crappy plan anyway."

"Still haven't heard one from you."

He sat back. "Honor and what?"

Coburn sighed.

"Honor and why don't you shut the hell up."

NOTHING HAPPENED FOR THREE HOURS.

Coburn was getting antsy, and becoming more annoyed with Joe Pickett by the minute. The evening sun was dropping below the tops of the trees, casting deep shadows through the golden light. The smell of the cool pines seemed to intensify. The temperature had dropped ten degrees. It would be dark in two hours.

His shoulder had gone from screaming pain to what was now a low throbbing. If he sat still, he could stand it. But when he moved, even when he took a deep breath, he had to clench his teeth to keep from moaning, groaning, or cussing a blue streak. Despite the chilly air, he was sweating. Only an act of will, and his training for covert missions, prevented him from shivering. He had no doubt he could do what he needed to do with the .45 in his left hand. Especially at close range.

But he wasn't sure he'd even get the chance.

The game warden sat still.

He worried that Pickett had fallen asleep. He stared across at the man who seemed to be looking at nothing. Face stoic. Or was it empty? He wasn't sure which, but either way it was getting on his nerves.

"Blink if you can hear me, Pickett."

"I hear you."

"What are you doing?"

"Thinking."

"Please don't strain yourself, but could you speed it along so I don't bleed out?"

"I've been waiting for Rojo to come back."

"Rojo?"

"My steed," Pickett said, with an embarrassed smile. "It doesn't look like he's coming."

"No, it doesn't."

Pickett was quiet for a long time. Then said, "Do you hear anything?"

He perked up, but when he tried to straighten his shoulders, pain pulsed through them.

"No," he said. "It's perfectly quiet, except for a little bit of wind."

"Right," Joe said. "We've been waiting three hours and the natural sounds haven't come back. No birds, squirrels, anything. Meaning, those guys are still up there."

He was more than a little impressed that the game warden had determined that. Coburn had engaged in guerrilla warfare in Central America. When the birds quit calling and the monkeys stopped chattering, you unsheathed your machete because somebody was close.

"It also probably means they aren't exactly sure what they're going to do," Pickett said. "Otherwise we would have heard something. Low talking. A branch snapping underfoot. Something. I think they're still up there, but confused."

"By what?"

"Think about it," Pickett said. "It was around noon when they were peppering us with gunfire and watched us take cover here. But because they've only seen you, they might assume I was hit and died in here. They haven't even caught a glimpse of me. They're pretty sure you're hit. And since that happened we haven't shown ourselves. For all they know there are two dead men down here."

He gave a curt nod of agreement.

Pickett asked, "Have you ever hunted?"

"You mean game?"

"What else?"

He turned his head aside, looked into the darkness, and said quietly, "Men."

"Only bad men, though."

"Sort of depends on who you ask, doesn't it?"

Pickett said nothing for a moment, then cleared his throat. "I was thinking elk or deer."

"Long ago in Idaho, with my dad," he said.

He'd been twelve years old. His father shot a mule deer from the window of their truck before the sun came up, which was illegal. In the headlights, his dad had put the wounded animal out of its misery by hitting it on the head with a shovel.

"Didn't like it much," he said.

"Maybe you can still relate to my point."

"Which is?"

"You can spend weeks in a wilderness like this, going after elk or moose. Stalking. Camping. Moving on foot. The first few years you hunt you're filled with bloodlust. It's how men are wired. We want to blast away and kill something and get our hands bloody. But it gets frustrating after a while because these animals we hunt are prey. That's how they're wired. They aren't particularly smart, but they know not to charge into a confrontation. Instead, they avoid 'em."

"What does that have to do with us?"

"Maybe nothing. But from what you tell me, these One Nation guys are just dumb rednecks. If they were smart, they'd hightail it out of these mountains while they've had the chance. Either that, or they'd wait until morning and sneak down here to make sure we're dead. But these guys are dumb. And violent. They have bloodlust. So they're itching to confirm their kills, bury our bodies, and get to working on this building again so they can go back to inciting a race war. In other words, they don't have much patience and they're probably hungry, like I am." Pickett chinned toward the coolers and canned goods in the shadow of the trees. "They want their Dinty Moore stew."

Coburn saw the logic in what Pickett said. Besides, in the shape he was in, he couldn't launch an attack on a butterfly, much less two idiots with firepower and a cause.

"So we wait them out?"

"Till they make a move," Pickett said.

"Or I drain dry of blood."

"Whichever comes first."

•◆•

"EMILY."

Pickett opened his eyes.

It had been an hour and a half since either of them had spoken. They had thirty minutes of light left, although it had been a while since they'd seen the sun. The dark walls of trees seemed to be closing in, and because the breeze had stopped it seemed incredibly still and totally silent except for Coburn's whisper of a name.

"What?" he whispered back.

"Honor and Emily."

He was puzzled. "That's a new one."

Coburn shook his head. "Honor is the name of my . . . woman. Emily's her daughter. Five years old."

He tried to keep his surprise from showing. "So you have a family?"

"Barely."

Joe waited for more that didn't come. Finally, he said, "I've got a great wife and three daughters. I don't mind admitting that, if it weren't for them, I don't know what good I'd be."

Coburn looked over hard at him. "You mean like me."

"I didn't say that."

"You wouldn't be far off the mark. She and I have only been together three months."

"Marybeth and I met in college."

Coburn shifted uncomfortably. "Honor and I met under more un-usual circumstances."

He waited for more.

"I crawled out of a swamp into her yard, held her at gunpoint, threat-ened her life, and tied her up."

"Never would've taken you for such a romantic."

Coburn puffed a laugh. "She was involved in this case I was working."

He motioned toward Coburn's belly. "Is that when that happened?"

"Yep. Didn't know if I'd ever see her again. I started going out to the airport every day." Coburn paused. "Anyhow, that asshole I told you about? My boss. Hamilton? Honor threatened him with bodily harm if he didn't tell her where I was. She would've been better off staying in Louisiana. But one day there she was. With Emily and Elmo."

"That sounds like a happy ending."

Coburn shrugged. "Maybe for a guy who wants to settle down. Maybe for a guy like you. A guy who knows who Elmo is."

He chuckled. "A little girl, huh? So you're awash in estrogen."

"You could say that."

"Sometimes I think of my place as the 'House of Feelings,'" he said. "It can be quite a shocker to spend the day alone out in the field and return home to that."

"Four of 'em," Coburn said, shaking his head. "I have trouble handling two. I've spent my whole life on my own. Keeping my own company. Not sharing anything with anybody, especially space. Now I'm having discussions about things like curtains. I don't care what color they are. I just want to know if they shut."

He nodded. "I hear you. And what's the thing with throw pillows?"

"Hell if I know."

They pondered the imponderable for a few seconds.

"Can Honor cook?" he asked.

Coburn smiled. "Oh, yeah. And don't get me wrong. She's wonderful. I can't keep my hands off her. It's the other stuff I gotta work through. I keep asking myself, Can I do this?"

"That's not the question you should be asking."

"Enlighten me."

"Do you want to do it?"

He gave him time to answer, but nothing came, so he said, "You can do it, Coburn. If I can put up with a mother-in-law who never fails to remind me that her daughter married down, you can put up with curtains and throw pillows. Builds character. Maybe Honor will take the edge off you."

"That's what I'm afraid of."

"With all due respect, you could be less of a hard-ass. And one other thing. When we get out of this thing, go have Emily's name added to your arm. Don't chicken out this time."

Coburn glanced at his still seeping wound. "If we get out of this thing."

"We'll find out soon enough, I think."

By eight thirty a sliver of moon had wedged between the spindled tops of two pine trees, the sky overhead almost cloudy from the countless stars. A sight Pickett never tired of seeing.

Two men stepped out of the trees on the south side of the clearing. One was stocky and short with a barrel chest. The other cadaverous, and he pulled his left leg behind him as he walked. Silver light reflected off the barrels of their rifles.

The stocky man whispered, "You gonna make it?"

"I better," the skinny man said in a southern twang. "Ain't never tried to walk on a shot-up leg before."

The stocky man chuckled.

They moved deliberately across the clearing toward the walls of the lodge. Condensation puffed from their mouths with every breath. They kept low as they neared the log walls.

When they were leaning against it, the stocky one whispered, "One, two, three."

And they both sprang up and looked over the wall, their rifles sweeping the dirt floor.

After a beat, the stocky man said, "Where the hell did they go?"

"Right behind you," Coburn said, raising the .45 with his left hand.

Joe didn't even have the stock of the shotgun up to his cheek before there were two loud booms and orange fireballs erupted from the muzzle of Coburn's weapon. Both the rednecks were thrown into the wall by the bullets' impact. The skinny man fell like a puppet with his strings clipped. The stocky one regained his balance, turned, and raised his rifle. Coburn shot him again and the man dropped to the ground.

Pickett's ears rang.

He barely heard Coburn say, "I think I forgot to say freeze."

⁃◆⁃

COBURN EYED PICKETT IN THE AMBER LIGHT FROM THE CAMPFIRE. The game warden had finally stopped talking and had settled in to shoveling spoonful after spoonful of canned stew into his mouth.

"I can't believe I'm so hungry," Pickett said. "Usually when I see a dead person, I get sick."

"Then drink," Coburn said, extending a bottle of bourbon they'd found in the One Nation cache.

Pickett grabbed the bottle, sucked a long swig, then grimaced.

"Good, huh?" Coburn said, taking it back.

The liquor dulled the pain from his shoulder but not as much as he would like.

"How did you know they wouldn't see us leave that shelter to hide in the trees?"

"The darkest time of the night is that ten-minute window after the sun goes down, and just before the moon comes out. It takes a few minutes for your eyes to adjust. You learn that by chasing poachers around. That's why we left when we did."

He nodded.

Smart thinking.

Something emerged from the trees.

Like a ghost, twenty feet from the fire, startling them both.

"My steed," Pickett said, definitely pleased. "Rojo."

The horse snorted.

Pickett stood with a grunt and led the animal closer to the fire, tying him to a tree trunk and fishing a radio out of the saddlebag.

"I'm going to contact the Teton County Sheriff's Department. When the good guys get here, do you want to go straight to the hospital?"

"Where else?"

"Thought maybe you'd want to roust your tattoo guy first."

Coburn savored another deep drink of the bourbon.

And grinned.

VAL McDERMID AND PETER JAMES

VAL McDERMID TELLS ME THAT THE IDEA FOR THIS STORY CAME while she was having her feet worked on by a brisk German reflexologist. While lying there she kept thinking about how most people consider feet unattractive, and yet for some they're a powerful sexual fetish.

A thought occurred.

What would happen if a foot-fetishist reflexologist confronted a pair of feet so perfect he wanted to keep them forever.

And the story was born.

Both Peter and Val are British crime (thriller) writers. But their novels are set at opposite ends of the country. Val's principal characters are a detective and a psychological profiler. Peter's is a pure detective. For them both, the whole world of foot fetishists was a relatively unexplored subject. Learning about the weird and wonderful world of feet, as objects of eroticism, seemed a bit mind-boggling for them.

But there was an element of fun to it too.

Peter wrote the skeleton of an outline. Val then fleshed it out and drafted the opening, setting the scene and the tone. Together, they then worked back and forth, each writing segments of about a thousand words.

Val counted on Peter for all the police procedural elements, which gave her free rein to have some fun with the characters. And they both had "a bit of a giggle" at each other's terrible puns about feet.

The result is something quite unique.

Footloose.

FOOTLOOSE

A WATERY RED SUN WAS STRUGGLING TO DEFEAT SKEINS OF CLOUD above the moors of either Lancashire or West Yorkshire, depending on personal allegiance. A narrow ribbon of road wound down from the high tops toward the outskirts of Bradfield, its gray sprawl just emerging from the dawn light. Gary Naylor steered a van crammed with bacon, sausages, and black pudding from his organic piggery down the moorside, knowing his bladder wasn't going to make it to the first delivery.

There was, he knew, a lay-by round the next bend, tucked in against a dry stone wall. He'd stop there for a quick slash. Nobody around to see at this time of the morning. He pulled over and squirmed out, duckwalking over to the wall. He had eyes for nothing but his zip and his hands and then, oh, the relief as he directed his hot stream over the low wall.

That was when he noticed her.

Sprawled on the far side of the gray drystone dike lay a woman.

Blond, beautiful, dressed in a figure-hugging dress, wide-eyed and indisputably dead.

Dead and covered in his steaming piss.

•—◆—•

DETECTIVE CHIEF INSPECTOR CAROL JORDAN OF THE REGIONAL Major Incident Team had already been awake when the call came in. She'd been halfway up the hill behind her converted barn home, exercising Flash, her border collie. She walked; the dog quartered the hillside in a manic outpouring of energy that made her feel faintly inadequate. She took the call and turned, whistling the dog to follow. Five yards in and Flash was in front of her, heading like an arrow for home.

She let the dog in and called to the man who shared her home but not her bed.

Dr. Tony Hill emerged from his separate suite at the far end of the barn, hair wet from the shower, tucking his shirt into his jeans.

"What's up?" he asked.

"Body of a woman found up on the moors. A fresh kill, by all accounts."

"And it's one for ReMIT?"

"Oh yes. It's definitely one for us. She's got no feet."

Carol Jordan and Tony Hill were a better fit in their professional lives than they'd ever managed personally.

He was a clinical psychologist who specialized in unraveling the motivations of the twisted killers who wanted to express themselves again and again. She was the kind of detective for whom justice matters more than any other consideration. Now she'd been put in charge of ReMIT, he was at the heart of the tight-knit team she'd built to deal with major crimes across six police areas. So when they turned up at the lay-by on the moors, there was a perceptible lowering of the level of tension among the local officers who'd been called to the scene first.

They could relax a bit.

This wasn't going to be down to them if it all went tits up.

The detective sergeant who'd been on duty when the call came in introduced them to Gary Naylor, sitting hunched in his van with the door open.

"I'm sorry," Naylor said. "I'm so, so sorry. I never saw her till it was too late."

For a moment Carol thought she was hearing a confession.

But the DS explained. "Mr. Naylor urinated on the woman's body. Then when he realized what he'd done, he threw up." He tried to keep his voice level, but the disgust showed in the line of his mouth.

"That must have been upsetting for you," Tony said.

"Have we taken a statement from Mr. Naylor?" Carol asked.

"We were waiting for you, ma'am," the DS said.

"Have someone take a statement from Mr. Naylor, then let the poor man get on with his day."

An edge to her voice stung the DS into action.

They took the marked path to the wall and looked down at the woman's body. Even stinking of urine and vomit, it was possible to see that she'd been attractive. Pleasant enough face, though nothing out of the ordinary. Good figure. Shapely legs. Except that where her feet should have been there was a puddle of blood-matted grass and heather.

"What do you make of that?" Carol asked.

Tony shook his head. "I'm not sure what he's saying to us. Don't think you can run away from me? You'll never dance with another guy now? Impossible to know until I know a lot more about the victim."

She gestured to the forensic technicians working the scene. "Hopefully they'll have something for us soon.

"How's it looking, Peter?" she called out to the crime scene manager.

He gave her a thumbs-up. "It'd be easier if the witness hadn't voided most of his body fluids over her. On the plus side we've got a clutch bag with a credit card, a business card, a set of keys, a lipstick, and forty quid in cash. The name on the credit card is Diane Flaherty. The business card is for a model called Dana Dupont. The contact number is an agency in Bradfield. I'll ping the details to your e-mail account as soon as I can get a strong enough signal. It's a nightmare up here."

"What's the agency called?"

"Out on a Limb."

Tony raised an eyebrow. "Interesting."

She nodded. "Let's get down to the office and see what Stacey can dig out about Diane Flaherty and this agency."

She tossed Tony a warning look.

"And don't tell me to put my foot down."

• ◆ •

MOST DAYS SARAH DENNISON RECKONED SHE HAD THE BEST JOB IN
the world, but today it felt like the worst.

The worst by a million, backbreaking stinky miles.

And it was getting even worse.

This would have been a perfect day for it to have rained and a howling
gale to have blown, as it seemed to have done for most of this summer.
Instead, under a searing midday sun and beneath a cloudless sky, the air in
the West Brighton Domestic Waste Recycling and Landfill Site stood still,
rank and fetid. The waste was literally steaming, the methane gas rising
from it offering her and her colleagues a headache.

Sarah was a sergeant in Brighton and Hove Police, and part of her spe-
ciality training was as a POLSA. Police search advisor. Normally she loved
the challenge of searching, particularly fingertip searches at the scene of a
major crime, looking for the one incriminating strand of hair or clothing
fiber on a carpet, or maybe in a field. It was always looking for needles
in haystacks and she was brilliant at spotting them. But today it wasn't a
needle, it was a murder weapon, small fire extinguisher that had come out
of a van and been used to strike a man on the head after a row over a girl
in a nightclub.

And this was no haystack.

It was twenty acres of rotting bin bags full of soiled nappies, rotting
food, dead animals, with aggressive feral rats running amok.

She and her five colleagues lined out to her right and left, steadily
working their way through the rubbish, were constantly having to fend
off rats with the rakes they were using to tear open and sift through the
contents of every single bag. They'd been here since 7 a.m., and her back
was aching like hell from the constant raking motions. It was now 2 p.m.
and they would keep on going into the evening, for as long as there was
light, until they found what they were looking for, or could conclude, for
certain, it wasn't here. She'd not eaten anything since arriving here, nor
had any of her colleagues.

None of them had any appetite.

"Skipper," a voice called out.

She turned to see PC Theakston at the end of the line to her right, dressed as they all were in blue overalls, face masks, gloves and boots, signaling.

"You'd better come and take a look at this."

His tone was a mixture of excitement and revulsion, in equal parts. Perhaps more revulsion.

And she could see and smell why.

Through a mist of buzzing blowflies a rat was gnawing hungrily at one of two severed human feet, cut off above the anklebones, lying on the ground. The terrible, rancid, cloying smell of dead flesh filled the air all around them, and Sarah yanked a handkerchief from her pocket and jammed it over her nose. The feet were intact, but some of the flesh had turned a mottled green color. Specks of pink varnish dotted some of the nails.

"Where's the rest of the body?" she said, wondering aloud.

"Done a runner?" the constable said.

•◆•

NORMALLY, DURING HIS WEEK AS THE ON-CALL SENIOR INVESTIGATING officer, Detective Superintendent Roy Grace, who was a few weeks shy of his forty-second birthday, wanted nothing more than a challenging homicide inquiry—a *Gucci* job, as he called them—that he could get his teeth into. One that would attract national press, and where he might have a chance to shine to his superiors. Most of the murders in the city of Brighton and Hove in recent months had been anything but. Lowlifes on lowlifes. A street drug dealer knifing another. Then a small-time drug dealer locked in the boot of a car that was then torched. Both of these, like most of that kind, were solved within days. A blindfolded monkey could have solved them in his view.

He knew it was wrong to be hoping for a good murder. But that's what every homicide detective secretly, and sometimes not so secretly, was after. As he sat at his desk poring over the trial papers of a suspect he had arrested the previous year, a highly evil female killer, whose case was coming up at the Old Bailey next month, his phone rang.

He answered and listened.

Then hung up.

He should wish for things more often.

An hour later, accompanied by his colleague and mate Detective Inspector Glenn Branson—tall, black, and bald as a bowling ball—Grace drove up to the entrance to the West Brighton Recycling and Landfill Site. A marked police car as well as a white CSI van were pulled up beside a Portacabin that housed the site office, and there was a line of blue-and-white police tape across the road, with a uniformed officer standing in front with a clipboard.

Grace was pleased to see that the site was already secured. But the site manager, a burly harassed-looking woman in a yellow uniform, with the name Tracey Finden on her lapel badge, clearly was not. She strode over before they were even out of the car. As Grace rolled down the window, introduced himself, and showed her his warrant card, she replied, "You can't do this, sir. We've got lorries and the general public coming and going all day. This is going to cause chaos."

"I do understand that and we'll be as quick as we can."

"I thought your officers were looking for a bloody fire extinguisher."

"They were—and still are. But now you have to understand this is a potential murder inquiry, and I'm treating this place as a crime scene."

"For how long?"

"At this moment, I cannot tell you. It could be several days."

"Several days? You're joking?"

"I don't think a dead human being is something to joke about."

"It's a pair of feet, right? That's all."

"That's all?" Grace replied.

"They could have come from anywhere. You don't seriously think whoever they belong to is wandering around the site looking for them, do you?"

"I don't think anything at this stage," he replied calmly. "Until I have more information. But I am going to need your help, Tracey. Is there CCTV here?"

"Yes, six cameras."

"How long do you keep the recordings?"

"Two weeks before they're automatically recorded over."

"I'm going to need the memory cards. Also the details of all lorries that you've logged in the past month and any information you can give about them and their drivers."

The two detectives climbed out of their car, wormed their way into their protective onesies, followed by overshoes, gloves, and face masks, then they signed the scene log and ducked under the tape.

"Yugggggh," Branson said, wrinkling his nose at the stench.

Grace too had to swallow to stop himself from gagging.

Then they followed the long length of police tape that had been laid on the ground, guiding them in a straight line through the garbage toward a small knot of people in uniform, standing amid a cloud of buzzing flies.

Unsurprisingly, the home office pathologist, pedantic Groucho Marx look-alike Dr. Frazer Theobald, declined the opportunity to view the feet in situ at the waste site, requesting them to be recovered and taken to the mortuary. Sarah Dennison and her colleagues had completed their search by late afternoon and no other body parts had been found. This, both Grace and the pathologist agreed, indicated the place was more likely to be a deposition site than the crime scene itself.

Assuming it was a crime scene—and Grace was always wary of assumptions. *Ass–u–me makes an ass out of u and me* was something he frequently liked to remind people of. The feet could have come from a hospital mortuary, taken in a sick prank by medical students. Things like that had happened before. Or some sicko might have stolen them from an undertaker. A funeral director would be loath and probably too embarrassed to report such a theft.

He stood with DI Branson, gowned up in green protective clothing and white clogs in the Brighton and Hove City Mortuary, along with his wife, Cleo, the chief mortician. Or senior anatomical pathology technician as the role was now known. Darren Bourne, Cleo's assistant, a coroner's officer, a crime scene photographer, and the crime scene manager.

So far Dr. Frazer Theobald had established the feet were female, size seven, and at some time recently, presumably prior to being severed, had been pedicured. He wasn't able to date how long they had been severed precisely, and his best estimate from the deterioration of the flesh, and the generation of blowfly larvae, was somewhere between three to five weeks. Tissue had been sent to the DNA lab with an urgent request. But it would be a couple of days before they would know if the owner of the feet was on the national database. The absolute priority for both detectives was to identify that person.

One thing the pathologist pointed out to Grace and Branson, with the aid of a microscope, was the surgical precision with which the leg bones had been sawed through. There were tiny, matching serrations on both feet. What that indicated to him was that the feet had not been hacked off in anger, or as some form of torture or revenge. They'd been removed by someone with medical skills, or possibly with butcher training. But beyond that the pathologist could offer no further suggestion at this stage. Nothing that would help answer the one burning question Roy Grace had right now.

Why?

At 6 p.m. that same evening, Grace sat in the Major Crime Suite conference room at the police HQ near Lewes, where his department was now based. Glenn Branson, DS Norman Potting, and several other members of his regular team, including a HOLMES—Home Office Large Major Enquiry System—analyst, an indexer, and a researcher sat around the oval table.

"This is the first briefing of Operation Podiatrist," he read out from his notes. "The investigation into the discovery of a pair of female feet found at the West Brighton Domestic Waste Recycling and Landfill earlier today, which I am treating as a homicide investigation."

Norman Potting began sniggering. Under Roy's withering glare he raised an apologetic hand. "Sorry, Chief. Operation Podiatrist? Feet?"

Several others around the table also grinned.

No one could accuse the police computer, that randomly produced operation names, of not having a sense of humor.

Grace fought back a smirk too. "I don't imagine the lady who's missing them is finding it quite so funny."

"I should think she's hopping mad." Potting chortled, looking around for appreciation, but all he saw were stony stares.

"One immediate line of inquiry," Grace said, "is to see if there is anything similar out there on the database. We need to take a look on the Serious Crime Analysis Section system and also log everything we have so far on Op Podiatrist on it. Another will be to map out the exact area of the city all the refuse lorries collect from, and their delivery times to the site. One thing we do know is that it's only refuse lorries that have access to the site. I want an outside inquiry team to list and interview all the refuse crews."

Jack Alexander, a young DC, raised a hand. "Are you considering utilizing the volunteer search team for the other body parts?"

"Not at this stage, Jack," Grace replied. "We have no idea where to begin. We don't even know how far and wide the other parts could be scattered. If at all."

"Seems to me," DS Potting said, "that the victim's giving us a right old runaround."

•◆•

IF IT WAS IN CYBERSPACE, CAROL JORDAN WAS CONVINCED THAT DC Stacey Chen could find it. Barricaded from the rest of the room by an array of six monitors, Stacey's fingers moved over her keyboard more quickly than the eye could follow. Nobody, Carol thought, was ever going to pick up her pin number shoulder-surfing at a cash machine. By the time they got back to the office, Stacey already had results from the scant information Carol had passed on to her.

She flicked a finger at the bottom right-hand screen.

"Out on a Limb is a specialized model agency." Stacey caught Tony's single raised eyebrow and gave him a long hard look. "Not that kind of specialized."

Tony opened his eyes wide in a look of mock innocence. "I never said a word."

"What kind of specialized?" Carol asked, cutting across the banter, eager to get to the point.

"I suppose you'd call it extremities," Stacey said doubtfully. "They do hands and legs and feet, not whole bodies. Their clients sell shoes, tights, stockings, jewelry, that kind of thing. They've even got a selection of ears for modeling earrings."

"I'd never thought about it. But I suppose it makes sense," Carol said. "So is this Diane Flaherty on their books?"

"Not that I can see. But Dana Dupont is."

Stacey tapped a trackpad and another screen rearranged its pixels. A shapely pair of calves appeared. Another tap and the image changed to elegant ankles and a pair of feet that appeared to be free from any of the myriad blemishes that most people's feet reveal. No hard skin, no corns, no bunions, no dry skin, no fungal infections, no ingrowing toenails, no oddly shaped toes. Just a pair of immaculate, enviable feet that looked as if they'd never so much as bent a blade of grass.

"Anything on Diane Flaherty at all?" Carol asked.

"There's a Diane Flaherty with an address in Bradfield. Self-employed, no criminal record, drives an Opel Corsa. Nobody else listed at her address." Stacey woke up a third screen with an address and a driver's license photo.

"That's the dead woman," Carol said. "We need to get a team round there, see what we can dig up. And I need to talk to somebody at Out on a Limb. You coming, Tony?"

He started, dragging his attention away from the pictures of Dana Dupont's feet.

"Yeah," he said absently. "And you need to get a list of people they send their catalogs to. If I was a foot fetishist, or I had a thing about ears or whatever, their catalogs would make me a happy bunny."

"It takes all sorts," Carol muttered.

"Otherwise we'd be out of a job," Tony said, following in her wake.

•◆•

THE PHYSICAL PREMISES OF OUT ON A LIMB WERE A LOT LESS GLOSSY than their catalog implied. A narrow doorway on the Halifax road between a kebab takeaway and a cancer charity shop led up a steep staircase to a Spartan office where strenuously artificial air freshener battled with the smell of stale fat.

So far, the fat was winning.

The woman who had buzzed them up leaned against the desk in what might have passed for a provocative pose in someone twenty years younger and two stone lighter.

"You said on the phone you were the police?" she said, her voice surprisingly warm and almost seductive. "Can I see some ID?"

Carol produced her warrant card and Tony smiled. "I'm not actually a police officer."

"Dr. Hill is a consultant," Carol butted in before he could say anything unfortunate. "And you are?"

"Margot Maynard," the woman said. "Out on a Limb is my business."

"I'm afraid I have some disturbing news, Ms. Maynard. This morning, a woman's body was found on the moors. In her bag she had a card belonging to one of your models." Carol proffered her phone, where she'd taken a photo of Dana Dupont's business card.

Margot Maynard paled and nodded. "That's one of ours. Dana is our most successful foot model. You're not telling me she's dead?"

"We believe the dead woman is called Diane Flaherty. Do you know a Diane Flaherty?"

"Diane is Dana Dupont. It's her working name. Oh my God, what's happened? Are you sure it's Diane? That can't be right."

Margot Maynard looked as if she might faint. Tony stepped forward and, taking her arm, led her to the office chair behind the desk.

"Can I get you anything? A glass of water?" Carol asked.

"No, I feel sick as it is. Diane? Dead? What happened? Was it a car crash? What?"

"I'm sorry to tell you that we're treating Diane's death as suspicious."

"What does that mean?"

Tony squatted down beside her. "Diane was murdered, Margot. And the killer took her feet."

She reared back in her chair. "Her feet? Oh my God, I always knew it would come to this one day."

*   *   *

They drove back to the police station in glum silence, turning over what they'd learned.

After she'd calmed down, Margot Maynard had explained that the agency had been plagued over the years by an assortment of what she called "weirdos and perverts." Men whose sexual fetishes focused on particular body parts. Feet, shoulders, even ears. The photographic studio where Out on a Limb did their catalog shots was across the landing from the office, and these strange, obsessive men haunted the street below, sometimes following the models after a photo shoot.

"Talk to the local cops," Margot had said bitterly. *"They must have a record of all the times we've called them because one of the girls has been harassed. You wouldn't believe the disgusting things they've suggested to our models."*

Tony knew precisely the kind of thing those poor women would have been subjected to. *"Was anyone ever arrested?"*

"There were a couple of men, a few years ago now. Mostly they back off when the police caution them. They've generally got too much to lose. Wives, jobs, reputation."

Carol's phone rang and she took it on speaker.

"Stacey here, guv. I've thought I might take a quick look at the SCAS—"

"Serious Crime Analysis Section," she muttered for Tony's benefit.

"I know I'm rubbish with acronyms but I do know that one," he said.

"If I could finish?" Stacey showed a sign of irritation.

"Go on," Carol said. "SCAS?"

"There's a report here from Sussex Police. They found a pair of feet on a rubbish tip in Brighton. It can't be our victim's feet, because they weren't fresh."

"But we don't believe in coincidence at ReMIT," Carol said. "Nice work, Stacey. Who's the SIO?"

"DST Roy Grace."

"I'll call him as soon as I get back. When's the autopsy?"

"They've bumped it up the list. They're doing it this afternoon."

Carol ended the call. "Weird. Maybe while I'm talking to Brighton and attending the autopsy you can check out the foot fetishists."

Tony nodded. "I'll take a look online. Most people with fantasies like these are pretty harmless. In my experience they tend not to be violent. They're often socially inadequate, shy, poor at forming relationships. They want to kiss and touch, not possess. Elvis Presley was one. So was Thomas Hardy."

Carol gave him a baffled look. "How do you know things like that?"

He shrugged. "Pub quizzes?"

Exasperated, she shook her head. "Go and find me an Elvis imperson-ator with homicidal tendencies, then."

•◆•

TONY WAS ACCUSTOMED TO SPENDING HIS DAYS TRYING TO EMPA-thize with the messy heads of murderers and rapists. But an afternoon on the trail of body part fetishists left him feeling more grimy than the average working day. There was something deeply unsettling about the transference of the sexual urge on to isolated bits of bodies. He found it dehumanizing and reductive. The more he read on forums and dis-cussion groups, the clearer the picture became. Men, for it was almost invariably men, posturing to cover deep feelings of inadequacy. If you couldn't handle a whole woman in her challenging complexity, how about her feet?

Or her hands?

Some even tried to rationalize it as a form of safe sex. Tony, who was used to a wide range of extraordinary rationalizations among serial of-fenders, thought that was right out there on the edge of daft, a technical term he used only when talking to Carol.

Whenever he came across someone who seemed to him to lean to-ward more salacious tendencies, he punted their details across to Stacey who performed her black arts to track down their location. Everybody who worked in the ReMIT team knew that Stacey had ways and means that went beyond the narrow confines of the law. But nobody cared be-cause she knew how to cover her tracks and the intel she produced was worth more to them than being on their best behavior. Raiding people's privacy for intel that could lead to evidence was a small transgression compared with murder and rape.

By the end of the afternoon, Stacey had run checks on half a dozen possibles, and they were both growing weary of their subjects' apparent respectability outside the murky world of online fetishists. But as Tony browsed yet another chat room, Stacey abruptly called his name.

"I'm pinging something across to you."

Tony glanced at the info sheet Stacey had sent, then sat up straight in his chair as he absorbed the key points.

Leyton Gray was a reflexologist based in Bradfield. A man whose profession necessitated the touching and manipulation of feet. A perfectly respectable calling, provided you weren't also spending hours of your free time online looking at feet and talking to other people whose sexual urges were awakened by them.

But there was more.

One of his clients had complained to the police about his behavior. In her statement, Jane Blackshaw said he'd appeared to become sexually aroused while supposedly massaging her feet to treat a problem with irritable bowel syndrome. He'd left the room in the middle of her treatment and returned a few minutes later, flushed and out of breath. Stacey had tracked down a photograph of Jane Blackshaw, who was an unexceptional-looking woman in her early twenties.

Leyton Gray had been interviewed and had denied that anything inappropriate had taken place. He described Jane Blackshaw as an attention seeker and pointed out none of his other clients had ever complained either to his professional body or to the police. It was his word against hers. So the file was marked No Further Action.

But the clincher as far as Tony was concerned was the final paragraph in Stacey's report. It had been snipped from the program of a complimentary therapy festival in Brighton.

"Returning by popular request, Leyton Gray will be talking about new developments in reflexology techniques. Leyton has been a regular speaker at our events and his sessions are always sold out. Book early to avoid disappointment."

Leyton Gray, it appeared, was no stranger to the town where a pair of feet had turned up on the rubbish tip.

●◆●

"*HAPPY FEET.* REMEMBER THAT MOVIE?" GLENN BRANSON SAID BREEZILY as he entered Roy Grace's office shortly after 9 p.m., carrying two mugs of coffee.

More breezily than he or his boss felt.

Grace frowned. "No, I don't."

"It was brilliant. Animated. With penguins dancing."

"Lovely," Grace said, distractedly.

"Awesome cast. Robin Williams, Nicole Kidman, Hugh Jackman. Your kid would like it."

"Noah's eight months old."

"Yeah, maybe wait a few years." He paused, then pulled up a chair in front of Grace's desk, turned it around and sat, resting his hands on the back. "I've had a thought."

Grace opened his hands, expansively. "I'm all ears."

"Forensic gait analysis. That specialist guy, Haydn Kelly, we've used on previous cases. Maybe we should bring him in. He knows more about feet than anyone on the planet, and he has a massive database. Worth a shot?"

"Good thinking, if he's around."

Kelly had developed software that, from a single footprint, could enable someone to be picked out in a crowd from his or her gait. Everyone walked in a unique way; every human being's gait was as unique as their DNA.

"Call him and see if he's in the country and available to come down. I know he's abroad a lot."

His phone rang.

"Roy Grace," he answered.

"Detective Superintendent Grace? This is DCI Carol Jordan of the Northern Regional Major Incident Team."

A strong, pleasant, if a tad formal, northern voice.

And the name rang a bell.

"Was it you involved with the Jennifer Maidment case?"

"I was, yes."

"That's where I know your name from. How can I help you?"

"Your inquiry team entered a pair of feet on SCAS. We have a female body up here missing her feet, and although we've had a man in for questioning, we didn't have enough evidence to hold him. So any support-ing info would be helpful."

He felt a beat of excitement and gave her all the information he had, informing her that tissue had been sent to the lab for fast-track DNA anal-ysis.

"From what I've read on SCAS, I'm pretty sure we won't get a DNA match to your victim. Our body here is fresh. Your feet sound a few weeks old, which doesn't tally with our time of death estimates or last-seen evi-dence."

"They are old. I can't give you a precise date. About two to three weeks is our pathologist's educated guess from the generations of insect larvae."

"Those serration marks you've just described interest me," she said. "Could you send me photographs? If we could establish whether the same, or a similar instrument has been used to sever both pairs of feet, we might make progress."

"I'll have them to you in a few minutes."

Carol Jordan thanked him and told him she would call back as soon as she had confirmation, one way or the other.

Ending the call, he turned to Glenn Branson. "You're a movie buff. What films can you think of where people have had their feet severed?"

"*Misery.* In the book the batty woman chain-sawed off one of his legs and cauterized it with a blowtorch. But they tamed it down in the film and she just shattered his legs with a sledgehammer."

"Anything more helpful?"

He was feeling tired and fractious.

Branson yawned. "There was some horror movie I saw years ago, but I can't remember the title. They hacked this guy's legs off and fed them to a pig in front of him."

"It had a happy ending?"

"Not exactly. They fed the rest of him to the pig, too."

"Let me guess, then they ate the pig?"

"You saw it, boss?"

•◆•

AT 7 A.M., GRACE WAS BACK IN THE CID HQ FOR THE DAILY MANAGE-ment meeting, prior to the next briefing on Operation Podiatrist. Just as he was entering the room, accompanied by Glenn Branson, his phone rang. Answering it, he heard the excited voice of the duty inspector, Ken "Panicking" Anakin.

"Roy, something that might be of interest to your current inquiry. A uniform crew got called to a firm of undertakers on the Lewes Road at 2 a.m., in response to an alarm and reports of lights on in the premises. It sounds like someone, maybe a drunk, broke in and disturbed some of the bodies in coffins prepared for funerals today. There's one in particular that might be significant. A young deceased woman in her early twenties, whose feet are missing."

"Can you give me the name and address?"

Anakin provided him the details and he jotted it down. "Is anyone there now?"

"The keyholder and proprietor. Mr. James Houlihan is quite upset."

"Meet me there in fifteen minutes," Grace said.

He brought Branson up to speed as they hurried out to the car park and into his unmarked Ford Mondeo, then with the DI reaching forward and switching on the blue lights and siren, ripped the five miles into central Brighton. Heading past the row of funeral directors' premises along Lewes Road, they slowed. A short distance along they saw a neat-looking building, with the sign announcing HOULIHAN AND SONS, ESTABLISHED 1868. There were crimson curtains in the windows either side of a grand front door, and a smaller sign with an arrow that indicated parking in the rear.

The two detectives stopped right outside and walked swiftly toward the front door. As they reached it and Grace rang the bell, a marked police car drew up behind theirs. Ken Anakin, wearing his inspector's braided cap, and a yellow high-viz over his uniform, looking as ever as if the world was going to end in five minutes, hurried over to join them.

The door was opened by a portly, balding man in his late fifties, so-berly dressed in a charcoal suit and black tie and wearing unfashionably large glasses. He looked agitated.

"Thank you for coming; this is all quite distressing," he said, in a mournful voice honed and toned by a lifetime of consoling loved ones and advising them on the decorum of funerals. It was the voice of a master salesman of quality coffins, and all the accoutrements for the funeral of a lifetime you had always promised yourself.

The two detectives introduced themselves and showed him their warrant cards, which he barely glanced at.

"Come in, please. What am I going to say to all my clients? What a disaster. Who would do such a thing?"

Grace and Branson, accompanied by the uniformed inspector, entered a small reception area. It had a deep pile carpet, ornate vases of flowers that looked too real to be real, and framed testimonials on the walls. Houlihan led them on through a door, along a corridor lit with sconces adorned by pink tasseled shades. He stopped outside a closed door.

"Our viewing room is there," he pointed. "We call it the chapel of rest. That has not been violated, fortunately."

It was strange, Grace thought; he didn't mind the mortuary, and postmortems never bothered him, but there was something about funeral homes that gave him the heebie-jeebies. He could see Branson looking uncomfortable, too.

The proprietor opened a door a short distance on, pressed some switches, and led them into a large workspace. Grace smelled glue, varnish, and a strong reek of disinfectant. He heard the click-whirr of a refrigerator, and a steady tick . . . tick . . . tick . . . of a clock or a meter of some kind. He saw a row of health and safety notices taped to one wall, and a drinking water dispenser nearby. Several coffins, some plain, others more ornate, rested on metal trestles, with their lids lying randomly on the floor beside them. In the far corner of the room was a tiled alcove. There, a cadaver lay on a steel tray beneath a white cover, with one darkened, shriveled foot protruding. A large glass container filled with what looked like pink embalming fluid sat on a table, amid several neatly laid out surgical instruments and a long rubber tube.

"It is this one over here, gentlemen," Houlihan said.

Grace walked past several coffins.

He saw a tiny old lady in one, her face so white it blended, ghostlike, with her hair color. The undertaker had stopped beside a plain pine coffin. Lying inside, between the cream, quilted satin sides, wearing a plain shroud, was a very attractive young woman, with flowing, titian red hair.

Pulling out a pair of protective surgical gloves from his pocket, he snapped them on, then with the undertaker's nodded assent, he lifted away the shroud completely. Everything else of her beautiful and well-endowed body was intact. Crude stitches right down her midriff showed she'd had a postmortem, and further marks were visible at the start of her hairline.

But her feet were missing.

They'd been severed at the ankles by an instrument that both detectives could see, with their naked eyes, had a serrated blade.

A pile of what was obviously her clothing lay alongside the coffin so she could be dressed for the funeral.

He found his phone and snapped several close-up photographs of the leg stumps. He e-mailed them to the crime scene manager and asked him to send them straight to DCI Carol Jordan.

"What can you tell us about this young lady, and the circumstances," he asked Houlihan, as he watched the e-mail sending on his screen.

The undertaker led them through to his small, overly cozy and plush office, Grace dropping his gloves in a trash can on the way. There were more flowers on display, pictures of a smiling woman, presumably Houlihan's wife and two small girls, also happy, and a stack of leather-bound books, which Grace presumed contained photographs of coffins, urns, and other funeral accoutrements. They sat in red leather armchairs in front of his desk, while Houlihan settled on the far side and glanced down at some notes.

"Her name is Sarah O'Hara, twenty-three, a waitress in Brighton, who was trying to become a fashion model. Tragically broke her neck when her boyfriend crashed his motorcycle."

"What about the break-in during the night?" Glenn Branson asked.

"When I first got here to deal with the alarm, and everything, I thought it was vandals. Drunks. Kids. We do get a bit of trouble here in this area. I thought maybe they'd just been fooling around with the coffins." He broke off for an instant. "How rude of me, I've not offered you gentlemen anything. Tea, coffee?"

"I'm fine, thanks," Grace said.

Branson smiled at him. "I'm good."

"But the thing is after finding this terrible thing, this dreadful des-ecration of this poor young lady's body, I've begun to change my mind." Houlihan cradled his head in his hands and fell silent for some moments. "How am I going to tell her family? What am I going to say? This will ruin my business. One hundred and forty-nine years my family has run this company, and we've never had a problem, ever. We were planning big celebrations for next year. Now will we even be in business?"

"I'm sure there'll be ways through this for you. But if we could just focus for now on establishing the facts we need."

"Of course."

Grace pulled out his notebook. "You don't believe it was vandals, you said? What are your reasons for that?"

"I was called out because the alarm was ringing. But I'm not the first keyholder contact. That is my embalmer, Rodney Tidy. I have a deal with him. I pay him a little bit of cash to come out if the alarm goes off. It's worth it not to have a disturbed night. Usually it's something silly, mice chewing through the wire, or a spider's web across a sensor that's set it off—that sort of thing."

"Mr. Tidy's away, is he?" Branson asked.

"No, he is not. So this is the strange thing. I got telephoned by the alarm company because they said they could not get an answer from Rodney."

"This was around 2 a.m.?" Grace asked.

Houlihan nodded.

"Late for someone to be out on a midweek night," Branson com-mented.

"Extremely unusual behavior for him."

"What do you know about him?" Grace asked.

"He's a bit of an oddball. But then again, embalming isn't everyone's cup of tea, so to speak. He's somewhat of a loner. Not married and he really does not have good social skills."

"You haven't been to check up on his address, to see if he's ill or any-thing?" Ken Anakin asked.

"I did. About 4 a.m. I waited here just to ensure whoever had done this didn't come back, but I was careful not to touch anything, as I was instructed by the officers who attended. Then I went to his address over in Portslade, but I couldn't find his house."

Grace carefully watched the man's face and his body language. It wasn't surprising he was in an agitated state, but it seemed there was something the undertaker was holding back.

"Couldn't find it?"

"I thought I must have written it down wrong. But when I got back here and checked it, I had it down correctly."

Grace let it go for a moment. "How many people do you employ here?"

"Just a few. We are a real family business. My wife, Gudrun, my son, Kevin, his wife, Gemma, my bookkeeper—her name's Eleanor Walker— and Rodney Tidy."

"This may be a difficult question for you to answer," Grace said, continuing to watch him carefully. "Could this have been done by a member of your staff."

Houlihan leaned forward, lowered his voice as if scared he might be overheard, and said, "There is only one person who could possibly have done this. Actually, there is something odd. When I was called here, because the alarm was ringing, the first thing I did was switch it off. Then I went around the entire premises with the two police officers and we couldn't find any unlocked outside doors, or open or broken windows."

"Meaning someone either had a door key or picked a lock?" Grace said.

"After the officers left, I checked the alarm. I know a bit about technology. On the control panel you can access the history of when it has been switched on and off." He raised a finger in the air, conspiratorially. "Here's the strange thing: The alarm was switched off at 1:10 a.m. this morning, a full fifty minutes before it was set off."

"Someone came in, switched the alarm off, did the damage, perhaps including sawing off the feet, then activated the alarm and left. Is that what you're saying?" Glenn Branson asked.

"Either activated the alarm accidentally, or perhaps deliberately to make it look like there had been a break-in."

"What time is Rodney Tidy due in for work?" Grace asked.

Houlihan checked his ornate antique watch. "He should have been in over an hour ago. We start early here, because sometimes relatives or partners want to come in on the morning of a funeral to view their loved one just one more time before they are interred or cremated."

"Did you ever check on Rodney Tidy's address previously?" Grace asked.

"Never had any reason too. He had excellent references when he applied for the job. Like I said, he's an oddball, but always a hard worker."

Grace looked at Branson. "I think we should go and pay Rodney Tidy a visit."

Houlihan provided them the address.

"I know roughly where that is," Branson said.

"In the meantime, I'd appreciate you not touching anything in the room where the coffins and the bodies are," Grace said. "We're going to need to seal your premises."

"Seal them?"

"I'm afraid so. This is potentially connected to a murder inquiry, so I'm declaring it a crime scene."

"But I've got funerals today, Detective."

"And I have a murdered young woman who may be connected to this."

"At least let me ship the bodies out that I have here."

"I'm sorry, I can't allow anything to be moved. But what we'll do is check those due for funerals today first, and see if we can get them released, although I can't promise anything at this stage."

"I can't tell six families there's going to be no funeral today."

"I'm sorry, you'll have to. I'm sure the dead bodies won't mind waiting."

Instantly he regretted making such an insensitive remark.

"This is outrageous. I want to speak to your superior, at once."

"His name is Assistant Chief Constable Cassian Pewe. Good luck with him, sir."

The three police officers left the building. Grace asked Anakin to remain until a scene guard was in place and to ensure Houlihan followed instructions.

Moments later Grace and Branson approached their car.

"You drive, Glenn," he said. "I need to make some calls."

"Okay, boss."

"And no jokes about legging it?"

"Absolutely not. I'd hate to do what you just did and put my foot in it."

•◆•

CAROL LOOKED OVER TONY'S SHOULDER.

He'd logged into what seemed to be the most popular foot fetishist forum as Doctor Sole and was browsing the comments. There seemed to be three or four others online, swapping resources for podiatric porn.

"I've just had Roy Grace on from Brighton," she said, filling him in on the raid at the undertaker's. "The embalmer seems to be on the missing list. Name of Rodney Tidy."

"Nobody uses their real names on here," Tony said. "But an embalmer would fit the bill. He'd have access to bodies. Most funerals are closed-coffin affairs, so he could help himself to the best feet after the lid was screwed down and nobody would be any the wiser. He could have been doing this for years."

"So why mess it up last night? Why set off the alarm and leave the coffin open so anyone could see what he'd done?" she asked.

"Maybe he didn't," Tony said. "Maybe it wasn't down to him. Maybe Rodney did what half the world seems to do on the Internet these days."

She frowned. "What do you mean?"

"Maybe he made a date online. He could have met someone in a chat room or a forum who shares his fetish. Not just lovely feet, but dead feet. Who knows? Maybe there's a secret place on the darknet. A Grindr for fetishists. Footr. Archr."

Carol groaned. "Make it stop. Okay, supposing you're right, what do you think might have happened?"

"Tidy could have invited him back to the undertaker's to show him round. Perhaps they'd made a pact to take a pair of feet together. Tidy insists they have to leave after they've done one. His new friend doesn't agree and bursts back inside, setting off the alarm." He shrugged one shoulder. "It does feel to me like somebody else's presence precipitated a different set of behaviors from Tidy." He raised his voice. "Stacey? That analysis you were doing of the chat rooms? Did you find anybody posting about embalmed feet?"

The sound of fingers whisking over keys could be heard. Then, from behind the bank of monitors, Stacey said, "About a dozen."

"Can you find out if any of them is Rodney Tidy?" Carol asked.

Before Stacey could respond, Carol's phone gave its text alert.

"Message from Roy Grace," she muttered. "They can't trace Rodney Tidy. The address he gave his employer doesn't exist. He could be anywhere."

"He uses the site you're on right now," Stacey said. "His handle is Cold Feet. He was last on two days ago, talking about a beautiful specimen who had walked into his world. He seems most friendly with Arch Lover, but I can't track his ID. He comes on through a proxy server in Belarus."

Carol paced back and forth across the incident room. "We know Leyton Gray goes to Brighton. And we know he's been accused of behavior that amounts to foot fetishism. Am I reaching to think there might be a connection? Can we put them together? Do we know where Gray stays when he's there?"

Stacey rolled her eyes. "We had him in here for three hours. What do you think?"

"I think you've already accessed his credit cards and his Internet history," Tony said.

Stacey tutted. "You should know me better than that. A teenage boy could manage that. I've also mirrored his phone. So I can tell you there's no record of credit card payments to any hotel or B&B in Brighton. But I can also tell you that three months ago he googled directions to an address in Kemptown. And he's referenced it twice since."

Carol's phone pinged.

"There you go, boss. It might be worth Superintendent Grace getting his team round there."

•◆•

AN HOUR LATER, ROY GRACE AND GLENN BRANSON DROVE THEIR plain Ford Escape slowly past a row of four-story Regency terraced houses, with railed-off basements, just off the seafront, all of them badly in need of a lick of paint. In Victorian times each would have been a single dwelling, with servants quartered down in the basements and up on the attic floors. But now they'd been broken up into flats and bedsits.

"Number fourteen, boss," Glenn Branson said, pointing through the side window.

Grace nodded and carried on a short distance, then pulled into an empty space behind a marked police car and climbed out in the blustery, salty wind.

Four uniformed officers in the marked car climbed out, also: the duty inspector at John Street police station, Ken "Panicking" Anakin, and three PCs, two male and one female.

One of the males was a man-mountain.

Anakin's nickname was well deserved. He panicked about pretty much everything. He approached Roy and Glenn with a twitchy smile. "Good to see you both."

"And you, Ken."

Anakin unfolded a large-scale map of the area, struggling to hold it steady in the gusting wind, and the three of them peered at it.

"Roy, this is the street behind." He ran a finger along. "Mews garages, but behind them are the rear gardens of these houses, so it could be an escape route. It's the basement flat, right?"

"That's the information I have; 14B sounds like a basement address," Grace replied.

"I think we should cover the rear," Anakin said.

Anakin dispatched two of the uniformed officers, then, accompanied by the man-mountain, followed the detectives up to the front and down the shabby basement steps, past the dustbins. In contrast to the rest of the building, the front door to the basement flat was well presented, recently painted a gloss white and with polished brass letters.

14B.

There was a modern Entryphone system with CCTV.

Grace pressed the bell.

They heard a buzz from the interior, but there was no response. After a brief pause, he tried again.

Still no response.

Ken Anakin radioed the officers he'd dispatched to the rear, asking if they could see into the flat. After a minute his radio crackled into life.

The woman PC spoke, "Sir, it's hard to see in because there are no lights on and it's dark. But it looks like there's a man in an armchair. We've rapped on the window a couple of times, but he's not reacted. I think he might be a G5."

That was the police terminology in Brighton for a sudden death.

Anakin thanked her and relayed the information to Grace and Branson.

"Push the door in," Grace said.

"I've got a bosher in the car," the man-mountain said.

"May not need it."

Branson braced himself, then kicked out hard with his size eleven boot, straight below the keyhole. With a splintering crack the door swung open, part of the frame going with it, the bottom of the door sweeping over a pile of mail that lay on the mat.

Grace breathed in a rank smell.

Not the smell of death that he'd been expecting; this was more a laboratory smell.

Preservatives. Formalin?

He entered first, followed by Glenn Branson, Anakin, and the man-mountain. They were in a narrow but smart hallway, with a red carpet, and recently painted cream walls, hung with professionally framed photographs of feet.

Ladies' feet.

Extremely beautiful feet.

The toes of one were curled around a snake. A lighted cigarette was held between two toes of another. As they walked toward the far end of the hall, the rank smell grew stronger.

Grace walked through an open door at the far end, into a large, elegantly furnished living room, and froze.

Directly in front of him, seated in an armchair with his back to the window, sat a man, staring at him, a hand resting on each arm of the chair.

Motionless.

He was in his early fifties and had the air of a provincial bank manager.

Short, neat, graying hair. A gray pin-striped suit, a pale gray shirt, and one of those rather naff matching tie and pocket handkerchiefs, both in purple. All that was missing were his shoes and there was a good reason for that.

His feet were missing too.

His legs ended just below the bottoms of his trousers, in two blackened, cauterized stumps. Darkened bloodstains lay on the carpet beneath them. In the man's slowly blinking eyes, Grace could see a vision of hell.

He could see something else too, as his eyes became increasingly accustomed to the dimness in here. One entire wall of the room was full of rows of glassed-in shelving, like in a museum. Lined along each row of shelves were perfectly preserved human feet.

"Rodney Tidy?" Grace asked.

"Help . . . me."

The voice was weak and parched, more a faint croak.

Grace ran forward, and it took him only moments to realize why the man was motionless.

Arms, hands, the back of the head, shoulders, and the entire spine were all bonded to the chair.

With superglue.

•—◆—•

LEYTON GRAY, ACCOMPANIED BY HIS SOLICITOR, AN INTENSELY SERI-ous woman in her early thirties, sat opposite Carol Jordan and another colleague in the small, starkly furnished interview room.

For the benefit of the CCTV recording Jordan announced, "DCI Carol Jordan and DS Paula McIntyre interviewing Leyton Gray under caution in the presence of his solicitor, Susan Ansell. The time is 10:05 a.m., Wednesday, July twelfth."

Then she leaned forward. "Mr. Gray, can you tell us your relationship with Mr. Rodney Tidy?

"Rivals. We've always been rivals."

Ignoring his solicitor's signals for him to keep quiet, he went on.

"I had to stop him. I had to, somehow. He always beat me to the best feet. He just always did. He told me once how much he loved to stare at feet. That he loved nothing more than to sit in a room and look at his latest trophies. So I obliged him. I've stopped him from ever getting to feet ahead of me again, and he gets his dream, to sit and look at feet. Did you see his own up there? They're not exactly beautiful, but I thought it would be a nice touch. That is, of course, if he's smart enough to understand my signal. Rodney, old boy, you've been de-feeted."

KATHY REICHS AND LEE CHILD

WAS FIRST PUBLISHED IN 1997 WHEN *KILLING FLOOR* INTRODUCED the world to a quiet wanderer named Jack Reacher. Kathy Reichs also came along in 1997 when *Déjà Dead* brought us forensic anthropologist Temperance Brennan.

Kathy freely admits that both she and Temperance have the same curriculum vitae. Getting the science right is important to Kathy, and she routinely turns to her own real-life experiences as a forensic anthropologist when writing a Temperance Brennan adventure. With Reacher I'm constantly asked if he's based on me. Truth be told, there's a lot of me inside him. It's almost unavoidable that a character created by a writer not be a little autobiographical. Reacher is pretty much a wish fulfillment for both me and the reader. What I (or they) would be, if we could all get away with it. How he acquired his name is simple. Both I and Reacher are tall. So back in the 1990s, while writing *Killing Floor* and grocery shopping, my wife remarked that "if the writing didn't work out I could always be a reacher in a supermarket."

Talk about fortuitous.

In creating our story, Kathy and I both agreed on the rough outline, then we wrote in turns. She likes things all planned out. I prefer to wander.

But we found a happy medium in which to work. I must confess to being a little nervous working with her, given her reputation for thoroughness, but we discovered that our actual writing styles are somewhat similar. This sometimes happens with collaborations. It helped that we've both written screenplays. Kathy with the television series *Bones,* which is based on her characters, and myself with my daughter. There's a process to fashioning a screenplay that's different from crafting a novel. Much more give-and-take is there between the various contributors, since rarely is a screenplay written by only one person. Luckily, we were both comfortable with that process.

And the result is an intriguing adventure that involves—

Faking a Murderer.

FAKING A MURDERER

"OVER THE PAST DECADE, THIS ACADEMY HAS TAKEN A GOOD HARD look at itself. We have evaluated the theory and methodology underlying each of our disciplines. Formalized statements on ethics. Developed clear and open paths toward board certification."

The hall was dim, the stage blazing like a Hollywood set. She could see little from the podium. Rows of shadowy heads. Here and there, a triangle of white bisected by a tie. A wink of reflection off a plastic-sheathed badge.

"No longer can unqualified individuals hang out their shingles, call themselves experts, and practice without oversight. Without adherence to rigorously verified standards."

The other speakers sat behind her in well-behaved silence. To either side of them, screens displayed projected images of the logos of the American Academy of Forensic Sciences and the Marriott Wardman Park Hotel. Flanking the screens were stairs to ground level.

"This year's conference is titled 'Reliable Relevant and Real Forensic

Science.' Anthropology. Pathology. Toxicology. It doesn't matter the section. That trifecta is the goal of everyone here."

At the base of each set of steps, an electrified sign indicated an exit. In her peripheral vision, she noticed two men shape up in the red radiance shed by the one to her right.

"As each presenter in this plenary session has so aptly demonstrated, we are working hard to achieve that goal. For law enforcement. For the courts. For justice. I thank you for your attention. And I wish you an informative and enjoyable conference."

There was a swell of applause as the houselights came up. More than the usual courteous clap. Long and heartfelt. Those behind her rose and gathered their notes, faces saying they were pleased with themselves. And relieved. The presentation had been well received by a very tough crowd. Their colleagues. The audience began to disperse. The aisles filled and the murmur of voices picked up volume.

As she closed her laptop, the two men climbed the treads and crossed toward her. Each wore a navy suit, white shirt, and tastefully understated tie. Black socks, shiny shoes.

Approaching the podium, the pair fanned out slightly. The guy who stepped left was tall and burly and had a nose that looked like it might have been broken. More than once. His shaved scalp gleamed like polished mahogany under the stage lights.

The guy who stepped right was close to her height. He had heavy dark brows over very small eyes, thick black hair, olive skin.

"Dr. Temperance Brennan?" Dark Brows's voice was surprisingly deep for a man of his size.

"Yes." Guarded. She suspected their purpose, accepted consults only through formal channels. "And you are?"

"Special Agent Pierre Dupreau." Displaying a badge to prove it.

"Bonjour," she said.

No hint of a grin.

"I speak English," she said.

Nope.

She looked at Broken Nose. He badged her with the same wrist motion employed by his partner. Special Agent Byron Szewczk. She wondered if Szewczk envied Dupreau his abundance of vowels.

"Are you armed, Dr. Brennan?" Dupreau, little eyes scanning her body for telltale bulges.

"Excuse me?"

"Are you carrying a—"

"The question was clear. I want to know why you posed it."

Sensing tension, a few stragglers eyed them while pretending not to.

"We'd like you to come with us," Dupreau said, voice lowered a hair.

"No."

"I'm afraid we must insist." Dupreau, steely.

"I'm afraid I must decline." Brennan, steelier.

Dupreau withdrew a photo from one navy pocket and handed it to her. A beat to indicate annoyance, then she glanced down at the image.

The subject was male, white, probably midforties. His hair was center parted and held back with a binder. Black plastic-framed glasses sat low on his nose. A camera hung from his neck. He looked like a middle-aged uncle who enjoyed shooting wildflowers in his spare time.

Brennan's eyes rolled up, one brow cocked in question.

"Don't pretend you don't know him," Dupreau said.

"I don't know him," Brennan said.

Dupreau's gaze cut to his partner. Szewczk wagged his head slowly, clearly disappointed.

"Lose the theatrics," Brennan said. "Who is he?"

"Jonathan Yeow," Dupreau said. "Until yesterday, an investigative reporter with the *Washington Post*."

"Why are you telling me this?"

"Yesterday, Yeow's house cleaner found him in his kitchen, asphyxiated with a plastic bag over his head." Delivered with an impressive level of disgust. "Murdered."

"I'm sorry for the man's misfortune." Handing back the photo. "But his death has nothing to do with me."

"Au contraire." Flick of a smile, no humor. "Your prints were on the plastic bag."

"That's impossible."

"Let's go." Dupreau's tone now carried an aggressive edge.

"May I phone my attorney?"

"I definitely would."

WEDNESDAY, FEBRUARY 22, 1320 EST

THE D.C. METRO PD STATION TO WHICH SHE WAS TRANSPORTED WAS
on Indiana Avenue in northwest Washington. It was a solid concrete bunker in a neighborhood of solid concrete bunkers, some more so than
others. Small red plaza out front, swatches of lawn that would look better come summer, ditto the few optimistic trees. Old-timey lampposts.
Droopy flags.

They parked her in an interview room containing the usual table,
chairs, wall phone, two-way mirror, and audio-video recording equipment. An hour of fuming, then the door opened and a woman entered.
She wore her hair drawn back in a very tight bun, a black pantsuit, size
elf, and sensible pumps. Her briefcase said lawyer. Her visitor tag said
V. Luong.

Brennan had explained the situation by phone. They got straight to
it. As Brennan talked, Luong listened, ears sharp. Attorney ears. Now and
then she asked a question.

"You're certain you've never met Mr. Yeow?"

"Absolutely. But I know the connection these yaks have jumped on.
Yeow was investigating a suicide that occurred back in the eighties. A man
named Calder Massee."

Luong's eyes rounded in surprise. "The air force bird colonel who
shot himself in Germany?"

"Yes. Massee was discovered dead in his car behind the Hotel Bremer-
hof in the town of Kaiserslautern in March of 1987. The coroner's ruling
was death by self-inflicted gunshot wound."

"Who performed the autopsy?"

"A German pathologist."

"Were you even out of grad school in '87?"

"Just. But I wasn't involved in the original analysis."

Brennan worked the keys on her laptop. Which she'd managed to retain thanks to Luong's intervention.

"The Massee family went ballistic. They insisted the suicide finding was a cover-up because Calder had been wrongly accused in an espionage case. They claimed he'd been shot in the back of the head, execution style. Said they had an eyewitness to prove it."

"I remember this." Luong was jotting notes on a yellow legal pad. "Some relatives were very adept at working the media."

"That's an understatement. They called press conferences, volunteered for interviews, appeared on every talk and news show airing at the time."

"So where do you come in?"

"Massee had three brothers. The youngest was obsessed. After the media lost interest, he took out ads, wrote op-ed pieces, set up blogs and Internet pages, put pressure on his senator and congressman, you know the drill. Over the years, every conspiracy theorist on the planet joined in the fight to have the case reopened. Long story short, in 2012, a government commission was formed. I was recruited to direct an exhumation and examine the remains."

Brennan double-clicked to open a document. A header gave a case file number, date, and the name Calder Massee.

"This was my final report to the commission." Scrolling down. "I won't bore you with the details. Take a look at these images."

The first was an anterior view of a skull. Brennan pointed to what had once been the nose.

"Note how the midfacial region is fragmented." Moving her finger to the forehead. "The radial fracturing on the frontal bone."

New image.

"This is a close-up of the roof of the mouth. Note the blue-green staining on what remains of the palatine process of the maxilla."

"I see it."

"That's due to copper oxidation."

"The bullet was copper jacketed."

"Yes. On its path through the head, a tiny sliver broke off, lodged, and oxidized there."

Brennan moved on to the teeth.

"This shows the lingual, or tongue side of the upper dental arcade. Note the cracked first molar and the dark areas on that tooth and the one beside it. The discoloration was caused by heat when the gun discharged."

The fourth image showed a hole in the crown of the skull.

"That defect was created when the bullet left Massee's head. Note that the exit point is high on the crown."

Tight shot.

"Note that the edges of the defect are beveled on the skull's outer surface. That means the defect is an exit hole."

Brennan leaned back. Gestured at the screen.

"The pattern is consistent with trauma resulting from a self-inflicted gunshot wound."

"Or someone shoved a gun in Massee's mouth and pulled the trigger." Luong, playing devil's advocate.

"Doubtful. The bullet trajectory was straight up and out the top, so Massee's head wasn't moving. Also, there were powder burns on his right hand and no drugs in his system."

"Why is the lack of drugs significant?"

"Massee was a big guy. Hard to stick a muzzle in a big guy's mouth if he doesn't want it there."

"Which I suspect he did not." Luong flipped a page. "So your opinion corroborated the original coroner's report."

"Yes."

"The brother wasn't happy."

"No."

"What does all this have to do with Yeow?"

"According to Dupreau and Szewczk, Yeow was working on a story that would prove my analysis was flawed. That I was either inept or bribed."

"So you killed him to save your reputation."

"That's their theory."

Luong thought about that.

Then, "Why were your prints on the plastic bag?"

"I have no idea."

WEDNESDAY, FEBRUARY 22, 1830 EST

JACK REACHER WALKED OUT OF THE BALTIMORE BUS DEPOT INTO A world of frozen streets and dirty snow. The sun was weak and watery and very low in the sky. He headed toward it, west, down a wide street, on the traffic side of a high berm of plowed snow, with his thumb out. Every car passed him by. Which he expected. Hitching rides in town was hard. Especially Baltimore. He would do better when he got to the highway ramp. His goal was I-95 South, for however many hundreds of miles it took to get fifty degrees warmer. Maybe as far as Miami. Or all the way to Key West. He had been there before. Always had a good time. Except it was the end of the line. Which meant the only way to leave was to double back. Which he didn't like. He preferred forward motion.

As always he had decent shoes, and for once he had a decent coat, so the weather didn't bother him. He had known colder. Korea in the winter, and the advanced units on the German plain. And some American bases. Baltimore in February was balmy by comparison. But even so, he couldn't afford an all-nighter. In the summertime he could sleep under a bridge. But not in February, however balmy. Happily the traffic was heavy. Rush hour, all across the civilized world. Lots of potential benefactors. But Reacher was a large man, and not especially attractive. Lots of rejection, too, for all kinds of gut-level reasons.

But the sheer weight of numbers and the overall odds were with him, and, sure enough, inside an hour and twenty minutes a guy in a rental Impala pulled over and agreed to take him as far as Savannah, Georgia, right then, a straight shot, as late as it took. Maybe conversation would keep the guy awake. That seemed to be the motive behind the offer. So Reacher climbed in, and they took off. The driver was a dark fleshy man who could have been forty. He had a black five o'clock shadow against what in better days would have been pale and papery skin, but was now dark red and swollen with capillaries. Which was a problem all its own. Reacher could stop the guy falling asleep, but he couldn't keep him alive from a heart attack. He wasn't a doctor.

There was no conversation at first. The guy had the radio playing, on a mostly sports talk station, where all kinds of mostly wonderful things were happening. Then at eight o'clock a different voice in a different acoustic read out the local news from Baltimore, just as they were leaving it, and then the voice called upon expert opinion to expand on and explain the news, in the form of respectful conversation, as if between the best of friends. Reacher tuned it out, until he heard a name he knew, and then one he didn't.

The anchor asked a question, and the expert answered, "You're absolutely right; to understand this case, you have to understand the Calder Massee case, and some say the dispute about that case's original findings has now gone on so long we should take the issue seriously at last. The official line has always been suicide, and indeed the government's last communication on the subject dates from four years ago, when it said it welcomed what it called Dr. Temperance Brennan's meticulous and independent analysis, which as expected confirmed conclusions made at the time, and therefore the case was now closed."

Reacher had never heard the word *Temperance* used as a name before.

The anchor said, "But Jonathan Yeow claimed it was more than a dispute. He claimed to have definitive proof that Massee was executed."

The expert said, "You're absolutely right, even to the point where there was a strong rumor Yeow had an actual copy of the illegal 1987 order to deploy the assassin. And don't forget, Yeow was a very well respected reporter. He was from the *Washington Post*. He was the heir to a grand tradition. What he was going to say would have carried some weight. If he was right, Dr. Brennan was either ordered or coerced or bribed to falsify her second autopsy, and if that was true, her career would be over. All her previous testimony would be worthless. She would be a laughingstock. I mean, just this morning she gave the keynote at their convention at the Marriott Wardman down there in D.C., telling hundreds of other forensic scientists to keep it reliable, and relevant, and real."

"Is that enough reason for homicide?"

"Professional ruin is a powerful motivator. Stranger things have happened. And sources inside the FBI suggest there is physical evidence, perhaps in the form of fingerprints."

"But Dr. Brennan hasn't been formally arrested."

"Before she even left the convention ballroom, she hired Veronica Luong. Brennan's supporters say that's appropriate, in terms of their respective professional achievements, but others say you don't hire the hottest hotshot in town unless you're in trouble. Either way it seems Luong negotiated a special arm's-length own-recognizance relationship with the FBI, at least for these initial stages of the investigation. Some are calling that a professional courtesy, and others are calling it the start of another cover-up."

Then the anchor moved on, to the price of gas.

Reacher looked at the driver and said, "I'm sorry, I have to get out now. I changed my mind. I'm not going to Savannah anymore. I'm going to D.C. instead."

WEDNESDAY, FEBRUARY 22, 2100 EST

REACHER GOT A BUS ON GEORGIA AVENUE AND GOT OUT WHERE HE thought the convention hotels might be. He asked a girl passing by if she knew the Marriott Wardman, and she did what they all did, thumbs flashing over a thin flat telephone the size of a paperback book, and then she showed him the screen, which represented their current location as a blue pulse, and the Wardman as a red blob, like the plastic head of a pushpin shoved in a map. South and west, two blocks down and three blocks over.

It was a big brassy place, with a lobby the size of a football field, still busy in the middle of the evening. Reacher figured however courteous and arm's-length Brennan's current relationship with the FBI might be, it would inevitably include a don't-leave-town provision, which meant extra nights in her convention room, plus no doubt a deal breaker on the FBI's part, in the form of an agent right outside her door, just in case she decided to run for it. No hotshot lawyer could negotiate that one away. So Reacher rode the elevator as high as it went and then walked back down the fire stairs, stopping at every floor to take a covert glance up and down the corridor. He saw two turndown carts, and three maids walking, and plenty of crusted trays of room-service leftovers. But no federal agents.

Until the fifth floor. Like in a movie. An old guy in a fold-up chair, right next to a door. Reacher pulled back and walked down to four, and came back up again to five in the elevator, like a normal person would. He stepped out and pretended to study the sign, these numbers this way, those numbers that way, and then he walked toward the seated agent, and said, "I'm Dr. Brennan's paralegal. From Veronica Luong's office."

The old guy didn't get up.

He said, "Got ID?"

Reacher gave him his passport.

The old guy said, "According to the number, this passport was issued direct by a certain office inside the State Department."

"It came in the mail," Reacher said.

"And now you're a lawyer?"

"Not quite. Paralegal, from the ancient Greek *para*. Like parachute. Not quite a fall."

"What do you need to see Dr. Brennan about?"

"Her Sixth Amendment right to assistance of counsel."

"Now you're the pro bono intern too?"

"You haven't arrested her. You can't stop her having visitors. You can put my name in the log. Which could help you in the end. We might want to switch to the Fifth Amendment later, and think about due process instead. Or as well."

The old guy handed back Reacher's passport.

He said, "Knock yourself out, kid."

The room door had a panel on the wall, close to the handle, with a red light for *Do Not Disturb,* and a green light for *Make Up My Room,* and a pushbutton for the doorbell.

The red light was on.

Do not disturb.

Reacher pressed the doorbell button. He heard a chime inside the room, muted and polite. A woman's voice said, "Who is it?"

Reacher said, "Your paralegal. Ms. Luong sent me."

The door opened on the chain. Reacher saw a third of a face, a green eye, the sweep of dark blond hair. Not tiny, not tall.

He liked what he saw.

He said, "Are you Temperance Brennan?"

The woman said, "Yes."

"Great name."

"Who are you?"

Reacher said, "I'm here to help."

"How?"

"Any way I can, which is what you're going to need, because this is the Massee family we're talking about here."

"Do you know them?"

"From a distance."

"Who are you?"

"My name is Jack Reacher."

"And?"

"I was in the army in March 1987. Serving in Germany, as a matter of fact."

Brennan was quiet for most of a minute.

Then she said, "You better come in."

• ◆ •

BRENNAN'S ROOM WAS A STANDARD RECTANGLE ALL GUSSIED UP with brass and wallpaper, so it could be priced as deluxe or executive. It had two club chairs under the window, either side of a small round table. Reacher sat down in one of them. Less threatening.

Brennan said, "What do you know?"

"I can't tell you," Reacher said.

"Then why are you here?"

"In case a rock meets a hard place. Which it might not. But you shouldn't underestimate the trouble you're in."

"I wasn't bribed and I didn't make a mistake. Massee shot himself."

"You know that scientifically."

"Yes, scientifically. Jonathan Yeow was wrong. Why would I be scared of him?"

Reacher said, "I'll stay the night in this hotel. My advice would be to call Ms. Luong and have her contact me first thing in the morning."

"What are you going to tell her that you won't tell me?"

"Nothing. This is all just in case."

"Of rocks and hard places?"

"Yeow is a dead journalist, which will drive all the other journalists batshit crazy. He's one of them. He's their hero now. It will become a question of stamina. Sooner or later the DOD will throw you under the bus just to shut them up."

"Who are you?"

"Just a guy passing through."

"What kind?"

"I was a military cop."

"They say Yeow was suffocated with a plastic bag."

"Uncommon method."

"They say my prints are on the bag."

"But they haven't arrested you."

"I don't think they buy it physically," Brennan said. "Yeow must have struggled. He was bigger than me. Almost certainly stronger."

"And because you're a major player."

"I suppose."

"How did your prints get on the bag?"

"I don't know."

Reacher got up and walked out of the room. He nodded to the old man in the fold-up chair and headed to the elevators, where he rode down to the lobby and hiked across an acre of marble to the reception desk. He bought a room for the night, using his passport for ID, and his ATM card for money. The room was on the third floor. Neither deluxe nor executive. No brass, no wallpaper. But it had a telephone, which rang within forty-two minutes.

A woman's voice said, "Mr. Reacher?"

Bright, intelligent, possibly lethal.

Reacher said, "Yes."

"This is Veronica Luong, Dr. Temperance Brennan's attorney. I assume you have classified information that proves the suicide case. I further assume your sense of duty makes you very reluctant to reveal it, but your sense of conscience makes you equally reluctant to see an innocent woman falsely convicted."

Definitely lethal.

Reacher said, "Something like that."

"You're a paralegal."

"I only said that to get in the door. Actually I'm unemployed."

"No, I mean you're a paralegal. As of now. With my firm. Officially employed."

"Is this an attorney-client thing?"

"I want you where I can see you," Luong said. "Starting at eight o'clock tomorrow morning, at the precinct house on Indiana Avenue, Northwest."

THURSDAY, FEBRUARY 23, 0837 EST

SAME WINDOWLESS CELL. SAME AV GEAR, WALL PHONE, TABLE AND chairs. Brennan was seated in one. Luong was beside her.

They'd been there forty minutes when Dupreau entered and tossed down a file. It landed with a *tic* and puff of stale air.

Dupreau stared at Brennan, skin sallow beneath the humming fluorescents. Brennan stared back, telegraphing the anger trip-wiring in her brain.

A few beats, then, "Thank you for coming."

"I had a choice?" Controlled, calm.

Dupreau pulled out a chair and sat. Opened the file. Slowly sorted and organized the contents. Neither Luong nor Brennan was impressed. Both were familiar with the old trick.

Dupreau checked that the AV equipment was on and working.

"This interview will be recorded. For your protection and mine. Do you have any objection to that?"

"And if I did?" Brennan glared at the mirror, certain Szewczk was on the far side.

Dupreau hit a button. "Present at this interrogation are Special Agent Pierre Dupreau, Federal Bureau of investigation, Internal Security Unit, Dr. Temperance Brennan, and legal counsel, Veronica Luong."

Dupreau provided the date and time, then drew a sheet from one of his stacks and pretended to read.

Brennan knew what he was doing. And why he'd left them cooling their heels. But the ploy wouldn't work. She hadn't become anxious or vulnerable as some suspects might. She'd grown furious. For Brennan, that translated into laser focus.

Dupreau laid down the paper.

Some interviewers like to put their subjects at ease, gain their trust, then take advantage. Knowing that wouldn't work, Dupreau went straight for the kill.

"Calder Massee was a bird colonel in the United States Air Force, a career officer with access to highly classified information. Many believe he was executed for a crime he didn't commit. He was wrongly suspected of being a traitor. They said he was actively engaged in spying for foreign governments. But he wasn't. The suicide story was a government-backed cover-up for the mistake."

"Many believe aliens landed at Roswell."

"In 2012, you oversaw the exhumation and reanalysis of Massee's remains."

"I'm impressed. You can read."

"This year marks the thirtieth anniversary of Massee's death. Jonathan Yeow was about to go public with proof of your involvement in the whitewashing of his murder. We believe you killed him to prevent that happening."

"Very creative."

"Incompetence, complicity, greed. Doesn't matter the reason. Exposure would ruin you."

"Seriously. You should write a pilot, shop it to Hollywood."

A long humming moment.

"According to the ME, Yeow died between midnight and seven Tuesday morning. Where were you during those hours?"

"Asleep in my room at the Marriott."

"Can anyone verify?"

"That's a rather personal question." Icy.

"Murder is a rather personal crime."

"I was alone."

"Your prints were on the plastic bag used to asphyxiate Yeow. That bag came from a CVS pharmacy. You were caught on surveillance video at four fifteen Monday afternoon at a CVS pharmacy on Connecticut Avenue."

"It's illegal to buy toothpaste?"

"Did you retain the bag that held your"—Dupreau hooked quotation marks—'toothpaste'?"

"I keep all my trash. Don't you?"

"Can you explain how your prints came to be on that bag?"

"I cannot."

"Dig deep."

"Kiss my—"

Luong jumped in. "My client has a busy schedule. Can we move this along?"

"Your client's attitude is causing me to lose patience." Little eyes drilling Brennan. "You don't want that."

Brennan took a breath to respond. Luong hushed her with a raised palm.

"Have you anything else, Special Agent Dupreau? An eyewitness? Evidence of contact between Dr. Brennan and the victim? Cell-phone records? E-mails?"

"The investigation is ongoing."

"Were Dr. Brennan's prints found elsewhere at the scene?"

"What scene?"

"Any scene."

No response.

"Was Dr. Brennan seen near Mr. Yeow's home? Caught on Yeow's security system? That of a bank? A school? A parking lot? A neighbor?"

Things moved behind the little eyes, but Dupreau said nothing.

"I take that to mean no," Luong said.

"The investigation is ongoing."

"I see. Will you be charging my client at this time?"

No response.

"I thought not." Luong rose. Brennan rose. "My client has nothing further to say."

Luong grabbed her briefcase, Brennan her purse. Both headed for the door.

Dupreau spoke to their retreating backs. "Dr. Brennan."

She turned, one hand on the knob.

"Until further notice, you are to remain in Washington."

"I'll cancel my trip to Chernobyl."

They left Dupreau gathering his meaningless papers.

•◆•

REACHER WAS IN THE HALL. LUONG LEFT BRENNAN STANDING ON her own for a minute. She walked over and Reacher said, "How was it?"

Luong said, "It was good, but not real good. I've seen people go to prison for less. Sometimes things go crazy. Nothing you can do."

"But they still didn't arrest her."

"Not yet."

"Got any paralegal work for me?"

"Yes," Luong said. "You know the law from a cop's point of view. You've got to stop her giving them a reason. You're her personal legal counsel. Don't let her say the wrong thing."

Luong walked away, and Reacher stepped across the hall to where Brennan was waiting.

She said, "What?"

He said, "Apparently I'm your personal legal counsel."

She didn't reply. Just walked. Reacher followed. They exited onto the small red plaza. The sky was leaden and appeared to be contemplating snow. Maybe sleet.

Brennan thumbed her phone for an Uber. The app promised Miguel in a Honda in seven minutes. He pulled up in six. They were back at the Marriott by ten.

Neither Brennan nor Reacher had eaten. Both were hungry. They crossed the football field lobby and found a restaurant that was serving breakfast.

Every table was full, but two women were leaving. Each wore a pantsuit made of polyester born at the dark end of the spectrum, solid shoes. Each carried a canvas bag bearing the AAFS logo and wore a neck lanyard dangling a badge. One identified its owner as S. Miller, the other as T. Southam. Colored ribbons hung from the badges. Miller had more than Southam.

Brennan ordered a cheese omelet. Reacher got pancakes with eggs and bacon. Both asked for plain coffee. Which seemed to disappoint Marsha, the waitress. Her badge was bronze and pinned to her ample chest.

"What is it you intend to do, Mr. Reacher?" When Marsha was out of earshot.

"That depends."

"Let's go at it differently. Why are you here?"

"To help."

"Me?"

"I believe you're going to need it."

"So you've said."

"I have."

"That's why you've agreed to work for Luong."

"I'm doing it for the money."

Brennan didn't laugh.

"Being employed by Luong legitimizes my presence," Reacher said.

"I didn't fudge data or make a mistake," Brennan said. "Massee shot himself."

Their food arrived. They peppered and salted and accepted refills on the disappointing coffee. Which was pretty good.

"How did you learn about Yeow's murder?" Brennan asked, when Marsha had again withdrawn.

"A radio news report."

"A Washington station?"

"No."

She waited for Reacher to elaborate. He didn't. But she grasped the implication. Media coverage wasn't just local. Not good. The story would catch fire, the press would go raw dog and she would end up their meat.

"You really think the DOD plans to make me a scapegoat?"

"I think it's a strong possibility."

"To hide the fact that it ordered Massee's execution."

"To stop people talking about it."

"Did the report say I'd been arrested?"

"It implied that was coming."

"Now that you've heard the evidence against me, will you move on?"

"Do you think I should?"

A man wove toward the table beside theirs. Brennan and Reacher both tracked him. Same reflex. Same discreet eyes.

"What if the radio hadn't been on?" Brennan asked, voice even lower than before.

"I read yesterday's papers."

"And you felt duty bound to come."

"Yes."

Brennan chewed on that. And her eggs. Reacher dabbed yolk with his toast. Around them people argued chain of custody and DNA and bitemark analysis. Some consulted programs. Some talked on cell phones.

"You said you were in the army in March of 1987. Stationed in Germany."

"I was," Reacher said.

"Did you know Calder Massee?"

"I knew of him."

"I don't like drama, Mr. Reacher." A note of something. Annoyance. Frustration. Unease.

"I don't do drama."

"There are things you are unwilling or unable to share."

Reacher nodded.

"Yet here you are."

"I am."

"What *can* you share?"

"You were right."

"About what?"

"Massee shot himself."

"How could you know?" Dubious.

Reacher laid down his fork, bunched his napkin, and leaned into his chair back.

He said, "I was there."

Over more plain coffee, Brennan and Reacher agreed on three main points.

A media frenzy would destroy Brennan's career. Maybe get her charged, perhaps convicted.

Dupreau and Szewczk were under pressure from forces far up the pay scale. She could expect no help from that quarter.

To clear her name, and avoid jail, she needed to find Yeow's killer on her own.

Reacher repeated his desire to help. Brennan admitted her skill set was better suited to the lab than the streets. Reacher assured her he had that end covered. That her analytical thinking would be their biggest asset.

For the first time that day, Brennan smiled. She liked Reacher. She accepted his offer.

That made four points.

They debated options. Concurred that a logical starting point was Yeow's editor.

Five points.

She ordered an Uber and they headed for the lobby.

• ◆ •

BRENNAN AND REACHER PUSHED THROUGH THE GLASS DOORS AND stepped out under the portico. The air was cold and heavy with moisture off the Potomac. The clouds, though darker and more bloated than earlier, still refused to commit.

A babble of voices and car horns caught their attention.

To their left, portable barriers stretched across the drive sweeping up from Woodley Road. Hotel personnel were checking vehicles before waving them on to the broad paved area used for loading and unloading guests.

Brennan and Reacher glanced right.

Same improv security.

A nanosecond of surprise, then understanding.

Beyond the barriers, a Barnum and Bailey scrum of cameras, mikes, booms, and journalists was expressing its discontent at being denied access to the hotel.

Figuring the sharks were sniffing the blood of some politician caught banging his intern, or a starlet not A-list enough to be at the Ritz, and that their driver hadn't a chance of reaching them, Brennan and Reacher decided to head downhill on foot.

"That's her!" As they approached the barrier. "That's Brennan."

Word spread through the scrum. Cameras popped onto shoulders. Lights ignited. Booms shot toward their mouths.

"Dr. Brennan. Ted Sanders, CNN."

"Would you care to make a statement?"

"Did you kill him?"

"Did you go along with the fake suicide? Or did you just blow it?"

"Are you about to be arrested?"

Brennan stopped short, face saying she'd shoot if she had a gun. Reacher took her arm and steered her back up the drive. Though bristling, she let him. Questions hammered their retreat.

"We'll wait thirty minutes, then go out through the kitchen," Reacher said when they were in the lobby.

"Bastards," she said.

"Yes," he said.

"It's all bullshit," she said.

"Yes," he said.

"I expected calls from the press, but this—" Arm arcing toward the door. "This is insane."

"Yeow was a journalist," Reacher said.

"They have the sensitivity of lice."

"Lice don't avenge their own."

"That must be it," she agreed.

They were both very wrong.

THURSDAY, FEBRUARY 23, 1345 EST

FOR DECADES THE *WASHINGTON POST* LOOMED LIKE A GIANT GRAY hive at the corner of Fifteenth and L. Its new address was 1301 K Street. Or One Franklin Square. The paper and the postal service were still hashing that out.

Yeow's editor was a guy named Albert Thorsten. A directory told them Thorsten's office was seven floors above the lobby with its zillion-inch screen. Brennan and Reacher ascended in a noiseless elevator and proceeded down a corridor flanking a newsroom the length of the U.S.-Canada border.

Five yards, then they saw Thorsten through an expanse of glass, seated at a desk that matched everything else in the building. The door was open. Brennan and Reacher entered. Both did their habitual scan.

The room wasn't big, wasn't small, wasn't drab, wasn't bright. Despite the fish tank wall, an overabundance of papers, printouts, files, and books made the unexceptional space feel tight and claustrophobic. A warehouse print hung behind Thorsten's head—a wooden pier, gulls, and a boat. It blended well with the blah.

Thorsten looked about fifty going on heart failure. Gray hair, saggy eyes, saggy gut. He raised skeptical brows on seeing Brennan. Apparently Luong had mentioned only her paralegal. Or maybe it was Reacher's size. Or gender.

"The lady of the hour," Thorsten guessed. Or knew, from press photos. Then the questioning eyes slid to Reacher.

"I'm the paralegal."

"Sure you are." Thorsten pointed at the two chairs facing him. They looked like the desk, except they were chairs.

Reacher sat. Brennan sat. Thorsten directed his next comment to her.

"Word is you burned one of my reporters." Voice dry and flat as the Kalahari.

"Word's wrong."

"And I'm blessed with your presence because?"

"I intend to find the bastard who did."

Thorsten thought about that. Then, "Yeow learned some interesting facts about you."

"Such as?"

"Beats me."

"He didn't brief you on his investigation?"

"Yeow was a veteran. We operated on a need-to-know basis."

"I need to know."

Another tense silence as they stared in two directions across the desk.

Thorsten's gaze was impersonal. Brennan figured years had passed since empathy last wormed into it.

"You're aiding Luong with the doc's defense?" Thorsten asked Reacher.

"I am."

"Paralegally."

"Yes. It would help to have the names of people Yeow was interviewing."

Thorsten laughed, as Brennan and Reacher both knew he would. "Please. I can't reveal sources." Realizing his mistake. "If I knew them."

"Yeow never told you what they said?" Brennan asked.

Thorsten shook his head slowly.

"He never showed you his notes? Asked for authorization? Requested travel money? Inducement money? Lunch money?"

The head kept wagging.

"What *can* you reveal, Mr. Thorsten?" Reacher, the diplomat.

"Yeow promised me one hell of a piece."

"Guess you're out of luck on that." Distaste coated Brennan's tone.

"Or the story's become much better."

"Be very careful, Mr. Thorsten."

"Is that a threat?"

"Journalists often pretend they know more than they do."

Thorsten shrugged. Whatever.

Brennan glanced at Reacher. He dipped his chin. They both stood.

"I didn't kill Jonathan Yeow," Brennan said, looking down at the editor. "And I didn't make an error or take a bribe in the Calder Massee case. When I prove those two facts, and find Yeow's killer, my first call will be to the *New York Times.*"

Brennan drew a card from her shoulder bag and winged it onto the desk. Then she and Reacher turned and left. Along the corridor overlooking the very long newsroom. Down the quiet elevator. Through the lobby out onto K street. Which wasn't quiet.

They decided to take the Metro. Were waiting on the platform when Brennan's cell phone rang. Caller ID displayed an unfamiliar number. She answered anyway.

"You didn't hear this from me." The Kalahari voice was muffled, as though Thorsten's mouth was cupped with one hand.

"Hear what?"

"Ian Massee."

"Calder's youngest brother."

"Ian thinks the suicide was a DOD-ordered execution."

"So do a lot of people."

"The guy's a lunatic."

"You've spoken to him?" Locking eyes with Reacher, who was listening to her end of the conversation.

"Many times. Until I stopped taking his calls."

"Do you think he could be violent?"

"He loathes the government."

"So do a lot of people."

"In my opinion, Ian Massee's the next Sandy Hook waiting to happen."

"Why would he kill Yeow? Yeow was going to prove him right."

"Follow the money," said the Kalahari voice, muffled, like a dust storm.

Then the call clicked off.

Reacher said, "Our Mr. Thorsten is a versatile character. One minute Mr. Cautious Corporate Editor, and the next minute Mr. Watergate Deep Throat."

Brennan said, "I don't want to have to talk to Ian Massee."

"Maybe we won't have to. Why would Thorsten change his tune like that?"

"You tell me."

"Maybe he dreams of the old days."

"Or?"

"He dreams of the money. He runs a newspaper. He's got a great story that just got better. He could sell a lot of extra copies. He could get all kinds of syndication deals. Maybe a movie. Except he doesn't know what the story is. Not yet. He knows the sources. But he doesn't know what they said. He's trying to get us to do the interviews all over again. To keep the dream alive."

"Doesn't work," Brennan said. "Thorsten wouldn't benefit. I'm sure Ian Massee sold the movie rights years ago. It's his project. And Watergate is ancient history. Journalists are different now. They know better. A hack like Yeow would sign up with Massee's people ahead of time, and in his own name. He'd cut Thorsten out. He'd want all the profit, not just a percentage."

"You're following the money."

"To where?"

"To wherever Ian Massee sold the rights. Some movie company somewhere knows the whole story. As a contractual requirement, I'm sure. Before making their substantial investment."

Brennan said, "Which would make them protect Mr. Yeow, because he's the golden goose. They can't possibly be suspects."

Reacher said nothing.

Brennan said, "And obviously they're not. But I suppose a rival might be. If someone wins, someone else loses. Suppose the someone else doesn't want to lose. People tell me show business is tough. Kill Yeow, you kill your competitor's bid for glory. And you make him waste his investment. That comes off his bottom line. It's a win-win."

"Follow the money."

"Which means television, not movies. People tell me that's where the money is these days. In which case there are hundreds of companies and therefore potentially thousands of one-on-one ratings wars. Millions, actually. It's a math thing."

"I understand," Reacher said. "I went to West Point. Which is a kind of college."

"It's an academy."

"We could all read and write."

"We would need to start where Ian Massee sold the rights. And work outward from there. Which means talking to him anyway. We're back where we started."

"At least we know what to ask him. We don't have to beat about the bush."

•◆•

THEY RODE THE METRO TO WHERE BRENNAN'S INTERNET PHONE told them Ian Massee maintained his office. Which turned out to be a storefront with a yellow painted-over window, between a post office and a bilingual tax preparer, in a mall about equidistant from the best and the worst the metro area had to offer.

On the inside the office was a plain rectangular space, and it was empty, except for a woman at a reception desk, just inside the door. She was backlit with gold, from the sunlight coming through the painted window.

Reacher stepped up and asked, "Is Mr. Ian Massee in the office?"

The woman looked at him with a pleasant receptionist-style smile, warm and friendly, except her eyes said *It's an open-plan office with only me in it. What part of that don't you understand?*

She said out loud, "Not at the moment, I'm afraid."

"Is he due back?"

"Not today, I'm afraid."

"Where is he?"

"I'm not at liberty to say."

"You should call him on the phone."

"Why?"

Reacher stepped aside and Brennan stepped up.

The woman said, "You're her."

Brennan said, "Call him."

She did. They heard the local end of the conversation, which started with repeated answers to what must have been are-you-sure questions, and then continued with arrangements around a place called Sammy's, which from the sound of it could have been anything from a strip club to a noodle shop, but which turned out to be a television production company.

Ian Massee was in a meeting about his documentary.

Temperance Brennan was welcome to come right over.

In fact they would send a car.

"No," Brennan said, and called an Uber.

•◆•

THE PRODUCTION COMPANY WAS ONE OF A DOZEN SHARING SPACE IN Crystal City. They went in assuming every microphone was live and every camera recording. Ian Massee met them in the corridor. He was a fair-haired version of the guy who had driven Reacher out of Baltimore. No doubt once a chiseled and slender youth, now bloated and rotted by stress and anger and bad food and too long in the bar.

But in the moment he was pleasant enough. He took Reacher to be Brennan's bodyguard, which he seemed to expect, as if it would be crazy for her to come without one. At first he seemed stunned to be in her presence. She was the key to the conspiracy. He was face-to-face with the woman who knew everything.

He was face-to-face with the woman who had killed Jonathan Yeow.

Then eventually he spoke, by asking politely if they would precede him into an office. He held a door. Reacher went first. Brennan followed. It was a multipurpose space. Technical equipment was stacked all around. There were white laminate desks. There were two men sitting on them. One was a wild-eyed guy with long gray hair and a four-day beard. He was very tall and very thin, and he was dressed in a fine-wale corduroy suit, gone all pouched and baggy from constant use. He was wearing fingerless gloves. Maybe the wintertime equivalent of wearing sunglasses inside.

The other guy had a missing hand.

He was short and solid under an impassive face, wearing a blue suit, sitting straight, all slabs and angles, all symmetrical, except on one side was a hand and on the other was a hook. Or, to be fair to the scientists who developed it, a sophisticated prosthesis ending in two controllable fingers, normally held an inch apart, but capable of being clamped. The fingers were shaped like hooks. For efficiency. The pirates had it right from the beginning.

Ian Massee introduced the wild-eyed guy with the long gray hair as Paul Warwick. He was an award-winning documentary maker. Then Massee introduced the one-handed guy as Samuel Rye. He was the money. He owned the production company. The three of them stretched the introductions into self-effacing laments about what they could lose. Warwick could lose his reputation. Rye could lose his fortune. Massee could lose his chance to tell the truth.

Brennan said, "It's not the truth. I don't understand how you think it could be. You know nothing. You've seen nothing."

Massee paused a beat, preparing a reply, but Warwick jumped in first, all restless energy. He said, "We have plenty of evidence."

"You don't. There is no evidence."

"We have travel orders. A second person left the same base at the same time."

"Traffic in and out of bases is constant. It doesn't imply a connection. It's a meaningless coincidence."

"There was trace evidence of a second man in the car where Calder Massee was killed."

"Where Calder Massee killed himself," Brennan corrected. "I'm sure it was a staff car, or a rental. Hundreds of men had been in it. That's another red herring."

"There's more than that."

Brennan sat down on a third desk.

She said, "Tell me."

Reacher stood behind her.

Warwick said, "Calder Massee was an air force colonel with a security clearance. That was a jackpot combination in 1987. The Cold War was still on. The air force had all the cool toys. They had the bombers endlessly prowling overhead. But someone was leaking. Calder Massee was wrongly suspected and falsely accused. While in custody he was badly beaten. When the real leak was found, Massee was killed too, to cover up the embarrassing mistake."

Brennan said, "That's a speech, not evidence."

"We have the order deploying the assassin."

"We?"

"Yeow has it. Or had it."

"Where is it now?"

"We don't know."

"Are you going to do the program without it?"

Warwick didn't answer.

Massee said, "My brother was a patriot and an honorable man. He was not a spy."

No one answered.

Reacher looked at Samuel Rye and asked, "How much money will you lose?"

"It's not the money," Rye said. "It's truth and justice."

"Big words."

"My company is built on them."

"Truth is Dr. Brennan never laid eyes on Yeow."

"If you say so."

"I do."

"So the government did it."

"The government wouldn't use a plastic bag," Reacher said. "Believe me."

"So who?"

"Would a rival do it to hurt you?"

"To kill my show? It's possible."

Rye went quiet for a long moment.

Then he said, "But you know what? Screw them. I just decided. We're going to do the show anyway."

Warwick punched the air. He said, "Great decision, Sammy. Real cutting edge. Because losing Yeow doesn't really hurt us. It actually helps us. We'll be totally up front about it. We'll say, this is the story, and brave Jonathan Yeow was murdered while confirming it. The audience will draw its own conclusions. Don't you see? The message is even stronger with a dead guy."

Brennan said, "You're disgusting."

"Says the killer," Massee said.

It got tense for a second. Then Reacher stepped out from behind Brennan's desk. Six five, two fifty, hands the size of dinner plates. He figured he could snap Warwick in two like a pencil, and then tear Rye's prosthesis off and stuff it down his throat. He figured Massee would have a heart attack all by himself, before throwing his first punch.

He said, "We're leaving now. But I'm sure we'll see you again."

• ◆ •

THEY WALKED A BLOCK TO A NEUTRAL CORNER AND WAITED FIVE minutes for another Uber. Brennan spent the time on her phone, bouncing from link to link, following industry gossip about Samuel Rye's rivals. Then she hit a trade paper headline that said "Rye Signs Controversial Documentary Maker." There was a picture. Mad eyes, long gray hair, beanpole build. Paul Warwick. She started reading.

The car came and they got in. She said, "Warwick sounds like a piece of work. There are numerous complaints he routinely bullies witnesses, fakes documents, and completely ignores any information that doesn't fit his story."

Reacher said, "How did your prints get on the bag?"

"I don't know."

"How thorough was your examination of Calder Massee's remains?"

"What, now you think I'm incompetent too?"

"Did you limit it to the head?"

"Of course not. I examined the whole skeleton."

"Any broken bones?"

"No."

"Did you read the original German report from 1987?"

"Of course I did."

"Any contusions, lacerations, or other injuries?"

"No."

"Therefore, your report also proves he wasn't badly beaten while in custody. Believe me, I know how that goes. I've seen the results. But Warwick needs to believe it. It's important to his story. In his opinion the government's motive is its embarrassment over mistreating the wrong guy. Maybe Yeow told him to cool it on that. Maybe Yeow showed him the original German report. Which diluted Warwick's narrative. Maybe a couple other details too. Yeow might have been a little more scrupulous than Warwick. He was with the *Post*, after all. That might still mean something."

"You think they argued?"

"Maybe worse than that."

"Go on."

"Warwick strikes me as the type who wouldn't like his grand design to be watered down. And he wouldn't like someone contradicting him in public afterward."

"Is that enough reason for homicide?"

"That's what they asked on the radio," Reacher said. "About you. The consensus was stranger things have happened and professional ruin is a great motivator."

"Seriously?"

"He said losing Yeow helped him."

"But only a little, surely. They have their basic story. A couple of extra lies won't make much of a difference. Not enough to kill someone for."

"I didn't like his gloves."

"Meaning?"

"Look at it from Yeow's point of view. He's standing in his kitchen, the bag goes over his head, it's wrapped tight around his neck, and the world starts to go fuzzy. What does he do?"

"He scrabbles at the killer's hands, to break the seal. Data show that in cases of strangulation or suffocation, it seems to be an almost universal reaction."

"Human nature," Reacher said. "But dumb. Better to use your thumb-nails to tear a breathing hole. Or grab the guy's nuts. But people grab their hands instead. They haul and scratch and scrabble. They leave marks."

"Hence gloves the next day."

"Exactly."

"That's a long shot. I don't see enough motive."

"He might not need much. He seems very intense. I expect he has the soul of an artist. But overall I agree. It's a long shot. But it's the kind of long shot a person wants to cross off the list. Human nature."

"So go take his gloves off."

"I will. But this is a big deal. As your legal counsel I would advise if we screw this up, we're dead and buried. We need to be fireproof. I need you to get a look at Yeow's autopsy notes. No point finding scratches on Warwick's hands if they didn't find skin under Yeow's nails."

"I can't get a look at his notes. They're probably not even tran-scribed yet."

"Can you phone whoever did the autopsy and ask for a favor?"

"They might not take my call."

"You probably trained them. They must know this is bullshit. They'll help. Ask about the nails. We're going to have Szewczk and Dupreau all over us. Better to have both ends of the deal in place. One scratches, and one gets scratched. The whole story, right there."

"Now?"

"This evening. Under the radar. I'll go back to Crystal City and speak to Warwick, and when you get the news from your medical friends, you can call me there with the outcome, and then either I'll bring Warwick in, or I'll give him his gloves back and pat him on the head and disappear."

"You don't have a cell phone."

"I'm sure they have a switchboard. It's a production company. Someone will put you through."

"While you're holding Warwick hostage, after hours?"

"I won't be. Unless he has scratches."

THURSDAY, FEBRUARY 23, 1825 EST

NOT WANTING TO PROVIDE A CLOSE-UP FOR SOME CARRION-EATING reporter with a superzoom lens, Brennan got another Uber and had the driver take her to Cantina Marina in the district's Southwest Waterfront area. She ordered the fried clam and shrimp basket and a Diet Coke, then settled at a table in a far back corner.

Her first call was to Bernie Rodriguez, a forensic anthropologist consulting to both the D.C. and Baltimore ME offices. She and Rodriguez had known each other since grad school. Still, she worried about his reaction. If he even answered.

Her worry was unfounded. Rodriguez picked up on the first ring, said he'd seen the media swarm, assured her that everyone in the section thought the accusations were rat shit. From the background hubbub she guessed he was still at the Marriott.

Brennan asked who'd done the autopsy on Jonathan Yeow. Rodriguez didn't know, promised to check and ring back.

She was finishing her last mollusk when he did. The pathologist was Helen Matias. Brennan knew Matias. They'd taught body recovery protocol together when such courses were still offered at the FBI Academy in Quantico. Matias was impartial, skilled, and kick-ass smart. The two women shared a mutual respect. And a love of George Carlin.

Still.

Rodriguez offered Matias's cell number. Brennan said she had it, thanked him, and disconnected.

Brennan checked the time. Six twenty-five. Not good. The ME office was undoubtedly closed for the day.

She dialed.

Four rings, then she was rolled to voice mail. She left a few words. Mainly her name.

Brennan looked around the cantina. It was packed with office workers in suits and ties and panty hose and trench coats. With locals in running gear and sweats. With tourists in sneakers and ball caps with cameras and guidebooks.

Matias called exactly four minutes after Brennan left her message.

"You'll do anything to get your name in the papers." The voice was low slung, the vowels broad and languorous. Definitely not New York.

"I'm thinking of dancing naked outside the White House."

"Might work. How the hell are you?"

"I've been better," Brennan said.

"Yeah. This whole Yeow thing's a real pants pisser."

So Matias knew.

"I didn't kill him."

Matias didn't reply.

"I understand you did the autopsy."

"I did." Revealing nothing.

An awkward silence filled the line while Brennan thought and Matias waited. Brennan decided to dive straight in.

"I'm wondering if there's any way I could—"

"I'd like you to take a look at him."

"What? Who?"

"Yeow. I found troubling marks on his shoulders."

"Troubling."

"Yes."

Brennan gave Matias room to expand. She didn't.

"You want my opinion."

"Unofficially, of course."

"When?"

"Tonight."

"Suits me."

"401 E Street. That's in Southwest. I'll meet you in the lobby at eight."

"I'll be there."

"Tempe. No one can know that you're viewing the body."

"What body?"

"Good. Because a leak could get both our faces on the eleven o'clock news."

•◆•

BRENNAN KILLED TIME SIPPING COFFEE. AFTER THE DIET COKE, WITH refills, the last thing she needed was more caffeine. But the restaurant was crowded and she wanted an excuse to stay.

By googling the address on E Street, she learned that the distance from her current location was about three-quarters of a mile. Bristling with pent-up energy, she decided to walk.

At seven thirty, she set out. Wired on java and Coke and adrenaline, she barely noticed her surroundings. The park, the school, the church. The Potomac Place Tower apartment complex. The Capital Park Tower. The Southwest Freeway overhead. The smell of the Potomac strong in the air. Walking up Fourth Street, all she could think about was Matias's reference to the strange marks on Yeow.

In her mind, she visualized the attack. The killer placing the bag over Yeow's head. Pulling down hard and gathering the plastic tight. His hands slamming Yeow's neck and shoulders. Maybe his chest.

Or her hands.

She reasoned that a tall assailant would leave marks resulting from an impact coming directly down on the deltoid. A shorter assailant, stretching in a more upward direction, would leave marks farther toward the front or rear, depending on his or her position relative to Yeow. She concluded that it might be possible to rule Warwick in or exclude him based on his height.

At E Street, she turned left. D.C.'s Consolidated Forensic Laboratory stretched the entire north side of the block. Multistory, lots of steel and glass grillwork. The same hopeful landscaping as at the cop shop on Indiana Avenue. Less dog shit. Identical flags.

A Hyatt faced off from the opposite side of the street. Government buildings sat at the remaining two corners. Thanks to Google she knew the behemoths housed, among other entities, the National Aeronautics and Space Administration, the Centers for Disease Control and Prevention, the USDA Economic Research Service, the Surface Transportation Board, and Casey's Coffee. Hot capitol damn.

Pulse humming, she opened the door to the CFL and entered.

• ◆ •

REACHER KEPT THE FIRST UBER AND TRACKED BACK TO CRYSTAL CITY. The charge would go straight to Brennan's credit card. No tip was required. Apparently that was how Uber worked. Which was fine with him. He had the military habit of assuming everyone he met was richer than him.

He got out a block from the shared TV building and moved to where he could watch the door. He stood in the cold February shadows and waited. People came out in ones and twos, dressed in jeans and puffy winter jackets. He saw Samuel Rye leave. But not Massee or Warwick. They were still inside. Still discussing their cutting-edge program, he thought, and how it was all the stronger now Yeow was dead. Disgusting, Brennan had said. He liked her for that reaction. There was a purity to it. As a forensic anthropologist she must have seen some pretty bad things done for some pretty bad reasons, but she wasn't cynical. Not totally. Which was unusual. Like her name. She was unusual all around.

And cute.

He waited.

By ten of eight he figured the building was as quiet as it was going to get. Massee and Warwick still inside. He went in and found the right corridor. Saw the right door up ahead. But it opened before he got there and Ian Massee stepped out.

He stopped and said, "You."

Reacher said, "Yeah, me."

"What do you want?"

"Warwick."

"Why?"

"None of your business."

"This whole thing is my business."

"This whole thing is bullshit."

"My brother was not a spy."

"Your brother was a piece of shit."

"In the end they said someone else was the spy. It's in the record."

"Were you out sick the day they taught thinking? There were two spies. Your brother and the other guy. Working together."

"That's not true."

"Yes, it is. I know for sure."

"How?"

"I watched him do two dead drops and meet with an East German government official. I was young, and I was army, not air force. He wasn't watching out for a guy like me. Which is why they sent me, I guess."

Massee was quiet a beat.

Then he said, "So he *was* executed."

Reacher said, "No, he wasn't. He put the gun in his mouth all by himself."

"We have the order."

"Do you have the response?"

"What?"

"They will have been paper-clipped together in the file. The order, and the response. The order said kill him, and the response said he was already dead when I got there."

"You?"

"Except that wasn't quite true. He was alive when I got there. We sat in his car and talked. I laid out the situation. He begged me to let him shoot himself. He wanted to spare his family the disgrace. I was okay with that. But then you went and dug it all up again. You should have let sleeping dogs lie."

"You were there?"

"Afterward I was deaf in my left ear for a week."

Massee went quiet again.

Went red in the face.

Wound himself up like a clock and swung a clumsy right hook at Reacher's jaw, powered by nothing but rot and bloat and furious anger. Reacher caught the fist in his left hand like a softball and crashed a low right into Massee's ample gut, which folded him up like a pocketknife, gasping and staggering on uncertain feet. Reacher waited until he stabilized and brought his knee up into Massee's lowered face. After which Massee collapsed, half backward and half sideways, onto the floor, and lay still.

Reacher stepped over him and stepped through the door.

Warwick was in the room. Evidently he had heard the commotion. He said, "What the hell is going on out there?"

Reacher closed the door and said, "Take your gloves off."

"What?"

"You heard."

"My gloves?"

"Take them off, or I'll take them off for you."

"Why?"

"I want to see your hands."

Warwick was too puzzled to protest. He simply peeled his gloves off, inside out, first one, then the other.

He held his hands up.

No scratches.

The door opened again and Samuel Rye stepped into the room.

●━◆━●

ALL MORGUES WEAR THE SAME PERFUME, A BLEND OF DISINFECTANT, refrigeration, and putrefying flesh. Eau de death.

All morgues are outfitted along the same lines. Gleaming tiles, cabinets, and counters. Stainless steel tables, sinks, lights, scales, carts, and instruments.

All morgues have the same coolers, some larger, some smaller, some more numerous. To Brennan's surprise, the one at the CFL had Braille lettering beside the sign saying 5205: BODY STORAGE. She wondered. Visually impaired pathologists or autopsy techs? Sketchy backup generators?

She didn't think about it long. The after-hours quiet was goosing her already jangled nerves. There were no Stryker saws whining. No phones ringing. No faucets pounding water into stainless steel sinks. No voices dictating, directing, or cracking jokes. She'd done her share of late-night autopsy room stints. It was never good times.

After badging her through security and escorting her upstairs, Matias had rolled a gurney from the blind-friendly cooler. They'd discussed her findings and reviewed her report. Then Matias had pulled surgical aprons, masks, and gloves from drawers and they'd both suited up.

"Ready?" Dark brows raised above the rectangle of fabric covering her nose and mouth. Which were also dark.

Brennan nodded.

Matias double-checked the tag, then unzipped the body bag. *Whrrrp.* The sound was like a snarl in the stillness. The stench of death wafted out. The odor bothered neither Matias nor Brennan.

Yeow lay naked and supine, the Y stitching his chest dark against the waxy, gray skin. One eye was half open, the pupil milky black. The base of his throat was mottled radish red.

From Matias's comments and autopsy notes and diagram, Brennan knew that the "troubling" marks were posterior, at the back of Yeow's neck.

"Roll him?"

Brennan nodded again.

Matias separated the flaps of the pouch. Together they tucked Yeow's arms and rotated his body, Matias at the shoulders, Brennan at the ankles. His forehead hit the table with a soft thunk.

Brennan leaned in. Saw nothing.

Matias pulled a surgical lamp close and thumbed the switch. Light flooded Yeow's head and upper torso.

The marks were subtle but definitely there, centered above the seventh cervical vertebrae, at the base of Yeow's neck. Two lines converging at a very slight angle.

"Perimortem?" Brennan asked.

"Definitely. The hemorrhaging means the injury occurred at the time of death."

"Looks like he was hit by something with a pair of long, thin edges. Or a pair of bars."

"Or he hit something."

"You think he fell?"

Matias shook her head. "I found no blunt trauma anywhere else on the body. No lacerations, no hematomas, no fractures. Nothing but this linear bruising and the abrasions on his throat."

"No defensive wounds on his hands or arms?"

"A few broken nails. But I have no way to tell when or how that happened."

"And there was no skin or tissue under his nails." Brennan knew that from Matias's notes. "No trace at all."

"It makes no sense. If conscious, victims of strangulation claw at their attackers' hands. Or at the ligature cutting off their air."

"Yes."

Brennan straightened and closed her eyes. Again played a mental holograph of the assault.

Yeow.

Warwick facing him with the plastic bag.

Or behind him.

Tall, skinny Warwick.

She pictured the two linear marks. Their position, spacing, and orientation.

The figure morphed. Grew shorter. More solid.

Sudden synapse.

Brennan's eyes flew open.

Not Paul Warwick.

Samuel Rye!

"These bruises were made by a prosthetic hand." Tone emphatically calm. "That's why you found no skin under Yeow's nails."

"A device with two hooks?" Matias spoke while eyeballing the patterned injury on Yeow's neck.

"Yes."

"That tracks." Nodding slowly.

Brennan stripped off and bunched her apron, mask, and gloves. "I know who did this."

"Seriously?" Matias, unconvinced.

"I have to go." Toe-slamming the pedal and tossing her gear into the biohazard bin.

"That's it?"

"My paralegal is in grave danger."

Brennan grabbed her shoulder bag and fired out the door. She thumbed her phone for an Uber as she hustled. The app seemed agonizingly slow. But eventually Fong promised to be there in a black Camry hybrid within eleven minutes. She pushed out to the street and ran, hoping her phone would bring Fong to her. She could be a mile away in eleven minutes. Maybe more. Then her phone buzzed in her hand. Caller ID displayed the same unfamiliar number she had seen before. Albert Thorsten. Yeow's editor at the *Washington Post*. The Kalahari voice.

It said, "I apologize."

"For what, dammit?"

No time for games.

"The Metro cops found Yeow's notes. They returned them to me. You were right. Calder Massee killed himself. He was a spy. There *was* an execution order, but the rest of the file shows Massee was already dead when the assassin got there. He shot himself in his car. Ian Massee and Paul Warwick were cherry-picking the evidence. Yeow's story was going to cut them off at the knees. They're the suspects now."

"No, it was Samuel Rye. Yeow's story was going to kill his show. I should have known. He said it wasn't about the money. When someone says that, it's always about the money."

She disconnected and dialed Veronica Luong.

Voice mail.

She said, "Tell Szewczk and Dupreau to get to Samuel Rye's place in Crystal City right now. Cops, SWAT, everything. Rye is the killer."

Then she saw a black Camry up ahead. She waved. It stopped. She got in.

•◆•

SAMUEL RYE STOOD FRAMED IN THE OPEN DOORWAY. SHORT, SQUAT, powerful. All slabs and angles. In his good hand was a Colt Python, which was a stainless steel six-shot revolver about the size and weight of a sledgehammer. Clamped in his hook was an open switchblade. Six inches of fine glittering steel, faintly blue in the fluorescent light. Not pretty. Not pretty at all. Reacher didn't like knives.

He should have known.

It's not the money.

It's always the money.

Rye said, "Sit down."

Reacher said, "No."

"I'll shoot."

"You won't. That's a very loud gun. The cops are coming."

"Says you."

"Brennan went to look at Yeow's autopsy notes. She won't find skin under the nails. She'll put two and two together. She's smart like that. And she has a cell phone."

Rye took a step into the room.

He leveled the Colt. The barrel looked the size of a water main. It was pointing at Reacher's center mass.

Stay alive and see what the next minute brings.

That was Reacher's motto.

He said, "How did you get her prints on the bag?"

Rye smiled. Pleased with himself.

He said, "I guess you don't watch much television."

"The Yankees sometimes," Reacher said. "When I can."

"My last program. All about 3-D printing. Very useful. But I hinted it could be used for bad purposes too."

"So how?"

"She arrived at the Marriott two days ago and had a room-service dinner. I bought her water glass from the waiter. Lifted her prints, scanned them, filled the printer cartridge with squalene, and printed them all over a brand-new bag, full size, about half a millimeter high."

Reacher nodded. He had heard of squalene. A Russian watchmaker had once told him all about it. It was a natural organic compound, found in shark liver oil and olive oil. And on human noses. The watchmaker used it to lubricate delicate mechanisms.

Rye said, "Sit down."

"No," Reacher said again.

He heard footsteps out in the corridor. Quiet and hesitant.

Getting closer.

Ian Massee appeared in the doorway.

He looked in bad shape. Bent over, limping, breathing ragged.

He said, "The bastard hit me."

Rye said, "We have worse problems than that."

Massee shuffled in. Stopped between Rye and Warwick. If Rye was the twelve on a clock face, Massee was the one and Warwick was the two. Reacher was the six. Outnumbered. A classic three against one.

The gun was still steady on Reacher's chest.

Rye said, "Is Brennan planning to meet you here?"

Reacher said, "No."

Then he sensed more movement in the corridor. Almost nothing. Just a faint disturbance in the air.

He looked at Rye and said, "You should cut your losses and get the hell out. Or shoot Massee, not me. He got you into this mess. He's as bad as his big brother."

Rye said nothing.

Behind his left shoulder Reacher saw a third of a face, a green eye, a sweep of dark blond hair. Brennan, peering around the doorjamb. Exactly the same as at the chained door of her hotel room, back at the beginning.

He said, "Time is ticking away."

Brennan moved soundlessly into the room. A yard behind Rye.

Reacher said, "I wish I was a woman."

Rye said, "What?"

"I would have a purse. I could swing it like a bat. I could knock your gun hand out of the way."

"What?" Rye said again.

And Brennan did exactly that. Reacher saw thirty-seven hours of anger and outrage and frustration in her face, channeling into some kind of deadly focus. She wound up like a discus thrower at the Olympics and swung her bag from behind and smashed it into Rye's forearm with all the strength in her body. Which was evidently considerable. The gun was swept all the way from the six on the clock face to the three. It fired with a deafening crash and a television monitor exploded, and simultaneously Reacher smashed a giant fist into the exposed side of Rye's head, jaw, ear, and cheekbone, and then he danced to his right and crashed an elbow into Warwick's throat. Rye and Warwick went down backward, and Massee sank to his knees clutching his chest. Maybe a heart attack, all by himself.

Reacher looked at Brennan and said, "Thank you."

Brennan took a breath and said, "You're welcome."

Then there were sirens outside and boots in the corridor and six men in FBI windbreakers burst into the room, followed by Szewczk and Dupreau, followed by Veronica Luong.

THURSDAY, FEBRUARY 23, 2310 EST

THEY BOTH NEEDED TO DECOMPRESS. AND REACHER WAS HUNGRY.

Certain the Marriott bars and restaurants would be packed with alcohol-buzzed toxicologists, pathologists, lawyers, and engineers, they opted for the Raven in Mount Pleasant. Brennan remembered it from her drinking days. The dive decor. The heart-stopping cheeseburgers and onion rings. She hoped it was still there.

It was. And a good choice. The interior was dim, lit mostly by neon beer signs. Bar to one side, booths to the other, each with its own miniature jukebox. The place, largely empty, had only one flaw. The syrupy stench of grease and stale beer.

They chose an alcove in the rear and climbed onto high chrome stools with cracked vinyl seats. Brennan climbed. Reacher simply straddled and dropped.

On the wall above their shoulders, his left, her right, was a bulgy-screen TV that looked like it had been mounted sometime in the '80s. The picture was on but the sound was muted.

After a brief wait, a guy slouched over and asked what they wanted. His tee, once white, was stained and stretched way too tight over his belly. On it was an unnaturally elongated Latvian flag.

Reacher asked for a burger, very rare, and black coffee. Brennan asked for the same, medium rare, double cheese. Perrier and lime to drink.

Their eyes met.

Reacher amended their order to two pints of whatever was on tap. The guy recommended some microbrewery IPA with an unlikely name.

The beer hit the table seconds later. Brennan took in a few molecules, mostly foam. Did the automatic alkie count in her head. How many months? Years? She'd be fine.

"What's an IPA?" Reacher asked.

"Damn good," Brennan said.

Brennan's eyes drifted to the ancient Sony above and between them. Read a headline below a grim-faced anchor. *Faking a Murderer.* To the anchor's right was a graphic of a middle-aged man in an air force officer's uniform.

"We've made the eleven o'clock news." Brennan echoed Matias's words.

As Reacher glanced left, the screen cut to video. Bathed in artificial light, Dupreau led a handcuffed Warwick from the Crystal City building. Szewczk followed with Rye. Massee was in the hands of a guy with *FBI* lettered on the back of his jacket.

The footage ended and the anchor returned. They watched her lips silently summarize the breaking story, Brennan's image now hanging where Calder Massee's had been.

Their burgers arrived. They added garnish and condiments. Ate in silence.

Brennan spoke when only lettuce remained on her plate. "Rye set the whole thing up."

"Two birds with one stone," Reacher agreed. "Eliminate Yeow, who was going to back your suicide finding, thereby killing his story. Hype attention for his documentary."

"Rye wanted it to hit big, like *Making a Murderer.* Or *Serial.*"

Reacher just looked at her.

"A TV documentary and a podcast."

Reacher said nothing.

"Everyone in America watched. Or listened."

"I'm on the move a lot."

"You headed south now?" Brennan changed the subject.

"I was."

"Good time of year for that."

"I often sleep outside."

"You sleeping outside tonight?" Brennan took another sip of her IPA.

"It's Luong's dime, so I'm staying one more night at the Marriott."

"As am I." Brennan studied Reacher over the rim of her mug.

"Shall we go there?" Reacher studied her back.

Brennan ingested another milliliter of beer. A long moment passed before she answered.

"Uber?"

Reacher nodded.

And they did.

DIANA GABALDON AND STEVE BERRY

D IANA GABALDON IS A FORMER SCIENTIST WITH FOUR DEGREES, including a PhD in behavioral ecology. In the 1980s she had a story churning in the back of her head. A tale about a mid-18th century Scotsman and a feisty Englishwoman. To really liven things up, she decided to add the element of time travel. The end result became the novel *Outlander,* which went on to be a massive bestseller with twenty-seven million copies in print across the globe. To date, there have been seven more installments in the adventures of James Fraser and Claire Randall. Now there's even a television series that has brought the characters to life for a whole new audience.

Diana's world thrives in the past, which made her the perfect partner for Steve Berry, who writes modern-day thrillers that rely heavily on something unique from the past. Steve's character, Cotton Malone, has starred in twelve novels. He's a retired Justice Department agent, living in Copenhagen, who runs an old bookshop. And much to his chagrin, his former profession keeps finding him.

As with Sandra Brown, Steve is also short story challenged. He can write them, but they take great effort. Likewise, as with C. J. Box, Diana is proficient. So, together she and Steve plotted the story, then Diana produced a first draft. Steve then edited and rewrote. Interestingly, this is the only story written for this anthology in the first person.

And present tense, no less.

But these two intrepid writers faced a complicated dilemma. How do they seamlessly meld the 18th-century world of Diana Gabaldon (including time travel), with Steve's modern-day hero Cotton Malone?

Their solution is masterful.

Fans of both writers are going to love—

Past Prologue.

PAST PROLOGUE

I LOVE SCOTLAND.

Always have.

Something about its collage of gray and green enchants me. I especially love its castles, and through the car window I study Ardsmuir, which looms out of the northern Scottish moor like something God himself hacked from the ancient rock. I have to admit, a less-welcoming pile I have never seen but, after all, centuries ago it had once been a prison. I've been driven straight from the Inverness airport and climb out of the car into a bone-chilling combination of driving rain and bitter north wind.

"Mr. Malone," comes a shout faintly over the roar of the storm.

I turn to see a man hurrying toward me across the flagged-stone courtyard, a red golf umbrella precariously clutched in one hand, a flashlight, or an electric torch as they would say here, in the other. I hustle toward the shelter of the umbrella, but not before retrieving my travel bag from the driver and leaving five pounds for a tip.

"So pleased you made it, Mr. Malone." The man with the umbrella shoves the flashlight under one arm in order to free up a hand for shaking. "I'm John MacRae."

"Call me Cotton." I duck under the umbrella. "And for God's sake, let's get out of this mess. Reminds me of south Georgia and the storms we get there."

Inside, the walls are more of the forbidding granite from outside, only here they serve as a matte for clusters of swords, shields, and stags' heads that dot the entrance hall. Thankfully, the roar of the wind and rain is gone. I set down my travel bag. MacRae hurries to take my overcoat, which I surrender, reluctantly, not accustomed to a manservant.

"The gentlemen—and lady," MacRae adds with a smile, "are all in the drawing room with Mr. Chubb. Let me show you the way, and I'll have your bag sent up to your room. There's a fire waiting."

I follow MacRae and enter the drawing room, a large comfortable space with dark-stained overhead beams and heavy furniture. More animal heads stare down from the walls. An unusual globe with a hollow interior catches my trained eye, its open ribs marking latitude and longitude. As advertised, a robust, crackling blaze, one suitable for roasting an ox, burns in the stone hearth. I make for it, barely pausing to shake hands with my host for the evening, Malcolm Chubb. I've crossed paths with Chubb before at various book auctions in London, Paris, and Edinburgh. During those times the Scot had been wearing a stylish Savile Row suit. Now he looks like a Christmas tree, ablaze in red-and-green tartan from waist to knees, and sporting a drape of the same fabric over one shoulder held in place with a striking bronze brooch.

"Wretched evening," my host says in apology, before thrusting a glass of single malt into my hand. "We didn't think you'd make it, but we're so pleased that you did."

I'm not much of a drinker, barely touching the stuff. But I know how the Scots feel about their malt. So I hold the glass up against the light and admire its golden murkiness. Then I allow the bitter liquid to lay a comfortable burn down my gullet, which thaws me enough to take stock of the room. A dozen or so booksellers and collectors loiter about, drinking more whisky, nibbling morsels from trays servants pass around, chatting to each other. A couple of them—a man named Arkwright that I know, and a woman I don't—doubtless "the lady" MacRae had mentioned earlier—are standing in front of a cloth-draped table at the far side, admiring the dozen or so books displayed within their velvet nests.

Strangers always raise my radar, and I keep a watchful eye on the lady, while saying to Chubb, "I wouldn't have missed it." I eye my host's tartan. "Clan McChubb?"

"Would that it was. No, the Scots blood is on my mother's side. Clan Farquarson. Isn't it dreadful?" Chubb flicks a hand at his blazing kilt, setting the tassels on his hairy sporran swinging. At a closer glance, I realized it's a dead badger, for God's sake. "You'll be relieved to know that we've set aside something a bit more subdued for you."

Was I hearing right? "For me?"

"Absolutely," Chubb says. "This is quite an occasion. We're expecting the media, though given the weather, it may only amount to a junior reporter from the *Inverness Courier*. But everyone, and I do mean everyone, including photographers, will be here for the book auction tomorrow. There will be plenty of time for an inspection of the wares later, but d'you want a quick look, before you go up to dress for dinner?"

"I think I would like that."

I finish off the rest of my malt and Chubb relieves me of the empty glass, passing it to a hovering waiter, then beckoning me toward the display table. Approaching close, an odd vibration shoots through me, one only a committed bibliophile could understand. I love books. And though my profession had been first a naval officer, then a lawyer, and finally an American intelligence operative, books have finally sunk their claws deep into me. Now retired from the Magellan Billet, a covert unit within the United States Justice Department, I own an old bookshop in Copenhagen, which has acquired a reputation for being able to find what collectors seek. And though my former profession as a spy has an annoying habit of revisiting me from time to time, books are most definitely my life now.

I step to the trestle table, catching the dry smell of old bindings, and admire some of what will be auctioned tomorrow.

A *Book of Deer*, straight from the 10th century a small information card notes. I know the volume. An Irish gospel text, one of the oldest-surviving manuscripts ever produced in Scotland. *The Book of the Dean of Lismore*, a compilation of 15th-century poetry, is a real treasure. Only a few editions exist. Its poems supposedly taken from the strolling bards themselves. A few of the other Celtic tomes are likewise rare. But second from the end is the book that really interests me. With luck, I'll even take it back to Denmark as I already have a buyer for it. The other offerings are all prime specimens, immensely valuable in their own right, but this is an incunabulum—which means it had been printed before 1501, in the days of movable type. It is also, so far as anyone knows, the only copy ever made of this particular book.

A grimoire. A book of sorcery.

That includes spells, alchemy, and what would certainly have been considered outright witchcraft in the 15th century. The label comes from the French word *grammaire,* which at first referred to all books written in Latin. Eventually, it came to be associated only with books of magic. I dare not touch it, though I want to. Per the usual practice at auctions such as this, it will be carefully displayed, page by page, during a detailed inspection right before the bidding, its pages turned by means of a swabbed stick held by gloved hands. For now, it is open to a page showing an exquisite wood-block print of a winged lion being either attacked or embraced by a wingless lion. The text in Latin on the opposite page, headed by a beautiful illuminated *O,* is twined with fruiting vines and serpents. To my surprise, this isn't the only grimoire on display, though it is by far the best. There are two others, one from the late 17th and another from the mid-18th century.

"These are all from a collection belonging to the last owner of this castle," Chubb says, from behind my shoulder, a pair of bifocals perched on the tip of the Scot's nose. "We think the one from the 15th century is a copy of a much older volume. Perhaps hand penned by Saint-Germain himself. *Le grimoire du Le Compte Saint-Germain.*"

There's a name. More legend than fact. At once a courtier, adventurer, inventor, pianist, and alchemist. Credited with near godlike powers and immortality. But nobody knows if he'd ever been real.

"That's quite a claim," I say. "Is there anything to support the idea?"

"Only hope, my good man," Chubb says. "Simply hope. The former owner of that grimoire had quite a taste for strange things. Both natural history and the odder branches of the occult. He owned many books on magic, though most of those aren't anything special. Not like this beauty."

"What was his name?" I ask, moving down the table to examine a spectacular double-folio edition of Albertus Seba's *Das NaturalienKabinett,* open to a pair of pages featuring an array of delicately drawn puffer fish, all looking surprised and annoyed.

"Appleton," Chubb says. "An Englishman. Strange man, I gather. He vanished quite suddenly one day without a word. The estate had to wait seven years to have him declared dead. That's why these"—he nods at the books—"had not come on the market before."

"He just vanished? Foul play?"

Chubb shrugs. "No sign of anything amiss, either physically or in terms of his affairs. The police investigated thoroughly. But you know, the cliffs are quite near. You could hear the sea now, if it wasn't raining so hard. And if he'd gone walking and fallen there, the currents are treacherous. The body would be swept out."

One of the servants approaches, bows, then murmurs something to Chubb, who nods and turns back.

"Dinner in twenty minutes. You'd best go up and dress. Nigel will show you the way."

Malcolm Chubb hadn't been joking.

Waiting for me, laid out on the poster bed, is a kilt, complete with sporran, hose, oddly laced shoes, and a short jacket. The tartan is a subdued gray with a faint blue check, everything crafted of fine wool. A low fire burns in the grate of the bedroom, casting a golden glow. It might technically be spring on the calendar, but it feels like winter, or at least late fall, outside. I'm actually not all that fond of the harsh Scottish weather.

But it's part of the charm.

The good with the bad, as the saying goes.

I undress and hesitate a moment over the question of underwear, but then shrug and don the kilt without it.

What the hell.

When in Scotland—

Back downstairs, Chubb introduces me to the other guests, all of them are wearing Highland dress too. Even the lone woman, who wears a full-length bodiced dress, a becoming muted tartan in shades of lavender and blue.

"Madam LeBlanc." Chubb pauses and bows, gesturing. "Allow me to present a valued friend, Mr. Harold Earl 'Cotton' Malone."

She's tall, with blond hair not her own as a trace of light brown can be seen at the roots. The color, though, suits her swarthy skin. Her smile reveals curious marks of fun that surround twinkling hazel eyes. I draw the conclusion that she's of money, accustomed to the finer things. She holds out a hand, and before I can decide whether I'm supposed to kiss it, she grabs mine and gives me a pleasantly firm clasp.

"Enchanted, Mr. Malone," she says. "Call me Eleanor, if you like."

I catch a faint French accent, but her direct manner is straight American business.

"Call me Cotton."

"Such a name. I bet there's a story there."

I grin. "Quite a long one."

I'd like to speak to her more, but Chubb is ushering me onto the next of the kilted guests. My eidetic memory, a gift at birth from my mother's side of the family, catalogs them all. There is John Simons, a London bookseller, short and spectacled, sporting a black kilt with a tartan tie. Wilhelm Fenstermacher, from Berlin, whom I met once long ago, of the Deutsches Historisches Museum. Nigel Soames from Edinburgh, a private collector, who I see now and then at Sotheby's. And Alexsandr Kuznyetsov, a saturnine sort whose predétente steel teeth clash with his Black Watch kilt. Most likely a private shopper for an oligarch, the people now with the real money in Russia. But who am I to judge. I too am here on behalf of others.

At dinner, I find myself seated next to Eleanor LeBlanc. She's adroitly dividing her attention between me on one side and Fenstermacher on the other, the effort made even more impressive as she is conversing in both English and German. Languages come easy to me, another benefit of my unusual memory. I'm fluent in several, so I catch all of her conversation with Fenstermacher. Finally, I ask whether she has a particular interest at the auction, as it's always good to know the competition.

"Most definitely," she says, tossing me a slight smile. "The same as yours, I believe. The incunabulum grimoire."

I had not been trying to disguise my interest, but I'm a little surprised that she'd been watching close enough to notice.

Her smile deepens, as she sees the question on my face.

"I have a personal interest in that book," she explains. "It was in my own family for generations. An impoverished ancestor sold it in the late 18th century, and it wandered, as you might say, for some time, owner to owner. I was excited to see it in the catalog here."

"So if you get it, you plan to keep it? Expensive bit of sentimentality."

She lifts one shoulder in a graceful shrug and twinkles at me. "Or perhaps I mean to use it. I'm told there are a great many interesting spells in that book."

I chuckle at her dismissal of my questions.

Conversation thereafter becomes more general, a genial dinner, but one at which the undercurrents of calculation are clear, everyone sizing up everyone else, deciding just how deep a given pocket might be. I love private auctions. They come with all the intrigue of my former profession without the risk of dying.

By the time the dessert plates are cleared a tiredness has crept over me, and I'm glad when the meal ends. Some of the guests ask for another brief look at the books on display in the drawing room, but I pass, leaving Madame LeBlanc to the others with a gallant kiss of her hand.

•◆•

I SLEEP LONG AND HARD, SURELY THE AFTEREFFECTS OF THE WHISKY, the dinner, and exhaustion from yesterday's travel from Denmark. I awake early, feeling fresh as the day outside. A bright sun shines through the slit in the drapes and, when I open them, the moor stretches out before me in a brilliant, rolling green under a cloudy sky.

A mass of crumpled shirts and creased slacks confront me when I open my travel bag. I'd been too tired last night to hang anything up. I glance again out the window and, shrugging, find the least-wrinkled shirt and an Arran sweater from the bag, pairing them with my kilt, sporran, and hose from the night before. Might as well stay in the mood.

A shower and shave refreshes me even more.

Downstairs, breakfast is full Scottish, meaning full English, with a choice of eggs, sausage, bacon, toast, muffins, fried tomatoes, grilled mushrooms, and a disemboweled haggis. A discreet notice advises the availability of porridge, which I think is probably the only thing saving the Scots from epidemic constipation. I help myself liberally from the groaning sideboard and place a request for the porridge, then make my way across to a table at which Madame LeBlanc has just sat down.

"May I join you?" I ask.

"By all means."

She's chosen a light breakfast of sliced melon with raspberries—obviously a special order from the kitchen as I've seen none of that on the buffet—with a tiny medallion of steak and a dab of baked beans.

She leans toward me. "Have you heard?"

"All I heard this morning was a lot of seagulls screaming on the roof."

She laughs. "I caught those too."

I butter my toast, add a few slices of bacon, a fried egg, fried tomatoes and mushrooms, then another slice of buttered toast and create my own Scottish Egg McMuffin. She observes me with an indulgent smile, but one that doesn't quite erase the deep line of concern between her brows.

"It appears that one of the books for the auction has gone missing," she tells me, glancing sideways to be sure she isn't being overheard. But the dining room is sparsely filled. Most of the guests appear to be sleeping in.

A thump of adrenaline forms in the pit of my stomach, one that has always primed me for action in my former occupation. But I also know the value of a poker face. So I keep my attention on the sandwich and ask, "I take it you don't mean mislaid? Missing as in gone?"

Her mouth twitches with mischief, but her eyes are serious. "Malcolm didn't want to raise an alarm. Not yet. He hasn't made an announcement, but I couldn't sleep last night, and when I came down about two o'clock, all of the lights were on. The servants were everywhere, quite plainly making a thorough search. Malcolm saw me on the landing and told me what had happened."

I listen as she explains that the books had all been locked inside their glass cases following the cocktail hour. Malcolm and his factor, John Mac-Rae, had come into the drawing room at midnight to see that all was in order for the detailed inspection to be held at eleven this morning. All had seemed to be as it should, but something had tingled Malcolm's antiquarian sense and he returned for a second look.

"It was the incunabulum. The little grimoire," she says. "There was a book in the case of the same size and also with a rough leather cover. But it had been put there so only the back cover showed. When turned over, it was revealed to be a first edition of Izaak Walton's *The Compleat Angler*. Certainly valuable, but nothing compared to the 15th-century grimoire."

My porridge arrives, fresh and steaming, along with a silver cream jug and a dish of sugar lumps.

"Oh, *that* looks good," Eleanor says, sniffing the heady steam that rises from the bowl.

"I tell you what. You have this one. I have to make a phone call. I'll order another when I come back."

I stand and place the bowl ceremoniously in front of her with a bow.

Then leave the breakfast room.

I'm concerned about the gun in my travel bag.

I flew in on a private charter that Malcolm Chubb arranged. In my former profession I went nowhere without a weapon, but in those days I carried an official United States Justice Department badge that granted me security exceptions. I still carry a badge, though unofficially, given to me by my former boss, Stephanie Nelle, since I often work for her as contract help. My display of it had satisfied Scottish customs. But the people in this house are another matter. Its presence will raise a lot of questions.

The first thing that occurred to me when Eleanor noted that the servants were searching the castle is that they'd certainly search the guests' rooms too. Most likely discreetly, after the occupants come down for breakfast. And, sure enough, I watch as one of the maids lightly raps at a door near the end of the hallway in which my own room is located, a stack of fresh towels in her arms by way of an excuse for her presence. I hang back behind a Victorian stand until the woman, receiving no answer to her knock, lays the towels aside and steps quietly inside. I quickly open my own door, find the Beretta, and tuck it into the kilt's internal waistband, concealing its presence with the baggy Arran sweater.

I descend the narrow zigzag stairway, one hand on the slick banister, back to ground level. More people are now around and I feel a suppressed air of consternation in the scraps of muted conversation I manage to hear. I don't think it will come to a physical search of the guests. Not yet, anyway. But I don't want to explain why I'm carrying a gun inside a remote Scottish castle. So I find the foot of the stairs and stride purposefully through the entrance hall, straight for the front door.

A young servant is on duty there.

Or maybe on guard?

"Off for a morning walk, are you, sir?"

I nod. "I thought I'd take advantage of the nice morning."

"Best move fast, then," the young man says. "Weather here changes every quarter of an hour. If you're going to walk along the cliffs, be sure to keep to the marked footpath. There's no missing it—some of the other guests went that way not ten minutes since."

I toss the guy a cheery wave. "I'll keep an eye out for them."

Outside, another servant at the front gate, this one wearing a Barbour jacket and flat cap with his kilt, evidently doesn't trust the weather any further than his pal inside. The young man adds the suggestion that if I mean to traverse the moor, I should stick to the road.

"It looks flat, but it's not," the young man says. "Up and down, it is. Lose sight o' the castle and ye won't know where ye are."

I assure him I will take care and set off up the paved road. The warning is a good one, though. I can feel the grade rise, then gently subside in the deceptively rolling terrain. I'm not afraid of getting lost, I just want to kill some time and give things back at the castle a chance to cool down. Once my room is searched and nothing found, I can replace the Beretta in my bag. Malcolm Chubb has to be in a panic. The missing grimoire is worth tens of thousands of pounds.

I walk for nearly an hour until I spot, in a hollow, a small cluster of pale boulders barely visible from the road. It's the first thing I've seen definite enough in the moor to make for a landmark, and I leave the pavement for a closer look. The going is rough, as stretches of spongy peat moss give way under my feet and soak my shoes and socks. Growths of scratchy heather and all kinds of other prickly plants grab at my hose and the hem of the kilt. Nothing that looks like a path leads to the stones, and it takes me a half hour to reach them. Why I feel the need to get closer to them baffles me.

It's just that I need to.

I stop for a moment and gather myself. A quick look back and I see that my passage through the brush has left no visible track, the moor so wild that it immediately swallows every trace of my presence. I'm also now out of sight of the castle, which had disappeared some time ago, along with the road.

I scramble down to the clearing, among the stones.

They might have once made a circle, but now they lie hither and yon, as the Scots would say, like teeth in a long neglected mouth, the remnants thick with lichens. Stonehenge, it isn't, but there is one that sticks up proud, like a hitchhiking thumb, and I make my way toward it. It has a faint mark chiseled into it, so faint I can't be sure what it is. Maybe a half circle with a cross of some kind above it? I spot a flowering plant on a slight mound at the base, its blue petals obvious among the muted heather. Then I notice that the heather is broken, several stems cracked and hanging loose. Fresh, too. None of the leaves have wilted. I squat and catch a glimpse of something that isn't a plant. A rock, maybe? No, not that either. I reach into a cavity that someone has dug under the heather and find a small rectangular package, tightly wrapped in clear, thick plastic.

A book.

About five by seven inches.

"Put that back where you found it," a voice says from behind me.

Which is startling, considering all I've heard for the past hour has been the wind gusting across the moor, tugging at my clothes. I stand and slowly turn, still holding the package in my left hand. The man who faces me is the Russian, Kuznyetsov, attired much like me, in a kilt and outdoor jacket, holding a gun, pointed my way.

I stay cool and assess the situation.

Obviously, this man has been here all along able to see my approach. Luckily, this isn't my first rodeo. I've faced down many guns.

"This yours?" I ask, motioning with the wrapped book.

"I told you to put it back."

I decide to see how much nerve this guy really possesses. "If you still want it, here."

And I feign tossing the book across the ten feet of air that separates us. At the same time I dive behind the sole standing stone, reach for my Beretta, and fire past the edge of the rock. A shot comes in return, which ricochets off the stone.

Chips and dust spew in my face.

I grab the stone to steady myself, bracing for another shot.

Everything turns inside out.

The rock, the heather, the sky, even me. It all flies apart in a strange, rapid disintegration. Like a jigsaw puzzle disassembling. I'm aware for a split second of being there, behind the stone, then in the next I fight to keep myself physically together. A blinding light sears across my eyes and I'm overwhelmed by an incredible force.

One I have never felt before.

And cannot fight.

●◆●

I WAKE.

Lying on the ground in a patch of wet peat moss, cold water wells up between my legs through the kilt. I roll over and push up onto my hands and knees. My head pounds and feels too heavy to lift and my thoughts make little sense. I see the wrapped book lying on the ground where I apparently dropped it. Then I realize that the gun is still in my hand, my fingers numb from gripping it.

I glance up at the sky.

More clouds have arrived, but the sun is still there, at about the same height. So not much time has passed. Things are coming back to me and, with a jolt of adrenaline, I remember Kuznyetsov.

I spring to my feet and look around. But no Kuznyetsov. I glance down at the gun and see shreds of blackened, melted plastic clinging to my fingers where the butt had once been. The gun itself is destroyed. The hammer fused tight, its form misshapen.

What the hell?

I shake away the plastic, as if it's an unwanted insect.

I bend down and lift the wrapped book. Through the clear wrappings I see that it's Chubb's missing 15th-century grimoire. How long have I been out? I glance at my watch. Magellan Billet standard issue with a GPS tracker. But the bezel has cracked with a hole the size of a fingertip, the watch face beneath showing a similar hole, black at the edges.

Then I notice something odd.

The edges of the hole in the watch face curl outward, as if something *inside* has exploded. Is this the cause of my confusion? Is that what knocked me out?

I unstrap the watch and toss it away, along with the useless gun.

My mind seems a blur of questions and I shake my head to rid a light-headed sensation. I need to think, but what I really need to do is get back to the castle. Kuznyetsov is gone. Either he'd been hit but is still mobile and heading back to the castle for medical help, or he hadn't been hit and is heading back to get his story heard first. More than likely, though, the Russian took a bullet. Otherwise, why hadn't he hung around to recover the book?

I hesitate for a moment, wondering if I should rehide the grimoire, but decide against it. My bringing the prize back will count in *my* favor and, luckily, I haven't freed the book from its wrappings. That means my fingerprints won't be there and, with any luck, Kuznyetsov's will.

I tuck the wrapped book inside the kilt's waistband at the small of my back. Then leave the stones and head through the moor, back from where I came, brushing scabs of heather off my sweater as I walk. I reach the road, which is different. Not paved. Dirt. Is this the same route? I'd been warned that it was easy to get turned around in the moor.

I set off at a jog, the wet kilt flapping against my legs. I maintain a good pace for a half hour with no sign of Kuznyetsov. Could the man have been hit seriously enough that he'd staggered off and collapsed? I'll find out soon enough, and increase my speed, wiping sweat from my eyes.

Castle Ardsmuir appears ahead.

But its hulk looks different. The big torches by the gate are gone and so is the paved drive. The castle itself appears damaged, strewn with debris of broken masonry, with gaping holes in the walls and one tower collapsed. No such disrepair had been there last night.

The castle gates swing open.

Instinct tells me to flee the dirt track and crouch behind a prickly gorse bush where I can observe out of sight. Creaking and clopping noises are at first faint, then louder as a horse-drawn wagon emerges, followed by a knot of ragged-looking men in filthy shirts and breeches.

Most wear manacles.

Prisoners.

Then three red-coated soldiers appear, each carrying bayoneted muskets angled on their shoulders. The soldiers are nearly as ragged and filthy as the prisoners. The scarlet uniforms all dirty, faded and patched. The day's breeze stiffens and the wind brings the repulsive stink of men who live in their clothes, never bathe, and lack even a rag to wipe their asses. All sense of time seems distorted, and I stare at the spectacle in numb fascination. A thought occurs that this is some sort of reenactment, but I quickly dismiss the idea, as another more outlandish conclusion is rapidly taking its place.

The wagon clanks away and the group marches down the road, passing close enough that I can hear snatches of talk among the prisoners. It isn't English, or any other language with which I'm familiar. The objective commentator in the back of my brain, which is already on high alert, a voice I've learned to trust, tells me that it might be Gaelic.

One of the prisoners staggers, stumbles, then falls flat in the dirt.

A tall, redheaded man in irons, built like an oak tree, runs toward the fallen man. All the other prisoners start to converge too, and the soldiers glance warily at each other then take a fresh grip on their muskets. Another work party—if that's what this is—shambles out of the castle gate. It looks as bad, if not worse, than the first one.

The big redheaded prisoner stands, crosses himself, and shouts toward the soldiers. "This man is dead."

In Scottish-accented English.

The soldiers relax into irritability, like this is a nuisance they've encountered many times before. One of them trudges over to have a look, poking the body gingerly with a booted foot, kicking it once or twice to make sure, then steps back.

"Get 'im off t'road."

Big Red seems not to like the order. He stands a foot taller than the runty soldier and draws himself up close to the redcoat, who makes a hasty retreat, then stops and points his rifle. No, it isn't a rifle.

His musket.

"We'll put him in the wagon," Big Red says in an even voice. "And bury him on the moor."

The soldier glances involuntarily over his shoulder and the oldest of the infantrymen shrugs, frowns, and nods.

Crisis averted.

The prisoners are already lifting the dead man, handling him with reverence. I hear clanking from inside the wagon as tools are moved aside in order to lay the corpse in the bed.

What is this?

All I know for certain is that Castle Ardsmuir may no longer be a place of safety. I knew that once, long ago, it had been a prison.

Was that now?

In the distance comes the boom of surf signaling the sea. Soldiers and prisoners alike seem preoccupied. So I seize the chance and, staying crouched, I duckwalk backward away from the road. Finally, I stand and run for it, bounding through the moor, then cutting back to the dirt road so as to move faster.

I hear shouts behind.

And the distinctive *pfoom* of a black-powder weapon.

• ◆ •

I STOP.

The shot hadn't come my way, but I decide not to wait around to see if my presence had been noticed. I keep running. I'm in good shape for a guy staring down fifty. Finally, I realize no wolves are in pursuit, so I stop to rest, wondering what the hell to do next. I've known from the instant I awoke by the stones that something is not right, and it's getting worse by the minute. My sense of logic keeps insisting that I'm just seeing things wrong, that I've made a mistake, taken a wrong turn somewhere, drawn the wrong conclusion. But my analytical brain tells me that I'm not in Kansas anymore. I recall that the village of Clebost is a half hour or so by car from Castle Ardsmuir, and the road I'm on leads there.

So the smart play is to head for the village and see what I can learn.

But after two hours of walking the only other signs of life I see are seagulls and a fox that crosses the road. The landscape casts a somber, eerie quality, tranquil but ominous. Then a pair of horses approach and I decide to flag the riders down.

A man and a woman.

The man is older and plainly not well, hunched in the saddle, half falling. The woman is tall, slender waisted, and buxom. Her complexion is a creamy blond with hair to match, done up in a loose coiffure, half hidden under a lacy blue cap. Her eyes are a deep shade of green and I catch a glint of interest within them as she looks me over. They are both dressed nothing like someone from the 21st century, their odd clothes as jaded as my nerves.

I decide to use some southern charm. "I beg your pardon. I wonder if you could tell me how far it is to Clebost?"

"Who are you?" the woman asks. Her long-lashed, slightly slanted eyes add a troubling, mysterious quality to her.

"My name is Harold Earl Malone," I say, deciding that "Cotton" might be hard to explain. "And you are?"

"Melisande Robicheaux," she says, with a one-sided curl of her mouth that makes me realize that is definitely not her name. "That's Duncan Kerr," she adds, with an offhanded nod toward her companion.

The old man slides off his horse with a moan, making a croaking, gargling sound, like speech, but inarticulate. He staggers into the bracken where he throws up and collapses.

"I told him not to risk the jellied eels," she says. "But do men ever listen? Where did ye come from, then?"

"Castle Ardsmuir. I drove there last night. From Strathpeffer."

"Did ye indeed?" she says, looking at me intently. "Ye drove, was it?"

I catch an instant of recognition in her question and my self-imposed restraint breaks down. "Do you know what I'm talking about?"

"Aye, maybe." Her lids are half lowered in thought. "If ye're staying at the castle, what is it ye're seeking in Clebost, though?"

I catch her evasion of my inquiry, but decide to go where she's leading. "I came out for a walk across the moor after breakfast and didn't pay attention to where I was going. I'm lost." I gesture at the vast expanse of undulating green. "If I can get to the village, I can make arrangements for someone to take me back to the castle."

I choose my words with great care, but I still have the impression that she understands what I mean by "drove." She slides off her horse in a flounce of petticoats, shakes herself into order, and steps close. I can't help but stare at the creamy skin that shows at the neck of her dress. She seems supremely aware of her femininity and notices my interest. The corners of her mouth turn up.

"I have a proposition for you, Mr. Harold Earl Malone. I find myself in urgent need of a man."

The hell you say, I think.

This woman radiates a sexual vibe I can almost touch.

But I'm not about to try.

Her expression looms easy and calm, but her eyes are intent on me, studying, judging. Her face shimmers in soft peach and vanilla tones and she tosses me a smile that shows her teeth but not her thoughts.

Then she gently touches my arm.

"Duncan's not able today," she says, with a careless wave at the other man, curled up in a heap amid the bracken. "And my errand's urgent. If you'll help me, I'll see you safe on your road home."

"What kind of errand?" I ask cautiously, and she motions toward the west, where I again hear the faint rush of an unseen ocean.

"I need a man to row me out to one of the bittie wee isles just off the coast. It's not far, but the current's tricky and it takes a strong back. It'll not take long," she adds, seeing my curious look. "I'll have ye back on dry land and on your way home before sunset."

Every radar synapse in my brain rings an alarm. I try to let my emotions subside, my mind to stop questioning the fantastical. A sense honed from my years as a Magellan Billet field agent tells me she's trouble, but what choice do I have? My options are severely limited. And experience has taught me that in every operation there comes only one course—blind risk—where trust has to be placed in something that might otherwise be senseless and all you can do is hope for the best.

Like now.

So I tell her yes, hoping she's not spotted any of my skepticism.

Pleased, she offers me the other horse, leaving her former companion lying in the bracken. We ride, with her in the lead, across the moor to the cliff edge and down a precipitous rocky path to a small settlement that huddles at the bottom. There she bargains with a fisherman in rapid Gaelic, paying him with coins. The man counts them carefully, nods, and gestures toward a small boat lying upturned on the rocky shore just above the tide line. She removes a saddlebag from her horse and, with a jerk of the head, leads me toward the sea.

"We'll take that one," she says. "The red-and-yellow one. It's painted that way to ward off the bad spirits and coax a good catch from the sea, aye?"

"You sound like an expert."

She shakes her head. "No but what I've heard."

The small wooden boat has no oarlocks, but I develop enough rhythm to propel us through the surf and out into open water. She sits on the gunwale, one hand shading her eyes. I glance back over my shoulder and spot at least six tiny islands ranging from a knob covered with birds to a couple big enough that it would take half an hour to traverse. Overhead the sky rolls with clouds bound to storm. Not here, maybe, but somewhere.

"Which one do you want?" I ask, and almost drop an oar when a wayward current slams into the stern and whirls us around.

She lets out a hoot of laughter at my mistake and points over my left shoulder. "That one. The silkies' isle."

I know a silkie is a seal. And I have already heard their hoarse barking, coming in snatches on the wind. A quick look, taking care to hold on to the oars and be mindful of the swells, and I see the island—a dark, rounded hump with flat ledges, packed with the sausage shapes of slickwet seals. After fifteen minutes of fighting the current, I ask her why she just didn't pay the fisherman to row her out.

"Because he lives here," she says. "I don't want him to know where

I'm going, nor what I do when I get there. You"—she smiles, as though to herself—"will be gone, away to your own place by nightfall."

The currents are murder, and a chilly breeze stirs the water to a froth. I'm relieved when we finally reach the island. I skirt the shore, searching for a landing place, fending off a few of the curious residents who pop up alongside the boat. Finally, I spot a small notch wide enough for the boat to pass through and nestle against a rocky ledge. A narrow, slitlike crevice eats up into the cliff face and winds a path to its top.

"Stay here," she says, hopping out. "Take care the boat doesn't get loose. It gets damned cold on these isles at night. Hand me the bag there, aye?"

She likes to give orders. But I actually like strong women. And even in this strange place, I still seem to attract them. So I hand her the saddlebag. She digs around inside for a few seconds before removing a wooden box, about a foot long and half that wide. It rattles and clinks with the unmistakable sound of coins. I glance up at her, but she says nothing, nor does she even look at me. She merely hands the saddlebag back, then hikes up her skirts and scrambles up the rock without a backward glance. I watch until she disappears from sight, then I wrap the rope of the painter around a thumb-shaped chunk of rock. My shoulders are tired and I hope to hell the tide will be going in when we head back.

A loud *wark* to my left makes me jump.

A big seal has decided to investigate the newcomer, the black-olive eyes intent with suspicion. I pick up one of the oars, ready just in case, but the silkie only offers some menacing head waving and more barking, backed up by a chorus from his nearby harem. After a cloudy exhale of fish-scented steam, the seal disappears beneath the water.

I sit for a few minutes.

The solid coldness of stone, sea, and wind leach the heat of rowing from my muscles. I blow warm breath into my palms. I'm growing hungry. Another half hour and I succumb to temptation, grabbing the saddlebag for a look inside.

And find food.

Flat oatcakes, like cardboard. A packet of strong-smelling dried fish. And a knob of rock-hard white cheese. I break off a chunk and eat the cheese with one of the oatcakes. Not the tastiest treat in the world, but filling.

The bag also contains a number of small corked bottles, each wrapped in rough cloth with Latin labels. I open one and sniff, catching a tangy, herbal scent from the dark liquid inside. A small wooden box with a sliding lid is full of dried seaweed, with a strong iodine smell. And another holds what looks like dead bugs. At the bottom I see something especially interesting. A small, square package, done up with paper and a layer of oiled silk beneath. I glance across the landscape of rock and seals, but there is no sign of Melisande. So I unwrap the bundle and find myself holding a book. I reach around and claw at my waist. Malcolm Chubb's grimoire is still there, safe inside its plastic cocoon.

The cover of the new book I hold is limp with no boards, made of a fine-grained leather. I gently stroke it. Unborn lamb, perhaps. Its pages are handwritten in French, but an archaic version, one I don't recognize, the book lavishly illustrated with drawn images, beautifully detailed, traces of the original gilding and color still clinging to many of them.

I catch their meaning.

Alchemy.

I scan more of the thin parchment pages, each in wonderful condition despite their obvious age. My brows go up seeing a remarkably explicit—though beautifully rendered—drawing of a woman having her way with a four-horned goat. I've risked enough exposure to the elements for this treasure, so I close the old book. As I do, I catch a glimpse of the title page.

Le grimoire du Le Compte Saint-Germain.

I free the other book from my kilt's waist band and compare the size and thickness. About the same. Nearly identical, in fact. What did Chubb say about the 15th-century grimoire? *We think it's a copy of a much older volume. One perhaps by Saint-Germain himself.* Is this the original manuscript from which the book I hold had been printed?

Suddenly I'm yanked from my thoughts.

By a scream.

●◆●

I STAND IN THE BOAT AND LISTEN, BUT CATCH NOTHING OTHER THAN the shriek of gulls. Perhaps I mistook one of their cries for something more human.

I carefully rewrap Melisande's book and replace it into the bag. I notice something else inside, bulky at the bottom. I dig down through the bottles and boxes and discover a flintlock pistol, loaded and primed, protected by a holster. Etched into the leather is a name.

Geillis.

I wonder.

Is that relevant to this woman?

Hard to say, but the flintlock is a fine specimen. Quite deadly from short range. Its presence raises a ton of questions about my benefactor, several of which I've already asked myself. So I decide to not take any chances. I withdraw the weapon and shake the cartridge and wad out into my hand. I stuff both into the sporran at my waist, then replace the weapon, now useless, in the bag.

An explosion of seal hysterics warns that someone is coming and I see Melisande pick her way down the rocks, now minus the coin box. Her movements are quick with a nervous vitality, and her shoulders rise and fall in concert with her rapid breathing.

"Let's be away," she says, stepping into the boat. "The tide's just on the turn."

I nod, not bothering with conversation. I'm as anxious to get back to the mainland as she is—possibly more so. The afternoon looms pale and without warmth and she's right. This is no place to be stranded. She's also right about the tide. It is turning, and the currents remain bizarre, pulsating and lifting us with each swell.

I keep my rowing in time with the shallow, jerking pitch.

Eventually we come to land and, with a final surge, the tide shoves us onto a pebbled shore. Close to the black cliff small thatched cottages stand, built of the same dark stone, smoke curling from holes in the thatch and the flicker of firelight just visible from a narrow window here and there. She bends to retrieve her bag as I scramble ashore to secure the boat to a barnacle-crusted iron ring sunk into the rocks. I just finish tying the

rope when I hear a click behind me and the immediate pop of a flash in
the pan, signaling the firing of a primed gun with no load. I turn around
to see Melisande, holding the weapon, aiming at me. Her expression bears
a mix of anger, contempt, and surprise.

Luckily, my suspicions proved correct.

"I'm not that stupid," I say to her.

Then I spot a package, wrapped in clear plastic, in the shadows under
the slats of one of the seats.

Damn.

I dropped Chubb's grimoire.

She leaps over the gunwale and I catch the glint of a knife in her hand.
She brings it toward me in a wide, flailing arc. I grab her wrist, but she's
strong, twisting like a snake. Her knee slams into my thigh and twists
me sideways. She jabs with the blade and I dodge her attacks. I grapple
with her for a few moments then decide enough of being a gentleman
and smash the back of my hand across her jawline. Her head flies up in a
cascade of hair that snaps her teeth together with a loud smack and makes
her totter backward. Her eyes go wide, then she moans and collapses onto
the beach, skirts blooming around her.

"Hoy!"

Shouts reach me from the water, and I stare out to see three boats
with men standing up, waving their arms. The doors to the nearby cottages open and more burly men flood out. Melisande suddenly rises to her
knees. Blood seeps from a gash in her lip.

"Help me. He's a murderer," she screams.

Rage fills her eyes.

This apparently is not going according to her plan.

No time to snatch up the lost book. So I retreat and make for the
trail, bounding upward in a wild scramble, scree sliding under my feet. I
reach the top winded and sweat drenched. A quick look below shows me
that Melisande is no longer lying on the beach and that a couple of the
fishermen and several of the other men are making their way up the trail.
I run off across the moor, with no idea where I'm going. I jog and walk
alternately, as fast as I can, my lungs pumping like bellows. After a while I
slow, fairly certain that nobody is following. God knows what that woman

is telling her saviors, or what she would have told them if she'd succeeded in killing me.

I'll have you on your way home by sunset.

Home, all right. Dead, more likely.

And now I know exactly why she didn't hire the local fisherman. She preferred a corpse nobody either knew or would miss.

I regret losing the grimoire, but there is no way to double back and retrieve it. Too many people around. I have to keep moving. I'm way past tired, my senses growing dull, my thoughts fragmented, the only constant the whine of the wind in my ears. Daylight gradually fades and I finally stop, overcome as much by confusion as by weariness. No amount of training could prepare anyone for this experience. Whatever *this experience* actually is. All sense of past and future seems gone.

Only the present matters.

I decide not to keep going any farther as darkness grows around me.

So I find a bit of high ground with no standing water, huddle up in the shelter of a clump of broom, and fall headlong into a dreamless sleep.

•◆•

I COME AWAKE TO A MORNING RAIN ACROSS THE TRACKLESS, ROUGH, uneven moor, the night's chill deep in my bones. The past few hours of impossibility flow with a calm finality through my mind. No visible sun aids my sense of direction, so all I can do is walk away from the faint sound of the distant sea and hope to find someone who might prove helpful. In the uneasy realms of sleep my mind seems to have accepted the insane notion that I have been displaced in time. Also it's clear that the ragged little group of stones has something to do with my dilemma. So that's what I need to find. The stones. And see what, if anything, might happen if I touch them again.

I walk for several hours, growing wetter by the minute. The few structures I pass seem as weathered and worn as the pitted road. I read once that the thick wool of a kilt and sweater traps body heat like a diver's wetsuit. I'm pleased to discover that the observation proves at least partially correct. I'm not comfortable, but I'm not freezing, either.

Just wet.

And hungry.

I should have eaten more of what I found in Melisande's saddlebag. Thinking of her, I spare a brief thought for Duncan Kerr. What on earth had led the old man to keep company with such a murderous bitch? Did she go back after him? Or had she just left him in the heather? I push aside those thoughts and trudge on.

Ahead, I hear faint voices.

I speed up, but skirt the side of the road, out of sight, and soon come upon another gang of prisoners cutting peat. Bricklike chunks of moss, decayed into a black, fudgy substance, are being hacked from the ground by poles with angled blades at the end. Their presence offers me hope. I could just wait and follow the work detail back to the castle, which was where they came from yesterday. Though not necessarily a place of safety, I don't want to risk spending another night on the moors. No red-coated guards are in sight. But I spot a small canvas shelter pitched away from the prisoners, a blue plume of smoke rising from a fire inside. Evidently the guards are keeping out of the wet.

I approach the work group cautiously, not sure whether to speak to one of the prisoners or one of the soldiers. Either could be friend or foe. Coming closer, I see that it is the same group from yesterday, and I spot the same tall redheaded man, wearing fetters, climbing up out of a wide dark scar of a pit in the green of the moor. Big Red sees me too and heads straight for me with a hasty stride. A clink of iron accompanies each step.

"How is it ye wear tartan, *a charaidh?*" the man says, giving me a narrow-eyed look. His voice is husky, with a slightly hollow tone to it.

I stand my ground. "It's Scotland, isn't it? Doesn't everyone?"

The man throws out a short, humorless laugh. "No one these ten years past, man. Ye risk being shot on sight, should the soldiers see ye in it. Or maybe only arrested and hanged later, if they're too lazy to shoot ye."

Big Red glances at the canvas lean-to and so do I. Voices raise from an argument inside.

"Come," the Scot says, grabbing me by the arm, hurrying me to the pit. "Get ye into the moss-hag. And keep still."

The Scot moves away and I follow the order, hopping down and pressing my back against the black wall of crumbling peat. I hear rapid Gaelic being spoken above and murmurs from the other prisoners. Distant laughter and the talk of the guards grows in intensity. Then the English voices recede and Big Red drops down into the pit beside me.

"Who are ye, man? Ye're no a Scot nor yet a German or an Irishman, and that's no a tartan from any Highland regiment I ken."

"My name's Cotton Malone. And yours?"

"I'm Jamie Fraser."

•◆•

I TAKE STOCK OF THE MAN STANDING BEFORE ME.

Fraser is tall, over six feet, and though he's as thin as the rest, his chest is that of a lumberjack, the forearms grooved with muscle. He has high cheekbones, a long, knife-edged nose, a strong jaw, and his long red hair is tied back in a tail that hangs below his shoulder blades. His eyes cast a dark blue gaze, open at first glance, disconcertingly wary at a second.

"Where are ye from?" he asks me.

I rub a hand across my stubbled face. There's no good answer to that question, so I decide to come to the point, "I've been lost on the moor for a couple of days. I'm looking for a group of stones. In a circle. Five or six, with a tall one standing high. It's got a thing carved into it that looks like a ring with a cross through it. Have you seen something like that?"

Puzzlement in the Scot's blue eyes is replaced by understanding. Fraser is soaked to the skin, the rags of his shirt clinging to him like cellophane, rivulets of water running down the side of his stout neck and off his broad shoulders. Suddenly his big hand shoots out and grips me by the shoulder.

The impassive mask crumples.

"Do you know of the year 1948?" he asks.

What an odd question in so ancient a setting. But it grabs my attention. At least I'm not the only one going nuts around here. His hard eyes stay fixed on me for a long time and I wonder if this man came from another time too. Then I decide to be more cautious in my reply.

"I know that year."

The Scot regards me with a look of astonishment and something that seems almost like excitement. "Then, aye. I ken those stones."

Excitement grows warm in my veins. But I have to know something. "What year is this?"

"1755."

Underlying my shock is a thread of awe. I am 262 years in the past. Unfrigging believable. With only one way out. "Can you tell me how to find the stones?"

"I can tell ye how to go."

I swallow the saliva of anticipation as we climb from the pit and he points out landmarks in the moor, invisible until I am shown them, by which to steer my course. "The clouds are shreddin'. Ye'll have the sun for another two hours and the moon's already risen. Keep it over your right shoulder as ye go."

Maybe, just maybe, the world might make sense again. I clasp his hand. It is deeply calloused and hard as wood. "Thank you."

He returns the shake, then steps back, suddenly ginger in his manner, as though he would rather not have made contact. But one thing is clear. This man understands my problem.

"If"—the Scot begins, then smothers his question behind compressed lips.

"Tell me. I'll do what I can for you."

"If when ye find your own place again. If ye should happen on a woman called Claire—" He swallows, then shakes his head. "No. Never mind." A sadness touches his face as he glances away.

"Speak your mind."

I allow my tone to take on the tinge of an order.

Fraser glances back at me, taking his time, but makes up his mind. He draws himself up to his full height, which is considerable, and speaks formally.

"Aye. Should ye meet with a woman called Claire Fraser—no, she'd be Claire Randall then—" A dark shadow crosses his face at the words, but he shakes it off. "A healer. Tell her that James Alexander Malcolm MacKenzie Fraser, the Laird of Lallybroch, blesses her and wishes her and her child both health and joy." His gaze goes far away for a moment, and he swallows again, before adding in a low voice, "Tell her that her husband misses her."

I should probe that statement more, but there is no time. So I simply say, "I will."

"Have ye a woman? There, I mean?"

I nod. "Her name is Cassiopeia."

Just saying her name makes me smile. She would have loved this adventure. He stares sharply at me, as though suspecting a joke, but seeing that it isn't, he nods soberly. "Think of her, when ye come to the stones. Go wi' God, and may Michael and Bride protect ye."

"Thank you," I say again, which feels wholly inadequate.

I turn to leave and my eye falls on the canvas shelter, from which a muffled, drunken song is now issuing. "Does anybody ever try to escape? Surely it wouldn't be that hard?"

He stares out across the endless moor, with eyes that seem incapable of illusion. "Where should we go? All that we knew is gone, and all that we have is each other."

•◆•

DARKNESS HAS FALLEN WHEN I FIND THE STONES, BUT A THREE-quarter moon, high on the scudding clouds, showers down a surreal ivory glow. I catch the quick, silent streak of a falling star across the southern curve of the heavens. A sign of good luck? Hopefully. But an owl hoots a sinister warning.

I stand for a minute, staring, afraid to look away for fear I am imagining them and the stones might disappear if I blink. A chilling air of pathos rises from the ruins. I have gone well past the point of feeling hungry, now more dizzy with tiredness than from a lack of food. I have no idea what I'll say, if it works and I am sent back to my own time. How will I explain Kuznyetsov? The lost grimoire? Where I've been, and all that happened? As a Magellan Billet agent I've been involved with some incredible things. But the past two days has climbed to the top of that amazing list.

I walk around the stones and begin to be aware of a low buzzing noise, like a hive of bumblebees. I didn't notice that before. Am I to utter some magic words? I smile at the thought. Then recall what Jamie Fraser said.

Think of her, when ye come to the stones.

The Scotsman had obviously been thinking about someone special. Claire. His wife. The memory almost painful.

I decide to take the man's advice.

Placing one hand on the tallest stone, I whisper, "Cassiopeia."

•◆•

MY EYES ARE CLOSED, BUT SCATTERED RECOLLECTIONS FLICKER though my mind, fading, then growing stronger. There's not as much motion or force in the journey like the first time—or maybe it's just that I know what to expect—more like a silent process of shifting lights and shapes.

My lips quiver.

A shiver of panic tries to free itself from my brain. Familiar faces I had almost forgotten swim in and out, blur, and disappear.

Then everything goes quiet.

I open my eyes to a dazzling radiance, bright to the point of burning my pupils. Shadowy figures hover over me. Faces approach, then recede. I raise an arm to shield my vision and hear a voice shout, "He's alive."

I struggle to focus and see that I'm being loaded into the back of a van. All I can see is the beam of a bright flashlight, which confirms what I need to know. I made it. Then I catch a stench of blood and death. Beside me in the van lies a huge dead boar on a sheet of blue plastic. A man scrambles inside. My mouth is dry and sticky, and the sudden roar of an engine drowns out the first words I try to say.

"You awake then, mate?" a Scottish voice says. "How ye feeling?"

It belongs to a man in his fifties, with a deeply weathered but friendly face, wearing a waxed jacket.

"Where are we going?" I ask, resisting the urge to swat the flashlight away.

"Aye, well, if your name is Malone, we thought we'd maybe take ye to your friends at the castle. If ye're no him, though, we should maybe carry ye down to the village. They've a wee cottage hospital there."

"I'm Malone," I assure him, then shut my eyes again, trying to gather strength, my memories a whirlwind of confusion.

Was the whole thing a dream?

Not real?

By the time the van turns into the paved drive that leads to the castle—once more ablaze with electric floodlights—I'm sitting up, passing a flask back and forth with one of my saviors.

"Archie McAndres, purveyor o' fine game," the man tells me, with a companionable slap on the flank of the dead boar. "The lad and I were headin' along to the castle, when we saw ye stagger out o' the moor. Thought ye were drunk, but then I remembered Mr. Chubb showin' me the wee photie of ye when we brought the pheasants yesterday."

"They were . . . looking for me?"

"Ach, aye. When they found your man Nyetski or whatever, lyin' dead on the moor wi' a bullet in him, there was a clishmaclaver from here to Inverness. When they found the things in his pockets, they thought ye maybe—"

"Things?" I ask. "What things?"

"Oh, I cannae just charge my mind, but it was bits o' ivory, maybe icons. Was it icons, Rob?" the man bellows toward the cab. "What the Russian fella had?"

"Jewels, I heard it was," Rob's voice comes back over the thrum of the motor.

The flask returns to my hands.

"Have another drink. Seems the dead one wasn't named Nyetski a'tall. He was one of the East European fellas. Known to the polis."

I pass on more from the flask. Talk of Kuznyetsov makes me think of the missing grimoire I found at the base of the stone. In the dream I tucked it at the small of my back, beneath my sweater. Then lost it on the boat. I reach around and feel, but no book is there.

The van stops and the rear doors open.

A blue sky overhead promises a new beginning.

I am back at Castle Ardsmuir.

●◆●

THE QUESTIONS COME IN RAPID FIRE, BUT I DECIDE A LIE IS BETTER than saying I may have traveled 262 years back in time. Besides, I'm not sure any of it ever happened. Kuznyetsov is definitely dead, though, but there is nothing linking me to that fact. Apparently, my gun has not been found. So it's better to just do a Sergeant Schultz. *I see nothing. I hear nothing. I know nothing.*

"Ye don't offer much," a local police inspector tells me, businesslike and composed. "Ye never saw the Russian?"

I shake my head.

"No idea how he got shot and dead?"

This is the fourth time we've been through it, but I know the drill. Have someone say something over and over enough until they mess up. "Like I've already explained, I have no idea what happened to him."

"Detective Inspector," Malcolm Chubb says, interrupting. "My friend is exhausted. He's been out on the moors with no food for nearly two days. For God's sake, look at him. Can't this wait until tomorrow?"

The finality of Chubb's voice seems to outlaw any further discussion, and the policeman doesn't look happy.

"Aye, for the present, sir. But I'll be back later."

The inspector leaves the drawing room.

"Do you want to clean up, old fellow?" Chubb asks. "I've organized some sandwiches and coffee, but say the word and we can do you some steak and eggs, jam omelet, you name it."

"Sandwiches and coffee sounds perfect."

The food arrives and I eat. Compared to the moor, the drawing room seems like an oasis. A crackling fire, comfortable chair, quiet warmth. Chubb sits watching me in companionable silence.

"We naturally put off the auction, after they found Kuznyetsov—or whatever his name turns out finally to be," Chubb says. "The guests had to stay to be questioned, and since everything seems to have quieted down, the police have agreed that we can have the sale tomorrow. If you're still interested in that old grimoire, I mean?"

I wash the last of a venison sandwich down with the first cup from the second pot of coffee.

Time to fess up.

But before I can, Chubb says, "Apparently that was the one thing Kuznyetsov actually *didn't* steal. We turned the whole castle upside down, as discreetly as possible, and were just considering how to question the guests when word came about Kuznyetsov's body being found. Then all hell promptly broke loose."

I wait for more explanation.

"You know how, when you've lost something, you keep looking over and over in the same place, because you can't really believe that it isn't there?" Chubb nods toward the glass cases across the room. "And blast me if it wasn't right there. Have a look. I wouldn't have believed it either, but there the bloody thing is."

I stand and walk over.

Chubb unlocks the glass case, slipping on a pair of white gloves and carefully lifts out the book, holding it like a relic. I stare in amazement. It is the incunabulum 15th-century grimoire—the same one Kuznyetsov stole, the same one I found at the stone, the same one that went with me to 1755.

The same one I dropped in the boat.

A chill bristles the hair on the back of my neck.

How is that possible? Then I know. *It was in my family for hundreds of years.* That's what Eleanor LeBlanc said. *Passed down, until some impoverished ancestor sold it.*

Passed down?

Chubb closes the case, seemingly pleased with everything.

A quote from Shakespeare rolls through my mind.

What is past is prologue.

Had Melisande Robicheaux apparently become the inadvertent owner of the incunabulum. Left in the boat by a man who rowed her out to the silkies' island, then passed down to her heirs, and they to theirs, through the centuries, until making its way here. That's nonsense. Ridiculous. It was all a dream. The missing book was simply found here at the castle, as Chubb said.

My host pours two generous measures of whisky. The silence in the room exaggerates the clink of the bottle against the rim of the glass.

"You're sure you're all right, old man? No need for a doctor?"

"I'm fine," I say, knowing that I can now keep the whole experience to myself.

I accept the drink and enjoy a sip. It is one of the peaty Highland malts with fumes that can clear the head of crazy dreams.

Exactly what I need.

But a thought occurs to me. The flintlock pistol in the boat. I reach down and open the sporran that hangs from my waist.

Inside lies the wad and load.

I smile.

Not a dream.

Then I wonder if someday the rusted remnants of my watch and gun will make their way inside some collector's case too.

GAYLE LYNDS AND DAVID MORRELL

G AYLE AND DAVID COFOUNDED INTERNATIONAL THRILLER
Writers, so it was only fitting they be teamed together for this
anthology.

Gayle's character, Liz Sansborough, appeared in her first novel,
Masquerade (1996). The story of an old assassin trying to come in
from the cold, the book was rejected some thirty times, largely because
publishers believed the market for international spy thrillers was as dead
as the Cold War. Plus, there was another problem—Gayle was female, and
as one publisher told her agent, "No woman could've written this book."
High-octane adventure and a geopolitical story that spanned the globe
was then a male-only field. Still, *Masquerade* went on to become a *New
York Times* bestseller, and *Publishers Weekly* has listed it among the top ten
spy novels of all time.

Rambo, of course, derives from the classic *First Blood*, which David
penned in 1972. That character has evolved into icon status. It's even now
an actual word in the dictionary. Few fictional characters can claim that
fame. There's not been a new Rambo story in print for over thirty years.
David has toyed with ideas, but none have "spoken to him," which is a pre-
requisite for him before starting any project. When asked to be a part of

this book we hoped that something might speak up and, thankfully, it did.

This story was a true collaboration.

David and Gayle e-mailed and talked on the phone many times, hashing out the plot, engaging in a vigorous back-and-forth reminiscent to them both of 2004 through 2006 when they were busy creating International Thriller Writers. David was a little apprehensive about using Rambo in a short story. He worried that whatever he might do with his character in the future might be compromised.

So he and Gayle devised a clever solution.

One that delivers on all fronts.

Rambo on Their Minds.

RAMBO ON THEIR MINDS

THE LONG SHADOWS OF MORNING DRIFTED ACROSS HIGHWAY 55. Forests clothed in autumn golds and reds pressed the road where a dusty five-year-old van cruised the speed limit, attracting no attention. In the front seat, the driver and his passenger—armed and alert—wore sunglasses and baseball caps pulled low across their foreheads.

From the vehicle's rear came the sounds of a moan and coughing.

The passenger peered back over his shoulder. His name was Rudy Voya, a muscular man in his midthirties, with a broad pale face and high Slavic cheekbones. "She's waking up," he reported. He carried a .40 Smith & Wesson in a shoulder holster under his leather jacket. At his feet lay his AK-47. "Looks as if you shot her up perfect, Max."

"Not like we don't have a lot of practice," the driver, Max Tariksky, said with a nod. He was Rudy's cousin, the same age and hearty build, but forty pounds heavier. His face was round, his nose a ski slope, and his hooded gray eyes steely. He carried a 9 mm Browning under his windbreaker.

They had snatched the woman when she was on her dawn run through Rock Creek Park in Chevy Chase. Her name was Liz Sansborough, and she was a professor of psychology at Georgetown. She should've been an easy mark, but she was also ex CIA and rumored to have been an undercover officer. Taking no chances, Rudy had pretended to lose control of a bicycle, crashing into her, knocking her to the ground, while Max had hurried from a bench to help her stand but instead had injected her with a fast-acting sedative. They'd shoved her and the bike into the van before anyone had a chance to realize what was happening.

Now she was curled like a lemon peel on the floor behind them.

The highway bent sharply left and crested a ridge. As a mountain valley unfolded below, Max slowed the van. No vehicles were in sight. On their right an asphalt lane came into view and he turned the van onto it, braking inside the trees. Ten feet ahead stood a reinforced security gate with barbed wire on the top. On either side a chain-link fence extended into the forest. The sign on the gate warned PRIVATE PROPERTY. NO TRESSPASSING.

Rudy jumped out, hurried to the gate, and pressed four numbers on a security pad. By the time he ran back to the passenger seat the steel gate had slid open. After Max drove through, the gate closed behind them. They now had complete control of the property's hundred acres.

The drive wound up through oaks, pines, and poplars for nearly two miles. In this part of the Blue Ridge Mountains hunt clubs were common. The family had owned this one for nearly twenty years and was considered a good neighbor. Which meant they minded their own business. In rural Warren County privacy was next to godliness.

Checking on Liz Sansborough, Rudy saw that she'd rolled over onto her other side. He studied her in her sleek, yellow jogging clothes, her auburn hair falling out of her ponytail. With her full lips and wide-set eyes she was pretty. Her hands were scraped from when she'd tried to cushion her fall after the bicycle struck her. Other than that, she didn't have a scratch or a bruise on her.

That will soon change, Rudy thought.

• ◆ •

HER EYELIDS FLUTTERING, LIZ HEARD HERSELF MOAN.

She felt dizzy, sick to her stomach. Where was she? What had happened? As the stench of exhaust burned her nose, she began to remember—two men in the park, a bicycle knocking her down, someone offering to help her stand, the sting of a hypodermic. Just before she passed out they'd thrown her into a van. The van. That must be where she was now.

The vehicle stopped.

So did the engine. Two doors opened and banged shut.

She forced herself up into a sitting position just as the rear door swung open. Two men stared at her, the same two who'd kidnapped her. One briefly aimed his AK-47.

Then they yanked her out.

Rallying, she slammed her knee in a *hizagashira* strike into the belly of the larger one. Swearing, he grabbed her and threw her down hard. Gravel bit into her palms. She felt dizzy again. She forced herself to lift her head and look around. The van had stopped in front of a two-story log house. Next to it was the berm of what appeared to be an outdoor shooting range. Farther over she saw a swimming pool, covered for cold weather.

What is this place? she wondered in a daze.

One of the men was aiming a cell phone at her, holding it so long that she realized he must be making a video.

"Say something," he ordered. "Say, 'Help me, Simon.'"

She hurt everywhere. Her vision was blurred. "Go to hell."

The other man swung his hand, his palm connecting with her cheek. "Say it."

Pain exploded through her face.

He swung the other hand and slammed the other cheek.

She pitched over, tasting blood.

"Say it. Goddammit."

Need to—

Her eyes closed. She smelled pine trees.

Escape.

She heard water trickling.

A stream?

A forest?

Some kind of camp?

WASHINGTON, D.C.

FOR THE TENTH TIME, SIMON CHILDS SCANNED THE ITEMS ON THE restaurant's breakfast menu. Yet again, he glanced past the hostess toward the entrance. Once more he looked at his watch—a vintage Rolex that Liz knew he admired and that she'd given him as a prewedding present.

Twenty minutes to ten.

He and Liz had made plans to meet here, in Georgetown, for breakfast at nine and then go to a final meeting with their wedding-reception caterer. He didn't understand why she hadn't phoned to tell him she was going to be late. He'd called her three times but had reached only her voice mail. Amid the clink of silverware and the murmur of conversations, a voice interrupted his worried thoughts. He looked up, surprised to see the hostess standing next to him.

"Mr. Childs, this arrived for you."

She handed him a small box wrapped in silver wedding paper. He frowned, seeing his name on an attached card.

"A messenger delivered it," the hostess explained. "He pointed toward you and said to tell you that Ms. Sansborough apologizes for being late."

"Thank you."

As she returned to greeting more guests, there was a faint buzzing sound from the box in his hand. It vibrated. In an instant, he realized why. He tore off the bow, ripped off the wrapping paper, and yanked off the box's lid. Inside was a cell phone. He pressed the Answer button and held the phone against his ear.

"Liz?" he asked.

"She's been detained," a female voice said.

His chest tightened. "What do you mean 'detained'? Who *is* this?"

"Someone who's concerned about your fiancée's welfare." The woman's voice had a Russian accent and the confidence of someone accustomed to exerting authority. "I sent you a video attachment. Unless you want to disturb people sitting near you, I suggest that you watch it out-side. I'll call you again in three minutes."

The transmission went dead.

He walked swiftly toward the door, sidestepped a couple entering, and hurried out to the parking lot. Ignoring the cold morning air he scrolled through the phone, found the video attachment and pressed it.

And saw Liz lying on gravel.

"Say something," a man's voice ordered. "Say, 'Help me, Simon.'"

Liz looked groggy, stunned. But managed to say, "Go to hell."

A hand with a jagged scar on it streaked into view, the palm crashing into one cheek, then the palm of the other battering her other cheek, drawing blood. "Say it. Goddammit."

The image abruptly changed to one in which Liz slumped on a pad-ded bench. There were zip-tie cuffs on her wrists that were looped around some kind of metal pole. Both cheeks looked raw and swollen. Blood smeared her nose and chin.

The same scarred hand clasped her injured cheeks.

"Let's try again. You know what I want." The camera moved closer, her blood-covered face filling the screen. "Say it."

The hand squeezed so hard that its knuckles whitened.

Her eyes widened.

She tried to scream, but the hand kept squeezing. Crushing.

She writhed, managing to say past the hand, "Help . . . me . . . Simon."

The video ended.

But he continued to see Liz's battered face.

The phone vibrated.

He jabbed the Answer button and said, "I will find and kill you."

"You don't have time for useless threats," the woman's voice said. "Last night, in Washington, the FBI arrested an associate of mine. His name is Nick Demidov. I want him released."

"We don't have anything to do with the FBI."

The woman's harsh laughter reminded him of an old Russian expres-sion—*the ruthless walk over the dead.*

"You're an MI6 operative on temporary assignment to the FBI for a special Russkaya Mafiya task force. And your fiancée used to work for the CIA, probably still does. I'm giving you less than twelve hours to get Nick free, so use your influence. Call in favors. It should be easy. He's not important. The FBI will admit that they just swept him up because they hope he'll lead them to someone higher."

"If he's that low level, why does he matter to you?"

"He's my brother. Our mother is upset, as am I. Poor Nick isn't smart, which is obvious, given that he allowed himself to be arrested. But he's family. You've got until nine o'clock tonight to deliver him."

"But—"

"Keep the phone I gave you. It has an open mic. Even when it's turned off, the phone transmits everything you and anyone near you say, so don't even think about warning your buddies at the FBI about what's going on. If I even slightly suspect you're playing games, the next video will show your fiancée's ears being cut off."

"I want a video report every half hour to prove Liz is alive and healthy," he demanded.

"Every two hours is often enough. Remember, the world won't end if the task force lets Nick go. But your world will end, if they don't. Give me my brother, or I'll give you your fiancée's dismembered corpse."

●◆●

LIZ AWOKE TO POUNDING PAIN IN HER FACE.

Keeping her eyes closed, she reached to hold her burning cheeks, but her wrists were secured to something. She was slumped on a padded surface. As she struggled to remember where she was, the sound of voices penetrated her foggy mind. With a chill, she recognized them as those of her kidnappers. Drifting in and out of consciousness, she'd heard them talk to each other and to someone else, a woman, on what sounded like a speakerphone. The woman had addressed one of them as Rudy and the other as Max. Breathing deeply to fight the pain, she made herself focus on them.

"John J. was on TV last night," Rudy was saying.

"'John J.'? What are you talking about?" Max asked.

"John Rambo. You know, *First Blood*," Rudy said. "When I was growing up in Moscow, I got better at English by watching the movies."

She noticed the slight hissing of his *s*'s, a characteristic of some English-speaking Russians.

"Rambo hardly says a word. How could you learn English from those movies?" Max asked.

"From the other characters."

"After the way the third Rambo movie made us Russians look, I'm surprised you watched any of them."

"I admit the third one isn't the best, but that first one was great."

She was learning nothing from them, so she forced her eyes open and saw that she was lying on a weight lifter's bench beside a massive Nautilus machine. As her mind cleared, she realized that the plastic zip-tie cuffs on her wrists encircled one of the machine's metal poles, holding her arms up. The restraint was so tight it cut into her skin. She studied the pole and the multigym station with its pulleys, handles, and weights, wondering whether there was a way to twist free. It didn't look hopeful, and if she succeeded, she'd still have to deal with the two bastards who'd grabbed her.

"If you wanted to learn English from Rambo, you should've read the novel," Max said.

"There's a novel?"

"He dies at the end."

"No, the police chief's still moving at the end. You can see him twitch when they put him in the ambulance."

"Not in the novel," Max said.

"The police chief dies in the novel?"

"And Rambo."

"Stop bullshitting me."

Following the sound of their voices, she peered across the room and saw that this was some kind of security center—the two men were sitting in the middle of a long curved desk, while above and around them rose five levels of closed-circuit TV monitors displaying views of a steel gate, a driveway, the exterior of the log house, and a chain-link fence, most in dense woods. Because the majority of screens showed the fence, she guessed it surrounded the property and there must be many forested acres.

Carrying a coffee mug, Max swiveled in his chair and headed toward a kitchenette. "I'm telling you Rambo gets killed in the novel. Colonel Trautman shoots him."

"No, no, no. Rambo can't die."

"That's what Stallone said. That's why the movie ends the way it does." Max poured coffee.

"Then why would Stallone end the novel that way? You're not making sense."

"Stallone didn't write the novel."

"You're starting to bother me."

"I'm telling you."

"Then who the hell wrote the novel?"

"I can't remember." Max returned to his chair and sat.

"You're making all this up."

As they talked, she studied the room.

On her left was an expansive gun cabinet in which a dozen M4 assault rifles stood neatly in a line. Boxes of ammo were piled on shelves. To her right a wooden staircase climbed upward. All four walls were made of concrete blocks. There were no windows. The place had the feel of not only being secure but underground.

She focused again on the men at the big console. They were watching a screen twice as large as the others. It showed a grid on which a green dot was slowly traveling along one of the lines.

"He's on the move," Max said.

Rudy laughed. "And he's no Rambo."

A phone rang somewhere in the chamber.

Max pressed a button on the computer, and a woman's disembodied voice reported from a speaker, "We've got Simon Childs on a leash. I need you to e-mail me a video of Sansborough every couple of hours to keep him motivated, until he delivers the package."

At Simon's name, Liz tensed, feeling fresh pain roll through her. Now she remembered. The men had made her beg Simon for help. So Simon was involved and there was a "package." What was so important that they'd kidnapped her to get Simon to do what they wanted?

"Not a problem," Rudy said. He turned and grinned at Liz. "You want us to hurt her some more?"

"Not yet. Maybe later."

Liz stared back at the asshole, refusing to show fear.

But they'd let her see their faces.

No way could they allow her to live.

• ◆ •

AS SIMON STARED AT THE PHONE IN HIS HAND, A CAR HORN STARTLED him. He jerked his head up, abruptly aware of the restaurant's parking lot. A taxi was stopping at the building's entrance and the passenger was getting out. He ran to the taxi, veered in front of a waiting couple, and lunged into the backseat.

"Hoover Building," he told the surprised driver.

While the taxi merged into the morning traffic, Simon examined the phone. The woman had told him it had an open mic. In that case Liz's captors would now have heard where he was going. But he'd been ordered to use his influence, so his destination shouldn't alarm them.

He hoped.

The time on the phone was 9:54 a.m.

Less than twelve hours remained.

He and Liz were scheduled to be married ten days from now, and by God he was going to make certain it happened.

The FBI's headquarters on Pennsylvania Avenue had been built with a rugged concrete exterior—to create a powerful, dominating impression. But after little more than four decades, the concrete was decaying, and nets enclosed the upper stories to prevent chunks from falling onto pedestrians.

Feeling that something might indeed crash onto him, Simon hurried inside the massive building. He tried not to arouse suspicion by looking impatient while he waited in a long line at the security checkpoint.

Another line blocked his way to the elevators.

A clock on a wall showed 10:28 when he finally entered the third-floor office where the Russian Mafia task force was located. The special agent in charge, a spectacled woman named Cassidy, spoke rapidly into a cell phone while a broad-shouldered man named Grant typed on a keyboard.

Cassidy ended her call and tossed Simon a puzzled look. "I thought you and Liz were finalizing your wedding reception today."

"The caterer postponed the meeting," Simon said, not daring to doubt that the phone did indeed broadcast the conversation.

He considered writing a note to alert them to what was happening, but he couldn't depend on them not saying something that would make Liz's captors suspicious. Instead he studied Grant's computer screen and pointed toward a new name on a list.

"Who's Nick Demidov?"

"Not sure yet."

Grant clicked on the name, opening an almost blank document that showed photographs of a dark-haired, fortyish man in a black leather sports jacket.

"The police grabbed him last night when they raided a warehouse stashed with stolen prescription painkillers," Cassidy said. "He has a Virginia driver's license, but all he claims to speak is Russian. So far there's no record on him. What's interesting is he had two hundred thousand dollars in the trunk of his car. A six-year-old car, no less. If he had that kind of money, he should have been driving the best. He seems to be a courier."

"We sent for a translator," Grant said. "Maybe Demidov can lead us to somebody important."

"You know, he's starting to look familiar," Simon lied again.

"Oh?" Cassidy asked.

"When I worked on the European task force, he was a bagman for a Russian money launderer in London. If I talk to him, maybe he'll drop the 'I don't speak English' act and tell me what he's doing in D.C. Where are you holding him?"

• ◆ •

LIZ FELT NAUSEATED.

Her head ached and her face still throbbed. Worse, whatever Max and Rudy had shot her up with had muddled her brain.

Dammit, enough whining, she told herself. *Focus.*

She heard Simon's voice. "Where are you holding him?"

She snapped open her eyes and realized his voice was coming from a speaker on the computer desk across the room. Beside it sat the large monitor where the green dot had been moving the last time she looked.

Now the dot was motionless.

They're tracking Simon.

Another man's voice sounded from the speaker, answering Simon. "Demidov is in a safe house out by Tysons Corner. Here's the address."

She heard someone writing on a piece of paper and tearing it from a pad.

In his chair at the security center, Max grinned. "I love it when a plan comes together. We gotta get Demidov away from the FBI before they figure out who he is. I'm e-mailing this to Marta in case she didn't pick it up."

"I'll be in touch."

Simon's voice again.

On the speaker, a man and woman said good-bye to Simon, and the sounds diminished to footsteps and distant voices.

Max chuckled and leaned back in his chair, hands clasped behind his head.

"That Simon guy is no Rambo."

Rudy headed toward the Nautilus multigym. "The first Rambo movie's okay, but I like the first sequel more."

He did some upper-body stretches.

"The one where he goes back to Vietnam?" Max asked. "You've gotta be kidding. Russians look like idiots in that one also."

"Hey, it was the Cold War. You need to give the movie some artistic license. How much weight do you think Stallone bench-presses?"

"More than you."

With a shrug, Rudy sat at the machine, gripped two handles, and exhaled as he pushed his arms out and away from his body.

Weights lifted.

Liz's wrists jerked up, her zip-tie cuffs caught in the mechanism.

Rudy noticed and laughed.

Inhaling, he returned to his original position and pushed out his arms once more.

Again her wrists were yanked up.

She stared at the cuff and realized it was being pinched. She wriggled her arms around so the tie was in the center between her wrists, and gritted her teeth as Rudy continued the exercise.

"Remember that scene where Rambo was tied to upright bedsprings," Rudy said, "while the Russian interrogators ran electricity through the metal springs, torturing him?"

"Where would they have found bedsprings in the jungle?" Max asked.

"You're starting to get on my nerves. I told you. Allow for artistic license. So Rambo starts shaking and shaking from the electricity, rattling the bedsprings, and all of a sudden the guys torturing him realize what's happening, and Rambo's so crazy with pain and rage, he—"

The sound of a car door being opened through the speaker interrupted them.

"Tysons Corner," Simon's voice said to someone.

•◆•

THE TAXI TOOK AN OFF-RAMP FROM THE RUSH OF TRAFFIC ON THE 495. Avoiding the huge shopping malls and corporate buildings that Tysons Corner was known for, it reached a quiet street of attractive houses and expensive landscaping. Conscious of how swiftly time was passing, Simon forced himself to follow protocol, giving the driver an address two blocks away. The watcher at the safe house would think it suspicious if he arrived at the front door in a taxi rather than first cleaning his trail on foot. Paying the driver, Simon waited until the taxi disappeared around a corner.

As dark clouds threatened rain, he pulled out the cell phone he'd been given and hurried toward his destination. He continued to assume that anything he said could be overheard, so he didn't bother using the number programmed into the phone and instead spoke directly to the blank screen.

"Prove that Liz is still alive."

•◆•

LIZ FELT A SURGE OF HOPE AS SIMON'S VOICE SPILLED FROM THE speaker.

"Send a video update. Now."

Max pressed a button on the console. "Marta?"

"Do it," the woman's Russian-accented voice ordered. "Let him see you damage her a little more."

"Cool," Rudy said.

Her stomach cramped as he turned toward where she was cuffed to the Nautilus machine, her arms stretched painfully above her head.

"Hey, Max, I've got an idea," the broad-shouldered Russian said. "Why don't we make our own Rambo movie?"

"What are you talking about?"

"Remember, when he was tied to the bedsprings."

"You should see a shrink. You've got Rambo on the brain."

"No, listen. When they weren't shooting electricity through him, the guys torturing him heated his knife and made it look like they were going to burn out one of his eyes."

• ◆ •

THE SAFE HOUSE WAS A SPLIT LEVEL, WITH A HUGE LAWN AND A TWO-car garage under lace-curtained windows. Walking toward it, Simon told the phone, "I said I want a video update."

"Your impatience is nothing compared to mine," the voice of the Russian woman replied.

The phone made a chiming sound that indicated a text message had arrived. Simon opened an attachment. With a mixture of fear and rage he again saw Liz positioned on the padded bench, but this time her arms were stretched above her head, her wrists still locked around the metal pole. More blood covered her face. Abruptly her arms jerked higher, the force great enough to slam her head back against the wall.

She groaned.

With equal abruptness, her arms fell, only to be jerked upward again as if she were a puppet.

Her head sagged forward.

The camera tilted down to reveal the scarred hand that Simon had seen earlier. The angle suggested that it belonged to the man who held the camera. The fingers gripped a long, saw-backed knife, holding its blade against the noisy blue flame of a butane blowtorch set on a table.

"Out there, you might be the law, but in here, we are," a voice with a Russian accent said. He seemed to be quoting from something. "Mess with us, and we'll show you a war you'll never believe."

"Yeah," another Russian voice said. "You don't want us to come for you, Murdock."

Who the hell was Murdock?

They sounded insane.

The point of the blade glowed red as the camera followed it toward Liz. She pressed her head desperately back against the wall. The fiery tip moved toward her left eye. She struggled to turn her head, but the blade went this way and that, matching her frantic movements. At once, it shifted toward her ear and branded it with the silhouette of the knife's tip.

Liz screamed.

The video ended.

"It's six minutes after twelve," the Russian woman's voice said from the cell phone. "You have less than nine hours to give me my brother."

He lowered the phone.

Struggling not to show how agitated he was, he put the phone in his pocket and approached the safe house's front door. As he pressed the doorbell, he peered up toward where he assumed a concealed camera watched him.

"Simon Childs," he said. "Cassidy sent me."

He waited while someone inside compared his face to the image in his electronic file.

A lock buzzed.

He turned the doorknob, entered, and showed his ID.

Thickly carpeted stairs led down to the left and up to the right. A man in a dark sport coat, a white shirt, and a loosened tie studied him from the bottom level. The open coat revealed a pistol in a holster on his belt.

"You looked like that phone call was bad news," the man said.

"I'm getting married in ten days. The reception's a logistical nightmare."

The man nodded sympathetically. "The second time I got married, the caterer had a heart attack two days before the wedding. Cassidy says you might have seen Nick Demidov before."

"His name isn't familiar, but his photograph is. I think he's someone the European task force picked up when I was in London."

"London? Then he's lying and he does speak English?"

"That's one of the things I came to find out."

He descended the stairs to a room that had a leather sofa and chair with plush cushions that showed no indication of having been sat upon. A coffee table was bare. At the far end, fake logs were stacked in a gas fireplace where blue flames wavered with artificial steadiness.

"Can't get the chill out of this basement," the man said.

"You're here alone?"

He pretended to sound puzzled, when he actually felt relieved.

"Until nine p.m. when my relief checks in. No need for anyone else. The way this place is set up, one agent at a time is all that's necessary. It's not as if Demidov's a heavy hitter and needs protection. But hey, maybe he'll lead us to somebody big. I'm John Fadiman, by the way."

They shook hands.

Then Fadiman led him into a room, where several video monitors showed the approaches to the house. Simon noticed a ring of keys and a cell phone next to a half-full coffee cup on a desk. He switched his attention to a glass wall that revealed an adjacent bedroom with little furniture. Wearing a black shirt and trousers, a dark-haired man lay on a narrow bed. His eyes were closed and his hands were folded on his chest. He had a heavy, expressionless face.

"That's all he's been doing since we put him in there," Fadiman said. "Either he needs a lot of sleep, or else he's been locked up before and knows how to pass the time."

"That's the man I saw in London. Are we visible to him?"

"It's a one-way glass."

"Then I need to go in there so Demidov can see my face. Once he recognizes me, he won't be able to keep claiming that all he speaks is Russian."

Fadiman nodded and stepped toward a door on the right. He pressed numbers on an electronic pad. With a soft click, the door unlocked.

The man on the bed sat up.

Fadiman opened the door. "I've got an old friend to see you."

Demidov shook his head, seeming not to understand the words Fadiman used.

"Hi, Nick. Surely you remember me from London," Simon said.

Again, Demidov shook his head, this time in what seemed genuine confusion.

"Yes, you and I and your sister had a long talk in London," Simon continued. "If you want to see her anytime soon, you need to do what I tell you. Do you understand? Do you want to see her? Say it in English so I know we're communicating."

There was a flash in Demidov's eyes. Anger? No, more disgust.

"My sister?" the prisoner asked.

"Damn," Fadiman said. "That's what I call fast results."

The agent suddenly groaned as Simon thrust an arm around his throat, pulled the man's pistol from beneath his jacket and pushed him into the room. Not knowing if Fadiman had a round in the chamber, Simon racked back the slide. Now, for sure, the weapon was ready to fire.

Fadiman held up his hands. "Are you fucking crazy?"

Standing inside the doorway where he could keep his pistol aimed at both Fadiman and Demidov, Simon ordered the Russian out.

Demidov moved smoothly past him and Simon followed, closing the door, making sure it locked. Through the glass wall he saw Fadiman charge toward the door and yank at the handle.

"Where's my bitch sister?" Demidov asked angrily.

"Waiting."

Simon whipped the pistol across his face.

●◆●

LIZ'S EARLOBE FELT ON FIRE.

Her shoulders and wrists throbbed.

But more than anything, she was filled with rage. Adrenaline pulsing through her, she'd heard Simon talk with someone named Fadiman about Nick Demidov, the man Simon had been asking about at the FBI. The sound of a scuffle was followed by someone groaning.

Rudy and Max listened intently.

From the room's speaker came Simon's voice. "Let's go, asshole. Your sister's waiting for you."

Max cheered. "He must've decked the FBI agent."

The transmission crackled, garbling what Simon and Demidov were saying.

"Cell phone must've gone out of range. Simon Childs isn't Rambo," Rudy said. "But he busted out our Rambo!"

"Yeah, Demidov's a hotshot," Max said. "But that's what it takes to run this outfit. Once he's back, things'll get normal again."

"Drugs and whores," Rudy whooped.

Max shook his head and laughed. "You're so lame."

Now Liz understood. Nick Demidov wasn't a mere courier. He was the head of their Mafia clan. That's why they'd gone to so much trouble to kidnap her and force Simon to help them.

Max set his coffee mug down on the security console. "I'm gonna celebrate the boss's escape by taking a leak." He hefted himself up and marched across the room toward the door on Liz's left.

"No prob. I've got lots of entertainment here."

Rudy cocked his head at Liz.

She looked away and made her voice small, frightened. "You're not going to slam my wrists up and down again, are you?"

"That's an idea." Setting the big knife on the floor beside the multigym, Rudy returned to the chest press. "You're a mess. Even if we let you live, your boyfriend would never marry you now." He gripped the handles and pushed his arms out and away from his body.

The weights lifted.

Her wrists jolted up.

Tears slid down her cheeks from the pain, but what Rudy didn't know was that while he'd been torturing her, the mechanism had been pounding her zip-tie cuffs. Earlier, she'd centered the tie. Since then she'd pulled her wrists wide apart to make the plastic taut every time Rudy used the machine.

Her wrists oozed blood.

Again Rudy slammed the chest press.

Clenching her jaw, Liz pulled, stretching the cuff. She thought of the Rambo movie that Rudy had described, Rambo tied to upright bedsprings, electricity making him shudder and writhe with pain and rage, furiously twisting at the rope that held him.

With a snap, the zip-tie broke, freeing her hands.

She lunged for Rudy's knife on the floor.

Her fingers were numb from lack of circulation. She needed both hands to grab the knife and keep from dropping it. Furious, she spun upward, slashing the blade across Rudy's throat. A deep cartilage split.

Blood spurted over her.

She stepped back. *Fuck you.*

Rudy fell off the Nautilus machine. She quickly knelt, preparing to turn him and retrieve the .40 S&W from his shoulder holster.

Somewhere in the distance, a toilet flushed.

Liz's numb right hand pulled Rudy onto his side. Her fingers seemed not to belong to her as she tugged at the pistol in his holster.

The pistol didn't move.

"Rudy, is something wrong?" Max said.

She pulled harder with her senseless fingers, but the pistol was snagged on Rudy's coat.

Heavy footsteps approached on the other side of the door.

No time.

Pressing the knife to her side to keep from dropping it, she rushed toward the iPhone on the desk and swept it into the pocket of her jogging jacket.

As if the dogs of hell were on her heels, she dashed up the stairs and through a huge room with an immense stone fireplace and antlered deer heads on the walls. Fumbling, she unbolted the front door and rushed outside. The van in which they'd brought her was still parked in front. But when she reached it, she saw that the keys weren't in the ignition switch.

A thick mountain mist drifted around her.

Chilled, she raced into it.

•◆•

"LET'S GO, ASSHOLE," SIMON SAID. "YOUR SISTER'S WAITING FOR YOU."

Demidov clutched the gash in his cheek, as blood dripped past his fingers.

Simon tore a sheet of paper from a notepad, crumpled it, and shoved it into the pocket that held the nosy cell phone. Whenever he moved, the crumpled paper would scrape against the phone, sounding like bad reception, making it difficult for anyone to hear what he and Demidov said.

"Yeah, I can't wait," Demidov rumbled. "Lead me to her."

He whipped the gun barrel against Demidov's other cheek. "First we need to have an understanding."

"Goddamn you." Demidov lurched back against the wall. "If you didn't have that gun—"

"But I do." Simon grabbed the ring of keys that he'd noticed next to the cell phone earlier. "Move."

Demidov walked ahead, passing the sofa and coffee table, and opened a far door. A black sedan occupied half of a garage. Simon touched the button on the key fob that unlatched the trunk. Seeing the trunk lid rise, Demidov stiffened, whirled, and lunged hard and fast, his shoulder slamming into Simon's chest, throwing both of them back against a workbench. Simon grabbed Demidov around the neck and shoved the muzzle of the pistol into his ear.

"You know what you have to do," he told him. "Get in the trunk."

"Bite my—"

He screwed the muzzle into Demidov's ear. "Maybe you'd like to bite this. If you get in the damned trunk, I'll let you talk to your sister."

There was a moment's hesitation. "Oh, I definitely want to talk to her."

"Move slowly," Simon ordered.

He relaxed his grip around Demidov's neck and eased the gun away from his ear. Without taking his eyes off Simon, Demidov stepped back, then crawled into the trunk. Simon saw a roll of duct tape on a bench and threw it to him. "Wrap this around your ankles."

"Why don't you wrap it around your—"

He picked up a length of pipe and whacked the Russian.

"All right. All right."

As Demidov bound his legs together with the duct tape, Simon removed the phone from his pocket. After activating the video camera, he focused on the blood-smeared face.

"What time is it?" Simon demanded.

"Time? Why the hell does *that* matter?"

"Believe me, it does." He aimed the pistol and the camera. "Tell your sister what time it is, or I'll use this pipe to break your knees."

"When this is over—" Demidov glared at his watch, telling the camera, "Twelve twenty-eight. Marta, I don't know who this guy is, but he's batshit crazy. You've really screwed up this time."

"Marta? Thanks for telling me her name."

Simon ended the video and sent it.

"Now what?"

"Roll onto your stomach." He jabbed Demidov with the pipe. "Put your wrists behind your back."

No sooner did he finish taping the guy's arms behind him than the phone buzzed.

"Hi, Marta," he said, mimicking the tone of an old friend. "The good news is that no matter how bad your brother looks, a minute ago he was still alive."

"You'll never see your fiancée again unless you release him."

Marta's voice sounded worried.

"I always assumed you'd kill her, so I'm not losing anything." He climbed into the car. "The thing is, that works the other way around too. You'll never see your brother again, unless you release my fiancée. So from this point on, I suggest you treat Liz gently. Because I swear to you, Marta, whatever you do to her, I'll do to your brother."

He pushed a button on a garage-door opener attached to the car's sun visor. The door rumbled open and gray daylight filled the garage.

"I'm moving the timetable up," he told her. "Five p.m. That's the new deadline for the exchange." He backed the car out of the garage and drove off along the quiet street. "At the Lincoln Memorial. Lots of witnesses if you try something stupid."

"I'll need more time than that."

"While you track me? Using the GPS on the phone you gave me?"

"I don't know what you're talking about."

"Hang on a second." Simon stopped the car across from a small park where city workers were gathering trash bags. He accessed the call history of the phone he'd been given and memorized the number it was linked to. Then he called that number, but this time he used his own phone. "Marta, that buzz you hear is me. It's coming from my personal phone. Answer it."

She sounded confused, but did as he instructed.

He resumed driving, came abreast of the city's open-backed truck, and tossed her phone among the garbage bags.

"I'm untethered, Marta," he said into his own phone. "Five o'clock. The Lincoln Memorial. Don't forget. Anything you do to Liz, I'll do to your brother."

•◆•

IN THE BACK OFFICE OF A DRY CLEANER'S SHOP IN MCLEAN, VIRGINIA, a tall woman with long blond hair, intense blue eyes, and strong Slavic features pressed the End button on her phone. She was in her midthirties and might have been considered a beauty if not for the cruelty around her mouth. She stared at a monitor where a pulsing green dot in Tysons Corner no longer moved. In the front of the shop, steam presses hissed and machines rumbled, but she barely heard them or registered the chemical smell that permeated the office.

Her brother had laughed at her when she'd suggested buying the business and using it as one of their fronts.

"What's so funny?" she'd asked.

"Don't you get it? Dry cleaning. That's what needs to happen to all the cash we bring in from the drugs and the gambling and the whores. We should buy a couple of laundries also. Just don't screw this up like you did when you bought those restaurants that gave people food poisoning."

Marta kept staring at the pulsing dot.

She heard the voices of what seemed to be workmen talking about the unusual amount of trash they'd picked up in a park. Obviously Simon Childs had thrown away the phone he'd been given and was now using his own.

Could she trust him not to have police and FBI agents positioned near the Memorial?

Hardly.

"Let's see how much you love your fiancée," she muttered.

She pressed the button for the phone at the hunting lodge.

• ◆ •

MAX OPENED THE DOOR.

"Rudy, what were you shouting about?"

He tensed when he saw the streaks of blood across the floor and then Rudy's body slumped next to the Nautilus machine.

He drew his pistol and spun to make sure he wasn't threatened, then rushed to his cousin. Rudy lay on his side, his crimson throat gaping. He couldn't possibly be alive, but Max felt for a pulse anyhow, shaking Rudy gently, hoping there was something he could do. But no one could have survived such a deep gash to the throat.

He spun and quickly checked the bunker.

Liz Sansborough wasn't there.

He raced past the monitors toward the stairs and charged upward. There was a chance she was hiding at the top, ready to slash at him.

Rather than approach cautiously, he rushed through the opening. But she wasn't there, and he kept running across the lodge's community room toward the open front door. Behind him, below in the bunker, he heard a phone ring, but he didn't dare stop to answer it.

The bitch was only thirty seconds ahead of him.

The outside air was gray and cool.

Mist encircled him.

Behind him, faintly, the phone kept ringing.

He heard something else, though.

Past the van.

Footsteps running across gravel.

• ◆ •

LIZ PLUNGED INTO THE MISTY FOREST.

The weather had softened the autumn leaves, but they still made noise, and thinking quickly, she veered toward the soft duff of pine needles, leaping over patches of leaves as she came to them.

Sensation was returning to her fingers. She used the knife to cut off the plastic cuffs, wincing as the tip dug into the skin under them. Then she pulled out the iPhone she'd stolen. She needed to use its GPS to determine her location and text Simon. She prayed he was all right. As she touched the icon activating the map, she lifted her head, listening. Feet were crunching quickly through the leaves behind her. It had to be Max, and he'd be armed with his pistol, while all she had was the knife.

No time to text.

"Liz Sansborough, where are you?" Max's voice boomed. "You're dead. Do you hear me? Dead."

Shoving the iPhone back into her pocket, she spotted a rotting log ahead. Now she wanted Max to hear her, so she ran hard, pounding through twigs and leaves. Then she yelled, "Stay away from me, Max."

To the right, a steep slope descended into the mist. At the log she dropped onto her back, braced her feet against it, and used the strength in her legs to push. The sound of the log rolling over the slope was at first hushed in the mist, but then it hit a rock and bounced off an unseen tree, the noise exploding as it crashed down into brush.

"I'm coming to get you," Max shouted.

She moved swiftly away in the opposite direction, into the trees again, leaping silently from one bed of pine needles to the next. She could hear him pounding down the slope, grunting and swearing and calling her name. Pauses told her he must have slid or fallen.

She smiled.

Hurrying as quietly as she could, she rounded an enormous boulder and saw the stream. It was about five feet wide and clear as glass. Desperately thirsty, she fell to her knees on the mossy bank. Cupping her hands, she scooped up water and drank. Then she splashed her face, the cold water, though stinging, like a tonic to her bruises and cuts. Wiping her hands on her jogging jacket, she took out the iPhone and touched the map icon again. No response. She frowned, checked the charge, saw it was good, and realized she had no reception. No surprise. She was out in the middle of nowhere. She had to get back to the cabin where there was wireless.

The forest was starting to come awake from the shock of human intruders. Unseen animals skittered through the underbrush. Birds complained in the treetops. The stream sounded extraloud. She'd heard it when she'd first arrived at the log cabin and realized it could lead her back there.

Abruptly, she heard Max searching for her, coming closer. Even in the mist, the yellow of her jogging suit would be obvious. The Rambo movies that Max and Rudy had talked about flashed through her mind, reminding her of the way the character always blended with the forest. Grabbing handfuls of mud, she smeared them over her face and her jogging suit. Soon her clothing was a monotonous brown.

She yanked the hood up and tied it under her chin, hiding her red hair.

Feeling the pressure of time, she ran along the moss and sand that edged the stream. She listened for Max, but he'd become silent once more.

That made her nervous.

With luck, he'd slipped and fallen, perhaps hitting his head on a rock on his way down into the hollow where he thought she'd run. If her luck were really good, the bastard was dead.

But she wouldn't count on it.

Creeping through the mist, she reached a stand of beeches.

She slowed and crouched. Listened. Watched.

Then took out the iPhone and studied the screen.

Finally, reception.

•◆•

MARTA LISTENED AS THE LODGE'S PHONE RANG AND RANG.

She didn't understand why no one was answering. Had she used the wrong number?

She pressed End.

Again, she called the number for the lodge, this time double-checking that she hadn't made a mistake.

One of several errors.

Nick would be furious.

It was her fault that he'd been arrested. He should never have been at the warehouse where the stolen prescription painkillers were delivered. She'd neglected to arrange for a go-between to pick up the money they were promised—so huge an amount that Nick himself had driven impatiently to the warehouse to retrieve it, only to be grabbed by the FBI.

And that wasn't the only screwup he would blame her for.

If she couldn't make this right, she didn't want to be around when he got out of prison.

After the twentieth time the lodge's phone rang, she impatiently broke the transmission and called Rudy instead of the lodge.

FEELING A SURGE OF HOPE, LIZ TOUCHED THE SCREEN'S MAP ICON and saw a green dot that revealed her location in the middle of a large, unmarked rural area. She expanded the image and discovered an orange line indicating a road, along with a number for Highway 55. She expanded the image even more, revealing the name of a town—Marsdon—southwest of her.

Her fingers trembling, she started to type a text message and let Simon know where she was. But all she managed was ESCAPED. OFF H55 N. Music suddenly blared from the cell phone.

Damn.

It sounded like the theme from the damned Rambo movies. The trumpets startled her so much that she nearly dropped the phone, touching the Send button before she intended to. As the rousing anthem reverberated through the mist, she flipped at the mute switch.

The sudden silence unnerved her.

Every animal in the forest seemed to have become paralyzed. Birds no longer complained in the trees.

Max didn't make a sound either.

No way he couldn't have heard the music.

RUBBING HIS SIDE FROM WHERE HE'D TUMBLED DOWN A SLOPE, MAX stalked through the forest.

Abruptly he heard music. Trumpets.

Rambo music.

Then he realized it was the ringtone on Rudy's phone. To the left. For a fierce moment Max almost charged toward it, but at once the trumpets ended, their echo subsiding into the mist.

He found an unexpected stillness inside him.

What would the big guy do?

Would he charge ahead?

No damned way.

The scum he'd hunted never knew where he was.

Rambo just struck out of nowhere and . . .

Listening for any sound that Sansborough might make, he changed his phone to mute.

Then he texted Marta.

BITCH ESCAPED. RUDY'S DEAD. HUNTING HER.

After studying the ground ahead of him, he stepped onto soft pine needles—exactly what Rambo would do—and moved silently toward where the music had come from.

●◆●

MARTA GAPED AT THE MESSAGE.

BITCH ESCAPED.

Without the woman, she had no way to rescue Nick. No way to prove that she could make up for her mistakes. No way to keep from being the target of Nick's fury. She desperately needed help, but the rest of the gang was in Texas, working on two hijack jobs that she hoped the police would blame on a rival gang—an idea that she hadn't told Nick about and for which he would surely now punish her.

She pulled a .40-caliber Sig Sauer from a drawer, made sure that its twelve-round magazine was fully loaded and that a round was in the firing chamber. She scooped an extra magazine from the drawer, shoved it and the pistol into her purse, and hurried from the office.

●◆●

IN THE DARKNESS OF THE TRUNK, NICK STRUGGLED TO BREATHE AS shallowly as possible. The stench of the spare tire and oily rags made him sick. He thought he smelled the bitterness of engine exhaust also, but if that were true, surely he'd be dead by now. His arms ached from the tight angle at which his wrists were duct-taped behind him, but no matter how much he squirmed, he couldn't loosen the tape.

Sweat streaked his forehead.

A bump sent a jolt of pain through the swelling gashes on his face. He was as furious about the damage to his handsome features as he was about anything else that the bastard driving the car had done to him. But he was even more furious because Marta's carelessness had gotten him into this mess.

Your sister's waiting for you, the man had said.

And she'll be sorry, he vowed.

• ◆ •

IN THE DRIVER'S SEAT SIMON BLENDED WITH THE RUSH OF VEHICLES on the Beltway. Back at the safe house, the FBI agent had said that he wasn't due to be relieved until nine tonight. So the police had no idea what happened and wouldn't be looking for the car.

In theory.

He tried to figure the best way to arrange the exchange and get Liz back. As he visualized vantage points around the Lincoln Memorial, he heard the ping of a text message coming through. He snatched up his phone from the seat next to him.

What he saw made him inhale sharply.

ESCAPED. OFF H55 N.

From a sender named Rudy Voya.

Who the hell is that? And where's the rest of the message? The name's Russian. Did Liz really escape, or was Marta playing with him? Trying to draw him and her brother away from Washington?

Knowing that H55 was the scenic highway west of Washington, he made an abrupt decision and took the first exit that allowed him to speed in that direction.

• ◆ •

LIZ CONTINUED ALONG THE SOFT BANK OF THE STREAM.

The trickle of the water hid the few sounds she made, but it also hid any sounds from Max. With trembling fingers, she typed the rest of her message to Simon.

NE OF MARSDON. A LODGE.

The moment she sent it, she tightened her grip on the knife and struggled to get control of herself. So far, she'd merely been fleeing. But she remembered what her CIA instructors had taught her during training exercises at the Farm.

If you're on the run—in the city, in the countryside, it doesn't matter—if you don't have a plan, if you're just reacting, you're going to lose.

Following the stream had the merit of giving her a course, but when she looked again at the map feature on her phone, she found an overhead photograph of the area. The stream meandered, sometimes curving back to the middle of the forest, where Max was surely searching for her. But if she veered from the stream with no landmarks to guide her, only the phone's GPS would keep her from wandering in the mist—and not for long. The battery-charge indicator was at twenty percent.

Soon the phone would be dead.

How long until the sun went down? Could she hope to find her way out of here by then, or would she be forced to hide in the dark?

The lodge.

Earlier, without cell-phone reception, she'd thought about heading back there until she came within Wi-Fi range and could contact Simon. But now that she'd been able to send a text, her only thought had been to put as much distance as she could between her and Max. It was counterintuitive for her to go back to the lodge. Max would never expect it. She thought about the weapons there and the communications equipment. She could lock the doors and send for help. The place looked like it had the strength of a bunker. Max and whoever came to help him wouldn't be able to break in before the police arrived.

Ready with the knife, she turned away from the stream, stepped warily over patches of leaves, and headed toward her best chance to survive.

•◆•

MAX RECALLED WHAT RAMBO HAD SAID IN THE SECOND MOVIE.

The best weapon's the human mind.

Yeah, right.

The guy's got a body like a chunk of granite and he wants to talk about his mind. But he decided the advice was good. He didn't know the first damned thing about chasing someone through a forest the way Rambo did, with his bow and arrow and knife like fucking Tarzan. It didn't matter. All he needed to do was be smart.

And use his phone.

He assumed that, when the outburst of Rambo music had suddenly ended, it meant that Sansborough had put Rudy's phone on mute. Not that it mattered. He and Rudy had each installed the "find" app on their phones, adding each other to the lists. When he opened the app and told it what to look for, son of a bitch, a map appeared. A dot showed that Rudy's phone was to his left, heading toward the lodge.

He knew what that meant.

She was trying to get to a gun.

He almost raced in that direction, but couldn't do that without making a lot of noise and warning her.

Be smart.

He picked up a rock and hurled it high into the air, throwing it as far as he could, way beyond where he estimated Sansborough might be. The rock crashed down through mist-cloaked branches, snapping twigs, thumping onto the ground and bouncing. Its trajectory was almost straight down. He hoped it would make Sansborough unable to guess from which direction it had been thrown. He used that noise to hide any sounds that he himself made while he simultaneously moved parallel toward where Sansborough was.

That's smarter than Rambo.

When he saw that the dot on his screen came to a stop in reaction to the noise from the rock, he grinned and hurled another in that direction, high and far. Again, he used the crashing, snapping noise to prevent her from hearing him step carefully toward the lodge.

Definitely.

Smarter than Rambo.

He tossed another rock.

With luck, he'd be waiting when she crossed the parking lot.

• ◆ •

WHEN SIMON SAW THE HIGHWAY 55 ROAD MARKER, HE RESISTED THE urge to drive faster, needing all his strength of will to continue to blend with the stream of traffic. If a policeman stopped him and wondered why he was driving a car that wasn't registered to him, if the policeman used that excuse to search the vehicle and looked in the trunk, it would all be over.

His phone chimed.

Another text coming through.

Again he felt pressure in his chest as he looked toward the seat next to him and saw that Rudy Voya had sent a new message.

NE OF MARSDON. A LODGE.

•◆•

ANOTHER ROCK CRASHED THROUGH UNSEEN BRANCHES BEYOND LIZ, breaking twigs and crunching down onto leaves.

The echo reverberated through the mist.

The afternoon's chill sank deeper into her, aggravated by her growing fear about whatever trick Max was planning. Obviously he was using the distraction of the rocks to hide any sounds he made. She doubted that he could have gotten ahead of her.

Which meant he was throwing rocks from behind her.

That tactic could work for her too.

She slipped the phone back into her pocket, freeing her right hand so that she could pick up a rock. She turned and threw it high in the air, imitating what Max had done. Maybe she'd get lucky and hit the bastard.

At a minimum she hoped to confuse him.

The rock struck an invisible branch and made more noise as it dropped past other branches. She used those precious seconds to risk the subtle sounds she couldn't avoid, as she clutched the knife and crept onward.

•◆•

MAX FLINCHED FROM THE CRUNCHING SOUND THAT HIS SHOE MADE on the gravel of the parking area. The forest had been a vague hulking presence in what was now a misty drizzle. Now all of a sudden there weren't any shrouded trees ahead of him. He stepped back onto soft earth and inched quietly to the right toward where his phone showed that Sansborough wasn't far from him.

He thought he heard her moving past trees.

But maybe not.

It didn't matter.

In a few seconds, she would step onto the gravel. The noise she made would give her away. She wouldn't be able to recover before he lunged toward the noise and shot her.

In the face. In each breast. In the stomach.

For Rudy.

He knew that Marta would want Sansborough alive, to exchange her for Nick. But the truth was, Max didn't like Nick. On the other hand, Rudy had been Max's cousin.

His friend.

No more watching Rambo movies with him.

No more joking around.

Close to him, a shoe stepped onto gravel.

Shouting to engage her startle reflex and momentarily paralyze her, he rushed ahead, firing.

•◆•

THE SIGN AT THE SIDE OF THE HIGHWAY—MARSDON 20 MILES—increased Simon's feeling of urgency.

So close.

The clouds darkened.

A misty rain blotted the countryside, obscuring the beauty for which the area was famous. He switched on the windshield wipers and glanced toward his phone, hoping to receive another text.

When he finally made it to Marsdon, then what?

There were a lot of woods out here.

A black SUV sped past him, hurling spray across his windshield.

•◆•

MARTA ADJUSTED THE WINDSHIELD WIPERS TO A HIGHER SPEED AND pressed harder on the SUV's accelerator.

•◆•

LIZ'S SHOE CRUNCHED THE GRAVEL OF THE PARKING LOT, THE NOISE seeming so loud that she recoiled, nearly dropping the knife. Someone suddenly shouted to her left.

Max.

His footsteps thundering toward her.

Gunshots roared.

A bullet tugged her right sleeve.

It would have struck her chest if she hadn't lurched back from the sound she made on the gravel.

Adrenaline broke her paralysis.

She saw Max's indistinct shape charging into view. She had a rock in her right hand, having planned to throw it and distract him one final time before she raced toward the lodge. Now she hurled it toward his increasingly clear face and ran into the forest.

The drizzle started to dissolve the mist.

Trees began to materialize.

Hearing Max curse behind her, she stretched her long legs farther, faster. Finally able to see where she was going, she zigzagged frantically through the bushes and trees.

•◆•

FOR A MOMENT MAX THOUGHT THAT HE'D BEEN SHOT, BUT THEN HE realized what had struck his forehead.

A rock.

He raised a hand to the already throbbing, swelling lump and felt blood.

"That's something else you'll pay for," he screamed.

His pain-blurred vision cleared.

He heard Sansborough crashing through the forest.

Let her run.

With the mist dispersing, it would be easy to follow her now. He fired once more in her direction, wanting to spur her into a panic, knowing that adrenaline would soon make her hyperventilate and sap her strength.

It wouldn't be long now.

He took the almost-expended magazine from his pistol and stuffed it into a pocket. He freed a spare magazine from his belt and shoved it home. A round was already in the chamber. He didn't need to rack the slide as so many stupid Hollywood actors unnecessarily did.

But never in a Rambo movie.

As the drizzle beaded on his windbreaker, he broke into an easy, confident jog, taking care that his breath rate didn't increase.

That was the secret.

If his breathing remained steady, everything else about him would be steady. It didn't matter how far Sansborough got at the start. He could easily track her down, using the "find" app. Ahead, beneath an evergreen branch, he saw something that made him smile.

Blood.

One of his bullets had struck home.

Now he had yet another way to know where she was heading.

● ◆ ●

LIZ LEAPED OVER A FALLEN TREE, LANDED ON WET LEAVES, SLIPPED, and nearly dropped.

Her right arm felt numb.

She wanted to clutch it, to try to stop the flow of blood, but she had to keep a tight grip on the knife in her left hand. Racing onward, she didn't understand why she felt out of breath. She'd run in marathons, for God's sake. With all her stress training, she shouldn't be breathing this hard this soon. But she'd never run a marathon after being shot.

"Sansborough, what you did to Rudy I'm gonna do to you," Max yelled behind her. "But you won't die as fast as Rudy did."

Her brain raced. How had he known that she'd headed back to the lodge? The only noise made had been when she stepped on the gravel. Nothing before that. Straining to fill her lungs, she veered around a tangle of bushes. Her legs almost buckled, but this time it wasn't because of slippery leaves.

"Bet you're feeling woozy from all the blood you're pumping out," Max yelled. "Won't be long now."

She glanced desperately over her shoulder and felt as though she'd been punched when she saw splotches of blood behind her. If the drizzle didn't wash them away fast enough, Max could easily follow her.

The question kept insisting.

How did he know she'd headed back to the lodge?

Running, she felt the lump of the phone in her pocket.

A wave of fury gripped her.

He was using that to track her.

She pulled out the phone and threw it away.

"You sound like you're running a little slower," Max shouted. "Legs feeling weak? It won't be long now."

Breathless, her legs losing strength, she peered down at the knife she clutched. She felt so light-headed she had to take care that if she fell, she wouldn't land on it. The blade had sawteeth on the back, reminding her of the knife in a Rambo movie she and Simon had seen on television. The damned things were broadcast every week, it seemed. Rambo had unscrewed the cap, revealing a hollow handle that contained a needle and thread with which he'd sewn a wound shut.

Running, Liz unscrewed the cap on this one.

The hollow grip contained nothing.

She remembered a scene in which Rambo had burst from the camouflage of branches and—

•◆•

JOGGING EASILY AFTER HER THROUGH THE RAIN, MAX GLANCED occasionally at the find app on his phone. Even though the noise Sansborough made was easy to follow—and to a lessening degree, the blood—it never hurt to be extrasure. Passing a tangle of bushes, he frowned when he saw that the dot indicated that Sansborough wasn't straight ahead as the blood track indicated but instead she was to his left.

Somehow he was passing her.

He stopped and aimed toward a tangle of bushes. Was she hiding behind them? But he didn't see any blood leading in that direction.

Wary, he took a step closer.

Another step. He tightened his finger on the trigger. Then he saw the phone on the ground. Dammit, she'd figured out what he was doing and thrown it away. Now he had only her blood and the sounds of her running to tell him where she was. But he no longer heard her running.

Had she collapsed from loss of blood and the shock of having been shot?

He returned to the trail she'd left and followed at a cautious walk. As water dripped off the brim of his baseball cap, he scanned the trees on each side. He passed a tall boulder and checked behind it. The rain had finally washed away the blood, but her footprints were more obvious, collecting water.

He moved faster.

He came to the stream and saw where she'd slid down to it. When she'd struggled up the opposite side, she'd made deep furrows in the mud. He stepped over a fallen log, eased down the slippery bank, started across the stream, feeling how cold the water was, and suddenly gasped from a blow to his back that hurtled him into the water.

• ◆ •

LIZ LUNGED FROM THE HOLLOW SHE'D SCOOPED FROM THE MUD under the log.

A few minutes earlier, she'd crossed the stream and entered the trees on the opposite side. There she found a dead branch that fit into the hollow grip of the knife. Then she circled back to the stream, walked through the water, and crawled under the log.

As Max descended past her, aiming toward the trees on the opposite bank, she had thrust with the rigged spear. Adding her weight to it, she pushed with all her remaining strength and plunged the blade deeper into him.

He groaned and fell facedown into the stream.

Her hands had shook. Her lungs felt starved for oxygen.

Springing toward him, she shoved the spear even deeper into his back. He raised his face from the water and struggled. Using her uninjured arm, she grabbed a rock from the stream and struck it against the back of his head. He slumped, his face partially out of the water. She struck his head again, feeling the softness of blood under his hair.

She struck a third time.

A fourth.

She heard his skull crack.

She hit him again and again.

The rock went deeper into bone.

Shrieking, she straddled his back and pressed his face into the water, holding it under until long after his death shudder had stopped.

She needed all her strength to stand and stagger backward. When she slumped on the muddy bank, she kept her grip on the rock in case she needed to use it again.

She couldn't stop shaking.

Finally, she decided to head back to the lodge and stop her bleeding. She placed a foot on his back and tugged the spear free. The effort of using her wounded arm made her groan. Max had dropped his pistol. She picked it up. As the rain fell, the forest again seemed enshrouded by mist, but she knew that the haze was really the consequence of blood loss.

She gave Max a fierce kick just to make sure he was dead.

Then she climbed the bank and followed her trail of blood.

SIMON DROVE OVER A RIDGE AND SAW AN ASPHALT LANE ON THE right, flanked by forest. He'd seen two driveways in the past five miles. They'd looked welcoming, with signs that advertised facilities for training and breeding horses. In contrast, this turnoff led to a reinforced steel gate and a fence with barbed wire along the top. He steered off the highway and stopped in front of the gate. A number pad was mounted to a pole.

He left the car and pressed the key fob, releasing the vehicle's trunk. After carefully raising it, he smelled the vinegar stench of carbon dioxide.

But it wasn't enough to hide another stench.

"You son of a bitch, I pissed my pants because of you," Nick said.

He lay on his side, his arms taped behind him.

"What's the code to open the gate?" he asked, ignoring the rain that struck him.

"Code? Gate? I don't know what you're talking about."

"Do you want me to close the trunk again? I'll keep it shut a lot longer.

Maybe the next time you'll do something else in your pants. Or would you rather see your sister?"

"My sister. Oh, I want to see my sister for sure. The stupid skank."

"Your happy reunion isn't going to occur unless you tell me the code to open the gate."

Nick recited four numbers.

He pressed them on the pad and heard a whir.

The gate started to open.

He returned to Nick and told him, "Bye for now."

He shut the trunk, hopped into the car, and drove through the open gate. In the rearview mirror, he saw it closing behind him. The lane continued through the forest for quite a while. Then Simon rounded a curve and abruptly came to a large clearing. Beyond a gravel parking area stood a two-story log house. A few small buildings sat next to a swimming pool that had been covered for the winter. A bermed area contained a shooting range with metal silhouettes of human-shaped targets.

A drab van was parked in front of the house.

The front door hung open, suggesting that someone had entered or left in a hurry. He stepped out of the car and drew the pistol that he'd taken from the FBI agent. Ignoring the rain, he scanned the clearing. He didn't dare call Liz's name, lest his voice attract whoever had been holding her captive.

He took a step toward the lodge.

Movement attracted his attention to the far side of the clearing.

A figure emerged from the trees, staggering.

Whoever it was held a spear and was covered with mud so thick that the rain hadn't dissolved it. The figure stumbled across the gravel and Simon saw blood on the right arm—and a suggestion of yellow on the figure's legs.

Liz's jogging suit was yellow.

He started to run toward her, only to be stopped by a gunshot and a bullet that tore up gravel in front of him. He spun toward the lodge's porch where a tall woman, with long blond hair and Slavic features, aimed a pistol at him. She wore a beige pantsuit and a brown suede jacket.

"Drop the gun," she told him.

He obeyed. "Marta?"

"Where the hell is Nick?"

"In the trunk."

"Alive?"

"How else would I be able to exchange him for Liz?"

"Show me."

At the edge of his vision, Simon was aware of Liz's grotesque mud-covered figure continuing to stumble across the gravel. She dropped to one knee, then planted the blunt edge of the spear into the gravel and used it to draw herself up.

"Never mind about her," Marta said, stepping closer with the gun. "Show me that Nick's alive."

He pressed the key fob and opened the trunk.

Peering in, he told Nick, "Your sister's asking for you."

Nick said something caustically angry in Russian.

He dragged him out and propped him on his feet. With legs taped together, the man had trouble standing.

"Cut him loose," Marta ordered.

"I'll need to reach for my pocketknife."

"Be careful."

He pulled out the knife and cut the tape that secured Demidov's legs. The Russian spread them, steadying himself. Simon sliced the tape that bound the wrists.

"Now drop the knife," Marta said.

He did so.

Demidov winced as he moved his arms slowly forward, giving the impression that his muscles were locked, then he removed the tape that remained on his wrists.

"This is all your fault."

"I'm sorry, Nick. I admit I made a mistake. But I corrected it. I got you out."

"The goddamned restaurants that the health department shut down. The courier you didn't send, so I had to pick up the money on my own, which is why the feds were able to grab me at the warehouse. That stupid dry-cleaning shop. Every time I leave the office, my clothes stink."

"Nick, I told you I'm sorry."

"Where the fuck *is* everybody? Why didn't you bring more help?"

"I couldn't."

"Couldn't? What do you mean?"

"They're all in Texas."

"What are they doing in—"

"Hijack jobs. It'll look like Texas gangs did it. No one'll ever suspect that—"

"You sent everybody to Texas? On your own?"

"I thought—"

"You stupid cunt, don't think. You're not good at it."

Marta shot him.

He took a step back and looked surprised.

She shot him again.

Then a third time.

Blood first seeped, then poured from the wounds.

Demidov collapsed to the ground.

Not moving.

She aimed at Simon.

Liz continued to stagger across the gravel. Except for the blood on her arm and the bit of yellow that showed on her legs, she was still covered with mud. With each halting step, she placed the blunt edge of the spear ahead, using it to support her weight. Marta switched her aim toward Liz, then back toward Simon.

The woman peered down at her brother, then lowered the pistol. "Look at what you finally made me do."

When Liz reached them, she wavered and remained standing only because she leaned on the spear.

"Where's Max?" Marta asked.

"Dead."

"I'm impressed."

"Rambo," Liz murmured.

"What?"

"Saw Rambo use his knife to make a spear. Saw him hide in a stream. Saw him do a lot of things."

"You'd better get her to a hospital," Marta said. "She's delirious."

"Hospital?"

"You kept your part of the bargain. Not that it matters." Marta stared down at Nick's body. "A lot of people are going to be angry about what I just did."

"Maybe I can help."

"How?"

"Protect you. Give you a new start. The FBI. Witness relocation program."

Marta laughed as if he were making a joke.

Again she stared down at her brother.

Liz's eyes closed, then she toppled. Simon grabbed her before she struck the gravel. She was terribly cold. He held her tightly, wanting never to let her go. When Simon looked up, Marta was gone.

A few seconds later a black SUV roared into view from behind the house and sped along the lane, disappearing among the trees.

"Sorry I missed breakfast," Liz managed to say.

He looked down.

She did her best to smile.

"Same time tomorrow?" she asked.

"On a hospital tray maybe. No more talking."

He picked her up, carried her into the lodge out of the rain, and laid her on a wooden bench.

She closed her eyes.

"Don't go to sleep. You've got to stay awake. Fight the shock." He tore open the right sleeve of her jogging suit, exposing a bullet wound, and found his cell phone. After calling for an ambulance, he searched the house and located a medical kit in a cabinet in the basement. He washed and disinfected her wound as best he could and bound it with a pressure bandage. She shivered, perhaps the first symptom of hypothermia. He pulled off her cold, wet jogging suit and covered her with a throw that he found on a sofa.

Then he held her.

"Rambo," she murmured again.

"What about him?" he asked, alarmed by her delirium but humoring her, trying to keep her from falling asleep.

"Died in the novel."

"Don't talk about dying."

"Bedsprings. Electrocution."

Simon couldn't figure out what she meant.

"Bedsprings," she repeated.

"Yes, sweetheart. Bedsprings."

"Rambo."

"Yes, sweetheart. Rambo."

"They said you weren't him."

He held her tighter, desperate to make her warm.

"But to me, you are."

He smiled.

Both at her compliment, and at the sirens approaching in the distance.

KARIN SLAUGHTER AND
MICHAEL KORYTA

WHEN KARIN SLAUGHTER AGREED TO BE A PART OF THIS anthology, she had two provisos. The first was the story would take place in the 1990s and, second, her partner would be Michael Koryta.

I readily agreed to both.

Thankfully, Michael agreed too.

The challenge here was for each writer to take their worlds back in time, to a point when their characters were much younger, just starting out in their respective fictional careers. Karin wanted to provide a look at Jeffrey Tolliver as a young man, from 1993. While writing him before, she always knew some things about his early years, but intentionally kept those close.

"It's fun to keep secrets from readers," she jokes.

This story allowed her an opportunity to share a few of those tidbits.

For Michael, this was the first time he's ever written from Joe Pritchard's point of view. He actually hasn't written about Lincoln Perry or Joe in eight years, and those stories were always told in the first person, from Lincoln's point of view. This story provided a chance to not only move the characters back in time but also to change the lens.

Michael notes that a pattern developed during the process. He would write something and hand it off to Karin. Then she'd write something a lot better and funnier and hand it back. It came to a point that he didn't want the story to end, because it became a lot of fun. One of the major characters is named after a bet he lost to the novelist Alafair Burke. I won't tell you which one, but the studious reader will know.

And here's the best irony.

Word-wise, this is the longest effort included in this anthology.

Yet it carries a curious title.

Short Story.

SHORT STORY

THIS WASN'T THE FIRST TIME JEFFREY TOLLIVER HAD STUMBLED around a dark hotel room looking for his clothes. His bare feet cut channels into the musty shag carpet. His hands blindly reached into the shadows. Alcohol permeated the air. And sweat. And sex.

Rustling came from the bed as the woman rolled over. She snored lightly, which might have been endearing if he knew her name.

Rebecca?

He smiled past his hangover.

Delta flight attendant. Ex-cheerleader. Long blond hair. Five nine, which was a good height for his six three. She had good numbers everywhere else, too, but then Jeffrey remembered that Rebecca had stood him up.

For two weeks, he'd worked double shifts so he could take a long weekend off. He had made the nearly four-hour drive from Birmingham only to find a phone message waiting about a storm coming through, the airline moving planes around, and that was how a hot weekend in the north Georgia mountains had ended with him slinking off alone to the hotel bar and drinking too much, then talking too much, then ending up in bed and doing too much with—

More snoring.

She was a slip of a thing under the sheets. A waist he could almost wrap both hands around, which had its pluses and minuses. Not as tall as Rebecca. Not as smart. Did smart matter? He'd like to think not, but then after a while, you needed someone with an imagination.

Shayna.

That was the woman in the bed. She was so country sticks came out of her mouth when she talked, but she knew that the hotel's name, the Schussel, was missing an umlaut—and she knew what an umlaut was—and that Schussel was German for "key."

Jeffrey found his boxers by the closed curtains. He slipped them on as he rustled the curtains, looking for the rest of his clothes. A sock made itself known. His sock? He made like a stork and shoved his left foot into the tube. He wriggled his toes. Definitely his sock.

This was what guys in his business would call a clue.

Jeffrey widened his search pattern from the last known sock. Bed, dresser, TV, chair. The Schussel Mountain Lodge was like every hotel room he'd ever awakened in, but done in a Bavarian style. Or Georgia's idea of Bavarian style, because for reasons unknown, the whole town of Helen was made to look like an Alpine Village dropped down in the foothills of the Appalachians.

His fingers brushed his wallet on the dresser. His keys. His pager. ChapStick. His shiny new detective's badge and somewhat older gun were locked in the wheel well of the trunk, though he'd had both out on the drive up from Birmingham in case of cops or robbers.

"Shit."

He hissed out the word a split second before a searing pain shot through his big toe, which had caught on one of the metal bed legs. He leaned heavily on the mattress. His hand gripped into a fist, and he realized that his fist was holding something that wasn't part of the sheets.

T-shirt.

"Y'all right?" the girl asked.

"Yes," he told Shayna.

Not Shayna.

Shayna was last weekend.

Jeffrey remembered a necklace with the name spelled out in script. Custom made, she'd told him, given to her by her stepfather to commend her high school graduation. He'd pretended this was a normal conversation for a twenty-six-year-old man to have with an eighteen-year-old girl in a downtown bar, and that he wasn't a cop, a newly minted detective, who should arrest her for underage drinking instead of having sex with her in the backseat of her Cadillac.

Her stepfather's Cadillac.

He fumbled for the switch in the bathroom, shutting the door as the fluorescent light flickered on. He checked his reflection in the mirror. He looked slightly more hungover than he felt. Or maybe he was getting better at being hungover, which was a skill that twigged off all the branches of his family tree.

He turned on the faucet. The handle came off in his hand. Water squirted sideways, up, down. He fumbled to fit the handle back on the nut. He watched the stream turn from brown to yellow to something close to clear before splashing his face with cold water.

Jeffrey looked up at the mirror again.

His T-shirt was soaking wet. A wet Maginot Line cut across his boxers where he'd leaned against the sink basin. His underwear was bright orange with blue-and-white AU's all over it.

Auburn University.

Rebecca the flight attendant had been a Georgia cheerleader. He'd worn the boxers as a joke but now the joke was probably on him because he hadn't packed a lot of clothes for the four-day retreat and he was pretty sure he was wearing his only underwear.

"Y'all right in there?"

She said "there" like "thar," which wasn't an indictment, especially to a man from south Alabama, but something in her tone set his teeth on edge.

He said, "Just gonna take a shower."

Before she could offer to join him, he reached behind the lank shower curtain and turned the handles. He stood in the middle of the small bathroom with his eyes closed. The hangover tapped at the bridge of his nose like an accusatory finger. How long could he keep doing this? He wasn't a kid anymore. It wouldn't be too long before his youthful indiscretions turned into full-blown, irreparable mistakes.

His eyes opened.

He cocked his head at a noise.

Outside the bathroom, but inside the room. Or maybe not inside the room so much as outside in the hallway, because he could've sworn he heard the door to the room click closed.

Jeffrey turned off the shower. He opened the door and turned on the light. No girl in the bed. No pager. No wallet. No keys.

She'd even taken his ChapStick.

"Motherfuck."

He could see every corner of the room, but he still checked on the other side of the bed, under the bed, looking for anything, but especially his pants. He found his right tennis shoe under the desk and jammed his foot into it on his way out the door.

Which closed behind him.

He patted his pockets for the key, but there were no pockets.

Somewhere not far away, a door opened on squeaky hinges. He looked up the hallway, which T-d off at the end, one side going to the elevators, the other to the exit stairs.

The door closed with the heavy, metal clunk of a fire exit door.

He bolted up the hall, lopsided on one shoe, each step jarring some truth into his hungover brain. That he wore wet, orange boxer shorts, a soaked white T-shirt, one sock, one shoe and no wallet, no pager, no ID, no car keys, and no fucking ChapStick.

He rounded the corner on his shoed foot, the waffle sole ripping shag from the carpet. He shouldered open the exit door and grabbed the metal railings of the stairs so that he could slide down on his palms.

Fourth floor, which meant that the sound of feet hitting the treads two floors below was the girl not named Shayna. He glanced over the side and saw two things. Her hand on the railing and the leg of his jeans flapping as she barreled down the stairs.

"Stop."

Jeffrey swung around the landing like a monkey in a Tarzan movie.

"Stop," he bellowed again, using his cop voice, which should be just as effective with thieves here as it was back in Birmingham.

Not-Shayna had hit the bottom floor. He saw the door close as his socked foot slipped across the last landing. He caught himself before he slid down the stairs. He pushed himself off the last step, exploding against the exit door, lunging into the lobby, ready to keep running in whatever direction the girl led him, but was stopped cold by a group of missionaries. Or he guessed they were missionaries, because their bright blue T-shirts shouted, ASK ME ABOUT BEING A MISSIONARY FOR JESUS.

"Jesus," he mumbled, because that was the word that stuck in his head.

There were at least thirty of them crowding the lobby, all blond with eyes as blue as their shirts, all teenagers, both men and women with cherubic cheeks lit up red with zeal for the Lord. He tried to look over the crowd, to discern which direction to go next, but there were no telltale swinging doors or arrows pointing the way.

One of the missionaries said, "Holy crap, mister. You're in your underwear."

"Running shorts," he said, resisting the urge to cover himself. "Training for a marathon."

"With just one shoe?"

"Half marathon."

Jeffrey made his way through the crowd of blue shirts, stepping over suitcases and duffel bags, scanning the floor for his jeans or his wallet in case these missionaries, by some miracle, were going to save him.

The woman at the front desk already had her lips pursed when he approached. He'd never met her in his life, but she said, "You again."

"Me again," he echoed, switching up the inflection so that it could be a statement or a question.

The corner of her lip trilled, but not like an old lady pucker, more like what you'd see from a pit bull right before it ripped off your nut sack with its bare teeth.

"Whatchu doin' down here in your underwear again?" she asked.

He chose to ignore the "again," asking, "Did you see that woman I was with come through here?"

"You mean my daughter?"

Jeffrey took a moment to collect his thoughts.

He'd taken reports off idiots who'd been rolled by women. At least Not-Shayna hadn't been a prostitute, though then again he'd had sex with her and she'd taken all his money, and on the other hand as a cop himself, he knew that no cop believed the guy in his boxers who said he was rolled by a woman who wasn't a prostitute. But goddamn, he'd never paid for sex in his life. He'd played football at Auburn for two years. He was pretty much guaranteed sex until they carted him off to the old folks home, and even then he was pretty sure there'd be some Tigers who would take care of his War Eagle. Though it pained him to say this, for right now, at this moment, the football didn't matter. Half of policing was knowing how to lay down a threat.

He could talk his way out of this.

He was in the process of opening his mouth when he heard the distinctive, guttural roar of a 1968 Mustang with a hole in the carburetor and a length of twine holding up the muffler.

"Shit."

He turned toward the front door.

The missionaries parted like the Red Sea for everybody except Moses, which was to say not at all. He shoved them out of his way, going faster than he ever had up the football field, which likely was why he'd only played two years for Auburn.

He ran through the parking lot, arms and legs pumping under the clouded glow of the receding moon. The Mustang had a healthy head start. It was already making a right onto the main road.

Jeffrey kept running, even as he became aware of three things.

One was that it was pointless to chase a car on foot. Even with two shoes, the car was always going to win.

Two took longer to register, and that was the knowledge that the temperature had dropped about thirty degrees from the day before. This didn't come as a revelation so much as a series of contractions. The muscles in his legs cramped. His abs cramped. His arms cramped. Other things started to shrink from the cold, too.

But none of this distracted from number three, which was the real killer. The Mustang was not his Mustang. It was likely a '68, and it had the same mixture of faded paint and primer, but his Mustang was sitting exactly where he'd parked it last night.

Somehow, Not-Shayna had stolen the wrong car.

He slowed to a jog.

The Mustang that wasn't his Mustang was turning again, this time into the adjacent parking lot. Another Alpine hotel. Another German word for its name. He checked over his shoulder. The moon was squinting over one lone peak, blue early morning sky casting an ominous shadow over the full parking lot. Every pant of breath out of his mouth showed a puff of air in front of his face.

The Mustang slowed as it weaved through the next door parking lot. Not-Shayna looked distracted, which was good because he ran parallel to the car, head low as he shielded himself behind a bunch of other cars. He ended up crouched at the front wheel of a big blue school bus that must have belonged to the missionaries because it too said ASK ME ABOUT BEING A MISSIONARY FOR JESUS.

The Mustang turned a third time, heading down an alleyway that separated the Schussel Mountain Lodge from the Schloss Linderhof, which was done up like a cardboard castle had thrown up on a Motel 6.

Footsteps.

A young black man holding a steaming cup of coffee was leaving the Linderhof lobby. He tipped his Cleveland Indians hat at Jeffrey as he continued down the sidewalk. You didn't see many Cleveland fans in Helen. Or black people for that matter. He nodded back like it was perfectly normal to be crouched in a parking lot wearing one sock and one shoe and orange underwear in a town built like an Alpine village.

He waited until the man was out of sight, then kept his knees bent low as he headed around the back of the Schussel Lodge on the opposite side of the alleyway. Without the parking lot lights, he could barely see more than a few yards in front of him. His entire body shuddered from the cold. The grass was wet because of course it was wet. His one sock got soaked, basically becoming a cube of ice as he made his way to the rear of the building. He saw the nose of the Mustang peeking out from the alley. Maybe fifty yards away. There was a dip in the pavement, a downhill dive to three giant green Dumpsters that stood sentry. The entire area was bathed in light from the xenon bulbs overhead. His ears tensed in that weird way that reminded him that Darwin had been right.

In the alley, there were some familiar sounds, not a car door opening or closing, but the dragging of a metal Auburn keychain across the rear panel of a car as a key clicked into a lock and clicked and clicked, because for whatever reason, the key to his Mustang had worked in the ignition of the Mustang that was not his, but it would not work in the not-his-Mustang's trunk lock.

But then it worked.

The trunk opened, the hinges squealing the same way they squealed in his car.

He moved fast because all he had was the element of surprise. He wasn't worried about getting shot. There were far, far worse things that could happen. Three months he'd had a gold shield. Three months he'd been in suits and ties instead of short-sleeved polyester uniforms with sixty pounds of equipment around his hips that beat into his legs and abs like a pile driver every time he chased some idiot perp through the streets of Birmingham.

He loved his gold detective's shield more than he'd ever loved a woman. Taken better care of it, too. And his lieutenant hadn't wanted to give him the promotion because he didn't trust Jeffrey, and Jeffrey didn't trust his lieutenant because he was an asshole.

Forty yards away.

He heard the solid thunk of a car door closing. He clip-clopped on his one tennis shoe, the cold in his socked foot working up his leg like a python. The sunrise was two scant hours away, but the temperature felt like it was dropping by the minute. How was that even possible? Two days ago, the thermometer had been in the seventies and now he felt like he was standing inside a commercial freezer.

Thirty yards.

Suddenly, he dropped flat to the ground, face and palms pressed to the asphalt.

Muscle memory.

His body had reacted faster than his brain could process the sound of a gunshot cracking like thunder in the thin, cold air.

Had Not-Shayna found a gun?

And accidentally fired a shot?

The reports he'd have to fill out on that one. Not that he didn't know how to fill out those reports in his sleep because he was a fucking vice detective and for the last three months, at least once a day, he'd taken a report from a stupid John who'd had his shit stolen by a hooker.

He pushed himself up.

Twenty yards.

Ten.

He crouched again, this time in front of the Mustang. He put his palms flat against the hot metal, trying to soak up the warmth. She had a gun, and the gun had been fired, and he was a cop so he had to do something about it.

Tires screeched in the alley.

He stood, shoulders hunched, so he could sneak a look over the top of the car. A blue Ford pickup, older model, peeled backward up the alley, leaving smoke and burned rubber in its wake.

He looked down.

His left foot was no longer freezing cold. Blood streamed around his sock, forming a lake, wicking into the material, soaking everything in its wake.

Steam came off the hot liquid.

He lowered himself down into a push-up and peered beneath the car.

Not-Shayna stared back, but not really.

She was caught in the in-between where life or death were the only questions going through her mind.

He'd seen the look many times before.

He scrambled around the car, head down as he made his way toward the woman because she had stopped being Not-Shayna the thief and had started being the victim of a gunshot wound.

He scanned the empty alley as he ran into the open. The woman was gut shot, one of the worst kinds of injuries. His Glock was in her hand.

He touched the muzzle. Cold as ice, so she hadn't shot herself. He took the gun and pointed it around the alley again, looking up for fire escapes or bad guys climbing into open windows.

The blue Ford truck.

Two people in the cab, one obviously the shooter. He'd seen them both—not their faces, but their shapes. One of them was wearing a baseball cap.

"Help. Me," the woman begged.

The hotel windows were closed, but there were guests inside who must have heard the gunshot.

He raised his voice, "Somebody call the police."

"Help," she repeated.

Her hand covered her belly. Blood rolled out between her fingers, a steady river of red that indicated an artery had been opened. He pressed his hands on top of hers, trying to stop the bleeding. She screamed from the pain, and he screamed over her, yelling, "Call the police."

She grabbed his wrist. Her mouth opened to cough. Blood sprayed out. Warm drops splattered his cold skin. Jeffrey laid his hand to her cheek. He looked down at her, aware that he had been above her like this last night, that just a handful of hours ago everything between them had been different. Her eyelids fluttered. He inhaled and the heat from her body reached into his mouth, traveled down his throat, and spread its fingers into his chest.

He shouldn't have drunk so much.

He shouldn't have talked so much.

He should have remembered her name.

"Don't move." The man's voice had cracked on the second word. "I mean it, mister. Just—don't."

Slowly, he turned his head.

A skinny beanpole of a kid riding high tide in his cop uniform was pointing a gun. Or at least trying to. The revolver shook in the boy's hands. His pointy elbows were akimbo. His knees kept locking and unlocking. He had to be at least six five, maybe one fifty after a good meal. His gun belt hung cowboy-style loose around his slim hips, but his eyes were wet with tears.

"Please don't move."

"It's all right." He read the man's name tag. "Paulson, I'm gonna put down my gun, all right? That's all I'm gonna do." Slowly, he laid his Glock on the pavement. Even more slowly, he raised his hands. "Paulson, you're holding that revolver the right way, with both of your hands in a standard grip, pointing at my center mass, but maybe move your finger off the trigger?" He waited, but the officer didn't move. "That's not how they taught you at the academy, is it, Paulson? What'd your instructor say? Keep your finger on the side, just above the trigger, so you don't make a mistake."

The boy's Adam's apple bobbed like a mermaid.

"Paulson, just think about what your instructor said. What'd he tell you about only putting your finger on the trigger when you're ready to shoot somebody?" He indicated his raised hands with a nod. "Are you ready to shoot me, Paulson?"

Carefully, with painstaking slowness, Paulson snailed his finger off the trigger.

"That's good." He felt his lungs finally relax enough to take a full breath. "Now radio your boss. Tell him you've got a dead woman and an unarmed man in custody, and that he needs to put out an APB for an older model Ford pickup, blue, two passengers, one likely African American, wearing a Cleveland Indians ball cap."

The kid started to do as he was told, but then Jeffrey made the mistake of relaxing his shoulders.

"Don't," Paulson screamed, his left hand going back to his gun, his finger tapping the trigger. "Don't move. I mean it." He seemed to realize his voice was more like a plea than an order. "Please, mister. I don't wanna shoot you."

"I don't want you to shoot me, either."

The statement gave them both pause.

A scuffling sound echoed down the alleyway. Another officer, this one more senior, came trotting toward them on what looked like a bad set of knees. His gun was out, but with a hell of a lot more self-assuredness. The chief of police, judging by the stars on his collar. He was barking into his radio, calling in the codes, alerting all available to get the hell over here.

"Don't fucking move," the chief ordered, sighting him down the nose of his revolver. "You try anything and I'll—"

"I'm a cop," Jeffrey said. "Birmingham, Eighth Precinct, Vice. My lieutenant is—"

"This ain't the time for talking." The old guy wasn't open to suggestions, and he couldn't blame him. None of this looked good for anybody. "Slow as molasses, I want you to lace your fingers on top of your head."

He did what the cop told him to do. "Please listen to me, sir." He talked to the chief because Paulson was leaning his shoulder against the wall like he was about to pass out. "You need to find a blue Ford pickup—"

"I cain't throw a rock without hittin' a blue pickup truck. Shit, my son drives a blue pickup." The chief was already reaching into the open trunk. Then he removed and held up a brick of cocaine. "You wanna tell me about this?"

His bowels turned liquid.

"Hoo-ee."

The chief had dollar signs in his eyes. Thanks to new federal laws, arresting agencies were allowed to keep proceeds from drug seizures. "You gotta 'bout ten grand worth of guns, a stack of cash, a hundred grand worth of coke."

"He killed Nora," Paulson said.

A small town like this, the young cop probably had gone to high school with the victim. He was crying for real now. His gun had stopped shaking. But his finger stayed on the trigger.

"You murdered her in cold blood."

"Steady now." The chief peeled his eyes away from the booty in the trunk. His smile said he fully understood the situation, or at least what he thought was the situation. "That why you shot her, boy? Come down here to peddle some guns and blow, but she got greedy?"

"Down?"

Jeffrey glanced at the car.

He'd seen it at the time but hadn't registered the fact until now.

Ohio license plates, front and back.

The cop dropped the brick of cocaine back in the trunk, then walked to the side of the car and opened the door and glove box. A stack of cash held with a rubber band fell out. The cop eyeballed the cash but didn't say a word this time.

"I can explain," Jeffrey said, the same three words he had heard from every criminal he'd ever arrested. "Please let me explain."

"Shut up until I ask you a question."

The chief bent down to search the car. His old knees popped, and he groaned as he pulled jeans from the floorboard of the backseat. He tossed them onto the ground, then a newspaper, the *Cleveland Plain Dealer*.

The chief looked at Jeffrey. "Cleveland, huh?"

All he could do was shake his head as the chief reached back into the car. The older guy groaned again as he bent his knees deeper to yank something out from underneath the seat. The cop grinned when he showed his prize.

A greasy brown paper bag.

The logo on front read "Duke's Grill."

The chief squinted at the receipt stapled to the bag. "Says here that six days ago, you were in East Cleveland on Eddy Road at 3:42 in the p.m." He nodded at Paulson. "Stretch, put the cuffs on this scumbag."

Like most cops, Jeffrey had a terror of being handcuffed. He worked to keep the quiver out of his voice. "That's not necessary. I'll cooperate fully."

"Shut up, you Yankee fucker."

Paulson walked toward Jeffrey, struggling to unsnap the handcuffs from his utility belt, but the belt kept shifting. The buckle was pulled to the last hole, but it was still loose because his hips were basically like a woman's.

"Gimme your hand."

Jeffrey didn't move.

Paulson wrenched Jeffrey's left hand off his head and twisted it around. Technically, the officer should've grabbed the right hand, and he should've cuffed it first, but teaching time was over. They were really going to push this? Arrest him for being some coke-dealing killer from fucking Cleveland?

Cleveland?

Motherfucker.

"Hang on, there was a black guy in the—"

"This ain't Ohio, buddy."

The chief nodded for Paulson to ratchet down the cuffs tight to the wrists.

"You can't just grab your nuts and blame the black guy."

CLEVELAND, OHIO
9:27 A.M.

THE DEA ARRIVED WITH PLANE TICKETS TO GEORGIA ON THE FIRST day Joe Pritchard had with his new partner, a kid named Lincoln Perry.

You were supposed to get to know your partners by working with them, but Joe had actually been watching Perry for a week, and not feeling optimistic about the pairing. Every night, Perry went drinking alone at a bar on Clark Avenue called the Hideaway. He was drinking alone because two weeks earlier he'd busted his childhood buddy, a guy named Ed Gradduk, on cocaine-dealing charges on the very streets where the two had grown up more like brothers than friends. To say that Perry was now persona non grata in his old neighborhood was an understatement. Given the chance to choose badge or buddy, he hadn't hesitated.

Thus the promotion.

Joe had heard the story and was impressed by it, but as he sat running surveillance on his own partner-to-be, watching Perry sip beer and stare into the middle distance as if unaware of the building rage his presence was creating in the bar, he was worried. Coming back down there, insisting on sitting down in the lion's den, was baiting trouble, and for what?

So on Friday morning he had a plan for the day, and the plan was his "no cowboys" lecture. Then the DEA showed up and told him he was packing Perry along to Georgia, cowboy or not, to try to find Antonio Childers.

Antonio Childers was a viral plague of Cleveland's crime scene, an east-side banger who'd spread his empire wide, pushing across town. He sold everything he could, from stolen cars to physical enforcement, but lately he'd made his name on Colombian cocaine. He was a suspect in more than a dozen murders in the past two years alone.

He'd also been missing for nearly a month.

For a week, maybe ten days, investigators had entertained the hopeful notion that he was dead and his body would turn up in the trunk of a car on Eddy Road, or maybe wash up in the Flats of the Cuyahoga River, or the Lake Erie breakwater. Joe hadn't shared that enthusiasm. None of his informants gave the slightest indication that there had been a power shift, or a power vacuum. The system purred on, and Antonio Childers remained at the wheel.

From where, though?

They'd heard a lot of rumors. Georgia wasn't in the mix. But here were two DEA agents with plane tickets. One of them was a stocky white guy with a crew cut who chewed Nicorette for the entire briefing, popping in fresh pieces but never removing the old ones, so that by the end of things he was working on a damn golf ball in the corner of his jaw. He didn't say much, but he nodded a lot and occasionally made a finger-gun pointing gesture when he agreed with something. The other was a tall woman named Luisa who had packed the brains while her partner packed his gum.

"The coke Antonio is moving has come through Atlanta for about nine months," she explained. She held a folder in her hands but kept it closed. "He's one of four, maybe five players working off the same supply. But they always transported it to him. When that stopped, he decided to head south himself."

"Why'd it stop?"

"We think they got a little uneasy about surveillance."

"That would be DEA surveillance?"

She nodded.

Joe thought this made sense. Antonio was not the type of guy who'd give up on a good thing when he found it. He'd be more inclined to go down and sort it out. If you stayed untouchable in your own neighborhood long enough, you could begin to think the same rules would apply elsewhere.

"You've known this for a while," Lincoln Perry said.

They nodded.

"You also know we've been looking for him for a while. Yet you didn't think it was worth sharing?"

"Let her finish," Joe said, but he didn't disagree with the kid. Still, feds were feds. He'd spent too many hours in too many meetings like this to want to debate what they should have shared and when.

All he wanted was Antonio Childers.

"Where is he?"

"He was in Atlanta," she said. "Blew out of town three days ago and our team down there figured he was northbound. They were partially right. He went north, but not far. Ended up in a small town up the mountains a couple hours northwest of the city. Best guess is he was waiting on a courier, or he was testing his back trail to see whether he was being followed. We're not sure."

"But he's still there?"

"Possibly."

That didn't sound encouraging.

"His car is there. This morning, local police found that for us. With a few bricks of cocaine, some cash, a half-dozen semiautomatic handguns, and . . ." She paused and opened the folder for the first time. "One Nora Simpson, now deceased, of Helen, Georgia."

She passed them a photo. It had come through on a fax and the image quality was grainy but you didn't need any better clarity to see the gunshot wound to the stomach.

"This happened this morning, or the car was found this morning?" Joe asked. "Or both?"

The crew-cut guy made the finger-gun gesture.

Joe figured that meant it was both.

"So you think our boy Antonio did the shooting, but now he's missing," Perry said.

Luisa nodded.

"Then the locals are also looking for him," Perry said. "Yet you want us to go to Georgia. With a warrant for a lesser charge. Explain that?"

Joe explained it for her. "They don't want him jailed in Georgia. Not yet, at least."

Crew Cut gave him the finger-gun again.

More points for the home team.

"We've got questions about the local police," Luisa said. "Not only that, but we have another officer in custody for the situation. A Detective Jeffrey Tolliver of Birmingham, Alabama. Originally from a little town called Sylacauga. Played football for Auburn. His lieutenant hates him, but he has a good reputation for the most part. A sheriff named Clayton Hollister speaks highly of him, too. Doesn't seem likely he was running cocaine with Antonio Childers."

"So what was he doing in Georgia with the dead woman?"

"Before she was a dead woman, she was a live woman with a hotel room," Luisa said. "It seems that even Mr. Tolliver's staunchest defenders will admit that he has a proclivity for finding his way into hotel rooms with women who may be, um, recent acquaintances."

"Happens to the best of us," Perry said, and Joe gave him a warning look.

"Listen," Luisa said, "what we need is to get Antonio Childers in custody in a hurry, but also in the right cell. We're giving the lead you've been looking for. Hell, we're even giving you plane tickets for the cause."

"Why so important that it's Ohio?" Joe asked.

She chose her words carefully. "Because we believe he has friends in Georgia who are a lot more important to us than he is, and we don't want them to get early chances with him."

"Police?" Joe asked. "You think your supplier involves police?"

If there was anything he loathed more than the Antonio Childerses of the world, it was a cop who'd help them.

"We just want him in Ohio," Luisa said without elaborating, but it was all she needed to say.

"So do we," Joe said. "Let's get to Georgia. How far is the drive from Atlanta to this town, Helen?"

"About two hours, usually. But there's snow coming in. Might slow things down."

"Hell," Joe said, "this is Cleveland. There's always snow coming in. We'll be fine."

He'd remember that statement often in the hours to come.

They flew direct to Atlanta and were in a rental car and northbound on I-85 by 2 p.m. There had been no four-wheel drives available at the rental counter; everyone was scared of the storm that hadn't arrived yet. There was no snow, and the temperature was near 50. Which wouldn't have been a poor Memorial Day in Cleveland.

But the air promised that was changing.

Changing to what nobody seemed to know, although everybody agreed it was going to be a mess.

The only thing they could find on the radio was dire news about the storm that was blowing up from Cuba and through Florida and what havoc it might wreak on Georgia overnight. That, and some goddamn song called "I Will Always Love You" that was the only thing more annoying than listening to meteorologists talk about barometric pressure shifts. They made it maybe twenty miles before Joe shut the radio off for good.

Once they were outside the perimeter, traffic opened up and they made good time heading north, the city and suburbs falling away behind them and the rural mountains opening up ahead. A light, misting rain was falling, trying to turn to ice. Farms, trailers, and churches dominated the roadside. They angled northwest and climbed higher in the mountains, and a pickup truck with a lifted suspension and oversized terrain tires growled past them, its tailgate a mud-splattered collage of bumper stickers pledging allegiance to God, guns, and the Confederacy. Perry began to whistle the dueling banjos bit from *Deliverance*, but Joe thought about that forecast and wouldn't have minded having the truck. Or anything that sat higher than the rented Chevy Malibu.

The road curled up and over a ridge and then they descended into Helen and Joe pressed on the brake.

The town was lined with Bavarian-style, multicolored chalets. Every home. Every business. He and Perry stared first at the town, then at each other.

"I wasn't paying attention," Perry said. "Where'd we pass through the wormhole?"

Joe drove slowly down the town's main street, looking for the sheriff's department. They passed a Wendy's, which featured the same exterior as the rest of the place.

Bavarian building code strictly enforced, apparently.

"Okay," Perry said, "so what's the plan? Do I distract the Nazis while you escape with the Von Trapps, or do you want to do it the other way around?"

"Maybe it'll be easy," Joe said. "Maybe every hour all these places pop open like cuckoo clocks and we just sit on the car and wait for Antonio to roll out onto a porch, fire his gun a few times, and get sucked back in until the next hour."

Perry pointed to the right. "There's a sign for the PD. Turn on, um . . . Alpenrosen Strasse. No shit, Joe, that's what it says."

"We gotta find some sauerkraut before we leave. God, I love good sauerkraut. If they don't have that, this place is nothing but a fraud."

"Maybe at the Wendy's?" Perry suggested, and Joe smiled.

The kid was all right.

Of course, Joe hadn't seen him under pressure yet. And if Antonio Childers was still anywhere near this place, they might run into pressure sooner than later.

They found the police located in a shared municipal office. They got out and walked through the rain to the building, and Joe noticed the temperature had dropped since their arrival in Atlanta. They were up higher now, and maybe that explained it, but, still, the air felt strange, and an uneasy wind blew the rain at them in gusts.

Inside, a black woman in a police uniform sat alone behind her desk. If there was any other presence in the police department, they were well hidden. Joe introduced himself, showed his badge, and asked to see the chief.

"He's up in Cleveland," she said, and he blinked at her, thinking for a moment that seemed like a definitively federal operation, sending Cleveland police to Georgia and Georgia police to Cleveland, before she added, "It's not far, just fifteen minutes. That's where the county sheriff is. And the jail."

"Cleveland, Georgia," Joe said. "Got it. Right. Did they handle the Nora Simpson shooting this morning?"

She seemed to puff up with righteous indignation. "No, they did not. That was our police department."

"My mistake. Which officer handled that scene?"

"All of them."

Joe glanced at Perry, who looked back at him with a cocked eyebrow as he said, "How many would that be?"

"Three," she said.

Joe considered that and said, "Nobody else has shown up? Feds, Georgia Bureau of Investigation?"

"Nope."

He sincerely doubted that the DEA's corruption concerns stemmed from a three-man department in a tourist-trap village, so if the GBI had been kept at bay this long, it suggested they were of interest.

"Is there someone we could speak to who was at the scene this morning?"

"Not right now. They all went up to Cleveland to talk to the sheriff. We got bigger problems ahead of us than this thing you all are so interested in, you know. There's a storm coming, supposed to be the all-time record. There was a public safety meeting in Cleveland. I expect they'll be back soon, though."

"In the meantime, who polices the town?" Perry asked.

She gave him a stone-cold stare. "That would be me."

Joe figured she'd do a fair-enough job of it, too.

"If you think they'll be back here soon, we'll hang out for a bit," he said, thinking that this was actually a hell of an opportunity to ask some questions around town without having the local law breathing down their necks.

God bless the blizzard.

"Fine by me. They won't be much longer, I'm sure."

"What happened to the guy you arrested, the cop from Alabama?"

"Still got him in a holding cell. And as far as I'm concerned? He ought to stay there."

"Yeah? You think he shot her?"

"I don't know about that." She looked at him primly. "But that man ran right through town in nothing but his underpants. Now, you tell me, isn't that some kind of crime?"

"Some kind," Joe agreed, and then he and Perry left and walked out into the cold. A few stray snowflakes were falling now.

"So we head for the closest Cleveland?" Perry asked.

Joe caught one of the snowflakes in his palm, watching it melt, and thought again that he would like to have rented a four-wheel drive. He didn't know what the all-time record storm was in Georgia, but it didn't sound encouraging.

"We could do that," he said. "Or could take advantage of a little time in town without a local deputy at our sides."

"I vote for the latter," Perry said. "I don't know what in the hell brought Antonio to a place like this, but my guess is, he stuck out once he arrived. People are likely to remember him."

"Agreed."

They didn't have to go far to find their first eyewitness, and they didn't have to interview her long to determine that she wasn't an eyewitness at all, but since she'd heard all about the shooting from someone who had talked to someone else who had probably seen it, she basically felt like she had herself, you know?

Pritchard assured her that of course he understood this, but all the same they'd like to talk to someone who actually had seen things. Police protocol and all that. It was a bitch that they couldn't just take her word for it, but, you know, it was the law.

"Ain't nobody going to say a single word different," she said with a pout. "He ran out of that motel in his underpants, and then came the shooting. He told the police she was trying to steal his car, but it wasn't even his car, so you tell me whether he's guilty or not? Answers itself. And doesn't matter if I saw or heard it, all of that's gospel, mister."

"It sounds authentic," Joe agreed, and then they thanked her and crossed the street to where she'd indicated the shooting had happened, an alley that angled downhill, behind the hotels. Outside of a hotel called the Linderhof, a guy wearing a long denim jacket that flapped around his legs like a duster was spreading snowmelt on the steps and smoking a cigarette. Maintenance man, probably.

"Want to see whether he, too, has heard the gospel?" Perry asked.

"I expect it spreads fast around here, but it might have some variations," Joe said. "We might as well hear them all."

They went up and badged him and he looked at them sourly while he smoked the cigarette.

"Cleveland, you say?"

"Cleveland, Ohio, yes."

"You interested in the black fella? I don't say that 'cause he was black. I say that 'cause he drove the car in."

"The car where Nora was shot?" Perry asked.

"That's the one. Sweet car. Older Mustang, maybe early '70s. Nah, that ain't right, not with those taillights. Late '60s." He took a long drag and then repeated, "Sweet car."

"Where was it impounded?" Joe asked.

"It wasn't. They just left it right where it was. There's police tape on it. I assume it's likely locked, too."

Perry glanced at Joe, clearly impressed by this police work, and said, "Was there anybody working here who might have had a view of what happened this morning?"

"Nope." Another puff on the cigarette, then, "I keep meaning to watch the tapes and see if there's anything useful on them. But, hell, with this storm, the manager keeps busting my balls about getting ice-melt down."

"You've got security cameras here?"

"Sure. A couple pointed right at the alley. I figure they might be of some use."

"I figure you're right," Joe said. "Let's take a look."

The security footage that hadn't been reviewed or even requested by the three-man Helen Police Department, currently occupied with plans for snowplow routes, offered more than a view of the car.

It showed the shooting.

"I'll be damned," the maintenance man said. "I wasn't expecting that."

Joe was starting to get a headache. He wondered how many homicides had been investigated in this town in the past century. Whatever the total was, it had to be matched exactly by the number of cold cases.

"Probably going to want to pass this along to the guy they've got in jail," Perry said as they watched the grainy-but-indisputable image of Antonio Childers opening fire on Nora Simpson. "It seems potentially useful to the defense team, what with the video of someone else doing the killing and all."

"How about the girl, though?" Joe said. "She's driving like she's expecting someone. Cruising slow through that alley. But she sure as hell wasn't expecting Antonio. She's cruising, and he's running. She seems surprised by him. If she just stole his car, that doesn't jibe."

"Remember what the girl who was spreading the gospel told us," Perry said. "The cop they locked up said Nora Simpson stole *his* car, but that he was lying about that, because—"

"It wasn't his car," Joe finished. "Right. Could be some of Detective Tolliver's testimony had been bent around the edges by the time it got to her. So let's say Nora sleeps with him, and then she steals a car. Problem is, it's Antonio's car. All fine. But how in the hell does she start it?"

"Hot-wire, maybe?"

"If she's hot-wiring cars, she doesn't need to steal keys."

"We need to chat with Detective Tolliver," Perry said. "I'd rather hear his version of things first. And alert him to the presence of this video. Seems like the kind thing to do, before they send him to the electric chair."

"Hang on," Joe said. "Can you go back?"

He had been focused on the shooting the first time through, but now as they watched it again he'd seen that just after Antonio Childers left the frame and just before the guy in one shoe and his boxer shorts arrived, there had been a blur of motion that looked like another vehicle pulling in. Pulling in too close to the scene not to have been part of it.

The maintenance man rewound and played it again. Joe put his finger on the corner of the screen. "Right there, Lincoln. You got better eyes than me, what's the make on that truck?"

Perry leaned forward and squinted. "F-150, I'd say. It's in and out awfully fast, but we can grab a still image and blow that up. Looks like an older Ford, though. Exhaust is custom. They don't have those big dual pipes coming out of the factory."

"Hell," the maintenance man said. "That's Paulson's truck."

Joe said, "You know who owns that thing?"

"Pretty sure. Like this fella said, those pipes stand out. Double Simpson put those growlers on. I remember that, because people said it should have been a, what do you call it? Noise ordinance violation, I think. But since it was Paulson's truck, and he wasn't likely to give himself a ticket, who the fuck cared how loud it was, right?"

They both stared at him.

Lincoln Perry spoke slowly, as if he had to use a second language with this guy. "That's a police officer's truck?"

"Sure it is. Matter of fact, it is that police officer's truck." He pointed at the screen where the surveillance footage was still running, and a tall, skinny, uniformed officer had a gun pointed at the guy in his underwear. Other than the gun and the badge he might've been mistaken for a telephone pole. He would've been the butt of the joke even in a movie. Despite his considerable height, he didn't look old enough to shave and probably had needed to add holes to his duty belt to cinch it up tight enough to hold the weight of the gun without his pants falling off his ass.

Joe said, "So Paulson's truck was in motion, but Paulson wasn't driving it. Who do you think was, mister?"

"How in the hell do I know?"

"Because you're batting pretty well already," Joe said. "So if you don't mind, keep swinging."

"I don't know. Paulson doesn't have a wife or a girl, lives by himself. I got no idea who'd be driving his car at the ass-crack of dawn while he's on duty."

"What about the guy you mentioned earlier, the one you said customized the exhaust on that Ford?" Perry asked. "Said his name was Double?"

"His full name is Thomas, I guess, but nobody around here has called him anything but Double since he was a kid. Not sure why, exactly. I think it's because whatever trouble you had in your life before he showed up, it doubled on you the moment he got there, you know? Matter of fact, I've heard it said it was his first-grade teacher who started that nickname. You know a kid is a problem when a teacher tags him like that."

Joe said, "Does Thomas, or Double, or whatever the hell he's known by, move drugs?"

"Probably."

"Coke?"

"I don't know. That boy walks down the sidewalk and I cross the street, right? I ain't exactly in his inner circle. But it surely wouldn't surprise me." The maintenance man grew reflective. "Matter of fact, I recall one story about him. Highway patrol stopped him somewhere north of Valdosta, and he was running something, I think maybe it was coke but I can't say for sure. Anyhow, between the time they ran his license and the time they made him get out of his car, he keistered it. The car search came up empty and they let him go with just a ticket for the expired plates."

"Keistered it," Perry echoed.

"It's when you shove the drugs right up your asshole."

Perry lifted a hand to ward off any further imagery. "I followed the mechanics, thanks. I was just unfamiliar with the term. I'll file that one away, though. So he does have a drug history, and he's close with the local police, particularly the officer who was first on the scene. Correct?"

"I wouldn't argue that. He runs a chop shop, everybody knows that, and Paulson surely does, but he hasn't done anything about it. In exchange, Paulson got a thousand-dollar set of pipes put on his truck, and a pretty bitchin' grill that you can't see in the video. It doesn't match the rest of the truck, but still, it looks tough." He said it with admiration and envy, and Joe cut in to bring his mind away from the truck and back to the murder scene.

"What are the odds this guy would have given Antonio Childers, that's the shooter's name, the black guy from out of town, a ride away from that scene?"

"Pretty slim, I'd think. Because he's Nora's brother."

There was a pregnant silence, and then Joe said, "The guy who worked on that truck was the victim's brother?"

"That's what I said."

"How many people live in this town?" Perry asked. "Five?"

"Just over three hundred."

The video was still running.

On the screen, Paulson and another officer, one who appeared to hold rank over him, were searching the Mustang and cuffing the guy in the one shoe, Detective Jeffrey Tolliver of Birmingham, Alabama. Every now and then Paulson would glance sideways, but his gun never traveled with him. Could be that he was checking to make sure there was no other threat in the area. Could be that he was checking to make sure his truck was long since out of sight.

"Somebody got Childers away from that scene in a hurry," Joe said. "But maybe we're looking at it backwards. We can't see what happened. The truck comes and goes, and Antonio comes and goes. Maybe with a friend. But maybe not."

The maintenance man had that reflective gaze going again. "You know, that's not a bad point."

Joe had never felt less validated by a positive review of his police work, but he pressed it. "Supposing that girl, Nora, was intending to steal the car, then her brother is the likely recipient, right? You said he runs a chop shop. So he'd be the guy who takes over once she's snagged the car."

The maintenance man nodded.

"Let's imagine her brother is waiting on her and sees what happens. Watches Antonio shoot his sister in the stomach. He's not just driving away then, is he? A guy like you described, he'd be all over the screen right now, he'd have killed Antonio, shot him where he stood, or at least stayed with his sister and waited for the cops."

That drew a frown and a slow, thoughtful shake of the head. "I can't say I agree with that, no."

"This guy you told us about, the hell-raiser, you think he'd just let it go? Watch his sister be killed and then clear out?"

"Oh, no. That's not what I meant, at all. I was just thinking. Old Double, if he did see all that? He'd have wanted to take some time on your boy, there, what's his name, Antonio? Double wouldn't have let that end easy for him. Not after what he did to Nora."

For a moment they were all quiet, watching Paulson arrest Tolliver on the screen, and listening to the rattling of snow and ice off the window.

Then Perry said, "Let's have a look around that car, Joe. Maybe there are more cameras, more angles."

Joe nodded, but he didn't turn away from the screen.

He was watching Nora Simpson's blood spread out over the pavement.

Double wouldn't have let that end easy for him, the maintenance man had said.

And he nearly smiled.

Antonio might have made one hell of a mistake leaving Cleveland for Georgia.

These crackers might not be all that easy to handle.

3:06 P.M.

JEFFREY PACED AROUND THE TINY HOLDING CELL IN HIS UNDERWEAR and T-shirt. He was still wearing one shoe and one sock. It was the only control he could assert over his person.

Thanks to his hangover, he had slept some, but now he was fully awake and fully freaking out. Claustrophobia had never been an issue for him until now. There wasn't enough saliva in his mouth. His heart was vibrating like a tuning fork. He was sweating profusely despite the cold that whipped past the single-paned, barred window high up in his cell.

Ten hours ago he had asked the Helen chief of police to call sheriff Hoss Hollister in Sylacauga so that Hoss could vouch for him. He knew that ten hours had passed because there was a giant clock on the wall opposite his cell, mounted over the empty desk that held a telephone, a fax machine, and a computer the size of a dog's coffin—corgi, not malamute—with a giant monitor on top of it. For the last ten hours, he'd listened to the tick-tick-tick of the clock, the second hand passing for something like Chinese water torture.

Occasionally, he heard voices in the next room, but nobody entered the holding space or sat behind the desk or checked on his welfare. Every once in a while the stainless steel toilet/sink inside his cell would gurgle, or his stomach would grumble, but other than the clock, those were the only sounds.

The phone never rang.

The computer wasn't even turned on.

He sat down on the narrow metal bed with no mattress, pillow, or blanket. They'd even taken the string out of his one tennis shoe. He clasped his hands between his knees, not praying so much as begging his brain to start working. There was a dead woman. Nora. Someone had killed her. She deserved justice. Some kind of acknowledgment that her life had mattered more than the last few seconds at the end.

Flashes of memories kept coming back to him.

The bartender had poured a little more generously when Nora had shown up. The room she'd taken him to was freshly cleaned, no toiletries or suitcase to indicate a guest was staying there.

What were these called?

Clues?

It was a scam, but then the scam had gone horribly wrong.

Nora had stayed the night. He wanted to think that was because he was damn good in bed, and not because she'd drunk too much and he'd not drunk enough. She was obviously a grab-and-dash kind of woman. Get the wallet, get the keys, go to the alley, and meet up with whoever was going to take the car for chopping.

But she'd stolen the wrong car.

Then there was the old blue pickup. The two shapes in the cab. The black guy in the Cleveland Indians baseball cap.

His head pounded out each memory like a chisel on a stone tablet.

He'd provided the Helen chief of police with Hoss's home phone number because he'd been close to the lawman his entire life. Hoss was the reason he became a cop. The guy had been a surrogate father, keeping him out of trouble, providing a nudge or a kick in the ass when needed. And Hoss would be a hell of a lot nicer about this current misunderstanding than his lieutenant back in Alabama, who would probably fax over a termination of employment letter the minute he hung up the phone.

But if the Helen chief had talked to Hoss, if he understood that Jeffrey was not, in fact, a murdering, coke-dealing, drug-running Yankee asshole from Cleveland, but an honest, God-fearing, law-abiding southern boy, the Helen chief wasn't letting on.

He stood and started pacing again.

Sock, shoe. Sock, shoe.

Tick tick tick.

If the Helen chief of police wasn't making phone calls, was he trying to build a case? By law, he only had forty-eight hours to hold a suspect before he had to charge him or let him go. The weekend was basically here. The courts would be closed for two days, maybe more if the storm turned bad. He should've been allowed a phone call, but in the last ten hours no one had been around to ask for that privilege. Today was almost a year that the cops who were accused of beating Rodney King had been acquitted of all crimes. If the Helen chief of police moved him to the county lockup, his life would be worth less than a pound of dog shit.

"Well, hello there, handsome."

A tall, willowy black woman in a tailored police uniform entered the holding area. She held a tray with grits, a biscuit, some eggs, bacon, and, because there was still a God in heaven, a large cup of coffee.

"You must be the underwear murderer."

He tried to smile the smile that usually won over women. "I never killed a pair of underwear in my life."

She chuckled as she placed the tray on the ledge by his cell. Her eyes traced the outline of his boxers. "You an Auburn fan?"

"Yes, ma'am." He crossed his arms over his chest. He knew a football fan when he saw one. "Played for two years."

"Is that right?" She started going through the keys on her belt. "What position?"

"Halfback," he said. "Like O.J., but without the athleticism or promising future."

She chuckled again, which he took as a good sign. "I can see you running through an airport with a briefcase."

She had found the key.

He watched the cell door swing open. The smell of sweet freedom put some warmth back into his body, even though she stood there with the tray in her hands, blocking the exit.

"You look like the kind of guy who would end up on the cover of *SEC Monthly*."

"Actually, I was on the cover of *SEC Monthly*."

"Roll Tide, asshole."

She dropped the tray on the floor.

The coffee exploded, much like his ego.

The cell door clanged shut.

He resisted the urge to fall to his knees and slurp the coffee off the dirty concrete. Instead, he sat back down on the metal bed. The cold didn't seep so much as drill into his bones. Whatever was happening to the weather outside wasn't good. He could practically feel the temperature dropping by the second.

The woman sat down at the desk.

She opened a drawer, took out a nameplate, and slapped it onto the desktop.

Sergeant A. Fuller.

She reached around and turned on the computer, then the giant monitor. A loud whir temporarily overwhelmed the ticking of the clock as the computer booted up. He rubbed his hands together. He was freezing, but he was also sweating. He thought of all the things he could say to Sergeant A. Fuller. *I'm a cop, too, bitch. Has your chief called the sheriff I told him to call? Why am I in a holding cell? With what crime am I being charged? I demand to speak to a lawyer.*

Go fucking War Eagles.

He reached down and grabbed the biscuit off the tray. Hard as a brick. Cold as his left foot. He shoved some frozen eggs and congealing bacon inside.

The phone rang.

A. Fuller picked up the receiver.

"Yes." Then another, "Yes." Her gaze slid toward him as she gave a throaty, "Uh-huh."

She stood up from her desk and picked up the phone base, stretching the cord across the room to the cell.

She held out the receiver a few inches from the bars.

Jeffrey pressed his palms to his knees and pushed himself up. He shoe-socked his way over to the front of the cell and reached out for the receiver. She pulled it just slightly out of his grasp before letting him take it.

He cleared his throat before saying, "This is Jeffrey Tolliver."

Hoss said, "Hey, Slick."

He could've wept. "Hello, sir."

"You had enough time to contemplate your many transgressions?"

He gripped the phone as he listened to Hoss chuckle. Obviously, the Helen chief of police had called the Sylacauga sheriff and they'd worked out a ten-hour penalty in the box.

"You told them to keep me locked up?"

"Aw, now, don't let your pride get in the way. I figger I did you a favor considering you was caught wet, hungover, and standing over a dead woman with a brick of coke and some illegal guns."

"That woman had a name."

"You remembering their names now?" Hoss paused, and he could practically see the old man frowning down the line. "Tell me, Slick. Ain't you gettin' a little old for this kind of behavior?"

"The thought had occurred to me earlier in the day."

"Nothin' wrong with settlin' down." Hoss sounded disappointed, which was far worse than him sounding angry. "'Course, what'll happen is, you'll meet some knockout gal, much smarter than you—which ain't hard—and you'll fall head over heels until you get her pinned down, then your eye will start wandering again and you'll fuck it all up." Hoss stopped to cough, which is what forty years of smoking cigars made you do. "On the plus side, she'll be a good excuse not to settle down with every other girl who comes after her. The one that got away. Your little redheaded girl, to put it into Charlie Brown parlance."

He leaned his head back against the bars. "I get the lesson, Hoss. Are you gonna let me out of here or not?"

"Chief Eustace DuPree is the man's name. Nice fella. Worked three murder cases in his thirty-two-year career, all of them domestics, which means he arrested the husband and that was that."

"Will he take my help?"

"Last I heard the DEA was sending some boys down from Cleveland to give DuPree a hand, but you know nobody likes that kind of help."

DEA meant federal. They wouldn't want help any more than the locals. Still, he lowered his voice. "There's a few things I can follow up on."

"Just try not to get arrested again."

He heard the phone click as Hoss hung up. For Sergeant A. Fuller's sake, he said, "I appreciate your confidence in me, sir. Thank you." He handed the phone back through the bars, but A. Fuller was already sitting at her desk.

She nodded to the phone base.

"Hang it up yourself, Slick. The door's not locked."

Jeffrey tentatively pushed at the cell door. It swung open. He shoe-socked to the desk and hung up the phone. "Did you find those two guys in the blue truck?"

"Nope."

"Did you find the black guy from the hotel?"

"You mean Homey D. Clown? Yeah, they got him locked up in the *other* jail."

Jeffrey ignored the sarcasm and looked down at his shoes so she couldn't see the hate in his eyes. "Does the chief want to talk to me?"

"I'd say that falls under the headline of 'When Hell Freezes Over.'"

"I want to help."

"I'm sure you do, Auburn, but we got it covered." A. Fuller pulled a large brown paper evidence bag from a drawer. She took out his left shoe and offered it to Jeffrey. He put it on. She handed him a sock. He took off his right shoe and donned the sock. She handed him his jeans.

"Really?"

He grabbed them, slid off his shoes, slipped on the jeans, then shoved his feet back into his sneakers.

"No wallet?" he asked. "Pager? Keys? ChapStick?"

She dug around in the bag, a blank expression on her face. Just when he was about to give up, she tossed him his keys.

"You're free to go, Mr. Tolliver."

He should've let it slide, but he couldn't. "Detective Tolliver. Good thing I didn't bring my Sugar Bowl ring on this trip to your beautiful town."

"You mean from back when you tied with Syracuse?" She snorted. "Weren't we the only team that beat you that year?"

"I don't remember seeing you on the bench, Sergeant."

She rested her hand on the butt of her gun. "I can put your ass back in that cell and nobody'll think to look for you till Monday."

He let it go and walked into what turned out to be an empty squad room. Two desks, each with a phone and stacks of papers. He guessed the nice leather chair belonged to the chief, and the Kmart special lowered about an inch from the ground belonged to Paulson. The kid wouldn't be able to stick his knees under the desk otherwise.

He gave the front door one push and it was immediately snatched out of his hand by a strong gust of wind. His T-shirt rattled against his chest. He squinted his eyes against the stinging wind. Of course the trek back to the hotel was straight into the wind tunnel. The gust came down off the mountains like a scythe. He jammed his hands into his jeans pockets, bent his knees, and forced himself forward.

His first stop was not at the Schussel Mountain Lodge but at the trash can on the sidewalk outside the building. He had seen the Mustang stop here for a second, and sure enough, Nora had taken the opportunity to dump his wallet. What a break it was still there. His cash and cards were gone, but Nora had left his driver's license and his key card to his hotel room. Next, he headed downwind to his Mustang. He unlocked the trunk, holding his breath until he found his badge and spare gun in the wheel well. He stuck the badge in his back pocket. The gun went into the waist of his jeans.

He felt whole again.

The lobby desk inside the Schussel was unmanned. Instead of waiting for the elevator, he used the stairs. His room was on the second floor, which happened to overlook the alleyway between the Schussel and the Linderhof. Once inside he pushed open the window overlooking the alley, his teeth chattering before he even had a chance to look down. The Mustang was two stories below, abandoned but for the police tape warning people away.

He saw flecks of white floating in front of his eyes. He blinked, thinking his brain was so tired it was throwing up hallucinations, but no—he really was seeing snow. In March. In Georgia. It was falling steady like you saw in movies, thick white flakes that looked like they had no intention of stopping.

He closed the window and rifled through his suitcase until he found some clean, nonnovelty underwear. He slipped on a new T-shirt and a flannel button-down that he almost hadn't packed because he was afraid the weather would be too warm. He stepped into the bathroom and brushed his teeth. Then washed his face, combed his hair, and looked at himself in the mirror.

His reflection in the mirror revealed a man who appeared even more hungover than he had this morning.

Hoss's earlier admonishments rang in his ears, but there was nothing he could do about changing his entire life right now. He left his room and took the steps down two at a time. When he opened the door to the lobby he found the front desk occupied by a teenager sporting a Chia-like goatee and a V-neck T-shirt that showed the top of a tattoo that probably read Damn Skippy.

The kid was reading *Catcher in the Rye,* because it wasn't disaffected enough to have a tattoo and a goatee. He looked up as Jeffrey approached. "You're the underwear guy."

He let the comment slide. "Where's the woman who was working here this morning?"

"Corinna?" The kid laid down his book. "At the funeral home. Nora was her daughter."

He scratched his chin. He'd forgotten to shave. "Did you know Nora?"

A derisive noise came out of the back of the kid's nose. "Not like you did."

He leaned over the desk.

Like a switch being hit, his hangover evaporated and his cop brain took over. The kid seemed to get that things were different now. He cowered away, quickly understanding that Jeffrey was ready to punch him in the throat if he didn't start talking.

"Nora was two years ahead of me in school, but I knew her."

He felt the color drain out of his face. The kid looked around fifteen. "How old was she?"

"Twenty-two."

He allowed some air out of his lungs. "Did she do this a lot?"

"What do you mean?"

The kid scratched at his hairless chest peeking out of the V-neck. A vein throbbed in his pimpled forehead. His visible fear heightened Jeffrey's aggression. He leaned farther across the counter and turned on the dead in his eyes.

"What I mean, you stupid piece of shit, is that they were working a scam. Corrina gets the signal from the bartender that he's got a live one. She sends in Nora. Nora gets the mark drunk, takes him up to an empty room, and pours more liquor down his throat until he passes out. Then she robs him, steals his car, and he wakes up the next morning thinking his only option is to lie to cops about how his car got stolen and get the hell out of town before his wife finds out he cheated on her."

"Don't sound like you passed out."

"Lucky for me," Jeffrey said, uneasy with his role in the situation. "Do the local cops know what you're running here?"

"No, sir." He held up his hands. "And I got no part in it. I promise on a stack of bibles."

He knew that was a lie, but didn't care. He glanced around the lobby. "Where did those missionaries go? I didn't see their bus in the parking lot."

"Left this morning before the storm came in. They had a long way to go."

"Where?"

"Michigan?"

At least he hadn't said Cleveland.

Jeffrey let his eyes travel around the empty lobby. Crappy leather couch. Overstuffed chairs. Card table by the door. A sign read COFFEE BAR but the urn was upside down and there were no cups, the same as it had been this morning.

He asked the kid, "Did Chief DuPree interview you?"

"Yeah. I told him I ain't seen nothing. I work the day shift. I was just pulling up when Corinna got the news about Nora."

"You were pulling up in your truck?"

"I wish. Drove in my mama's Camry this morning. My motorcycle's in the shop, which is fine by me 'cause the whole witch is cold today. You know what I mean?"

"Do you know anybody who drives a blue Ford pickup? Late model?"

He kept scratching his chest, like his brain was in there and could feel the stimulation. "Coupl'a three boys I went to school with. My grand-pappy. Pastor Davis. Mrs. Fields who owns the—"

"Where does Nora live?"

"With Corinna up the mountain. And her brother, Double. It's a fur piece, right up near the falls."

"Ruby Falls?"

"Yep, just take Millar Road before you get to the falls. They're the second trailer on the right, got an American flag outside—but, lookit, mister." The kid lowered his voice as if inviting him into a confidence. "I wouldn't mess with Double. He's the kinda guy who's always look-ing for trouble. Worse than his daddy, even, and his daddy's doing hard time down in Valdosta for a triple murder." He gave Jeffrey a knowing look. "That's where 'Double' comes from, on account of compared to his daddy, he's double trouble."

He knew the sort, and he wasn't scared. "Does Double drive an old blue Ford truck?"

"Black one. Brand-new."

That sounded a little too nice for a kid named Double. "He deal drugs?"

The kid balked.

"I'm from Alabama, buddy. You can snort your fucking way to the state line and I won't give a shit."

The kid started nodding. "Yeah, he's a dealer."

"Big fish or a little fish?"

"Medium fish, but he's always lookin' to get bigger. Since he was in kindergarten even." The kid cleared his throat. "I was in his class. He was hateful even then. Like, pull the wings off a butterfly hateful."

"Does he run girls?"

"Just his sisters. And a wall-eyed cousin. And that neighbor girl with the funny name. And sometimes his mama, but that takes a certain type of guy wants an older gal. You know what I mean?"

Jeffrey let that sink in. "There was a black guy with—"

"A Cleveland baseball cap?" the kid asked. "Yeah, the chief asked me about him, but I ain't seen him."

"Did Chief DuPree go through your guest register?"

"Sure did, but he didn't find nobody matching the description. Even knocked on the doors to double-check."

He had no doubt Corinna went off-book with cash-paying guests.

The kid leaned over, suddenly chatty. "See, I don't think there was a black guy in a hat. I think ol' DuPree was testing me, 'cause there's three black people in town, and Sergeant Ava, that's the chief's wife, is one of them, and her father and her mother are the other two, and if there was a fourth black person, she would know that fella, too, right?" He held up his hands. "I'm not being racist, all right? That's how it is."

"I get it," he said.

And he did.

He worked in the Titusville area of Birmingham, a poor African American area. Oftentimes, he was the only white guy on the streets. People knew him by color, not name.

The kid said, "I told the chief to check next door at the Hof, but Mr. Tucker, he don't rent to black people. Not that we get that many up here. Everybody knows they don't like the cold."

So much for not being racist.

"That's all I got," the kid said. "I promise."

He was still lying, but Jeffrey wasn't sure about what, or if it even mattered. Everybody lied to the police, even the ones who were trying to help.

Especially the ones who were trying to help.

He left the hotel.

The wind whipped at his clothes. In the twenty minutes he'd been inside, the ground had become thick with snow. He stuck his hands in his pockets, fighting the sensation of his skin being burned off by the wind. For once the weathermen had been right. This storm was going to knock the state on its ass. The sky looked worse than ominous, something stuck between a tornado and Armageddon.

Despite the arctic blast, he stood roughly where he had stood in the parking lot earlier that morning. He was pretty sure that the guy in the Cleveland Indian hat had come out of the Linderhof with his cup of coffee. He'd dismissed the event as random at the time, but with a dead body, nothing was random.

So maybe this is what happened.

Last night, Cleveland Hat stays at the Schussel Mountain Lodge. He parks his car close to the building, probably so he can see it from his room, which is at the front of the hotel because that's what he asks for. Cleveland's got the coke and guns with him in the room, but he wants to make sure no one is snooping around his stolen car—a cop, say, or an idiot kid looking for a joyride.

Cleveland stays the night.

Then goes downstairs in the morning to check out of the hotel, finds himself enveloped by cheery blond-haired and blue-eyed Michiganers for Jesus, which is bad, then finds out there's no coffee, which is worse, so he loads up his car, walks over to the Linderhof, grabs a cup of coffee, and comes out to find his Mustang gone and a half-naked man standing in the parking lot.

Cleveland had played it cool with Jeffrey. The man's casual tip of his hat said it all. This wasn't his first rodeo. You didn't get to be a black man traveling up the northeastern corridor with a carload of coke and guns without having a pair of brass ones. No wonder the DEA was on this guy's trail. The murder charge would bring even more resources into what was probably shaping up to be an interstate trafficking investigation, possibly a RICO charge. Cleveland could be either the tip of the iceberg or, better yet, the tip of the spear.

Jeffrey picked up the pace as he walked toward the alleyway. His sneakers became soaked with snow. His jeans wicked up the cold as he approached the Mustang that was not his Mustang. The police tape was floating in the wind, torn in two and flapping off the side mirrors like flags outside a used car dealership.

He stopped by the driver's-side door, took his keys out of his pocket, trying to think how Nora would've worked it. He imagined her running out of the Schussel, probably right when Cleveland was going into the Linderhof to score his coffee. She spots the Mustang parked out front, runs toward it, jams the car key into the door lock—

That wasn't right.

The door would've been unlocked, because Cleveland had used a slim jim to open the door. He could see where the gasket had been sliced by the flat, hooked piece of metal that had been used to pull up the locking mechanism.

So she opened the car door.

He did the same.

Then she'd climbed in.

So did he, giving himself a second to enjoy the sensation of not being battered by hurricane-like winds. The car was bright white inside from the snow on all the windows. He found the ignition switch. Dash mounted, the same as his. Some engineer at Ford had had the bright idea to add a little sidebar hole in the face of the ignition switch. You slide the key in the ignition and turned it to Accessory, then bent open a paper clip and shoved it into the hole. Voilà. The cylinder inside the ignition switch popped out.

You needed a key to do this, of course, but the thing about the ignition switch on a '68 Mustang is that it's twenty-five years old. He was twenty-six and wasn't holding up so well himself. The pins inside the cylinder weakened over time, so all you had to do was jimmy in a flathead screwdriver, or a pocketknife, turn it gently to the left, push in the paper clip, and pop out the cylinder.

A pro could do this in under ten seconds. A really smart pro, someone who wanted to be able to easily crank the engine again and again, possibly on a trip up from Florida, through Georgia, and onto farther points north with some coke and guns in the trunk, would shave down the tumblers inside the cylinder so that any key would turn on the engine.

Which he was able to do with the key to his own Mustang.

The engine coughed and sputtered against the freezing temperature. He pumped the gas to keep it going. While he was at it, he turned up the heater. Cold air blew in his face.

Now what?

He sat back in the seat, trying to consider his options. The kid at the hotel needed a second round, but not enough time had passed. Whatever he was lying about needed to fester like a rusted piece of metal inside his intestines.

Corinna was at the funeral home, but he doubted he'd get much out of the grieving mother, and besides, he wasn't exactly working with the blessing of the locals. There was a fine line between what Chief DuPree would see as helping and what might come across as hindering.

Double up on the mountain was an obvious suspect to follow—drug dealer, connected to the victim—but he knew better than to go into some desolate holler without someone watching his back.

Not to mention that the snow was accumulating, which to a person living in the South was the most bloodcurdling thing that snow could ever do. Cars would be abandoned. Children would be locked behind doors. Grocery stores would be purged of milk, bread, kerosene, toilet paper, and Cheetos—all the vital necessities.

Anna Ruby Falls was half an hour drive and a quick hike into the Chattahoochee National Forest. The kid at the Shussel had said Double and his family lived on Millar Road. Second trailer on the right. American flag. Double's neighbors would be watching out the windows. They might be involved in the family business, or making money off not being involved. Around these parts, crack was the new moonshine. The same people you saw in church on Sunday were the same people dealing on Monday.

He tried to turn on the wipers. The motor sent back a pained groan over the weight of the snow. He cut the engine and looked at his key, making sure the jimmied lock hadn't damaged it. He could see white breaths in the air in front of his face.

The radio clock read 4:01.

The roads would be locked up by sundown, not because of the snow, but because even when it was cold, it always got warm enough in the afternoon to melt the snow, then it got cold enough to freeze it and come rush hour, people who thought they were driving home in the snow realized that they were sliding across sheets of ice.

All this talk about snow made him think of something.

He reached down and pulled the trunk release. He got out of the car, shivering like a beat-down dog as the wind cut open his skin. He had to squint his eyes almost closed as he walked to the back of the Mustang and pushed up the trunk.

The guns were still there.

The brick of coke was still there, but there had to be more than one brick of coke, otherwise, why bother?

"Shit," he mumbled.

He didn't have to think hard about how this had gone down. The chief, freaking out about the murder, the death notification, the hit to his budget, the risk to his department's reputation, had run off to make phone calls, but not before telling Officer Paulson to secure the car. Paulson had put up the tape thinking that no one would violate the sacred words that beseeched all good citizens to DO NOT CROSS. Then he'd clapped his Jolly Green Giant hands together and ho-ho-ho'd off thinking job well done.

"Shit," he repeated.

He would have to call A. Fuller and tell her to come get the coke and the guns. And then he would have to listen to her tell him that Alabama was going to be ranked number one or two this year, depending on where Florida State fell.

"What have we got here?"

He turned around.

The question had been posed by a guy with a northern accent who stood like a cop, legs apart, shoulders relaxed. He had a sidekick, another cop, a little younger, with a Glock in hand.

Police issued, it seemed.

The sidekick said, "Looks like we've got a guy with a bunch of guns and some coke in his trunk."

The older guy said, "At least he's put on some pants."

4:04 P.M.

"HOLSTER THE SIDE ARM," JOE TOLD LINCOLN PERRY.

Joe had heard decent things about Detective Jeffrey Tolliver of Birmingham, Alabama, already from the DEA, and the surveillance video had proven beyond question that he hadn't killed anyone today. But more important, Tolliver hadn't packed up his shit and headed home once they kicked him loose from the holding cell. Joe had an idea that he was going to like the reason why.

"How long you been out of that cell?" he asked.

"Less than an hour."

"And you're here nosing around the car. Why?"

There was a little spark in the other man's eyes that Joe liked an awful lot when Tolliver said, "A woman was gut shot in an alley and left to die. They never charged me, never searched me or my room or my car, and never asked me why I was here or what I was doing. The fact that I was locked up until the second shift came on—which consists solely of the chief's wife—leads me to believe that the locals aren't all that good at the detecting business."

"So you came back here to work," Joe said, which was exactly what he'd have done in Tolliver's shoes.

Or shoe, as it were.

Tolliver nodded. "It's been made clear that my help isn't wanted, but it seems like they could use it."

Joe said, "Okay. Here's what I'd like to suggest. You close that trunk before we compromise the scene any more than already has been done, which would take some real effort."

Tolliver closed the trunk with his elbow.

"We've got a surveillance video that will clear you completely, if they're still talking about charges," Joe said. "But we've also got a few questions. We came down here from Ohio to serve a warrant on the guy who did shoot the girl. What we've been told is that you think she stole your car. But this isn't your car."

Tolliver told him about the shaved tumblers, his theory about Antonio going to get a cup of coffee at the wrong place at the wrong time. He ended with, "Nora probably saw the Mustang on my key, thought she had the right ride, and ended up making the last mistake of her life."

"The first cop who was on scene. What did you think of him?"

"Paulson?" He didn't look impressed. "Young. Built like a radio antennae. Real jittery."

"Jittery because he's young, or jittery because he was scared?"

"Both, I guess." Tolliver cocked his head and studied Joe through the falling snow. "Why're you asking?"

Joe blew on his hands to warm them and then said, "Why don't we talk in the car. Our car. We'll drive, you ride, we'll talk."

"Where are we going?"

"I've got three possible addresses in the mountains for a guy named Double Simpson, who may have been waiting to inherit a stolen Mustang from his sister this morning."

"I can pin that down for you. Millar Road near the falls. Second trailer on the right. I heard he's a small-time pimp, wannabe big-time pusher. Runs his own sister. And mother."

Joe winced. "Terrific. I was cautioned that the mother was the type who'd come out shooting if she saw a strange car pulling into the drive. You good to ride along with us? I'd like you to, and we can't stand here in the snow chatting. Got to move."

"You're acting like a guy who knows more than he's saying."

"I am," Joe said. "One reason is up there." He pointed at the gunmetal sky that was spitting snow. "And the other reason is that to my understanding the same police who managed to confuse a white cop from Alabama for a black gangbanger from Cleveland and neglected to review security cameras that were sitting right on top of the damned crime scene are due back in town any minute. At which point, I suspect my chance to get out of here without their escort diminishes dramatically. And based on the surveillance videos I saw, I do not want to be escorted into the hills by those boys. But we need to hear what you've got to say, Detective. Now, you want to ride along, or you want to stick here, or go on home and take a shower and get some sleep? I won't fault you that, with the day you've had."

"I'll go with you," Tolliver said, and Joe smiled.

He liked this guy just fine.

The debate about who was going to drive began before they even reached the rented Malibu. Tolliver said he should, because he knew the area. Joe wanted to drive because he held rank in the situation, out of state or not. He was the man with the warrant and the instructions from the DEA. Lincoln Perry, on the other hand, wanted the wheel because of the weather and his supposed skill in such conditions.

"It's coming down hard and only going to get worse," Perry said. "My father was an ambulance driver in Cleveland. I learned how to handle snow and ice. I'm not letting some southerner who probably gets gun-shy at the first flurry drive me off a mountain, and based on the way you rode the brake on the way up here, Joe, we'll take six hours to get six miles."

"Wouldn't have gotten here at all, if I'd been reckless."

"Christ," Tolliver said. "Give him the keys, if it'll shut him up."

Joe didn't love that. He hated to ride; the passenger seat always gave him an uneasy feeling. But he did want to talk to Tolliver while they traveled, and he couldn't take notes and drive at the same time.

He tossed Perry the keys. "Just don't pull a Barney Oldfield on us, now."

"Who's that?" Perry and Tolliver asked in unison.

Joe sighed.

Kids.

By the time they were ten miles out of town, two things were clear. Jeffrey Tolliver was a good cop plagued by a god-awful taste in women, and this storm was serious business.

The flakes fell from the sky the way only a hard rain should, more thundershower than snowstorm, and the accumulation rate was staggering. They passed only one home-brew utility truck, which consisted of an old guy sitting on the open tailgate, spreading sand and salt from five-gallon buckets. The roads were mostly empty, all the locals hunkering down to wait it out. That was about the only good thing that could be said of their conditions. The weather was bad, the road worse. They just kept climbing, winding up, up, up into the snow-covered mountains that suddenly looked as if they belonged to the Rockies, not north Georgia. Perry had turned the radio on and the announcer seemed in disbelief as he read the latest report.

"The National Weather Service is predicting an expected twenty inches in the Cleveland and Rome area, with heavier accumulations locally. Now, the same paper in my hand says that the all-time record is twelve inches, so that should speak for itself. Stay off the roads tonight."

Perry clicked off the radio. "It occurs to me that it might not have been a bad idea to let one of the locals know where we are going, no matter how dim-witted they seem to be. If we end up running into trouble with Double—Lord, did I really just say that?—if we end up having problems up here, it'll be a while before anyone can get to us."

"We'll be fine," Joe said.

"That's what the Donner Party told each other."

A gust of wind buffeted the car.

The Malibu fishtailed, but Perry steered it into the skid and kept his foot off the brake and the car corrected. Still, Joe had grabbed the armrest and moved his own foot toward an imaginary brake like a jumpy driver's ed instructor.

He should have insisted on driving.

"You just keep your eyes on the road, and let the Donners fend for themselves," he said, but he was regretting the rush out of town now, himself. The rush had been planted by that seed of distrust the DEA had shared, unwilling to tell him what cops in Georgia were dirty, but just that they suspected some of them were. Between that and the way the locals had handled the scene the only person with a badge he trusted down here was, ironically, the one who'd just been kicked loose from a cell.

No, there was more than that.

It was also the idea that Antonio Childers was close at hand. They'd come all this way and into this storm for the singular purpose of picking Childers up with their existing warrant, but what they had now—that surveillance tape of the shooting—was something that had eluded Joe for too long. Courtroom gold. Evidence that would not just put Childers in prison, but keep him there.

If he was still alive.

From the back, Tolliver cleared his throat. He clearly had too much pride to stick his head between the front seats like a dog. Joe was beginning to wish he'd given Tolliver the wheel. Perry had a lead foot and too much confidence.

"Listen," Tolliver said, "since we're all in this together, why don't you tell me a little bit more about this Antonio Childers. Are you thinking he's your bad guy, or a hostage?"

"Both," Perry said.

"Maybe both," Joe corrected. "Surveillance footage shows him coming and going fast, but if our local source was right, he came and went with Nora Simpson's brother. All the interesting dynamics of that family relationship aside, we're starting to believe that Double Simpson might not have been pleased to see his sister murdered."

"If nothing else, she was an earner for him," Tolliver agreed. "So you're telling me that we are heading into a potential hostage rescue wherein we're looking for a murderer and revenge-seeking sadist. Plus no one knows where we are and we've got three guns to our names. Let's hope we don't run into any Wampas."

Perry said, "I'll take three guns over a nervous Tauntaun."

Joe said, "Were those local Indian tribes or something? Or some sort of Civil War thing? I don't know the history of this part of the country that well."

Perry turned to exchange a shocked stare with Tolliver.

Tolliver shook his head in disbelief. "He hasn't seen *Star Wars?*"

Before they could push that dialogue further, the wind rose to a howl and the Malibu shuddered and shivered, the back tires sliding again.

Perry dropped the speed.

"Why don't you watch the road instead of thinking about *Star Trek,*" Joe said.

"*Wars.* Star *Wars.*"

"They're different?" Joe asked, and he was legitimately surprised to learn this, thinking that it explained a lot of confusion over the years.

Headlights rose behind them.

Joe was hoping for a plow, but the headlights were set too low for that. And coming on too fast.

"Son of a bitch," Perry said. "This asshole is really going to try to pass me, in this weather?"

"Then let him," Joe said, and right then the vehicle behind them turned on its police flashers, painting the white landscape with red and blue light.

"You've got to be shitting me," Perry said as he eased to a stop. There was no shoulder left to pull onto, only snowbanks, so he just stopped in the road.

"Just get your badge out," Joe said, but the police car behind them didn't stop, it just passed by. For an instant, they were side by side with it in the whirling white snow and fading gray day. It was still light enough to read the logo on the car's door panel.

Helen Police Department.

Then the car was by and the flashing lights went off. The driver had just turned them on to goose the Malibu out of his way. The driver was keeping up a hurrying speed, like he had places to get and people to see, weather be damned.

"Seems like we're outside of Helen's jurisdiction," Perry said.

"I'll tell you something else," Tolliver said from the backseat. "That giant stick behind the wheel was Paulson. He's the kid who stuck his gun in my face in the alley this morning. Didn't it seem like he was in a bigger rush to get up the mountain than we are?"

Perry looked at Tolliver, then at Joe. "Follow him?"

They both nodded.

The wind rose in the same proportion as the road, both of them crawling steadily higher. Perry was driving faster than Joe would have liked, but he had to do it to keep the Helen police car in sight.

"Any idea where we are?" he asked Tolliver.

"Not sure, but I'd say we're in the park."

"What park?"

"Unicoi State Park, which is inside the Chattahoochee National Forest, which is where Anna Ruby Falls is located." He looked out the window. "I would say pay attention to your surroundings, but everything is white."

"We didn't pass through any gate," Perry said.

"There aren't any gates. You just drive in."

Brake lights came on ahead of them.

The Helen police car was pulling to a stop.

"Drive past," Joe instructed.

His hand had crept to the butt of his gun.

As they drove by, the Malibu's headlights pinned two vehicles in the relentless snow. The Helen cruiser and a Ford pickup that was idling, the engine running to keep the heater going, probably. It was covered with snow, but the hood was warm enough to have left melted streaks across it that showed traces of the paint.

"Black, not blue," Joe said, disappointed. "Has a roof rack of lights, too. That's not the one from the surveillance video."

"I was told that Double Simpson drives a new black Ford," Tolliver said. "That one fits the bill."

"So what do you want to do?" Perry asked as he drove around a curve and the road plummeted down, the other vehicles falling out of sight in the mirrors. "Go back in the car, or go back on foot? If it's just Paulson and Simpson sitting there, with no sign of the blue truck, we're going to have to explain—"

His words faltered as the Malibu caught black ice and slid, the car drifting sideways as if the steering wheel was an unimportant thing. Perry spun it and slammed on the brake. Neither effort made any impact. They turned in a near 360, the spinning headlights illuminating snow-laden limbs, and then there was a muffled thump and a jarring impact as the back of the car smacked into a snow-covered bank. Perry slammed the gearshift into first and hit the gas.

The tires spun without catching.

"Kill those headlights," Joe said. "Kill it all, actually."

Perry shut off the lights and the engine.

The stillness was eerie, no sounds save the wind and the whisper of falling snow on the glass.

"I guess that answers your question," Tolliver said from the backseat. "We'll be going back on foot."

"For the record," Joe said, "Barney Oldfield was a race car driver who couldn't hold a curve. Maybe you'll remember him now."

He popped open his door and had to push hard to keep the wind from slamming it shut on him. Somewhere in the distance was a crashing, thundering sound that had to be the roar of the falls that Tolliver mentioned. In this weather it wouldn't be long before that water would ice into spikes and daggers. Cleveland, Georgia, had gotten confused with Cleveland, Ohio, today. He thought about the dumb-shit remark he'd made that morning to Luisa, the DEA agent, about how they wouldn't be troubled by the snow.

If only she could see them now.

Tolliver had found a flashlight in the back of the car. Perry had packed a go-bag, which seemed unnecessary at the time, but now that the car had spun out in the middle of nowhere, Joe was grateful for the supplies.

He was climbing out of the car when a moaning sound made him stop half in and half out of the car. For a moment, he thought it was the wind, low and mournful as it whistled through the trees. But then it returned, and while the wind might be able to moan, it was not able to cry out for help.

"That's behind us," Tolliver said.

He was already out of the car, standing nearly knee-deep in a drift, and had his gun in one hand and flashlight in the other. Perry got out carefully, taking care not to make any noise. The cry came again, and it might have been mistaken for the howl of a wounded animal if not for that single word it formed.

Help.

Tolliver handed Perry the flashlight and moved toward the sound without speaking. Joe followed, motioning at Tolliver to separate, and Tolliver nodded and moved laterally without hesitation, putting distance between them while Perry hung back, ready to provide covering fire. In this triangular formation they moved slowly through the snow. The wind gusted and a pine bow shed its weight, dumping fresh, cold powder across Joe's neck and shoulders, some of it sliding under his shirt and melting in a chilled slick along his spine.

The voice came again, crying for help, but it was weaker now, fading.

Joe was just about to say they might have gone in the wrong direction, that Tolliver had been mistaken about where the voice was coming from, when they crested a ridgeline and saw the man hanging by his arm from the tree.

Five steps farther, and Joe recognized him.

Antonio Childers was handcuffed to a low-hanging pine limb. His face was a mask of battered flesh and blood, and he wasn't dangling from the branch because he'd been hung too high for his feet to reach the ground.

He was dangling from it because his legs were broken.

Tolliver whispered, "What'd they do to him?"

"Whatever they wanted," Perry said.

Joe looked out into the wind-whipped snow and the gathering darkness and said, "Let's get him out of the tree and the hell out of here in a hurry. Before whoever hung him up there comes back."

He tossed Tolliver the handcuff keys. Tolliver caught them with one hand, tucked the Glock into the back of his pants, and went to free Antonio.

Perry said, "They kept him alive for a reason. They're not done with him."

Joe was about to concur when he heard a sound that made him look over his shoulder. Nothing in sight, but he wasn't sure how much that mattered. Thomas "Double" Simpson had grown up on these mountains.

Perry went to help Tolliver carry Antonio back toward the car. When they were close enough, Joe looked at the man's battered face and said, "You're a long way from Eddy Road, Antonio. Happy to see a familiar face?"

Childers, who'd once promised to kill Joe and all those dear to him, whimpered like a child.

Begging for help.

"Don't worry," Joe said. "We've come to take you home to Mansfield."

There was a snapping sound in the woods, and Joe whirled again.

Still nothing visible.

The roar of the falls in the distance had seemed to quiet, and the temperature was dropping fast. The blackness of night was rising even faster. The moon fought through the clouds, casting eerie white light on the snow. He'd never wanted to get away from a place more than this one.

"We're going to need shelter," Joe said.

He was trying to remember old survival priorities. First aid was priority number one, but the only member of the group who was hurt was Antonio, and there wasn't anybody in the group who was qualified to set broken legs. So let Antonio suffer a little longer, and move on down the list.

Shelter was next.

"Let's go back to the car, dig it free, and get the hell out of here," Tolliver said. "I don't want to sit and wait. Let the locals handle Double Simpson."

Nobody contested that advice.

Tolliver and Perry dragged Antonio through the snow, his bleeding, broken legs leaving a trail.

They'd made it halfway back to the car when headlights lit up the snow behind them.

6:13 P.M.

JEFFREY FROZE IN THE GLARE OF THE LIGHTS.

He glanced over his shoulder. The lights were high beam, casting everything behind them in shadow, but he could still make out exactly what he was expecting to see.

The black truck, and a figure holding a sawed-off shotgun.

Not Paulson, because Paulson was the circumference if not the height of a flag pole. This guy was solidly built, shorter, and had a hell of a lot more confidence about the weapon in his hand.

Had to be Double Simpson.

"Leave the black fella with me and I'll let you walk off this mountain," Simpson called out.

Pritchard, who came across as pretty cerebral for a Cleveland cop, asked, "Or we don't drop him and then what?"

Double slapped the short muzzle of the shotgun against his palm. The smacking sound echoed in the snowy silence.

Pritchard said, "Seems like we have no choice." His tone was convincing, but Jeffrey gathered the guy was like every guy on the Birmingham force, which meant two things. He was a consummate liar and he was never, ever going to let some thug tell him what to do.

Double said, "I'll give you sixty seconds to get back to your car and get the hell out of here."

Jeffrey let Antonio drop, which meant Perry had no choice but to do the same, and also meant that everyone had their hands free now.

Pritchard got it.

And gave Jeffrey a nod, moving toward the car, which was on his right. Jeffrey inched left, which was away from the car and toward a thick stand of trees twenty feet away.

Pritchard told Double, "You can have him. Just let us know where the body is when the thaw comes."

"What?" Antonio, who'd been content to play dead while they dragged his two-hundred-pound ass through the forest, was suddenly coherent. "No, man. You can't do that to me. This cracker's gonna—"

"Sorry about your luck," Pritchard said, and he kept making his way in the thick snow toward the car.

Perry seemed to be itching to make a stand, but he finally got with the program when Jeffrey moved left, following their lead. He understood that the plan wasn't to get to the car and go. The plan was to get out of the range of the shotgun because no matter what Double said, none of them were stupid enough to believe he was going to let them walk off this mountain.

"Please," Antonio begged. "Come on, man. You can't—"

Pritchard slipped around the side of the car.

Jeffrey darted into the woods. He heard a gun blast as he dove to the ground, the air cracking like lightning from the sky.

Perry oofed as he landed beside Jeffrey. He didn't move for a few seconds, and he wondered if the kid had been hit, but then Perry whispered, "Is Joe clear?"

He knelt on the lee side of a large oak, checking for Pritchard.

The moon gave off just enough light to make out shapes, but only if you knew what you were looking for. Pritchard was behind the Malibu's engine block, gun drawn. No eye contact was needed. Pritchard was doing his job and he expected everyone else to be doing theirs.

Perry said, "We need to surround this asshole. That's a double-barrel shotgun. He's already wasted one round. That leaves one shot left against three people. I like those odds."

"The shotgun's been modified," Jeffrey said, because young guys in small towns hack up their guns the same way they hack up their cars. "That second round couldn't hit a brick in a bucket, but we don't know what else he's got on him."

As if to illustrate the problem, a handgun was fired.

The bullet snicked into the trunk of the oak, about four inches above Jeffrey's head.

Perry hugged the ground again.

So did Jeffrey.

The snow was so deep and so wet that he had trouble pushing himself back up. He sneaked a look at the black truck. Double still held the shotgun, but he also now had a handgun. Nine millimeter by the shape of it. The magazine hung way down like an extra set of balls. He'd modified the stack so that he could double the ammo.

Perry had seen the extended magazine, too. "That ain't good."

Jeffrey said, "And Paulson's out there, too."

"Probably backing him up."

"Paulson's not so easy with a gun. If he's backing up Double, it's from behind. Way behind."

"I'll remember to watch my six," Perry said. "You go up the hill, I'll go to Double's rear. Joe's got the third corner of the triangle."

Those were good odds, because trying to sneak behind Double, maybe facing Paulson along the way, was clearly the more dangerous path.

He told the kid, "Wrong way around," and took off, heading away from the hill, parallel to Double and his truck. It wasn't the plan Perry had favored, but Jeffrey trusted he would move quickly to get into position.

Quietly, Jeffrey walked a wide circle around Double's truck, trying to slip behind him. He kept an eye peeled for Paulson, but he had a gut feeling that Paulson would piss himself before he took a stand. Two against three was more like one against three, and Jeffrey liked the odds of the three who were highly trained law enforcement officers.

Then again, maybe the playing field was evened out by the deep snow. His breath started to come in pants as he picked up his feet from thirty-inch drifts. He and Perry were around the same age. Jeffrey was probably in better shape, then again, he always assumed he was the guy in better shape. But Perry was probably more accustomed to moving in snow. Then again, Perry had said he was more accustomed to driving in snow too and look how that had ended.

There were too many *then agains* in this mix, and if any one of them went wrong, it was going to be a fucking bloodbath.

If they were lucky, they would get to their opposite ends of the triangle about the same time. Then it was just a matter of making Double listen to logic. Having three Glocks pointed at your head could make even the stupidest man see reason. The problem was, maybe Double was too smart to be stupid. The thug seemed to realize a move was being made. He turned off the lights on his truck and everything went black. Jeffrey felt his eyes squint in protest, but he kept them open, tracking Double as the man crouched down low, pulled the hood up over his head and somehow disappeared into the shadows.

He felt his heart thumping inside his throat.

Their bad situation had turned worse.

His gun was frozen in his ice block of a hand. He couldn't see Perry. He could barely make out the Malibu stuck in a snowdrift, let alone pick out Pritchard's location.

There was nothing to do but stick with the plan.

He kept moving toward Double's last known rear, making good time until he tripped over a fallen tree. He tried not to groan as he fell flat into the snow. Cold, sleety water went up his nose and mouth.

Over by the Malibu, Pritchard called, "Hey, Double. Let's talk about our options."

He was trying to locate Double, but their target wasn't stupid enough to let him.

Jeffrey closed his eyes and listened for the crunch of snow that indicated a man was walking toward him. All he heard was the soft pat of snow hitting snow, overlaid with the tinkling sound of water freezing in the falls.

He pushed himself up.

He flexed his hands, swapping his Glock back and forth, because he knew that if he had to pull the trigger, it would take functioning fingers.

The snow gripped his legs like a child trying to play a game. The weight was enormous. His lungs were heaving by the time he forced himself into a clearing. He guessed he was maybe twenty feet to the rear of the black truck. The question now was, Were they hunting Double or was Double hunting them?

A gunshot rang out.

He dove behind a tree, realizing too late that the shot had come downrange. He spat a mouthful of snow onto the ground, wondering why in the hell he kept opening his mouth every time he fell into the snow.

He listened for another shot, some indication there was gunplay. He didn't think Pritchard had pulled the trigger. He was too cool under pressure. Perry might have, but then again, Double could've been doing the same thing they were trying to do, only he'd sneaked up behind the Malibu.

The shot could've ended up in Pritchard's head.

He shook off the image.

Snow flew out of his hair. It was coming down hard and steady. He flexed his hands again. When he stood up it felt like the cold was pushing him back down. Still, he trudged on, edging toward the rear of Double's truck.

Paulson yipped like a dog.

He was behind the truck, holding on to the tailgate as he crouched down in the snow.

Jeffrey's cold hands had no problem pressing the muzzle of his Glock to Paulson's head. The kid was so thin that he could feel the bumps in his skull.

"Don't move."

Paulson flinched, giving another yip. He tried to cover his head with his hands. There was a rattling sound. In the faint moonlight, Jeffrey could see that Paulson was handcuffed to the hinge of the tailgate.

"Please, help me."

He put his hand over the kid's mouth, because he'd almost screamed the words. He waited until Paulson nodded before taking his hand away. Paulson was in uniform, but his gun was gone. So was his baton and mace.

"What happened?" he whispered.

"He killed Nora." Paulson's voice cracked on the girl's name. "I saw it on the security video, and I was going to arrest him, but he—"

He could guess the rest.

A guy like Paulson would need a tank to go up against Double, and even then, he would've bet against the beanpole.

He still had the handcuff key that Pritchard had thrown at him. He gave it to Paulson and whispered, "Get back to your car. Radio for help. Not your chief, but the DEA, the GBI, the FBI, the fucking EPA—anybody you can get on the wire. Do you understand?"

Paulson, wide-eyed, could only nod.

He didn't trust the terror in the young man's eyes. "I swear to God, Paulson, if you leave us up here on this mountain to die, I'll find you and put a bullet in your head. Do you understand?"

Paulson nodded in earnest this time.

His hands shook as he fumbled with the handcuff key.

Jeffrey didn't stick around to help him. Instead, he crept toward the cab of the truck. The wheels were the waffled semitrailer variety. The cab was high off the ground, almost to his waist. Double had left the door open. He swung around, Glock drawn, ready to pull the trigger on anybody inside the truck.

Empty.

Snow covered the driver's seat.

Double had left the keys in the ignition, which gave him a couple of options. He could turn the headlights back on, which meant he could see, but it would also signal that he was standing at the truck in case Double wanted to shoot him.

Or he could jump into the truck and drive.

Option two seemed likely to yield the biggest surprise. Double wouldn't be expecting to have his own truck used against him, and the big wheels would cut through the snow a hell of a lot easier than exhausted legs.

He used the back of his sleeve to knock the fresh snow off the windshield. His sleeve got soaked in the process, but he was pretty sure that it wasn't possible to get any colder than he already was. He moved the Glock to the front of his jeans and climbed into the truck. He put his hand on the key but didn't turn it. He stared ahead at the dark expanse. Snow had already started to accumulate on the windshield again. He squinted at the Malibu. Had Pritchard seen him get into the truck? Was Perry out there somewhere tracking his movements?

He rested his other hand on the knob to turn on the lights. He turned the key, pulled the knob, and the truck roared to life. The lights came on and he saw several different things at the same time that took about a second too late for his brain to figure out.

Number one was that Antonio Childers had managed to drag his sorry ass and two broken legs into the path directly in front of the truck.

Number two was that Pritchard was no longer behind the Malibu. He was no longer anywhere that could be seen.

Number three was that Perry had managed somehow to sneak up on Double.

The scene was almost like something out of a Wile E. Coyote cartoon. Perry, frozen in the headlights, was standing behind Double with the flashlight raised in the air, ready to bring down the butt on the thug's head.

Not just a flashlight.

A police-issue Maglite.

Twelve-inch aluminum shaft with four D-cell batteries and enough weight behind it to stop a horse.

Perry didn't know that Paulson was neutralized, and he wanted to take out Double without making a sound.

Which Perry did.

It was like somebody hit play on a paused movie. Perry's raised hand got unstuck, and he smashed the flashlight down, and Double fell hard into the snow.

"Christ."

He jumped and his hand went to his gun.

But it was Pritchard who'd said the word. So much for Perry's triangle. Pritchard had taken it upon himself to sneak up on the truck, too.

"I think I'll keep this kid," Pritchard muttered. "Paulson?"

"Scampered off like a giraffe with its tail between his legs."

"I thought that might be the case. I saw you give him the key to the cuffs." Pritchard looked around the truck. "Any reason you don't have the heat running?"

He turned on the heater but got out of the truck. "I'll go see if Paulson's still around. That cruiser looked like it had snow tires."

Pritchard smiled at the monster wheels. "I think even I can get this thing down the mountain."

He ignored the "I" because he wasn't about to get into a dick-measuring contest about who was going to drive.

Perry had already lifted Double, throwing him onto his back like a sack of flour. If the kid wanted to show off, Jeffrey wasn't going to stop him. He headed toward Antonio Childers. The hostage/fugitive hadn't gotten the memo that the struggle was over and the good guys had won. Or maybe he'd realized that the good guys winning didn't necessarily mean he'd get a happy ending. Even as Jeffrey approached, the guy was still pulling himself on his elbows, dragging his way toward the trees like he could make a getaway.

Antonio saw Jeffrey and quickly gave up the struggle.

"Please help me."

He glanced back over his shoulder. If Double was a sack of flour, Antonio was a sack of sheet metal. No way he was going to blow out his back for this murdering asshole. Besides, now that Antonio wasn't a hostage anymore, he was again a fugitive. He could wait in the snow while Perry cuffed Double in the back of the pickup.

"Bigger fish to fry," he said, heading toward the road. "Stay here."

"Fucksakes," Antonio said. "Where am I going to go?"

Jeffrey chuckled at his own joke as he walked through the thick snow. Then he stopped chuckling because his adrenaline was ebbing and the cold was rushing back in. His shoes felt frozen to his feet. The legs of his jeans had turned into concrete. His shins ached. His thighs ached. His balls ached. Why in God's name would somebody actually choose to live in a place where this kind of cold was a seasonal regularity?

He ran his fingers through his wet hair.

Tiny shards of ice came off in his hands.

Paulson was behind the wheel of his cruiser. He reminded Jeffrey of a praying mantis as he leaned down and tried to crank the engine. The engine did not reward the effort. They were going to have to abandon the cruiser with the Malibu if there was any hope of making it back to what passed for civilization.

He knocked on the window and made a rolling motion with his hand.

Paulson leaned down and started pumping the crank. The window squeaked against the frozen rubber gasket. Snow fell into the car.

"I got the GBI on the horn. They said to stay put, but I figger I should go down the mountain, bring them back up here so they know how to find you."

"I think we're better off if we all go down in Double's truck."

"There's an injured man?" Paulson's voice went up a few octaves. "I think we'll need air rescue."

He looked up at the sky, which was basically like looking into the business end of a saltshaker. Suddenly, Paulson wanted to be the hero.

Or did he?

Jeffrey's eyes slid over the backseat of the cruiser and he spotted two black duffel bags bulging with bricks of cocaine, a cardboard box filled with handguns, and two large stacks of cash in ClingWrap.

He looked back at Paulson.

Paulson had his gun pointed at Jeffrey's chest.

"Back up."

He sighed.

His gut had told him a long time ago that this idiot was going to be a problem. "You could've just said that you confiscated everything from Double to take back into evidence."

"Shit," Paulson mumbled, realizing his mistake. "Too late now."

Jeffrey thought of his Glock tucked snuggly down the front of his jeans.

Paulson thought of it, too, reaching over and grabbing the gun. The muzzle was so cold that it took some of the skin with it.

"What now?" he asked. "I mean past stealing Double's guns and drugs and money?"

Paulson snickered. "Mister, do you think Double's smart enough to set up a Yankee as the contact for his supply?"

He wondered if he was going to be killed by a guy who called him "mister."

"I didn't kill Nora," Paulson said.

"I know you didn't."

"That guy, Antonio, he's the one you want for murder." Paulson waved his gun. "But don't go thinking I don't know how to get rid of somebody who gets in my way."

He saw that his earlier guess about what went down in the alleyway was wrong.

New version of what happened.

Paulson had been in the parking lot that morning, too. It made sense because he'd arrived on the scene so quickly, playing Deputy Fife until Chief DuPree showed up. Probably, Paulson was waiting in his blue truck so he could do the meet with Antonio, get the coke and guns, then be on his merry way. Only Antonio had needed some coffee and his car had been jacked while he was in the Linderhof. Paulson had either seen the whole thing or rolled up just as Antonio realized that his car was gone.

"Nora went into the alley," he said. "You picked up Antonio in the parking lot and followed. Antonio shot her and then what?"

"This ain't no *Batman* movie, mister. I don't got to explain myself."

He cocked his head, wondering why Perry and Pritchard weren't looking for him. "Double was supposed to meet Nora in the alley so he could take the car to the chop shop. He saw you and Antonio standing over his dead sister and decided to kidnap the man who was responsible." He remembered a detail. "Only, Double's not so single-minded that he doesn't take the bulk of the coke with him, which is how you ended up here on this mountain."

Paulson climbed out of the car. "I woulda got away with it except for those meddling kids." The gun stayed on him as Paulson tried in vain to straighten his utility belt. "Oh, wait. I'm the meddling kid, and I am getting away with it."

He'd underestimated Paulson's abilities.

Or maybe motivations.

The guy hadn't seemed eager to kill another man in response to the cold-blooded murder of a girl, but he sure as shit seemed eager to murder a man over some coke, guns, and money.

"Turn around," Paulson said. "Start walking."

He did. It was slow going. The snow was piled up past his knees. He couldn't see the truck, but he could hear the engine. He hoped to God that Pritchard was as smart as he looked, and Perry was as cunning as he seemed, and they'd both figured out that something was not right. Though, considering his recent streak of bad luck, the two cops were probably warming themselves inside the truck, Perry explaining to Pritchard that Hoth is the sixth planet in some star system while Pritchard tried not to strangle him.

Not that Paulson was driving Jeffrey toward the truck.

The engine noise was actually fading.

"Where are we going?" he asked. "Doesn't seem wise to go deeper into the forest."

"Shut up."

He wasn't planning on shutting up, but then he felt the gun press into his head, and knew that Paulson had a habit of leaving his finger on the trigger, so he did.

Paulson said, "I don't want to shoot you."

The refrain echoed from the alleyway this morning, but out in the dark, cold woods, he realized that Paulson didn't have to shoot him to kill him.

"You just gonna leave me out here to die? Let's talk this out, Paulson. Those two cops back there ain't dummies. They're gonna figure this out."

"I'm betting they don't."

Then Paulson stumbled. His utility belt clattered.

The gun banged into Jeffrey's skull.

"DuPree ain't figured it out," Paulson said, "and I've been selling coke outta my squad car for years." Paulson stumbled again. "Stupid tourists come up here thinking they're gonna have some fun. They go to the waterfall, take a couple'a three pictures, then head back into town and ask what the fuck do we do next."

The waterfall.

He realized that the rush of water he'd heard when he first got out of the Malibu had slowed to a trickle.

"Through here," Paulson said.

He turned into a clearing and they were at the falls. Or what was the falls when the temperature wasn't in the polar region. He heard a weird noise and realized it was coming from the surface layer of the water. It kept freezing, cracking, then freezing again. The sound was like a squeaky basement door slowly opening in every single horror movie ever filmed.

There were no trees overhead, just an open, snowy sky with moonlight streaking down onto the frozen water. He'd read the brochure back at the hotel. Anna Ruby Falls was actually two waterfalls that were created by Curtis Creek and York Creek. The Curtis side dropped one hundred fifty-three feet. The York side fifty feet. They joined at the base of the falls to form Smith Creek. Jeffrey craned his neck to look over the side. Smith Creek was starting to freeze, a thin skein of ice making its way toward the falls. If you didn't want to shoot a man, but you wanted to kill him, this was the place to do it.

Paulson said, "Move."

He did, but only so that his toes were about eighteen inches from the edge of the falls. Again, he craned his neck to look over. They were on the Curtis side. One hundred fifty-three feet, most of it ice. What were the odds that he could survive the fall? Better than his odds of turning around, grabbing the gun out of Paulson's hands and beating the shit out of him?

Paulson said, "You wanna jump or you wanna be pushed?"

He riffled through his options. Paulson was a man who kept his finger on the trigger. Grab the gun and he would squeeze.

"You're gonna have to push me."

Paulson jammed his gun between Jeffrey's shoulder blades.

He didn't move.

Paulson jammed him again.

He still didn't move.

The math was against Paulson. He was taller, sure, but he was roughly one part bone and the other part gristle. Stuff like muscle and tendon had yet to develop.

"Come on, you're doing this on purpose," Paulson said.

"I need you to shove me harder than that."

Paulson used his free hand to push Jeffrey's shoulder, which torqued, but his feet stayed firmly planted.

"Jesus."

Paulson sounded exasperated.

He heard him jam his gun back into his holster.

Then two hands pressed flat to Jeffrey's back.

That's when he darted right and Paulson fell forward.

The plan was to catch the guy before he went over the side, but Jeffrey didn't count on his hands being frozen, his arms moving like they were in quicksand, his legs refusing to budge or Paulson, frankly, being so skinny that the only part of him that he was able to grab was the utility belt around his narrow waist.

Two fingers slipped inside the belt, which was actually a belt on top of a belt. The sixty pounds of equipment that a cop had to wear was so heavy that first you had to put an underbelt through the loops on your pants, then you attached two metal hooks that held the outer belt with all the equipment. When worn correctly, the belt system worked great when you were chasing bad guys. Not so much when you were teetering on the edge of a frozen waterfall.

"Help."

Paulson mouthed the word more than said it.

Jeffery leaned back, trying to dig in his feet. Paulson's belt slipped up to his armpits. He squealed. His gun clattered down the frozen falls. His arms windmilled.

"Don't struggle." Jeffery reached his other hand toward the belt and managed to loop in three fingers. "Stop struggling."

Paulson's mouth moved. He was praying. He kept flailing his arms. Jeffrey groaned. His fingers were going to snap in two. The muscles in his arms were like tightened wires. His shoulders were burning. Cold air stabbed his lungs.

"Listen to me," he told Paulson, using the same calming voice he'd used in the alleyway this morning. "Slowly, I want you to put one of your hands on mine. Then try to climb your way back toward—"

"Help," Paulson cried out. The bank of the creek was starting to give way. One of his feet slipped.

"Don't panic," he coaxed as panic filled every single cell in his body. "Just—"

He felt someone grab him from behind.

Pritchard.

Who held him in a bear hug.

Jeffery reached out for Paulson's belt, but it was too late. The ground fell out from underneath Paulson's feet. Jeffrey struggled to hold on to the belt as gravity took over. It all happened in slow motion, like the cold was trying to freeze them in place.

Paulson's narrow shoulders rolled.

The belt slid up higher, over the arms, past the head, then finally past the hands. Like watching a magician pass a hula hoop over his floating assistant.

Ice cracked beneath Paulson. Water poured out. Paulson screamed and groaned, then pitched down into the creek below. He must've been like a pine needle hitting the water straight on. There was barely a splash.

Time sped back up to normal.

Jeffrey fell against Pritchard, the belt still in his hands. Perry fell back, too. He held on to the belt as tightly as Jeffrey.

None of them had been able to save Paulson.

They all three got down on their knees and peered over the side.

The skein of ice had broken apart.

Paulson was floating on the top of the water. His hands were still over his head. His legs were splayed. He was trapped somewhere between a snow angel and a crucifixion.

Pritchard stood up and brushed the snow off his pants.

Perry was still staring at the river, even though Paulson was now out of sight.

Nobody spoke.

Paulson had been a piece of shit, but they'd all wanted him in a cell, not being dredged out of the creek whenever the ice thawed.

Jeffrey coughed. He'd swallowed more damn snow. Why did he keep opening his mouth when he fell?

"What now?" Perry said.

"I guess we deal with what we've got left," Pritchard said.

And Jeffrey nodded.

There was nothing they could do for Paulson except tell the coroner where to find the body. Double would have to be put in a cell. Antonio Childers, on a plane—once his broken legs were set at the hospital.

"One good thing about the snow," Perry said as he turned from the water. "The trail back is clear enough."

Jeffrey took one last look at the frozen falls. He shivered from the bitter cold. His fingers ached. His arms ached. His balls still ached.

He smiled.

The last part was easily fixable.

Nora hadn't been the only woman at the bar last night. There was another girl he'd talked to—tall, brunette, not so smart, but smart didn't really matter. She'd said that she was heading out of town this afternoon, but nobody in their right mind had headed anywhere this afternoon. Maybe no one would be leaving tomorrow, or the next day, or maybe for the rest of the week. If he was going to be trapped in this alpine version of hell, the least he could do was make sure he had a warm body to wile away the hours with.

He turned around and headed toward the truck.

Perry was right about the trail being clear. Even with the snow falling in waves, walking back the way he'd come was a hell of a lot easier than forging new ground.

Which seemed the story of his life.

At least so far.

CHARLAINE HARRIS AND ANDREW GROSS

THIS TEAM MAY BE THE EPITOME OF EVERYTHING WE STRIVE FOR with an anthology. Andy and Charlaine are nothing alike. Charlaine is a Mississippi girl, who cut her teeth on mysteries before making a name for herself with vampires. Andy is a born and bred New Yorker, who started off writing with James Patterson before forging a career of his own with what he calls "suburban thrillers." Their characters are likewise utterly different. Andy's Ty Hauck is a rough and gritty detective hailing from the land of the wealthy in Greenwich, Connecticut, while Charlaine's Harper Connelly is a young woman who, after being struck by lightning, is able to locate dead bodies, then visualize their last moments.

But it was all these differences that made everything click.

The idea for the story came from Andy. He'd taken a trip to Alexandria, Egypt, a city literally built on the bones of other ancient civilizations. Once learning of Harper's ability to communicate with the dead, he knew the story had to be set there. Charlaine was a bit dubious at first, but together they adapted both their characters, and individual styles, into a superb tale. Their only problem came with their personal generosity, each trying to give the other's character more page time.

But they found the right balance.

So let's—

Dig Here.

DIG HERE

THE WOMAN IN THE PALE BLUE HEADSCARF CAME OUT TO MEET him. She was around forty, attractive, in Western clothes, other than the blue hijab. "You're the American? Mr. Hauck?"

"I am," Ty Hauck said, standing up to meet her. He'd been in the outside waiting room of Sikka Hadid police station for an hour, and he'd been getting restless.

They shook hands.

"I'm Inspector Honsi, but everyone calls me Nabila. We're all a little rushed today. Some bigwigs are in town. Come on back."

Nabila took him into a large room crammed with rows of desks. It looked similar to a hundred other detective bullpens Hauck had seen in the States, down to the Siemens computers. Men in open shirts, jackets off. The temperature in the eighties, but the electric fans made the room comfortable.

"Welcome to Alexandria," Nabila said, pointing him to her desk. "First time here?"

"It is."

It didn't escape Hauck's notice that Nabila was the only female detective in the room.

"It's everyone's first time in Alexandria these days. Since the Arab Spring, Egypt has kind of been on lockdown to the world. There's a cruise ship in the port. First one in two years. We used to get two a week." They sat at Nabila's desk, which was crowded with folders and computer print-outs. "Now all tourists want to do is go to Cairo, see the Nile and the pyramids for a day, and then get out as fast as they can. May I offer you some tea?"

"No, thanks. I had some at the hotel. Mind if I take off my jacket?" He didn't want to offend Inspector Honsi by breaking local protocol.

"Of course not. It's not as hot here as everyone expects, since we're on the coast, but it's definitely a warm day. And I'm sure you are probably used to air-conditioning. Where are you from in the States?"

"Greenwich," he replied. "It's in Connecticut. Near New York."

"I know where Connecticut is," she said.

Inspector Honsi was pretty, her dark hair streaked with traces of blond highlights pulled back beneath her headscarf, one of a hundred mixes of the old and the modern he'd seen here in just a day. She had smooth, coffee-colored skin, and sharp, dark almond-shaped eyes. He didn't know if the glances the male detectives sent their way were because Nabila was pretty, or because they wanted to be sure an American minded his manners around an Egyptian woman.

"You've studied American geography?" he said, smiling.

She laughed. "I spent two years studying criminology in D.C. American University. I became a basketball fan there. And I fell in love with hockey. The Capitals. Imagine, an Egyptian. Here, you're lucky to get enough ice to put in your drink. Mr. Hauck, did I understand correctly that you're a police inspector?"

"I was." For twenty years, he'd been a detective both in New York City, and in Greenwich, where he'd been head of Violent Crime. "Now I'm a partner in a private security firm. And please call me Ty." He took out his wallet and slid his card across the desk.

"Talon," she noted. "Offices in Greenwich, New York, London, and Dubai. Sounds like a lot of employees?"

"It's a good size. We do a lot of forensic stuff in finance, IT. Some field protection work as well."

"And you are here to look into the disappearance of Stephanie Winters. I'm told you have some connection to the family?"

"Not personally," he explained. "My boss told me to come. Ms. Winters's father is a client of Talon."

"Talon must have a lot of clout," she said. "I was told by Chief Inspector Farnoush to make myself available to you and share what we know. Your boss talked to my boss, so to speak. The men upstairs. And here we are. Did you travel here from the States?"

"I happened to be in Tel Aviv on a money-laundering investigation. Fake antiquities out of Syria. The money was going somewhere in Connecticut. By the way, I was told there was another American consultant coming in?"

"Later today," the inspector said. She opened a drawer, pulled out a thick file, and slipped on her glasses. Pretty stylish. Fendi or Prada or some Italian brand. She opened the folder and her manner changed.

She looked defensive.

"I've been in your seat many times. Enough to know no one loves people looking over your shoulder," he said.

"You'll see we are pretty thorough. Not quite the third-world police investigators you expect."

Yes, definitely defensive.

She snapped the file shut and slid it near Hauck on the desk. "This is all we know. Ms. Winters was an intern at the Alexandria National Museum. I understand she was receiving her master's in archaeology at Columbia University."

"That's about as much as I know too."

He paged through the file. Photos. Evidence forms. Interview transcripts. Depositions. Much like they had in the States. Most of the documents were in English. He assumed this had been done for the benefit of Stephanie Winters's family.

Clipped to the front of the file was Stephanie Winters's ID photo from the museum. She wasn't beautiful, but she was attractive. Straight blond hair. Wide eyes. A strong and confident smile. She looked eager and ready to go.

And smart.

Hauck's managing partner, Tom Foley, had told him that Stephanie was top of her class. A young woman who'd had every reason to be pleased with her life.

Then she'd vanished.

The Winters family had resources and contacts. They'd pulled every string they had with the Egyptian government and the U.S. State Department.

And came up empty.

"She went missing when?" he asked.

"Two months ago." Nabila didn't have to look at the file to know. "The parents are divorced, as you know, but they've both been here several times. I understand their frustration. She was last seen in an Internet café on Mustafa Kamel Street. I'm told she had some interest in a young man who works there. A Croat. She was, by all accounts, an excellent student and a committed worker. According to Doctor Razi at the museum, they were doing work in satellite cartography. Do you know what that is?"

"You're talking to someone who barely got through eighth-grade earth science," he said with a smile.

"Electromagnetic cartography can map out formations of ruins that are still underground. All Egypt is built on layers and layers of such ruins. Greek. Hellenistic. Roman. Ottoman. Dig anywhere, we say here, you will find something."

"You might say we cops believe that sounds true for anywhere," he said.

"The world over. It is true. But here we are sitting atop buried civilizations. A graveyard of history. Watch your step, you may trip over Cleopatra's chariot wheel. I am kidding, of course. Anyway, we checked, regarding the girl. We don't have street cameras here, the way you have in the United States and London. But we interviewed everyone. Her roommates, her colleagues. We went through her apartment and office. We checked for hairs and DNA. We exhausted all our leads. Nothing."

"No chance she just ran off with someone?"

He had to ask, though it didn't seem likely.

"Without word? At work, Stephanie never missed a day. She and her parents would speak several times a week. And she was in constant contact with her brother and her sister on her WhatsApp account. They were all anxious, as you might imagine, a young American woman here in Egypt. Attractive. And Jewish, too, I was told."

"I was going to mention that," he said. "I don't know what the climate for that kind of hatred is, here. I know in Cairo—"

"In Cairo the temperature is even higher, as we say. For what is going on in the world. In the second and third century, Alexandria had the largest Jewish population in the world." She shrugged. "Even now, we have a reputation as a tolerant, multicultural city. There is still a small Jewish population here. But in today's world, violence can happen anywhere."

He had seen the aftermath of hatred more times than he cared to remember. "You're right. May I take a good look at this file in a room here?"

"You can keep it. I've made copies for both of you." Nabila glanced at the clock on the wall. "I already e-mailed one to your colleague, who is due to arrive soon."

"I've never met him," he admitted. "I was only asked to make sure things went smoothly for this guy. My boss told me he could be pretty unconventional. I assume he's a forensic guy?"

"Not a guy," the inspector said with surprise. "A woman. Were you not briefed?"

"Obviously not. It all happened pretty quickly. I was just asked to get down here as fast as I could, and get up to speed when I landed in Alexandria."

"Then I think you are in for a surprise," the inspector said. She smiled openly. "This young lady was sent by the Winters family, not by the police. I think you'll find she has an interesting specialty."

"And what is that?"

Nabila Honsi rose and slipped her purse over her shoulder.

"Apparently, she can speak to the dead."

•◆•

THE LUFTHANSA FLIGHT FROM FRANKFURT TO ALEXANDRIA PULLED up to the gate at Borg El Arab International Airport an hour late. Hauck was used to delays, used to waiting, but the drive from Alexandria out to the airport had been longer than he expected and he was ready for the plane to taxi up.

He watched men in light-colored business suits and open shirts, carrying val pacs and briefcases, who looked like they might well be in commercial fields like oil, textiles, or import/export, exit from the first-class compartment.

They were almost all native Egyptians.

Trailing behind them were two young Americans, perhaps in their twenties. The pale woman was wearing yoga pants and a denim jacket over her tank top. Her short dark hair stood up in spikes, though he wondered if that was deliberate or a result of hours on the plane. The man was in battered jeans and a cut-off UNC sweatshirt, and he wheeled a cheap carry-on suitcase behind him.

He looked past them, waiting for his colleague to emerge.

Every woman he'd met who claimed to deal with the occult had either been overly made up and glitzy, or of the gauze skirt and sandals type.

Nearly always middle-aged.

The two young Americans stepped up to Nabila Honsi, who held a sign reading HARPER CONNELLY.

"I'm Harper," the woman said. She looked first at Nabila, next at Hauck, as if she were recording them mentally.

"See, Harper, I told you they'd be meeting us," the man said. He had dark hair, too, and his face was scarred with the evidence of long-ago acne.

They grew up poor, Hauck thought.

"I thought you'd be at baggage claim," the young woman said.

"You've been sent by the Winterses?" Hauck said, unable to conceal his surprise.

It didn't seem to bother her. "Mrs. Winter. This is Tolliver Lang. My brother. And manager."

"Your manager?" Hauck said, meeting Nabila's surprised gaze.

They'd both noticed the different last names.

Was this woman married? He'd noticed no rings.

Nabila jumped into the conversational gap. "I'm Inspector Honsi of the Alexandria police. I worked on Stephanie Winters's case. And this is

Ty Hauck. He's from the Talon Company in the States. The Winters family asked Mr. Hauck to join us while you are here."

"Ms. Winters's father asked me to come along," Hauck added. "I've just flown in myself earlier today, from Tel Aviv. You came in from the States?"

"The longest flight we've ever been on," Tolliver said, stretching. His southern accent seemed more marked than his sister's. "A whole lot longer than from Los Angeles to Atlanta. That was our previous record."

"You're a lawyer?" Harper asked Hauck.

"Ex-policeman. But I have no official capacity in Egypt. I'm only here to make sure it's easy for you to do your job."

"We don't need help," she said evenly. "We're quite good at what we do."

"I'm sure you are. I meant help with the local bureaucracy," he explained.

He gave a slight wink to Nabila. This young woman was beyond cocky.

"I know it's been a long trip," Nabila said. "I'll take you to the hotel. We put you at the Four Seasons at the Winterses' request. I'm pretty sure you'll find it comfortable. You're staying there as well, Ty?"

"I am."

"Good. I'm sure you'll all want to shower and relax a few hours."

"Definitely a shower," Harper said, after a glance at her brother. "But we slept on the plane. I'd like to get started." She pulled her knapsack over her shoulder as if to say, *Let's go*.

Nabila looked at her with surprise. "Right away?"

They started to walk to the exit.

"Yes, we have to be in Charlotte on Friday," Tolliver said, falling in beside his sister.

Hauck said, "You have another case there?"

Harper nodded. "It's not an urgent one, like this. It's pretty certain the man was killed in an accident somewhere along his route home. He's missing, and so is his car. Plus he'd been drinking. But his family wants the body."

She spoke quite calmly, and he began to wonder what it would take to rattle her.

"You can converse with the dead?" he asked, after they climbed into a white, unmarked Ford sedan.

Tolliver and Harper sat in back. Hauck in front next to Nabila, who drove.

"Not converse," Harper said, gazing out the window at the Egyptian landscape. "Their bones call to me, so I can locate them. Then I see how they died."

"And what is it like?"

"What's what like?"

"How they communicate with you," he asked.

"They want to be found. I feel the hum. Kind of like the wind blowing through a wind harp, if you know what I mean. It can be overwhelming." She looked bleak, and much older, for a long moment. "This place is distracting. There are so many dead crowded here. Layers and layers and layers." She fell silent and closed her eyes. After a moment, she began to move in tiny ways, her head tilting, hand twitching.

Creepy as hell.

He didn't know if she was a fraud or, just remotely possible, the real thing. But she was good at selling herself. He glanced over at Nabila, but she was concentrating on the road, keeping her face neutral.

"Harper's solved many important cases," Tolliver said matter-of-factly. "Just last week we were in Knoxville, Tennessee, working with the police there."

"You found a body?"

"We didn't find one there. It was a bad case. A kid. But we had a strong case in Atlanta before that. Harper found a woman who'd been missing for ten years."

"And how did your sister get this power?" he asked, unable to keep the hint of skepticism from his voice.

Harper's eyes flew open.

They looked a fainter shade of gray than they had earlier.

"Lightning," she said.

"Really?" He couldn't hide the incredulity in his voice.

"I was struck by lightning as a teenager. I lived. Most people don't. Tolliver started my heart again." She took her brother's hand. "Since then

I've had this power. It was hard to deal with." She smiled, but it wasn't a happy smile. "I can see you don't believe me, Mr. Hauck. Many of the police are skeptical. At least, at first."

"I'm no longer a policeman," he said. "But I'll be interested to see you at work."

Which was the truth.

"Don't be so Western, Ty," Nabila chided him.

He figured she was trying to lighten the atmosphere.

"In Alexandria, we are all in a partnership with the dead. As I said, our city is built on prior civilizations. The dead are alive to us here. In America, when you dig, you strike oil or water. Here, we find two-thousand-year-old ruins. Even the person who founded this city, Alexander the Great—the legend is buried here somewhere. Though no one knows where."

"I thought he died in Asia? Babylon?" he said. "And no one knows for sure what killed him, right?"

"Alexander died in Babylon. Maybe he was murdered, poisoned. Maybe he had blood poisoning. Or an illness. His bones were on the way to Macedon when they were hijacked. Perhaps the hijacker was his leading general, Ptolemy, who stayed and founded the five-hundred-year Greek dynasty here. Of all the places Alexander conquered, he loved Alexandria the best. He wasn't the last Greek to rule Egypt. You know of Cleopatra? She was Greek. The last of the Greeks, as it turned out."

"Maybe Ms. Connelly will find Alexander's bones while she's here."

He turned back to her with a smile.

"Maybe I will," Harper said, staring at an open truck with an ox in the cargo bay. "If there are any bones left."

"Do we get to see any pyramids?" Tolliver asked, eyes wide, scanning out the window. But it was only a highway, with the same rushing traffic you would find anywhere in the world, the scenery relentlessly modern.

"No, there are no pyramids here. Those are farther west. Along the Nile. Out of Cairo." Nabila sounded as though she'd said the same thing many times, and it never made her happy.

He could understand her viewpoint.

Pyramids equaled tourist dollars.

Tolliver appeared disappointed and glanced at his sister, as if that was the reason they had taken this gig.

She patted his shoulder.

They were sure a bit touchy for brother and sister.

•◆•

THE FOUR SEASONS ALEXANDRIA WAS AS STRIKING AS ANY FOUR Seasons, and it was situated right on the harbor. Considering that Harper and Tolliver dressed inexpensively and in general gave such an air of having been brought up rough, Hauck expected the two to be more impressed with the gleaming lobby.

But if they were, they covered it up well.

An hour later the four met again in front of the concierge desk. Hauck could tell that Harper had had a shower. Her hair looked much calmer, her face fresher. Even Tolliver looked more relaxed. This time, Nabila drove them through the souk sector of the city, down a crowded market street. The brother and sister got a taste of the foreign there with the limbs of livestock hanging from hooks in the open air, stalls of fruits, melons, and dates.

"We have also a specialized market area called the Attarine, where you can find many antiques," Nabila told the newcomers. .

The two looked at her blankly, so she got to business.

"We are heading to three places. The Coolnet café, the last place Ms. Winters was seen. Then her apartment. After that, I'll take you to the museum. I've arranged a time to speak with Professor Razi, Ms. Winters's superior."

"Her bones are not going to be in her apartment, or the Internet café, or the museum," Tolliver said.

"We're also conducting a conventional investigation," Hauck said, beginning to be pissed off by the two Americans' indifference to the rest of the world, including anyone else's experience.

He addressed his next remarks exclusively to Nabila.

"So what do we know about her? Did she like to party? What about any relationships with men? Ex-boyfriends? Anyone who might have a motive for harming her. Was she active in local affairs? Did she go to the synagogue, have contacts there?"

"By all accounts she was like any of the students who come here," Nabila said. "Alexandria is a place that sets your spirits free. She went to some parties. Still, Dr. Omar Razi, her superior at the museum, says she was a serious girl and a dedicated worker. Her primary focus was the discovery of ruins of past civilizations."

The car wound down a narrow street.

"In fact, we are entering the old Roman part of the city. There is not much left from that era. What the Ottomans or earthquakes did not destroy, time has built over."

Hauck pointed at a tall column amid a walled-in field of white marble rubble. "What's that?"

"That is Pompey's Pillar," Nabila said. She pulled to a stop and turned to face all her guests. "You know the famous Roman consul? The Romans appointed him as Cleopatra's guardian. She hated him though. He fought Caesar and Anthony. When he was on the run from Caesar, he was assassinated here. His bones are rumored to be under the pillar, but in fact—"

"He's not," Harper interrupted.

"Not what?" asked Hauck.

"There's no one buried there. No bones, no bone powder."

"In fact, as I was about to say," Nabila said stiffly, turning to her, "you are right. It is now known that Pompey is not in fact buried inside the tomb. And also—"

"It's not even a pillar," Harper said. "It's round. Pillars have sides. It's a column."

"Yes," Nabila said, with a glance at Hauck, "that's what I was about to say. It's a column. Everything about it is incorrect."

Hauck grunted to himself. He was not a big fan of what he'd seen so far of the Winterses' consultant. Psychic bone detector?

"Maybe it's time for an Egyptian coffee," Nabila said, and started driving again. The car pulled up at a street-side café. "We are here. This is the Internet café that Ms. Winters patronized."

Inside, the place looked a lot like an American Internet café. Lots of young people sitting at the small tables, using their laptops. The click of the keys was louder than the conversation.

They all ordered coffees.

Tolliver and Harper, who hadn't eaten, ordered a Greek salad and chicken in yogurt sauce.

"Be careful of the salad," Nabila warned. "You never know how things are washed."

"No, we are good, madame," the waiter said. "You see, tourist menu."

"Very well," she said. "Still."

A tall, lanky young man of about twenty-five with a mop of light brown hair wearing a soccer T-shirt and jeans approached the table.

"You may sit," the inspector said, waving him to a seat. "This is Ivo Karilic. He works here. In the evenings, correct?"

"Night manager," the youth said in a hard-to-read European accent.

"Ivo was Stephanie's friend. He was here the night she disappeared," Nabila told Hauck. She turned to Ivo. "These people were hired by her family to look into her whereabouts. Ivo, why don't you tell them what you told me?"

The man tossed back his wavy hair. He was good looking and knew it. "We were friends. Stephanie was a good girl. Everyone liked her. Lots of students hang out here. We give them free Internet and some music they know. I saw her that night. She was with her usual friends. Tina, one of her roommates. Francois, I think she worked with. But I heard he's left and gone back to France."

"Something we should follow up on?" Hauck asked Nabila.

"We did, of course. As it turns out, Francois remained here until two a.m. that night. He never left."

"He was fond of her," the restaurant manager said. "We all were."

"How fond?" Tolliver seemed to have decided to join the conversation. His sister was distracted again, tiny twitches in her face and hands indicating she was listening to other voices.

Or other bones.

Ivo looked at Tolliver doubtfully. "You are a little young to be with the police."

"True," Hauck said. "But it's a fair question, so answer."

"Like I told Inspector Honsi," Ivo said. "Once, back in the fall, we hooked up. Stephanie and I."

"Only once?" Hauck added a lot of skepticism into his voice.

"One night. She wasn't into the whole boyfriend scene. She was only going to be here a year. She was serious about her work. Nothing interfered. That's the truth."

"When's the last time you and she hooked up?"

"Only that once, months ago. I have a girlfriend now. Flora. She's Albanian. She works nights with me."

"Anyone else have an interest in Ms. Winters?" Hauck asked. "An interest she didn't return?"

"You must be kidding. Everyone is all over everyone here. They're students. They're here for a while, in Egypt, and then they go. It's the song of the Nile."

Hauck said, "We're not on the Nile."

"Someone's song then. All the foreigners here are temporary, like me."

The salad and chicken came.

"You guys want a beer?" Ivo asked, returning to his professional manner.

"No thanks," Harper said.

"I'll have one," Tolliver said.

"If I were you, I'd watch the lettuce," Nabila warned him again. "Maybe stay with the tomatoes and cheese."

"Don't worry," he said, lifting his fork. "I have a cast-iron stomach."

Nabila shook her head, with a glance toward Hauck. "What is it you say? Famous last words."

•◆•

THEY WALKED A FEW MINUTES BEFORE GETTING BACK IN THE CAR. From their position on a natural rise in the land, Nabila pointed out the location on the water where the famous Pharos Lighthouse had stood on a promontory, maybe an island? Hauck couldn't tell.

"It was one of the wonders of the ancient world," she said. "But it was destroyed by an earthquake in 1480. "It isn't far from the location of our famous library."

"Can we please get going?" Harper said, after taking in the view. "You said we could go to where she lived?"

"Of course," the inspector said. "This way back to the car."

Harper turned and had taken a couple of steps before she stopped. Her face completely pale.

Tolliver leaped to her side.

She buckled.

Hauck grabbed her by the arm to keep her from hitting the ground. Her face had turned pasty, her eyes glazed and rolled up in her head.

"The food?" Nabila said anxiously. "I warned you."

"No." Harper shook her head as Hauck helped her back into a standing position. "It's not the food. This is different. Something's here."

"Meaning what?" Hauck pressed, helping her over to a parked car where she could lean.

Tolliver said, "Dead people."

"Stephanie?" Nabila asked. "Here?"

"No." Harper laid a hand to her head and blew out her cheeks. "Ten times stronger. A hundred times. Something's here. I don't think I've ever felt anything like it. It's as if my legs just gave out." Her color was still bad. She took a couple of deep breaths, trying to regain her composure. Then she pointed away from the harbor, blinking, a look of determination creeping on her face. "What's over there?"

"It's just a park," Hauck said, looking at a fenced-in area behind a short wall against a hillside with a small stone building in the center.

"No, it's not a park," replied Nabila. "It's Kom el Shoqafa. It means Mound of Shards. The catacombs."

"Catacombs?"

"From the first century AD. It was a burial place for ancient Romans." They all stared at her. "There were once hundreds of bodies discovered there. But they're all a hundred feet underground."

Harper still looked ashen and weak. She turned to Tolliver. "I've never felt anything that powerful in my life."

"Is Stephanie there?" Tolliver asked.

Hauck could see that the man was a true believer. No doubt his sister was for real.

"Nothing modern. Can you help me? I want to get a little closer."

With Hauck on one arm and Tolliver on the other, they helped Harper walk to the grounds' entrance. A tour bus was parked nearby.

"This is the strongest feeling I've ever felt. There must have been hundreds buried here? Thousands."

"That's right." Nabila regarded her with astonishment. "But you have to know, the bodies are all gone. They excavated this site in levels. There are three levels underground. In each, they found more bodies. But they're all empty now. The bone remains were all moved, years ago, to the museum of archaeology."

Harper gingerly walked over to the site. Struggling against the weakness that seemed to overwhelm her, she slowly seemed to gather herself. Then she just stared at the tomb for a long time.

"You say they dug this out in levels?"

Nabila nodded. "The last one was years ago. A hundred feet deep."

"There are more," Harper said.

"That's impossible. This catacomb is one of our most studied sites. Dozens of archaeologists have been through it."

"They should keep digging."

And Hauck, much to his surprise, found himself agreeing.

•◆•

HARPER SEEMED TO HAVE FULLY RECOVERED BY THE TIME THEY reached Stephanie's apartment. She'd lived in a Western-style building, seven stories high, that stood in contrast to the other structures on the street because it was so new. The honey-colored stone was clean, and there was even a lobby attendant in the modern entrance area. Hauck noticed that the people walking through were all European. This was expat lodging.

And maybe government as well.

"I assume this is pretty expensive housing," he said to Nabila.

She nodded. "There is parking behind and underneath the building with an armed guard at all times. We do our best to make foreigners feel safe here, whether native Egyptians or whomever." She was quite expressionless as she said this, and Hauck could only guess at her feelings. But he found himself thinking that, considering the income disparity between the average Egyptian and the students who could afford to study abroad, having an armed guard watch over the vehicles was simply a wise precaution.

Nabila talked to the doorman in rapid Egyptian. The man then made a phone call and nodded.

"The roommates are home and say we can come up," Nabila said.

"I'm not sure what good my going up there will do." Harper huddled, thin and tense, against her brother. "They're all alive."

Hauck stifled a laugh. "Maybe you should come up because you're Stephanie's age. You might be more tuned into her roommates than I'll be."

Harper's eyes narrowed. She seemed to suspect she was being cozened into the expedition.

"All right," she said grudgingly, and they entered an elevator.

At the third floor they exited into a hall that was clean and wide, but not elaborately decorated. Stephanie's door was to the right at the end of the corridor. In answer to Nabila's knock a short girl with permed red hair swung open the door and stepped back to admit them. Hauck figured she was in her upper twenties, and she was wearing clothes that looked expensive. Could be knockoffs, though, like Nabila's sunglasses. Hauck was no style expert.

"This is Jerri Sanderson," Nabila said, then she pointed to each of her companions and introduced them.

"Come sit down," Jerri said. "Can I get you something to drink?"

They all declined, then took seats in the small common living area.

"Have you found out anything new?" Jerri asked.

"Nothing," Nabila said. "Where is your other roommate?"

"Tina's on her way. She got held up at the university."

"Do you attend there as well?" Hauck asked.

Based on nothing all that tangible, he was not an immediate fan of Jerri Sanderson.

"No. I'm a working girl," Jerri said. An edge of anger had entered her voice. "I'm here as a gofer for an interior designer. He does places for Westerners. So they'll feel . . . *comfortable.*"

The door opened and a tall girl, no more than twenty, hurried inside, dropping a load of books on the dining table.

"Sorry I'm late," she said. "I'm Tina Peek."

She threw herself in a basket chair and looked at them expectantly. After introductions were done—again—Tina said, "I'm sure Stephanie is on a yacht somewhere with one of the millionaires."

Hauck was taken aback. "One of the millionaires?"

Out of the corner of his eye, he noticed Harper sit straight.

Then she rose from her chair and began wandering around the room.

"You know all kinds of rich Egyptians come here to go to the beach," Tina said. "Are you at the Four Seasons? That's prime stomping grounds. But Stephanie was a magnet for that kind of guy." She spread her hands, as if to say, *Go figure.*

Jerri looked away scowling.

"Can you give us a name?" Nabila asked. "And why do you think Stephanie in particular was a magnet? You didn't mention that theory when we were here last time."

"I can't give you a specific name. But there are sheiks and princes and whatnot vacationing here all the time. Stephanie was blond and cute. Just their type."

Hauck noted that Tina was neither of those things.

"She had guys after her all the time. But who did she actually take up with? That loser at the bar."

"Ivo? He says he only hooked up with Stephanie one night," Hauck said.

Tina gave a snort of laughter. "Really?"

Jerri tossed Tina a surprised look. "It may be true. I don't know that Stephanie was meeting up with Ivo every night she went out. I think she was doing something else."

"Why do you think that?" he asked.

In the kitchen area, Harper bent over and picked something up from a tiny space between the stove and the counter.

Jerri and Tina had their backs to her.

"She didn't dress up," Jerri said.

Harper wandered back into the conversation. "What did she wear? If she wasn't dressing up for a date?"

"Washed-out jeans and T-shirts that had gotten stained from the cleaning solvents at the museum," Jerri said.

Tina laughed again. "You're imagining that, Jerri," she said. "Just because she didn't wear a lot of perfume and a skimpy skirt."

This was clearly a dart that hit its target.

Jerri flushed and pressed her lips together.

"Can we look at her room?" Harper said.

"You can, but it's empty. Her family cleared out most of her stuff. Her rental car is still in the parking garage, but they looked through that too. We'll be glad when we can get a new roommate, but no one is exactly panting to live here now," Jerri said.

They took a look anyway.

Blank walls and empty shelves. A few cheap art prints and a tchotchke or two that didn't seem worth carting home.

"What's that?"

Harper pointed to an odd Egyptian statuette on the dresser. It had the body of a man, but the head of a bird with a pointy, curved beak.

"That's Anti," Jerri said. "The Falcon God. I guess he ferried the pharaohs to the afterlife or something. They left it though. Steph was obsessed with it. Anti, Ivo, Razi. She was obsessed with a lot of things."

Hauck looked at Harper, who shook her head in futility. But she looked as though there was something else on her mind. She seemed to be holding something she had found, and he noticed her slip it into her pocket.

When they were back in the car and on their way to their next destination, the museum, he asked, "What did you think of the two roomies?"

He expected to hear Nabila's opinion, and she'd opened her mouth to respond, when Harper cut her off.

"One of them was lying."

"How do you figure?" He was curious about her reasoning.

"Either Jerri was telling the truth and Stephanie was dressed for work, hard work. Or Tina was telling the truth and Stephanie was dressed for a date."

"It has to be an either/or?" he said.

"Both things can't be true. Especially since they don't like each other." Harper was observant, he'd give her that. Of course, if she was a con woman that would be part of the tricks of her trade. "Where were they the night she went missing?"

Nabila said, "Jerri Sanderson said she was out of town until late the next day, and we partially confirmed that with her employer. She was with him until eight at night, and she was there at nine the next morning. In between, who knows? Tina Peek said she was partying until two in the morning, and Stephanie was not in the apartment when she came home."

"They don't like each other, it's true," Nabila went on.

And Hauck noticed that something about the interview, or about the two women, had made Nabila thoughtful, as well.

"By the way, Nabila," he said. "Are either of the girls Jewish? Did they mention connections of Stephanie's through her synagogue?"

Nabila flushed. "The last synagogue in Alexandria is closed. There is nowhere she could have gone."

So much for Alexandria's record of tolerance, Hauck thought, taken aback by the way Nabila had misled him. Had it been simple loyalty to her city that had caused her to paint Alexandria in more flattering colors? Or did the police inspector know something about the case that she hadn't divulged? For the first time, he looked at Nabila Honsi with a feeling of doubt.

The policewoman concentrated solely on her driving, the crowded streets noisy with cars and pedestrians of all sorts. They were close to the harbor again when Nabila pointed to a white stone building with a green lawn in front.

"That's the museum," she said. "I'm going to have to let you out and find a place to park. Obviously, that's quite difficult here."

She'd lost the pleasant tone that had made her sound so agreeable, and Hauck realized that quite possibly that had been a façade. This beautiful inspector had layers he hadn't anticipated.

Like the city they were in.

As they scrambled out of the car and began to walk up the driveway, Hauck saw that Harper was watching after Nabila thoughtfully. Tolliver was looking pale and was sweating.

"What's wrong?" Harper asked her brother, and Hauck saw she was alarmed, maybe more alarmed than the situation warranted.

"I don't know if it's jet lag or the salad I had," Tolliver said. "I feel crappy."

"Do you want to get a cab back to the hotel?" Harper said. "Get in bed?"

"I better do that, or I'm going to be embarrassing to have along," Tolliver said, doing his best to sound jaunty.

Hauck undertook getting the cab, which was awkward since he didn't speak much of the language. But the driver understood "Four Seasons," and Hauck helped Tolliver into the backseat, at the last moment realizing the man needed local currency. He stuffed some in his hand.

"Watch out for her," Tolliver muttered. Then he reached into his pocket and handed Hauck a handful of Werther's Caramels and peppermints. "If she has a spell, give her one of these right away."

Hauck pocketed the candy and rejoined Harper, who was looking distraught.

"He doesn't have any money, he can't pay," she said anxiously.

"I took care of that. And I have candy in case you need it?"

She looked relieved. "He always watches out for me. I have something to give you."

But just then Nabila joined them and he noticed the subject was dropped. They all headed to the office of Dr. Omar Razi.

"I thought it would be bigger," Harper whispered to Hauck, as they crowded into Dr. Razi's office.

It wasn't a large space, but every inch of it was crammed with machinery, and papers and drawings. The walls were lined with open glass shelves crowded with interesting objects. Pots, spearheads, even pieces of bone. He wondered if Harper was vibrating like a tuning fork.

"This is not a huge museum, like your Smithsonian," Dr. Razi said, in crisp English.

Perhaps in his early or midthirties, the man seemed young for his position. He had a thick head of hair and a trimmed mustache and was dressed in a white linen shirt and khaki slacks. Handsome man, by most standards. And to overhear Harper's remark, the guy must be sharp-eared.

"But we are serious about discovering and excavating sites from the past that have remained undiscovered," Dr. Razi added, as he seated himself behind his cluttered desk. The rest of them chose straight-backed chairs that were none too clean.

"And that's what Ms. Winters was working on?" Hauck asked.

"More or less. She was learning the mechanics and analysis of satellite cartography under my tutelage."

"I understand that it can reveal buried sites that aren't apparent to the naked eye," Hauck said.

And Dr. Razi was off and running. Hauck didn't completely comprehend what the doctor was telling him, but he understood that satellite imaging had enabled archaeologists to see features of the landscape from above, features that had been buried hundreds or thousands of years not visible from the ground. There were specific programs to aid archaeologists in mapping these ancient sites and locating buried cities no one had suspected were there.

"I understand there's another circle close to Stonehenge that is much larger," Harper said, completely out of the blue.

"That's right," Dr. Razi said, his face lighting up at having discovered a kindred soul.

He showed every sign of launching into another monologue, but Hauck stopped him before he could hit his stride. "Please tell us about Stephanie."

Razi's face grew somber. "Of course. That's why you are here, and I want to help in any way I can. She was an intelligent young woman, and her death is a great loss. To the program. To us all."

"You're sure she's dead?" Harper said.

They all stared at her, but she showed no signs of being self-conscious.

"Sadly, what other conclusion is there?" Razi said. "Stephanie has been gone so long and has had no contact with her family. She was always on the cell phone to them. I had to speak to her about it more than once.

Work hours, you know. I can't waste the museum's money. History must go on."

"So she was slacking off?" Hauck said.

"I wouldn't say that." Razi seemed uncomfortable. "I don't want to speak ill of her, you understand. She worked hard. But she'd also come to Egypt to sample its life, its sights and sounds, and I suppose that sometimes her job could be boring in comparison with that."

"She was your intern," Harper said quietly.

Razi nodded.

"So you spent a lot of time with Ms. Winters?"

"I suppose I did. She worked in my department."

"And you say she was hard to supervise?" Harper persisted.

Razi obviously didn't like where she was leading. "No. Just a bit careless, perhaps."

"And you made note of that? On her evaluations?" Harper pressed.

Hauck wondered where she was leading.

"No," Razi said, backpedaling. "I didn't want to hurt her career in any way."

"So what did you think she was in Alexandria for? The nightlife, or the research?"

"Both. After all," Razi said, regaining his composure, "Ms. Winters came from a wealthy Jewish family. She was not used to being told what to do."

The fact that Razi had made a point of Stephanie's faith was unsettling.

"That's so strange," Nabila said, joining in for the first time, her dark eyebrows drawn together. "Dr. Razi, I understood that Ms. Winters was close to being an expert in satellite cartography."

He shrugged. "She was good, but she was inclined to be too excitable. History requires patience. There are a lot of false leads. You can't be rushing off to every site just because something is there. The funds are not there to support it."

Hauck leaned forward, his elbows on his knees. "So what is your theory, Dr. Razi? What do you believe happened to her?"

Razi hesitated. "I don't know. But I have assumed that Stephanie had gone into some souk or bar or gotten in a car with someone who tried to force themselves on her. And that she fought back and was killed. Sadly, things happen here. Governments come and go, but there is still a lingering resentment against the West."

"So she was a fighter?" Hauck asked. "In your opinion."

The Egyptologist almost smiled. "Oh, yes. Stephanie was indeed a fighter for what she believed in. And, my word, that girl could argue the leg off a table."

They rose to leave, but instead of stepping toward the door, Harper drifted to the glass shelves. Her thin white hand floated toward a partial skull. Before Dr. Razi could protest, one finger touched the rounded dome.

"That is a woman's skull from Roman times," Razi said. "I will have to ask you not to touch."

"Do you want to know what killed her?" Harper asked.

Her voice was eerily matter-of-fact.

"What?" Razi seemed confused, and he wasn't the only one. Nabila looked taken aback.

The hair was rising on Hauck's neck.

"She got an infection during childbirth," Harper said, her eyes still on the brown bit of skull. "She was twenty-one. The baby lived, at least for a while."

"And now we have to go," Hauck said briskly. "Harper's brother is ill, and we have to go check on him."

●◆●

THEY WALKED BACK TO THE ELEVATOR, DR. RAZI BEHIND THEM AS IF he were herding them out of the museum. The three kept silent until they were outside, amid the noise and bustle of Alexandria.

Nabila spoke first. "You frightened him."

"He shouldn't keep her head in his office," Harper said, "if he didn't want to know the truth behind it. And look."

Dr. Razi was leaving the building too, in a hurry. He hustled over to a car parked near the entrance, a white VW Passant, flicked the automatic lock, and climbed in. Then he drove away from the museum grounds.

"Not sure how I feel about that guy," Harper said.

Hauck nodded. "Amen."

Nabila dropped them off at their hotel, explaining that she had to return to the police station to wrap up a few things before she could leave for the day. Hauck thanked her and told her he'd see her tomorrow. By the time he'd said good-bye, Harper had vanished. Checking on her brother, he assumed. But he was surprised when she stopped him in the lavish lobby, amid the shadow of a pillar.

"Mr. Hauck," she said. "One of the roommates is waiting in the bar. I think she's waiting for you. Listen, come talk to me later. I found something."

And then she was gone.

Hauck moseyed over to the bar to see if it were true.

Tall Tina was trying to look at ease in the upscale lobby bar, but she was not succeeding. The room was designed to look like a posh living room, with plates displayed on shelves, a painting above the fireplace, velvet armchairs, dark wood tables, and the gleam of china and crystal. She looked young and awkward in that setting.

"I didn't think you were ever going to get back," she said as Hauck came to her table. "I've been here for an hour. Drinks here cost a fortune."

"It's a nice place to wait," he said, not about to apologize for being late to an appointment he hadn't made.

"Did you go to the museum?"

She pushed her brown hair behind her ears. She was wearing antique, Egyptian earrings, which seemed out of keeping with her outfit. She appeared edgy.

"I just came from there."

"Talking to Omar?"

"Naturally."

"Stephanie had a good job," Tina said.

"You're using the past tense. You're the one who believed she'd gotten on a yacht with a rich guy?"

"Even if Steph came back today, she wouldn't get that job back," Tina said.

"Did you come here to talk to me?"

He was ready to cut to the chase. It had been a very long day, and he wanted to shower, eat, and go to bed.

And he still had to stop by Harper's room.

"It's nice to talk to an American man, for a change."

"Tina, I'm close to thirty years older than you. What do you really want?"

She bit her lip. "You shouldn't sell yourself short. You're an attractive guy. But I do have a boyfriend. I came to talk to you about something else."

He waited.

"You know Stephanie was Jewish?"

He nodded.

"And you know Jews aren't exactly popular here."

She said it like some kind of inside scoop.

"That's been the case, off and on, for thousands of years," he noted. "This is the Middle East."

"Here's what I wondered. What if Stephanie went to the synagogue that's supposed to be so beautiful, the one that's closed? Elia something. What if she tried to get in? What if the guards caught her?"

"Tina, I don't know what made you imagine that scenario. From what I've heard, Stephanie was hardly observant. Her family certainly isn't. Eliyahu Hanavi would be the last thing on her list of sites to visit in Alexandria."

From the corner of his eye, he noticed a quick movement. He glanced in that direction and caught a glimpse of Stephanie's other roommate, Jerri. When she realized Hauck had seen her, Jerri moved more into his line of sight and drew her hand across her throat. He guessed she was telling him to get rid of Tina.

That was curious.

It didn't take long to accomplish the task. Tina ran out of conversational gambits, then offered to take him to a nightclub.

He declined.

Naomi Blum, who ran the Treasury's antiterrorist desk in D.C., and with whom he was off and on with, would have a chuckle at the thought Tina could tempt him.

"I really want to get to my room," he said.

"I'll say good night, then. Give me a call if you have some free time." She handed him a card with her number written on it.

"For sure."

He watched her leave. A young woman with an agenda. He only wished he knew what it was. Then her roommate, another young woman with her own agenda, threw herself into the same red chair Tina had just vacated. Though Jerri had not been exactly friendly or forthcoming at the apartment, he realized she was smarter and tougher than Tina.

"So here's what you need to know," Jerri said, not wasting time. "The truth is, Stephanie was a good person. And she knew all about that mapping thing she was doing. She was all over it. She loved it. She loved her job. She was trying to think of a way to keep doing it after her internship was over. Jobs in the archaeological world are hard to come by, and she understood that Egyptians would rather hire Egyptians. Government policy and all. She got that."

Jerri paused, and Hauck nodded, just to show he was paying attention. If Tina had been all over the place conversationally, Jerri seemed a laser beam.

"I can't pretend that Steph and I were close friends," she said. "But I do know that she was having some kind of crisis. She was really worried. And it wasn't boyfriend crap that was on her mind. It was something much bigger."

He was an old hand at keeping his reactions private. "Bigger, like artifact smuggling? Or faking antiquities?"

"Bigger, still. She found something."

"Like?"

"You know her area of expertise," Jerri said. "What do *you* think?"

And as quickly as she had started the conversation, Jerri ended it by walking out.

He ordered a bourbon and settled back in his chair to think over what she meant.

His cell phone rang.

"Can you come up to our room, Mr. Hauck?"

Harper sounded upset.

"Tolliver's too sick for me to leave him, and I have to tell you something. It's 709."

"Sure, why not?"

• ◆ •

ON HIS WAY UP IN THE ELEVATOR, HE NOTED THAT THIS SEEMED HIS evening to receive information from young women.

He knocked at Harper's door, and she answered it quickly, waving him in.

"How's your brother?" he asked.

"Not good. He only thought he had a cast-iron stomach. I can't really do much until the worst of it is over, which I hope will be soon." She looked both worried and exasperated and didn't invite him to sit. "Look, I found something at the apartment. I wanted to show you privately." She dug in her jeans pocket and extracted a Kleenex, unfolded it, and handed Hauck a tiny fragment.

"It looks like part of a tooth."

"It's Stephanie's. She's dead," she said in as matter-of-fact a tone as if she was making a bank deposit. "I felt a tiny buzz from it in the apartment. It was between the stove and the refrigerator, not even visible until I leaned down and looked. I don't think she was murdered there. It came to the apartment some other way. Maybe on someone's shoe."

"Surely the Egyptian police searched the place and tested for blood?" He was thinking out loud, and he wasn't too surprised when Harper didn't offer an opinion or comment. "We need to find the rest of the bones. Can you track them with the piece of tooth?"

"You suddenly seem to have a lot more belief in what I do than you did before."

"You've earned it," he said.

"Tooth is not bone, but it turns out it's close enough," she said. "I've never tracked a body that way. But I could try."

He shook his head, placing the wrapped-up tooth fragment in his shirt pocket. "You're quite the surprising gal."

"I am what I am." She shrugged. "But thanks. Now let me get back to Mt. Vesuvius in the bathroom."

"Be my guest."

Back in his room, Hauck spent the rest of the evening studying Nabila's file. Something didn't sit right. Poor Stephanie. He looked over her photo again.

Was she dead?

Jerri said she had found something.

Something big.

You know her area of expertise.

Electromagnetic cartography, he read from the file.

She could find what was under the ground.

Unable to rest, he threw on a jacket and took a taxi back to Stephanie's apartment building.

"You remember me, I represent the family," he said to the man in the lobby. He showed him Nabila's card with a two-hundred-Egyptian-pound note wrapped around it. "I want to check out her car."

"I go on break." The guard looked through a cabinet, taking the card and cash.

He handed Hauck a set of car keys.

"In twenty minutes."

• ◆ •

HAUCK WOVE THROUGH THE ROWS OF CARS TO THE BLUE FIAT Stephanie had leased when she'd arrived in Alexandria. The police had gone over it, Nabila had assured him, but found nothing suspicious. The contents of the car had not been significant, so they'd left them in a shoe box on the front passenger's seat. He took out his cell phone and switched on the flashlight app.

He looked through what was in there.

A grocery list, some notes on a museum exhibit in town, a city map, tourist brochures, and a small date book filled with appointments, sketches, some restaurant comments, and travel notes she had made on side trips to Cairo, Italy, and Croatia.

Nothing entered on the day she disappeared.

He turned on the car and checked the GPS memory for recent destinations.

It had been wiped clean.

Interesting.

Cradling his cell-phone light in his lap, he paged through the date book one more time. There were numbers scattered throughout. Prices, dates, addresses, shopping notes. Things so trivial she likely wouldn't have even bothered to enter them on her phone.

Two of the numbers stood out.

They weren't on the same page. Instead, they were some ten pages apart. One, on March 8, the other back in August. Both written in blue ink, instead of the more prevalent black. The first was an eight-digit number with two letters in front of it.

LO31.200092.

The second similar.

LA29.918739.

He turned the page, pretty sure he knew exactly what these numbers represented, and his heart stopped in his chest. There was a sketch of what looked like two statues, side by side. Each had the body of a man. A measurement to the side read 50´.

Fifty feet tall?

But that wasn't what stopped him.

It was the face.

The two of them side by side.

Anti.

Each had the body of a man and the face of a falcon.

It was a long walk back to his hotel.

A lot of the city was quiet, a few cafés were still open, people playing games or watching soccer on TV.

A few cabs rushed by.

In his room once more, Hauck booted up his laptop and entered the numbers as GPS coordinates, with a period after the first two in each sequence.

And struck gold.

•◆•

THE NEXT MORNING, AROUND 9, NABILA ARRIVED AT THE HOTEL IN her car. Hauck and Harper climbed in. Tolliver was still sleeping, though Harper said he was feeling much better.

The inspector turned to Hauck. "You texted me that you had a new itinerary today?"

He took out his iPhone, which was set to Google Maps. He'd entered the location of the numbers, which he now knew were GPS coordinates.

"It's in Abu Qir."

"Abur Qir? That's west. Maybe forty minutes, depending on traffic. Why do we need to go there?"

"Humor me."

"I don't have the time, Mr. Hauck, to be chasing shadows."

"Just this once?"

She complied, though she was clearly not happy that he chose not to explain. Harper sat in the backseat with the piece of Stephanie's tooth, which he'd returned to her earlier.

Her eyes were closed. She seemed to be taking a nap.

It took nearly twenty minutes to flee the city center. He was tense, and the closer the car drove to the designated site, the more anxious he grew. The landscape was now desertlike and far less populated, though there were settlements from time to time marked in Arabic and English on green road signs. He was all too aware that he was basing this bet simply on some numbers he'd happened on and a hunch. That, and the dubious talent of a woman who'd been struck by lightning.

They turned north a mile or so after they left the city, heading toward the Mediterranean. The landscape became arid and barren, the Sahara creeping right to the sea. Palm trees dotted the road like sentinels. The towns were smaller and poorer, the signage all in Arabic. When they were within half a mile of their destination, Harper took out Stephanie's tooth fragment and held it between her forefinger and thumb.

"What's going on?" Nabila asked.

"Jerri came to meet me when we got back to the hotel yesterday afternoon," he said. "She told me that Stephanie was on the trail of something really big. Razi never mentioned that, did he?"

Nabila turned while driving on the dusty, narrow road. "Not a word."

"She said Stephanie was obsessed with that statue we saw in her room. Anti. The Falcon God." He turned around to face Harper. "Feel anything yet?"

"Nothing."

He prayed this wasn't a wild-goose chase. If so, he'd probably have two Egyptian cops escorting him onto the first plane out of here.

Nabila said, "Feel what?"

"Last night I went back to the apartment and looked through Stephanie's car."

"How did you possibly get in?"

The inspector seemed annoyed.

"I gave them your card."

Nabila's dark eyes flared in anger.

"Plus a two-hundred-Egyptian-pound bill. Anyway, I found this notebook, among her things." He showed her. "No worries. No reason anyone would have thought it suspicious. But it had this sketch of Anti in it, you remember, the man-falcon god. Two Antis, to be exact. They look like statues. And two, separated, not meant for anyone to see together."

Nabila looked confused.

"GPS coordinates."

"And where do you think they lead?" the inspector asked, though as soon as the words were out of her mouth, her eyes widened with understanding of what Hauck meant.

Google Maps announced they had arrived.

"Here," he said.

They were next to a large dirt field. Maybe a farm that had dried up. Few structures were around. A couple of run-down stucco homes, more like shanty houses, outfitted with satellite dishes. And a domed stone building that looked like some kind of local community center. Two men were sitting at a table outside it, reading newspapers.

Nabila stopped the car. "You're saying these statues are somehow connected to these coordinates? Here?"

"Stephanie was an expert in electromagnetic cartography. She could see what was under the ground."

The detective seemed to finally grasp what Hauck was implying. "You're thinking Razi—"

"I don't know what I'm thinking yet. We're just—"

Harper gasped.

"What's going on?" Nabila demanded. "What have you found?"

"Let's get out," he said.

The car's rear door opened and Harper was out, on the move.

"Over here," she called, leading them away from the coordinates.

Her eyes were squeezed shut in concentration. She held the tooth fragment to her forehead, as if to help her mind listen more closely. She continued to walk, almost blindly, leading them into a barren crop field with a large mound of rock on the other side.

"The site's back there," he said, catching up to her.

Harper kept walking, as if following an inner radar. "That may be, but she's here."

Nabila picked up her skirt and tried to keep up with them. "Tell me what's going on?"

"Harper is earning her fee."

It was even hotter here than on the coast, and the sunlight was blinding. There were rocks ahead, and if you looked closely, you might conclude that they were not rocks, but building stones.

Palm trees stood all around.

Harper held out one hand, and Hauck understood he was supposed to take it. She pointed where she wanted to go, eyes still closed, and he led her, not breaking the trance. He started to say something, but she put up her hand and shook her head. The hill of rocks ahead seemed the target. She rounded the mound and stopped.

"There she is."

And he saw it.

A body.

The remains loosely covered by dirt and scattered rocks.

Whoever dumped Stephanie there had surely hoped some animal would make a meal. She'd been stuffed into a naturally formed cavity within the stones, which had then been sealed with smaller rocks. Unless you came around here, to the far side, looking for something, you would never notice.

Nabila stared, stunned.

Then she looked at Hauck. "You're saying Razi killed her?"

"I think Stephanie told him she'd found a promising new site. You heard what he said. She was impulsive, impatient. She always wanted to rush out to anything she found. But not just a site. A major Egyptian tomb, guarded by giant statues, which is what those Anti figures represent. The ferryman to the afterworld. And Egyptian, not Greek. The tomb of someone important."

Nabila nodded, seemingly stunned at the magnitude of Stephanie's discovery. "That would be quite a find."

"And here, near Alexandria. Not on the Nile. She'd discovered it, plotted the coordinates, mapped out what it was. Maybe it was her hope to bring it to the world's attention. Who knows? Maybe Razi wanted the credit for himself as the vaunted director of the program. Maybe he told her not to be looking here and now he would be completely shown up. Maybe she brought him here to finally show it to him."

"What about this tooth?" Harper asked.

"I think Tina told Razi that Stephanie was going to tell her family about what she'd found, and then the government. Razi would be the man who let a Western woman trump him. I'm sure he and Tina were an item. Maybe Tina put a drug in Stephanie's drink, at the apartment after she left the bar, or there was a struggle and then Tina and Razi brought her out here and killed her."

"How?" Nabila asked.

"Tire iron," Harper said. "That's what she's telling me. That's what killed her. It's out here somewhere."

She started walking away from Stephanie's resting place.

Hauck just followed.

"She's looking for the murder weapon?" Nabila said, disbelievingly. "Out here?"

"You're the one who chided me yesterday for thinking so Western. You have to believe."

Harper kept kicking up dust and dirt as if on the scent of something. Fifty yards away, as if she had a divining rod in her head, she stopped at a small clump of dirt in the arid earth. Hauck bent down and swept away loose dirt with his hands.

"There are fragments of her skull on it," Harper said, opening her eyes as if her work was done.

Hauck kept digging.

He removed a rock from the ground and pawed at the earth. Finally he came upon the edge of something promising.

Metal.

"Don't touch it," Nabila said.

"Been doing this twenty years."

He took out a handkerchief.

"I know what I'm doing."

Then he freed the metal from the ground.

A tire iron.

He winked at Harper. "Never doubted you."

"Can we head back to town now?" Harper said. "I really need to see about Tolliver. He might want something to eat by now."

Hauck grinned. "I think we can do just that."

•◆•

THEY WERE ALL GOING HOME IN THE MORNING.

Hauck to D.C. through London. Harper and Tolliver on their return trip through Frankfurt. Their work was done here. Stephanie's body had been found. Razi had been detained by the police. Whether or not there was enough evidence to convict him in a country like Egypt, a place of influence and power and family, who knew? Hopefully, they would find his fingerprints on the tire iron they'd uncovered. And it would be missing from his own car. Nabila promised she would press the case aggressively. Her eyes had definitely been opened in the past two days.

And so had Hauck's.

He'd said his good-byes over plates of spaghetti at the hotel's restaurant. Tolliver wolfed down the food like he hadn't eaten a meal in weeks.

"If you're ever in Greenwich, look me up."

He shook Harper's hand.

"We never seem to get that far north," Tolliver said.

"If you ever need a recommendation"—he laid his card on the table—"you know who to call."

He went upstairs, packed, and made a few calls. He left a message for Naomi he'd return by tomorrow night. Around eleven he came back down for a nightcap and thought he'd take a walk.

Experience the city one last time.

"American bourbon," he told the Egyptian bartender. He pointed. "That Woodford'll be fine."

"Interesting business in Alexandria?" the bartender inquired.

Hauck chuckled and savored a long sip. "You'd never guess."

"Then relax, sir, and enjoy yourself."

He sat back and let his mind drift to what lay ahead. At home he had a lot of choices to make, and Naomi was at the center of most of them. Greenwich or D.C.? As he was finishing his bourbon and thinking of going to bed, he spotted someone through the lobby, leaving the hotel.

Harper.

Alone.

Dressed in her jean jacket and college sweatshirt. It was going on midnight, not safe for a woman to be out alone. Especially a Western woman.

He signed the bill and ran after her.

On the street, she made a right turn toward the harbor with a fifty-yard head start. He followed. The night was bright, the moon exceedingly large. A warm breeze blew in from the Sahara to the south.

A sirocco, he recalled.

Harper kept for the harbor at a good pace, as if she knew precisely where she was going. At this late hour she certainly wasn't catching up on some last-minute souvenir shopping. He wanted to make sure she didn't find any trouble. Stephanie already proved what could happen.

Harper kept walking.

As if drawn, never looking back.

The streets were mostly dark and empty. The open markets shut up, the shops closed. Occasionally a café leaked music.

But Harper continued on her way.

As she neared the water, it began to grow cooler. The wind picked up. There were more hotels, cafés, and modern businesses. The new Alexandria library was out on the point, the previous one, one of the wonders of the ancient world disappeared centuries ago.

Finally she came to land's end at the seawall.

Nothing in front of her but the dark harbor.

She walked along the wall, the Mediterranean quietly lapping against it. Past a hotel and a restaurant, everything dark and quiet at this late hour.

At the end of the harbor, she stopped.

Something seemed to be guiding her.

She held out her arms.

The wind kicked up, brisk and warm, whipping her hair. She stepped closer to the water's edge. For a moment, he was worried she was going to do something crazy. He edged closer, now only about ten feet from her. He didn't want to scare her.

He was about to ask if everything was all right when she spoke.

"He wants to be found now, Mr. Hauck," she said, without ever turning around to acknowledge he was there. "He's ready."

More wind blew her hair. The moon bathed her in an eerie, almost holy kind of light.

"They brought him here, after he died. It was his favorite among all his cities. The city of his dreams. And it became so. He said it would unite the East and West."

"You're speaking of Alexander?"

"He was so young, but he had accomplished so much. There was so much more he wanted to do." She turned around. "I feel it in his bones."

"How?" he asked her.

He wanted clarity.

"I can feel his thoughts at his death. It's perfectly clear."

She halfway smiled.

Now Hauck's blood surged with excitement. "Where, Harper?"

"You know what used to be here, don't you?" She pointed. "The Pharos. The famous lighthouse from ancient times. A beacon to the entire world. That's where he is."

In the moonlight, Harper's skin was eerily white, like alabaster. "He wants to be found now, Mr. Hauck. He said it's time. He's ready. There's a lot of water all around him."

She walked to the edge, so close for a moment he thought one more step and she would fall into the sea.

But then she stood still, the water lapping over the wall, the wind taking her hair, and she pointed, to the earth that had buried so many civilizations, so many worlds.

"Dig here."

LISA JACKSON AND JOHN SANDFORD

ISA WANTED TO USE DETECTIVE REGAN PESCOLI FROM GRIZZLY Falls, Montana, in this story. The character is central to her ongoing To Die series. One of John's most popular characters is Virgil Flowers. He's an agent with the Minnesota Bureau of Criminal Apprehension, but he's also an avid fisherman and sportswriter.

So John had an idea.

Send Virgil on a fishing trip to Montana, Regan Pescoli's home turf, where a crime would draw the two characters together.

Lisa freely admits that John started the story and ran with it. They didn't toss it back and forth, or pit one scene against the other. John wrote the entire draft, then Lisa added scenes, filled in details, and tweaked. She's a huge fan of John's Lucas Davenport series, but she'd never read any of the Virgil Flowers books. To prepare herself, during the months between agreeing to write the story and actually finishing it, she devoured five Virgil Flowers's novels.

Here's another interesting detail.

At the end of Lisa's 2017 novel, *Expecting to Die*, a pregnant Regan Pescoli finally has a baby. But when this short story was written (in 2016), Lisa had no idea of the child's sex, as that was to be determined through a contest her publisher was running. Since this story would be released a few months after *Expecting to Die,* Lisa had to go ahead and make Regan a lactating mother of a newborn, sex unknown.

A final thought.

Lisa loved the way John ended the story. It actually provided her with some great grist as she continues the Regan Pescoli series.

Now it's time to found out just who—

Deserves to Be Dead.

DESERVES TO BE DEAD

IRGIL FLOWERS AND JOHNSON JOHNSON SAT ON THE CABIN'S
narrow board porch, drinking coffee and looking out at the empty
golf course. A fine mist was sweeping down from the mountains
and across the tan grass of the first fairway. The dissected remnants of
three newspapers lay on the table between them. Four fly rods hung tip-
down from a rack on the wall.

Two other fishermen, whom they'd met the day before, wandered
by in rain jackets, aiming in the general direction of the bar, and Johnson
said, "We got like a gallon of hot coffee."

"We'll take some of that," Rich Lang said, the shorter of the two
guys.

He looked soft around the middle with about a week's worth of graying stubble on his face. The two guys took the other chairs on the porch,
and the four of them sat around talking about fish and politics and personal health, as they admired the rain.

The other guy, Dan Cain, said, "Shoulda gone to Colorado."

"Can't afford Colorado," Lang said. "Besides, the fish are bigger
here."

The personal health issue involved Cain, who'd taken a bad fall on a river rock the day before, shredding the skin on his elbows and upper arms. Nothing serious, but painful, and his arms were coated with antiseptic cream and wrapped in gauze.

"Pain in the butt," he admitted.

"That's what happens when us big guys fall," Johnson said to Cain. They were both six six or so, and well over two hundred pounds. "Virgil falls down, it's like dropping a snake. I fall down, and it's like Pluto rammed into the earth."

"Pluto the planet, or Pluto the dog?" Virgil asked.

It went back and forth like that for twenty minutes, Lang and Cain browsing halfheartedly through the abandoned newspapers.

Cain eventually said, "It's looking lighter in the west."

Virgil, Johnson, and Lang said, almost simultaneously, "Bullshit."

Johnson checked his cell phone and a weather app for a radar image of the area.

"We won't get out this afternoon," he said. "It's rain all the way back to Idaho."

"What about tomorrow?" Lang asked.

"Thirty percent chance of rain," Johnson said. "When they say thirty . percent chance of rain, that usually means there's a fifty percent chance."

"We could go into town, find a place that sells books," Virgil said. "Check the grocery store, get something to eat tonight."

"Or find a casino, lose some money in the slots," Johnson said. "Did I ever tell you about the casino up in Ontario? I was up there last month with Donnie Glover, and it was raining like hell."

Johnson launched into a rambling story about a Canadian casino in which the slot machines apparently never paid anything, ever.

The four of them were at WJ Guest Ranch outside of Grizzly Falls, Montana, possibly the smallest dude ranch in the state at seventy acres. Sixty of those were dedicated to a homemade, ramshackle executive golf course. The other ten acres had nine tiny chrome-yellow cabins, a barn with four rentable horses, the equine equivalent of Yugos, the owners' house, a larger cabin with a bar that had six stools, three tables, one satellite TV permanently tuned to a sports channel, and a collection of old books and magazines that smelled of mold. The place had two secret ingredients. Access to a trout stream stuffed with big rainbows and browns, and price. The WJ was cheap.

They were all half listening to Johnson's story when a girl started screaming, her shrill voice rising from the owners' house.

Not screaming in fear. She was out-of-control angry.

Johnson broke off the story to say, "That's Katy."

"Sounds a little pissed," Cain said.

Katy was the oldest of the owners' kids, a skinny blond fifteen-year-old about to start high school. She was in charge of horse rentals and, on sunny days, ran a soda stand on the fifth hole of the golf course. At night, she worked illegally as a part-time bartender. They hadn't had much contact with her, but from what they'd seen, she wasn't a girl you'd want to cross.

"More than a little pissed," Lang said. "Hope she doesn't have a gun."

The angry screaming, peppered with a few choice swearwords, continued, and Jim Waller, the owner, stuck his head out of the bar, then trotted over to his house, holding a piece of cardboard box over his balding head to fend off the rain. Tall and lean, he disappeared into the house, where the shouting got louder.

Two minutes later, the side door exploded open and Katy charged out, heading straight for their cabin. Rain splattered the ground around her, creating puddles, but she didn't seem to notice. A moment later her father ran out behind her, trying and failing to catch her. She climbed up on the porch, looked straight at Johnson, and demanded, "Did you steal my money?"

Jim Waller arrived, shouting. "Katy. Stop it." And to Johnson Johnson and Virgil he said, "I'm sorry, guys."

"I want to know," Katy said, her eyes snapping fire. "Did you?"

"Shut up," her father shouted.

"You shut up," she yelled back.

Johnson Johnson jumped in. "Whoa. Whoa. Why do you think I stole your money?"

"We know everybody else here, and they wouldn't do it, and you look like a crook," she said.

"What?"

"You heard me." Her hair was damp, darkening the blond strands, rain drizzling down her face.

Jim Waller grabbed his daughter's arm and tried to drag her off the porch.

Virgil shouted, "Hey, hey. Everybody stop."

He could see Waller's wife, Ann, and another one of the kids, a girl, peering at them from the screen door of the owners' house.

He was loud enough that everybody stopped for a moment, so he said, to Katy, "Johnson does look like a crook, but check his truck. It's a Cadillac. He's rich. He owns a lumber mill. He doesn't need your money. And I'm a cop."

Johnson turned to Virgil. "Wait a minute, did you say—"

Virgil said to Johnson, "What can I tell you, Johnson?" And to Katy, "What about this money?"

She was still boiling. "My pop money. From selling soda pop all summer. More than six hundred dollars and it's all gone." She was getting mad again, glaring at the men.

"Somebody took it out of her chest of drawers," Jim Waller said.

Then Katy asked Virgil, "What kind of cop are you?"

"I'm an investigator for the Minnesota Bureau of Criminal Apprehension."

"It's like a state version of the FBI," Johnson added.

Katy didn't care. She just seized on the word *cop* and focused on Virgil. "Could you find out who took the money?"

Her father said, "Katy, goddarnit, he's here to fish."

"We're not fishing with this rain," Cain said.

Johnson nodded. "He's right: Why don't we take a look, Virgie? It's something to do."

Damn that Johnson.

They were all looking at him, and Virgil said to Katy, "You know, it's enough money that you should call the local cops."

"That's not gonna help," she said. "The deputy we got out here, he couldn't catch a cow on a golf course. His main job is giving speeding tickets to tourists."

"Let's take a look," Johnson said, as Lang and Cain made their way back to their own cabin.

Katy led Virgil and Johnson back to the house, trailed by her father, who kept saying to Virgil, "We really appreciate this, but you don't have to do it."

Virgil agreed, but shook his head and said, "It's okay."

He asked Katy when she'd last seen the money.

"Day before last. I got ten dollars off the golf course and stuck it in there."

The Wallers had six children, four girls and two boys. Their house, made of two cabins joined together, had three small bedrooms for the six kids, and one shared bathroom for all six. Virgil guessed those rooms and half of a long living area had been one cabin, while the dining room, kitchen, master bedroom, and another bath had probably originally been in another cabin with a common wall.

On their way to Katy's bedroom, Jim Waller explained to his wife that Virgil was a cop. To that she started saying, "Oh, geez," and didn't stop until Virgil was inside the girls' room. The bedroom had two beds, a wooden chair, and a chest of drawers, with a window that looked out the back of the cabin toward a line of trees that hid the trout stream.

Virgil, Johnson, Katy, and her parents all crowded into the bedroom and Katy pointed at the bottom drawer of the chest. It contained a couple of flannel nightgowns, winter wear, some shirts, a couple of belts, and a dozen pairs of socks rolled into balls. Three pairs of white athletic socks had been unrolled. Two pair were lying on top of other clothing in the drawer and one pair was lying on the floor.

"I put the money in a pair of white socks. That's where I always keep it," Katy said. "It's gone. It's mostly in one- and five-dollar bills, so it makes a big lump. I couldn't believe it when it was gone. I checked all the socks, even the black ones."

Virgil dug around in the drawer for a moment, then turned and asked Ann Waller, who was watching from the doorway, "Could you get me a little wad of toilet paper?"

"You find something?" Katy asked.

"Dunno."

He was kneeling by the chest, and a moment later, Ann Waller reached over and handed him the toilet paper. He touched his tongue to it, then dabbed at the side of the drawer.

He asked Katy, "When you were digging around in here, did you cut yourself? Cut your hands?"

She examined her hands, front and back. "No, I didn't. Why?"

He held up the toilet paper. "There're some spots of blood in the drawer, and it's fairly fresh." He then approached the window and saw that it was unlocked. "You lock this?"

"All the time, when it's down. It's always down, unless it's a really hot night, but then, we're always here when it's up, me'n my sister, Liz. The screen's always hooked, though, all the time. It should have been locked."

He pushed the window fully open and checked the nylon screen, which had a hook lock at the bottom. The hook was undone and when he pressed his finger against the screen, he found a slit right along the bottom of it.

"The screen's been cut, to get at the hook," he said.

Jim Waller was astonished. "Son of a bitch. Somebody broke in? That doesn't happen around here."

Virgil said, "You really need to report this."

Jim Waller said, "To who? Katy's right about the deputy. Couldn't you do something?"

"Out of my jurisdiction by about two states," he said. "But I'll tell you what. How about if Jim and Ann come and sit on my porch for a few minutes. And then Katy, separately. To talk. Johnson can wait in the bar."

Back on the cabin porch, Virgil said to the Wallers, "I don't want to embarrass anybody, but with this kind of thing the money is usually taken by somebody in the family. Do you think somebody in the family, maybe one of the kids, might have borrowed it?"

The Wallers looked at each other and then Jim Waller blurted, "No way."

Ann said, "We don't have much money, but we've been harder up than we are now. Katy was saving that money for school clothes and makeup and things. She's getting to be that age. We wouldn't take it." A lean woman with springy blond hair and big eyes, she was nearly a foot shorter than her husband. She looked tough. Tanned, a little weathered, not an ounce of fat on her. She stood in front of him, arms folded under her breasts, faded blue work shirt tucked into equally faded jeans.

"What about one of the other kids?"

They both shook their heads.

"Never," Ann said. "We go to church and the kids never miss Sunday school. Even little Nate knows his bible."

Virgil doubted a three-year-old could quote much out of Proverbs or St. Mark, but kept his opinion to himself. He also did not mention that the church might frown on a fifteen-year-old serving alcohol.

He was told that the four daughters were "good girls" and the only one who'd ever given them any trouble was Katy, the oldest. Liz, Ellie, and Lauren were model children, did well in school, obeyed their parents. As to the boys, eight-year-old Jimmy was "a bit of a handful" but Nate, the baby, near perfect. In fact, that boy had slept through the night at two months and to this day rarely cried.

They talked for a few more minutes, but the Wallers were adamant.

Nobody in the family took the money.

Jim and Ann wanted to stay and listen to Virgil talk with Katy, but Virgil insisted that he speak to their daughter alone, and unhappily they shepherded the rest of their brood inside and closed the door. The girl was still angry as she settled into the chair across from him on the porch, one thin leg bouncing in agitation, rain still drizzling from the sky and gurgling in the leaky gutters.

"Here's where we have the problem, Katy," Virgil said, leaning forward, elbows on his knees. "Somebody cut the screen, which means he or she probably entered the room from outside the house. But you say the window is always locked, and it's not broken, which means somebody from the inside had to unlock the window. Why would somebody cut that screen to push the screen hook out, if he or she could open the window from the inside? It doesn't make any sense. So here's my question, do you know if somebody was in your bedroom, who might have unlocked the window without your knowing it, and who then might have come back some other time and cut the screen to get in? Maybe while you were tending bar last night?"

Her eyes went sideways, a hand went to her throat. "Oh, no." She was slowly shaking her head, almost as if she were trying to convince herself.

"That's probably the person who took it," Virgil said. "Who was it? A friend?"

She didn't say anything for a long time, then, "You can't tell my dad or he'll kill me. I mean it. Besides, nothing happened. But he won't believe it."

"Tell me."

She hesitated, then sighed and looked away.

The night before, she said, the rest of the family had gone into town to shop. A boy who lived up the road had come over and they'd sat in her bedroom to talk.

"Like I said, nothing really happened. We were just hanging out."

She was looking at Virgil directly, nodding, her blond curls bobbing around her face. She seemed earnest.

"I believe you." But he wasn't sure. "Do you want to go talk to this kid?"

She nodded again. "Like I said, nothing happened. He's cute, and we're friendly, but that's all." She must've sensed Virgil's doubts, because she added, "Really. But if he took my money—" Her lips pursed and her eyes narrowed as she considered what she'd do to the thief. "I just want my six hundred dollars back. That's all."

"Okay."

The kid's name was Phillip Weeks, a sixteen-year-old who lived with his father in a mobile home a half mile up the dead-end road that passed the WJ Ranch.

"The place is owned by a rich guy named Drake from Butte, and Phil and his dad are caretakers," she said. "I don't go up there because his father creeps me out. Kinda scares me, ya know? I think he beats up Phil, too. Last year, Phil had these big black eyes and he wouldn't say where he got in a fight, and nobody in school knew of any fight. I think it was his father."

"The old man's name?"

"Bart Weeks." She gave a little shudder.

He hoped she wasn't right, but her instincts were probably dead-on. "Let's go talk to your dad and tell him what we figured out. See what he wants to do."

"Don't mention that Phil was inside. Liz doesn't even know. No one does. No one can. If Mom and Dad found out, they'd freak. So just say that we figured it out."

"I got it."

Inside the house, the older boy was wrapped up with Legos in his bedroom, the baby asleep, and Virgil caught a glimpse of Liz, one of Katy's younger sisters hovering near the doorway, pretending to read a book, but probably eavesdropping. Ann braced herself against a counter that separated the kitchen from the dining area and Jim sat in a recliner angled to an oversized but bubble-faced TV tuned into a muted baseball game. Virgil and Katy explained what they thought happened. Without admitting that Phillip had ever been in Katy's room. The parents bought the story without too many questions, so Virgil didn't have to lie.

"Never liked that guy," Jim Waller said, flipping down the footrest of the recliner and getting to his feet. He eyed his oldest daughter and shook a finger at her, "If I ever see that kid around here . . ." He let the sentence trail off, but by the looks of it, Katy got the message just about the time Johnson showed up.

What Jim and Ann Waller wanted Virgil and Johnson to do was to go up the road and confront Bart Weeks, the father of Phillip.

Virgil said, "I'm not a cop here in Montana, I'm just a guy. A guy who's up here to fish."

"But you're a police officer," Ann Waller said, glancing nervously at her husband. "Wouldn't someone with authority scare him? Make him tell the truth?"

"It's not like it looks like on TV. People just don't open up to cops because they flash a badge."

"Jim and I, we're not good at confrontation."

"We aren't?" her husband asked, perplexed. Scratching at his beard stubble, he glared at his wife, and Virgil noticed their younger daughter, Liz, shrink farther into the shadows.

Hiding?

"We have a business to run," Ann reminded him. "Neighbors to get along with."

"Hell, we're great at confrontation," Johnson said with a wide grin. "We'll be glad to do it."

"We will?" Virgil asked.

"Absolutely. C'mon, it's raining, we got nothing to do. Don't be a pussy." Johnson glanced at Ann and Katy and said, "Sorry about the language there."

•—◆—•

VIRGIL DIDN'T WANT TO DO IT. "THAT'S WHY I GO FISHING, SO I DON'T have to do this shit," he told Johnson as they trudged back to the cabin to get their rain suits. The drizzle had increased, puddles widening in the sparse gravel yard, the big Montana sky opening up. "I don't appreciate you signing me up for this shit."

"But we're helping out a hardworking girl," Johnson said. "I don't understand how you could even think of saying no."

"Fine." But Virgil was still burned.

When they got out to Johnson's Escalade, Katy, now in a rain jacket herself, was leaning against the rear passenger-side door.

"I'm going," she said.

There was some talk about that, but she went, because she said if they didn't take her, she'd walk, and making her walk in the rain would be mean.

The Drake place consisted of a two-story log cabin that sat on a high rocky bank over the trout stream. A hundred-yard-long pool backed up into a natural stone dam. There were two outbuildings. A machine shed, in which they could see the back of a BMW truck and an older Jeep, and another square log building that might be a guesthouse. A huge silvery RV was parked on a gravel spur off the house and a wrist-thick black electric cable snaked from the house to the RV.

"Nice place," Johnson said, nodding his approval.

"Yeah, he's rich, Drake is," Katy said. "The Weekses live right at the end of the road, a little farther."

They drove on and found the Weeks place, a broken-down single-wide mobile home set up on concrete blocks, well back in a notch in the woods. A stream of smoke seeped out of a can-size chimney on top. Virgil pulled in, and they all got out. He led the way up to the front door, climbing the graying stoop while Johnson and Katy waited below, and rapped on the door.

He heard feet cross the floor inside, and then a man yanked the door open, peered out, saw Johnson and Katy behind him, looked back at Virgil and asked, "Who are you?"

Weeks was a tall, thin man, with ropy muscles in his arms and neck, big battered hands, and small suspicious blue eyes.

"I'm with the MBCA," Virgil said.

"What the hell is that?"

"The Minnesota Bureau of Criminal Apprehension."

"Minnesota?"

And Virgil gave him a look at his badge.

The man's eyes narrowed. "Y're a long way from home."

He ignored that and said, "Katy Waller here lives and works down at the Wallers' ranch." He turned and motioned at Katy. "Somebody stole more than six hundred dollars from her chest of drawers, probably last night. We're hoping that Phillip Weeks could help us figure out who took it."

"Can't help you," Weeks said. "Little asshole ran off last night, said he ain't coming back, took his clothes and he's outta here. And he *ain't* coming back. He shows up here again, I'll kick his ass and throw him right back out. Time he was workin' on his own anyway."

At sixteen. Sure.

Weeks started to close the door, but Virgil said, "Do you know if he took the money?"

"Shit. I don't know about any money," Weeks said. "I didn't take it, and I told you, he's gone. Now get off my fuckin' porch."

"Do you know where he might be headed?"

"I don't know and I don't give a shit."

A Montana cop might have had more to say about that, but Virgil didn't, because he wasn't one. Weeks slammed the door and Virgil backed down the steps and said to Katy, "I think I believe him. I don't have any resources here to try to track the kid. If he really took off with that money, he could be on a Greyhound halfway to California or Seattle by now."

"Goddarnit," she groaned. "I was gonna buy clothes."

"On the way out," Virgil told Johnson, "let's stop at the Drake place. I'll ask if anybody talked to Phillip before he left."

Back down the short road Johnson pulled in behind the RV, gave a low whistle, and said, "A Rosestone recreational vehicle. Never seen one in the flesh, but I thought about buying one of 'em. Those are the Cadillacs of RVs."

"But you've got the Cadillac of Cadillacs, why would you want the Cadillac of something else?"

"Think of where you could go with that thing," Johnson said, eyeing the big rig, practically salivating.

"No place too far from an interstate highway or a gas station," Virgil said. "Almost as close to nature as Grand Central Station."

Virgil and Katy walked up to the door of the cabin, while Johnson made his way slowly around the RV, giving it a closer look, running his fingers over the smooth finish. Virgil knocked, and a minute later, a young-ish, soft-faced man opened the door, looked out, and asked politely, "Can I help you?"

"I'm looking for Mr. Drake."

"I'm Michael Drake."

He was an inch or so over average height, slender, and older than he looked at first impression. Somewhere around forty-five, he was wearing black slacks with pleats, a black dress shirt, and tasseled black loafers. An expensive-looking watch circled one wrist, a turquoise bracelet on the other.

Virgil told him about the missing money and looking for Phillip Weeks, and halfway through the explanation, Drake started shaking his head. "I haven't seen Phillip at all this trip. Don't see him much anyway."

He shoved his hands into the pockets of his slacks. "Have you asked his father about him? He lives with Bart."

Drake hitched his chin in the direction of the mobile home.

"Yeah, not a lot of help. He thinks Phillip might be off looking for a job."

There was a fuss out at the RV. A small, round woman in jeans and a sweater had come to the back door. Her short, dishwater hair was spiked and she wore half glasses. Her eyes, over the lenses, were focused like icy lasers on Johnson. "You get away from there. You hear me? Move. Who the hell are you?"

A flustered Johnson backed away, said, "Sorry, there, just interested in the RV."

"Yeah. For the love of God, don't go peeking into our windows."

And she slammed the door.

Virgil said to Drake, "Sorry about that; Johnson really does like the RV."

"Cheryl gets a little spooky," Drake explained, casting a what're-ya-gonna-do smile at Virgil. "She'll cool off. No worries."

Virgil nodded, not thinking the woman was going to calm down any time soon. Spooky? More like going ape shit. She was mad. "Thanks for your time, we'll be on our way." He motioned to Johnson and they headed to the Escalade.

As Johnson drove Virgil twisted so he could see Katy in the backseat. "Listen, even if the local deputy isn't any good, you've got to report the theft. If they can show this Phillip kid took the money, and he's not eighteen yet, his old man might be held responsible by a court, and you'd get the money back. Some of it, anyway. Or if your father has homeowners' insurance."

"That could take forever," she said, lower lip extending, looking miserable. Lost in her thoughts she drew on the condensation on the Escalade's window, and Virgil decided to give her some space as the Escalade bounced down the rutted road to the dude ranch.

They dropped off Katy, then headed into Grizzly Falls, the local town, where Virgil bought a copy of every newspaper the convenience store had, and Johnson bought some tourist crap that he planned to give to his girlfriend. The town was tiered, a newer section built on the crest of a hill, homes and businesses running along the ridge, the older part of town in the lower section spread out on the shores of the river where falls fell across shelves of flat rocks.

They stopped at a restaurant called Wild Wills where a stuffed grizzly bear stood on display in the lobby. Not only did the thing seem to be on guard near the front desk, it was dressed in a witch's costume, black hat tilted jauntily on its head, the brim dipping below a glass eye, black cape tossed over its huge shoulders, a broom tucked under one forearm. A black pot with steam rising from inside sat beside the thing's huge feet.

"What the hell is that?" Johnson asked, recoiling as he stared at the bear's shining claws and teeth gleaming, frozen in a perpetual scowl.

"The official greeter," Virgil guessed.

"Man, this is one weird fuckin' town. All those statues of Big Foot lining the street and now this." It was true, they must've passed half a dozen statues of Sasquatches on their way into town, including a ten-foot-tall wooden image in the parking lot of the convenience store where Johnson had bought the touristy crap.

They ordered cheeseburgers and fries and ate them in silence.

On the way back to the dude ranch, Virgil said, "You've gone kinda quiet. What's with that?"

"I dunno," Johnson said. "Thinking things over, I guess."

"That doesn't sound like Johnson Johnson. Thinking things over."

On the way back, the Rosestone RV passed them, going in the opposite direction.

They didn't wave.

At the ranch, Johnson said he was going to take a walk.

"In the rain?"

"I can't tell it's raining; this is a seven-hundred-dollar rain suit," Johnson said.

"Still thinking things over?"

"Yep."

Johnson rubbed the back of his neck and looked across the golf course where two men in Gore-Tex were chipping near a soggy green.

The door to the owners' cabin burst open and Katy, carrying a water-proof bag, leaped across the porch to dash through the drizzle. Ignoring the rain, she grinned widely. "You guys won't believe what happened."

"From the way you're smiling, I'd say you found your money," Virgil said.

"Nope." She was shaking her head. "Phillip's dad came down here."

That didn't sound like good news.

She went on, "He said Phillip called from the bus station and said he was going to Minneapolis and wasn't coming back. He told his dad he'd taken the money for a bus ticket but felt bad about it. And then Bart Weeks told my dad he didn't want any trouble, and he wanted to pay it back." Her grin widened and she blinked against the rain, oblivious to the fact that she was getting wet. "So he did, every penny of it. In cash."

Virgil said, "That's a little hard to believe."

Johnson spread his arms and said, "Hard to believe, but we'll take it. We're gold."

Katy said, "Yes, we are. I want to thank you guys for what you did. Thank you so much."

Then she looked directly at Johnson.

"I'm sorry I said you look like a crook."

•◆•

THE NEXT DAY WAS COOL, THE SKY STILL TINGED WITH DARKNESS, the remaining clouds occasionally spitting some drizzle, but they could see stars far to the west, the cloud cover breaking up as night surrendered to dawn. Virgil and Johnson got their gear together and pulled on rain jackets, then took the insulated bag from Ann Waller who had made sandwiches and filled a thermos with coffee for them.

"An extra thanks for helping with Katy," she explained. "It's a big deal to her. To us."

They were on their way to the Escalade for the trip to the river when Dan Cain stepped out on the porch of his cabin with a cup of coffee in his hand and called after them, "Good luck. Leave a couple fish for us."

Johnson stopped, turned, and asked, "You coming?"

Cain shook his head. "Not yet. That fuckin' Lang had one too many last night. He's just getting up now. We'll be a half hour behind you."

The river was shallow and quick, with occasional pools, and it was gorgeous, with the stone-cut bank on the far side looking like a piece of petrified wood rising a hundred feet above them, the dawn coming, sunlight glinting on water. As dawn gave way to daylight Virgil spent almost as much time looking at the landscape as he did fishing, and the fishing was decent. A little after eight o'clock they stopped to sit on a rock and eat the egg-salad sandwiches that Ann Waller had made them for breakfast, when they heard a pop from upstream.

The report of a rifle echoed over the water.

They both stared downriver and waited.

No second shot.

Nothing to disturb the silence but the lapping of the water and the cry of a blackbird, its red wing visible in the brush on the shore.

"That was a rifle, a center fire," Johnson said with a frown. "What the hell was he shootin' at?"

Virgil didn't know, and he had no idea what was in season for a hunter here in Montana. "If that was target shooting, the shooter was easily satisfied."

"I don't like the idea of people shooting around in heavy brush when there are lots of folks out on the river, fishing," Johnson said. "It gives me an itchy feeling between my shoulder blades. Like we oughta be wearing our blaze orange."

They finished their sandwiches as the sun rose over the eastern horizon, then climbed back into the boat and went down the river. Fishing. Catching nothing for half an hour.

And then a man started screaming.

"Virgil Flowers. Where the hell are you?"

The voice sounded frantic, scared as hell.

They both looked back upstream, trying to pinpoint its location.

*   *   *

They'd just pulled their boat to the side of the river and were heading toward the sound of the shouting, when Jim Waller, driving a John Deere Gator on what was little more than two ruts in the brush, found them. His face was grim, his lips compressed.

He didn't bother climbing off the idling utility vehicle but shouted, "Dan Cain's been shot. He's dead. For the love of Christ, some dumb ass shot him in the back."

"You call the cops?" Virgil asked as he and Johnson slogged through the reeds, mud, and bitter brush to Waller's vehicle.

"Yeah, but they'll be half an hour." Waller said. "We told them you were here, they want you to go up and take a look at the body."

There was nothing to see.

No crime scene.

Virgil's gaze swept up and down the river as he stood over the body and listened to a barely coherent Lang who had been fishing with Cain, the men in separate boats.

"I don't know what happened. I mean, he was trailing me down the river about a hundred yards or so." He was sweating and breathing hard, though it wasn't from the temperature. Exertion and adrenaline had turned his face beet red. Fear rounded his eyes and he kept swiping at his forehead, wiping away the sweat.

The man was freaked.

As was Johnson.

He wasn't good with dead bodies, and at the first chance he took off along the road, heading back to the spot where the car was parked.

Virgil listened as Lang explained in short bursts, his gaze traveling from the body to Virgil, along the river's edge and back to the body.

He had looked Cain over, the shot had gone through his back, exited his chest, probably caught him right through the heart. *Good shot,* Virgil thought, *if Cain really was the intended victim. If the whole thing was an accident, then both Cain and the shooter were damned unlucky. But if it were an accident, why hadn't the shooter showed himself? Run for help?*

A kid? Or just a coward?

Or a cold-stone killer?

Cain had been trailing Lang down the water by a hundred yards. Lang had gone around a bend in the river when he heard the shot. He'd gone on, but when Cain hadn't reappeared around the bend, Lang, now worried, went looking for his friend and found him out of the boat, in the river, already dead, aground on some shallow rocks.

Lang said he'd dragged Cain's body to the riverbank and pulled it up on shore. He believed Cain was dead, but wasn't sure, and he'd run to get help.

"I found Jim, here," he said, pointed at the owner of the ranch who was standing near his Gator, taking in the entire scene. "And we called 911."

"That's good." He paused. "You own a gun?"

"A rifle?" Lang asked.

"Any gun?"

"Nothing."

"Don't keep one in the car."

"No, and Dan didn't either. Neither one of us hunt and I don't believe in that self-protection crap. Too many people get killed with their own weapons." His gaze strayed to the body again. "Oh, Jesus, who would do this? Why? God, it must've been an accident, right? Some asshole with a rifle."

"That's what we'll have to find out," Virgil said. "Now, everyone step back onto the road. Clear this area."

He could do nothing but keep people away from the body, keep them out of the woods along the river, where the shooter might have been.

And wait for the local cops.

A deputy arrived a few minutes later, parked away from the area, and walked in. He was a tall man and introduced himself as Pete Watershed. He wore aviator sunglasses and a scowl. Virgil told him what he'd done, which was almost nothing aside from clear the area around the body and where a shooter might have been potentially hidden. A couple more deputies arrived, then the sheriff, Hooper Blackwater. About six feet, he was all compact muscle and carried himself as if he were in the military. Short-cropped black hair, coppery skin, and high cheekbones suggested he might be part Native American. He was all business. He surveyed the area, frowned, barked out some orders to his men, took a closer look at the body, then pulled Virgil aside and after checking his ID said, "You're an investigator? You do this kind of thing all the time?"

"When I'm on the job."

And often, when he wasn't. Like now.

Blackwater asked, "What do you think? What happened here?"

"Haven't figured out where the shooter was or if this was an attack or an accident. If it was intentional, it's hard to figure out why. Random target? Paid assassin? Some nutcase getting his rocks off? Someone with a grudge? So far that's all unknown. I talked to Lang; he and Cain are from Bismarck, and they really don't know anybody here but the Wallers. They've been at this camp a couple of times. This trip up they haven't left the camp since they got here, day before yesterday. They fished the first day, sat out the rain yesterday, and got back at it today. Mr. Waller said there'd been no trouble at all at the camps, no arguments, nothing like that."

"And you and your friend think it was a rifle shot."

"We both have experience with all kinds of firearms. It was a rifle."

"What happened to the guy you were with?"

"He went for the car. He doesn't do well with this kind of thing."

"Not a cop."

"Lumber business. You can catch up with him back at the WJ Guest Ranch if you want, but I'll vouch for him. He was with me the whole time."

The sheriff rubbed his forehead. "We'll want to talk to him." Then he asked, "Got any theories?"

"Too early. Lang found him in the river, dragged him out. Cain's a big guy. Would have been easy to see in the woods, as it was light. There was only one shot. I suppose somebody could have been poaching deer. We've seen a couple."

"That's pretty thin. One shot, hits the guy through the heart from the back, and the shooter disappears."

"It's thin," Virgil said. "I kinda think he was murdered. You need to get an investigator in here, soon as you can. Start looking at their backgrounds. Lang doesn't really have an alibi. He seems real. I mean, looking and listening to him, I buy his story. Still, I'd hate to think it was something else, that you might have a crazy out there."

"We've got a detective on the way," Blackwater said. "I'll ask her to stop and talk to you, your friend, Cain, and Waller when she gets here, which ought to be pretty soon."

The sheriff's lips compressed as he surveyed the area again.

"This is bad business. Real bad business."

Johnson Johnson wasn't at the cabin when Virgil got back and his Cadillac was gone, so Virgil grabbed a Coke from the refrigerator and went into the bathroom to shave, shower, and put on fresh clothes. He was just pulling on his pants when he heard a truck pull up in front of the cabin, and then a second one. He looked out the window and saw Johnson Johnson getting out of his Escalade and a woman shutting the door of a Jeep.

She was tall and solidly built. She had a good figure but wasn't slim. Nor was she heavy. Just solid and athletic-looking. Her hair was light brown with hints of red, pulled away from her face and tied at her nape. Her lips showed a hint of gloss and when she shoved a pair of sunglasses onto her head, he saw that her eyes were greenish, with flecks of gold. From habit he noticed the gold band on her left hand.

Married.

Had to be the detective.

Here to do her job.

Regan Pescoli was pissed as she drove into the parking area of the WJ Guest Ranch.

She'd already stopped by the river where deputies had blocked off what appeared to be the crime scene. She'd viewed the body, got all the particulars from Blackwater, then headed here to talk to Virgil Flowers.

This morning wasn't the first time she'd been here. Her daughter

Bianca knew the oldest Waller girl, Katy, and had spent some time here a few years back. The dude ranch and golf course hadn't improved much. In fact, it looked more dilapidated than ever, as if surviving on a shoestring.

The apparent homicide of a fisherman was the first case she'd caught since returning to work three days earlier and already Blackwater, the prick, was stepping into it. She'd never gotten used to working with the acting sheriff of Pinewood County, but she had no choice.

She parked next to a newer Cadillac SUV with Minnesota plates. The driver, a big man, was just getting out, hopping to the ground and trying to avoid stepping in a puddle. Thankfully, for now, the rain had stopped and sunlight, filtering through the stand of pines surrounding the cabins dappled across the sparse gravel.

She slammed the door to her Jeep and asked, "Are you Virgil Flowers, from Minnesota?"

"No, I'm Johnson Johnson from Minnesota. Trust me, I'm much larger, better looking, and more intelligent than that fuckin' Flowers."

"Johnson Johnson?" she repeated.

"Right."

"You with Flowers?"

A nod. "I'm his fishing partner. He's probably inside the cabin."

"Is he a bullshitter too?"

"Bullshitter? I speak nothing but the honest truth. Who're you?"

"Detective Regan Pescoli, Pinewood County Sheriff's Department." To prove her point, she opened her wallet and flashed her badge.

"Okay. Good. Get this off Virgil's back, will ya? We got more fishin' to do. C'mon in."

She followed Johnson Johnson up the steps, across the porch, and through a screen door. Inside, a tall surfer type with damp blond hair was buttoning his shirt. He was barefoot, apparently just out of the shower.

Johnson introduced them.

Regan and Flowers shook hands, and Flowers asked, "Have you been down at the scene?"

She gave a quick nod. "Just now. Talked to Mr. Lang. He seems freaked enough that I buy his innocence. For now. Until I learn different. The sheriff tells me you think it might have been a murder, not an accident."

"The more I think about it," Flowers said.

"Then we're on the same page," said Regan. "You told him the shot was a few minutes after eight o'clock?"

"I looked at my watch," Flowers said. "The sun was up."

She pulled out a notebook and jotted down the details as Flowers laid them out. Including what Cain had said to them as they passed the cabin earlier in the morning, where they all were relative to each other, the timing of the shot, when Lang raised the alarm, the arrival of the first deputy.

"We didn't work through the woods looking for the brass. One shot from a rifle, I suspect it was a bolt action," Flowers said. "If it had been a semiauto, the killer would have pulled the trigger again."

She glanced down at her notes for a moment, then said, "If it was a bolt action, probably won't find any brass. Not near the scene, anyway. Cain was almost certainly shot from this side of the river."

"How do you know that?" Johnson asked.

"The slug hit him in the middle of the back and came out on the same level in front," she said. "If the shooter had been on the other side of the river, he would have had to have been on that high bank, and the shot would have been angled down."

Flowers nodded. "You looked at the wound?"

"Yeah. Looks to me, and the ME should be able to tell us for sure, that it was a pretty heavy caliber. Not a .223 or anything like that."

"Wasn't a .223," Flowers said. "It went boom, not bap."

"Probably a hunting rifle," she said. "The crazies around here usually go for those .223 black rifles with the rails and all that crap on them, but maybe this was something different. You seem to think so." Flowers clearly knew about guns, that much was obvious. "Regardless of the caliber, I think this was a hunter."

"Who mistook Lang for a bull elk?" Flowers asked.

"Who shot him, either by mistake or intentionally. First we find the guy, then we find the motive." Her smile was ice. "Unless it works out the other way around."

She checked her watch and frowned.

That feeling again.

Time to stop by the house and feed the baby, or find an out-of-the-way place to pump her breasts.

"Look, I gotta go work the phones for a while. Thanks for this. I might need to come back and talk some more."

She started for the door, but Johnson raised a hand and said, "I kinda need to tell you something. May be nothing, but I'm worried."

She asked, "About this?"

"Yeah." Johnson looked down at the floor, guilty of something but she couldn't guess what. "The shooter might have made a mistake. I've been thinkin' about it, and I believe that maybe he thought he was shooting at me."

"Why's that?" she asked.

Flowers was shaking his head and staring at his fishing buddy, reading the other guy, guessing something, and it wasn't good.

"Johnson," Flowers said, "what have you done?"

They all took chairs around the kitchen table and Johnson, appearing slightly shamefaced, rubbed his knees nervously, looked at Regan and said, "First, I've got to tell you about a break-in we had here at the ranch. Somebody stole six hundred dollars from the lodge owner's daughter."

She listened as Johnson told the story of the theft, how they'd gone to Weeks's mobile home, meeting Bart, who'd thrown them off his property. How they'd stopped at the Drake residence and met Michael Drake, the rich dude who owned the log cabin. How he'd looked at the high-end Rosestone RV parked nearby, and how Weeks had shown up later in the day to repay the stolen money.

"What in God's name does all that have to do with the shooting?" Flowers asked. To Regan he said, "Johnson has a tendency to bullshit a little."

"Okay," she said, but sensed the guy was getting to something. To Johnson she said, "I'm listening."

Johnson turned to Flowers and asked, "You remember that woman who screamed at me from the RV? What was her name? Cheryl?"

"Because you were peeking in the window. Yeah, I remember."

Johnson's face reddened, which surprised her. For one thing Johnson was so tanned that a blush would normally have been invisible. "I didn't mean to peek," Johnson said to Regan. "I've thought about buying an RV like that and I wondered how it was finished inside. I'm tall enough that I could see through the window, and when I looked, there was this girl, and she didn't have much clothes on. She wasn't naked but pretty close."

Flowers said, "Uh-oh."

"Yeah," Johnson said. "I probably woulda never said anything to anybody, because it was embarrassing. I was peeking, even though I didn't mean to. But I've got this image in my head of this kid, she was maybe twelve or eleven. Shit, maybe even younger. But she was wearing one of those things that you see at Victoria's Secret, this red thing, real low V in front, almost down to her crotch."

He waved his hands around, trying to demonstrate, and finally Regan helped him out. "A teddy." She took out her cell phone, tapped a bunch of keys with her thumbs, waited, then turned it around so Johnson could see the photos that came up.

He nodded. "That's it. It was one of those. And the thing is, she was all made up, you know. Rouged cheeks, eye shadow, lipstick."

"Jesus, Johnson," Flowers said. "Why didn't you say something?"

"Because it was embarrassing, and you know how it is with girls these days, all made up, you can't really tell how old they are, but it bothered me. I was going to tell you after I thought it over some more. Anyway, I'd decided to let you know, today, I swear. Later. When we got back."

Flowers glared at him, and Johnson went on, "Anyway, so we're out on the river this morning, right? All of us. All wearing rain suits, and fishing and all."

"Yeah?" Regan said, wondering where the hell this was going.

"The thing is, Cain, he looked like me, if we were all in rain suits and geared up, you know? Big guy, my size, staying at the ranch to fish."

"Oh, man," Flowers said, leaning back in his chair.

Regan glanced at Flowers. "If you're thinking what I'm thinking, that our shooter was aiming for Johnson, here, and not Cain and it's because of what he saw, then we've got ourselves a motive and it's not pretty."

"I hate this shit," Flowers said.

"Not as much as I do."

Inside she was coldly furious. She'd dealt with a lot of sickos in her day, lowlifes who preyed on weaker victims, but the ones who targeted innocent children? Those fuckers could go straight to hell and Regan would be glad to help them along.

"I had a bad feeling about some of this," Flowers said, leaning forward again. "Let me tell you about this Weeks character. Giving six hundred bucks back is the last thing I would have expected. He didn't want any cops up there poking around. If we're both thinking the same thing, he's in on it."

She said, "I need to talk to some feds. And that kid who ran away, we need to find him. He could be key here."

Flowers rubbed the back of his neck, appeared to be mulling things over. "You know, I'd be willing to give you whatever help you need, but this isn't my territory."

"You want to just step away? Hide behind legality and jurisdiction?"

She was incensed. What a prick.

"I'd like to get back to fishing. Not to be rude, but this is really your problem, not mine."

"It's not entirely my problem," she said, getting to her feet.

Damn. Her breasts hurt. She really needed to get to a spot where she could pump.

"Johnson's still alive. When the shooter finds out he got the wrong guy, he could be back."

"Could have gone all day without hearing that," Johnson said. "Might be time to fish somewhere else."

She said tautly, "Look, Flowers, this is child porn and homicide. You're a pro. Or supposed to be. I'd appreciate it if you'd stick around for a couple days. You and Johnson are the only ones on our side who've seen the woman, or the RV, or even that Drake character. And without Johnson's statement about seeing the girl in the teddy, we don't have a lot to go on."

Flowers didn't argue. "So, look, I'm going to try to run this kid down, this Phillip, and try to find that RV." To Johnson she said, "I don't suppose you took a cell-phone picture of it . . . one that would include the tags? Was it local? Montana plates?"

Johnson was shaking his head. "Didn't notice and no, no picture, but I did see an advertising plate on the side. It said Luxury America Motor Tours, or something like that. I believe it was a rental: I kind of made a mental note, in case I wanted to try one out."

She jotted the name in her notebook. "You're smarter than you look."

Johnson said, "I'll have to think about that for a while."

"I think it was a compliment," Flowers said. "But I'm not absolutely certain."

She ignored them. "One more thing, if there's something going on with the girl, there are different possibilities. One would be that she's been prostituted. The other is they're making child porn."

Her stomach tightened at the thought.

"Or both," Flowers said. He, too, was grim. "But since she's way out here, I'd say child porn is the better possibility. High-quality child porn. You'd need space, time, lights, decent cameras, plus the kids. And you might want to shoot some stuff out in the woods, as well as interiors. Sex, you could do almost anywhere. Photography, not so much. Especially video."

"Describe Cheryl for me and Michael Drake," she asked. "I'll try to run 'em down."

They did and she took notes.

"Tell you what. Since Johnson doesn't want to get murdered, you guys could help out by scouting around up there. I can't do that without a warrant, which would warn everyone. If you find something, just as tourists walking around in the woods like tourists do, I'll get a warrant and we'll swarm the place. We bust everybody in sight, and you guys are good to go fishing. While you're doing that, I'll find the Weeks kid and get a fix on the RV."

"Walking around in the woods could be a little touchy," Flowers said. "We're not armed."

"Maybe you're not," Johnson said.

Flowers stepped back. "Ah, Jesus, Johnson, you brought a gun?"

"You can't go driving around the countryside without at least a nine," Johnson said. To Regan he said, "Virgil doesn't like guns."

"And you're a cop? Really?"

"Not your usual brand."

"Mr. Kumbaya, huh." She shrugged. "If you do happen to stumble across something, armed or not, I'll be on my cell."

"Me 'n' Johnson will talk about it," Flowers said and he actually seemed faintly amused at her ire.

• ◆ •

TRUTH TO TELL, REGAN DIDN'T QUITE KNOW WHAT TO THINK ABOUT the cop and his friend from Minnesota, but they were better help than the local deputies who were like no choice at all. And if the RV was rolling away, and if Phillip Weeks was on his way to somewhere else on a Greyhound, she had to get on it.

She started by talking with Katy and getting a physical description of Phillip Weeks, along with two pictures Katy texted to Regan's phone. But there was little more. Everything Katy knew Regan had already heard from Flowers. Her parents weren't any help, either, but she wondered about Jim Waller, a man who admitted to being a hunter, a man who had no trouble showing off his collection of rifles and shotguns.

But why?

He claimed to know nothing about the Weeks family or Michael Drake other than he was "a rich guy and drives a fancy car." They'd seen RVs on the property a time or two, but had no other information, thought the vehicles probably belonged to friends or family of Drake.

With no answers she drove back to the station and thought about the case, the girl, the murder, the chance that Johnson had stumbled upon the illegal operation and someone had tried to murder him. It all seemed far-fetched, didn't quite hang together.

Yet.

Back at the sheriff's department she ordered a be-on-the-lookout for the RV, asked Sage Zoller, a junior detective, to track down Luxury America Motor Tours, then took twenty minutes in the women's room to pump her damned breasts. Afterward, she placed the bottles in a pouch marked with her name in the refrigerator in the lunchroom and thought about someone finding them.

Like Blackwater. Or Watershed.

Go for it, she thought.

Blackwater would be able to handle it.

Watershed, a misogynist if ever there was one, would freak.

She drove to the Greyhound station, which had been built sometime in the 1950s and looked as if it had never been updated. The clerk at the desk, a girl all of eighteen, hadn't been working the day before and wasn't too interested in helping, but the manager overheard their conversation and bustled over. "I think I can help you. I remember him. Tall, thin, long hair, looked like he'd been in a fight? This was the night before last, right?" The manager had a bushy copper-colored mustache and reddish hair that reminded Regan of a cartoon character, though she couldn't remember which one.

Ah, Yosemite Sam.

"He got here too late to catch the bus that night, so he came back the next morning. He might have slept outside somewhere, because he spent some time in the restroom washing up. Then he bought his ticket, with a full-day layover in Butte. Said he wanted to stop and see his grandma. If that's the kid you're looking for, he'd be catching the bus out of Butte tonight at seven o'clock, and will be in LA tomorrow night around eight."

Good information.

She called the Butte cops and arranged to have a patrol car check for Weeks when the LA bus was loading up that night.

"Could have information on a homicide investigation," she told the Butte desk sergeant.

"We'll make it a priority," he said.

Back on the road, she was driving up Boxer Hill to the upper part of Grizzly Falls when her cell phone rang. Seeing it was from the department, she clicked on.

Sage Zoller was on the other end of the line.

"Luxury America Motor Tours rents Rosestone RVs out of Las Vegas," he said. "I could go to Vegas and check it out."

"I'll call them on the phone."

"And blow a perfectly good excuse to go to Vegas?"

"Nice try. I'm on my way in. Find out what you can about a guy named Virgil Flowers. Surfer-dude type who works for the MBCA."

"Already done. I figured you'd want background on the guy you were meeting."

"And?" Regan asked, spying a coffee kiosk and turning in.

"He's kind of a big deal. One of their best cops."

"Really," she said. "Thanks."

She ordered two oatmeal cookies and a coffee, then zipped across traffic and ended up following the slowest pickup on record up Boxer Hill. So Virgil Flowers was a big deal in Minnesota, she thought heading up the hill.

Who would have guessed.

The truck in front of her lugged down even farther, and she considered flipping on the light bar to get him out of the way. Instead she called and checked on the baby, talked with her husband a few minutes, hung up and ate one of the cookies all the while following the lumbering truck.

Finally, back at her desk, she picked at the second cookie and sipped at the coffee while she fired up her iPad and clicked onto Google maps. She found out that Las Vegas was fourteen to fifteen hours away, if driven straight through. Flowers and Johnson had seen the RV on the road almost twenty-four hours earlier. When she called the Luxury America, the manager of the RV rental company told her, "Got it back at eleven o'clock this morning. That was three days early, actually. Surprised me. But they paid an early-return penalty, no problem."

"Credit card?"

"Let me look." She heard clicking as he worked his own computer. "No. They paid cash, but they had to provide a credit card and government ID before they could take it out. Hold on a sec. Wait. You're sure you're a cop?"

"I looked at my badge about three or four minutes ago, so I'm pretty sure."

"I'd give you the information, if I could see it, but I can't see it."

She provided the guy her badge number and invited him to call the Pinewood County Sheriff's Department. She'd just taken the final bite of her second cookie when her desk phone jangled and she answered it. Sure enough, Luxury America was calling, the manager having satisfied his need to verify that she was who she said she was.

"Sorry about that. We have to be supercareful. These days with all of the hacking and identity theft and fraud."

"I get it," she cut in. "Tell me what I want to know."

"The credit card you're asking about was issued to Clark and Delores Foley of Riverdale, California."

"Was there another woman with them, named Cheryl?" She checked her notes. "In her fifties, dirty-blond spiked hair, under five five, a little on the heavy side. Sometimes wears half glasses?"

"No other woman that I saw, but that sounds a lot like Delores."

She scribbled down the address and a contact number. "Did they have any kids with them?"

"Yup. Good-looking kids, too. A boy and three girls. I think. Tweens or younger. I asked them if they were in the movies."

"What'd they say?"

"Mmm, nothing. Their mom hustled them off to their car."

"Delores? A little old for kids that age, isn't she?"

"Could be their grandmother, I s'pose."

"You got a tag on the car?" she asked. "In your rental agreement somewhere."

"No, but the car was registered in California, I remember that much. It was an SUV, Japanese, I'm thinking."

"That's pretty broad."

"Yeah, sorry. But let me tell you what I do have. When somebody comes in to rent an RV, we've got a video camera out of sight behind the desk. We don't tell 'em we're taking their picture, but we are. It goes back a month. We've got them on video."

Finally, a break.

"Find that video. Somebody will come by to pick it up, either the Vegas cops or the FBI."

"You got it."

They talked for another minute, but the manager didn't have much more. As soon as she hung up she rang the FBI, identified herself, got switched to the Violent Crimes Against Children program, identified herself again to the woman who answered the phone, got switched to an agent, identified herself a third time, and told him about the sequence of events.

She hadn't always had the best of luck with the feds, and wasn't that crazy about them. But in this case the agent named David Burch said, "I'll get on to the Vegas office and have them pick up the tape and get the manager to ID these guys. If we've got good head shots, we'll run it through a facial ID program and see what pops up. Most of the time, nothing does, but if this is as high end and well organized as you're making it sound, then maybe something will. These people sound like they've been doing it for a while."

"How long before I hear?"

"Tomorrow morning, probably. We'll push it hard. I hate these guys. Hate 'em," Burch said.

"Amen." Her anger hardened at the thought of the kids trapped in whatever the hell scam it was. "So, David. Can I call you David?"

"Yes, ma'am."

"And you can call me Regan or Pescoli. The ma'am thing makes me feel old. The thing is, I need to talk to you off the record."

"We're off."

No hesitation.

Deciding to trust him, she launched into her story and told him about Virgil and Johnson, and about Phillip Weeks. "I have a feeling that the Weeks kid may be running from whatever was going down. The sex, or porn, movies, pictures, whatever."

"Nothing good."

"You got that right. I'm going to try to corner him tonight and see what he knows. He's also running from his old man, who could be in on it. I think the dad uses his son as a punching bag."

"Needs to be put in jail."

Agreed. "While I'm handling the kid, Flowers and Johnson are going up to snoop around the Drake place where they saw the RV. Anything in particular they should look for?"

"If they were making movies or taking photos, we could use pictures of the inside of the studio, or whatever they're using as a studio. We got a million miles of digitized film. What we'd be looking for is identifiable marks or structures inside the studio, like an identifiable window with a particular kind of latch. Anything like that. We can run a new image against the digitized film and it'll kick out any exact matches. If we get a match, we'll be all over them."

"I'll tell Flowers. I don't know exactly how reliable these two are."

"I started running Flowers as soon as you mentioned his name," Burch said. "The DEA has been trying to recruit him for years. He's been involved in some heavy stuff in Minnesota. There's a note here that says he doesn't much care for guns."

"That's the guy," she said.

"Looks to me like you can lean on him," Burch said.

"Good to know," Regan said.

So Mr. Hang Ten was the real deal.

"Something else. He's a part-time writer, mostly for outdoors magazines, but he's had stories in both the *New York Times* magazine and *Vanity Fair*. Play your cards right—"

"I'll keep it in mind," she said dryly.

She rotated the kinks from her neck and decided she had to head to Butte, which was about a hundred and fifty miles from Grizzly Falls. That meant over two hours by car. She didn't look forward to the drive, but had to go for it. The case had taken a serious enough turn that even the feds were scrambling. She stopped by Alvarez's office. Before her maternity leave she and Alvarez had been partners, but they hadn't been reassigned together.

Not yet, anyway.

Alvarez, always thin and lithe, was doing some yoga pose over her desk, her jet black hair rolled into a tight bun and gleaming under the ever-humming fluorescent lights. The position looked painful and ridiculous, but Alvarez swore by it. Alvarez had always been Regan's diametric opposite. Into health foods, green tea, worked out at a gym and, of course, yoga.

"I'm stopping at home to see the kids and Santana for a sec, then heading for Butte. On the Daniel Cain case, the fisherman found shot in the river near the WJ Guest Ranch."

Alvarez nodded.

"It's gone from homicide to a much wider investigation. Got the feds involved. Zoller can bring you up to speed. Aside from what I'm doing we'll need to look into who would benefit from Cain's death. Insurance, wife involved in an affair, him involved in an affair, business problems, known enemies. The working theory was that he was killed by mistake, but I want to cover all my bases."

Alvarez rolled back her desk chair, rotated her neck, then her shoulders. "I'll work with Zoller."

"If you find anything interesting, call my cell."

After stopping by the house, depositing the bag of breast milk into the refrigerator and spending half an hour feeding and cuddling the baby, she kissed her husband good-bye, assured him that she would be fine and that, though she missed her family terribly, she loved her job and would call them from the road.

"We have to talk about this," Santana said.

He was taller than she by half a foot, a cowboy type who actually worked on a ranch and was tough as nails. His hair was black, his eyes dark above a hawkish nose, his smile, when he rained it on her, an irreverent slash of white.

"We already did."

"Then we need to talk about it again. You're exhausted, the baby needs you, the older kids, too. Hell, I need you."

"I'll be back as soon as I can."

"Make it sooner," he said and kissed her on the lips, a long slow kiss that turned her inside out, just as it had the first time. She weakened, wanted to melt against him, wanted the feel of him inside her, but that would have to wait.

"I'll try," she promised.

Then she took off.

On the way to Butte, she called Flowers and brought him up to speed as the miles rolled by. She told him what FBI agent Burch had said about getting photos of the inside of the studio.

"That's what we need. Pictures of the place. Something that will nail them, connect the RV or house or some landmark up there to pictures that have already been taken."

"We'll go up there after dark," Flowers said. "Give us a call later on, around midnight."

• ◆ •

IN BUTTE, REGAN FOUND PHILLIP WEEKS SITTING IN THE CORNER OF a drunk tank, where the Butte cops had put him after picking him up at the bus station. A Butte detective named Charlie Tarley unlocked the door and pushed it open. Weeks, looking terrified, slowly rolled to his feet.

Tarley, African American and looking as if he worked out regularly, said to him, "You got a visitor."

She stepped forward, into the kid's range of vision, and held up her badge. "Detective Regan Pescoli. Pinewood County Sheriff's Department."

Fear showed in Weeks's eyes.

He was tall, unnaturally thin, weathered in the way of street people, farmers, and lumberjacks. He bore a fading bruise below one eye.

Tarley said in a calm voice, "C'mon out, Phillip. Detective Pescoli made a long drive to see you. We all need to chat."

"What'd I do?" Weeks asked.

"You probably took six hundred dollars from a young girl at the WJ Ranch, but your old man paid it back, so that's not it," Regan said. "But I think you might know why you want to talk."

Weeks shoved both hands in his jeans pocket and stared at the floor a second, then looked up through the dark strands of the hair falling over his forehead. Pinning Regan with his suspicious gaze, he said, "He paid it back?"

She nodded.

Weeks shook his head. "Where'd he get the money? He was drinking and didn't even have enough cash to buy a box of cereal. I know he didn't have six hundred dollars."

"He gave it back. All of it. So you're good on that score," she said. "C'mon out of there."

Shuffling reluctantly Weeks followed Regan along a short hallway to an interview room, Tarley trailing behind, talking on a cell phone. The square, windowless room had a table and four chairs. Regan sat directly across from the boy with his downcast eyes, Tarley on her right.

"I'm going to read you your rights," Tarley said.

"I didn't do anything!"

"Just listen," she ordered. "Hear him out. This is all part of the deal."

Weeks sullenly let Tarley go through his spiel. When the detective finished, the room was silent apart from the rush of air through the vents. She peered at Weeks for a long intense moment and remembered when her own son had been held for questioning. She felt some empathy for this kid, whatever he was wrapped up in.

"Tell me about Michael Drake, and what he's doing up there in the woods."

Weeks's Adam's apple bobbed a couple of times. He brushed his long hair back from his eyes and shrugged. "He comes up and fishes."

"You know that's not what I'm talking about."

A muscle worked in the boy's jaw. He looked at Tarley and said, "My old man paid the money back. You heard that. Can I go now?"

Tarley said, "If you burglarize a place, you don't get a free pass for giving the money back. And then there's the murder."

Weeks's mouth dropped open. He blinked and stared at Regan again. "Who was murdered?"

"A completely innocent fisherman from North Dakota," she said. "We believe whoever did it shot the wrong guy. The man they were trying to shoot saw a nearly naked girl in that RV at Drake's, and whoever was behind it decided they had to get rid of him."

Weeks stared at the table. "Oh, God. Shit."

"What do you know, Phillip? Who are those people?"

He glanced wildly around the room, as if searching for a way out. "They'll kill me, too. If I talk. They said it. That they'd kill me if they ever saw me talking to a cop."

Tears welled in his eyes.

She said, "It'll be hard for them to kill anyone, when they're doing life without parole."

"You can't keep me safe."

"I can."

He looked to Tarley who nodded his assessment.

"Okay," he finally said. "Okay."

A moment of silence passed.

"What happened to them kids?" Weeks asked. "The girl that the guy saw. The one who was almost naked. What happened to her? Is she there? Is she okay? Are the other ones okay?" He was frantic now, both legs bouncing crazily under the table. "Carla and Al are mean people. Are the kids still up there?"

"I thought the woman's name was Cheryl," she said. "Or maybe Delores."

"Not if they were in that RV. That was Carla and Al," he said urgently. All his arguments about not talking seemed to have vanished.

"Do Carla and Al have a last name?"

"I think Al's is Dickens or, no, Dicker. That's it. I don't know Carla's. I never heard. I don't know much about them." He squeezed his eyes closed in concentration. "Except maybe they're from Nevada. I think I heard that once, but I'm not sure."

"How often have you seen them at Drake's?"

"A bunch. They come up four, maybe five times a year, in the RV."

"And what do they do?"

He looked at Regan as if she were slow on the uptake. "They make movies, ya know, and take pictures either in the cabin, Drake's house, or out in the woods around there."

"You've seen them?"

He nodded.

"Children having sex?"

"Sometimes, the older ones with Al, mostly, and with each other," Weeks said, his voice going low.

"Were you ever involved in that?"

Weeks looked away, scared, maybe, shamed for sure. Then he nodded. "Not for a long time. Not for a couple of years. I got too old. Are you going to put me in prison?"

Her heart bled for the kid, for what he'd been through. Who knew where his mother was, or if she was alive or dead. The old man abused and beat him, then used him for profit, forcing him to pose and have sex.

"No, Phillip. What we'd like to do is to get a complete story from you.

Everything you know about Michael Drake and Carla and Al, and then, someday, we'll want you to talk about it in a courtroom," she said. "But you won't be going to prison. You're a victim here."

But the people who did this?

Hell wasn't bad enough for them.

Tarley got sandwiches, chips, and soft drinks, and though there was an out-of-sight recorder covering the interview room, he'd also brought out a small digital recorder that Weeks could see. They talked for an hour, leading the kid through a basic statement. As Regan had expected, Weeks had left his home before Flowers, Johnson, and Katy Waller had been to Weeks's father's trailer and to Drake's log cabin, so Phillip knew nothing about the events that led to the shooting of Cain. His father knew about the child porn but had nothing to do with its production.

"He doesn't know anything about cameras or lights or any of that shit," he said demolishing a ham and cheese, then washing it all down with a huge swallow of Dr Pepper. "He just took care of the property when Drake wasn't there."

His father had guns, Weeks said. Both rifles and handguns, and he was a hunter.

"It's not a big deal though. Everybody up there's got guns. Everybody hunts. That's why you're up there," he said, then finished the final half of his sandwich and tore open a small bag of Doritos.

"So Drake has guns?" she asked.

"I never seen one. Maybe he's the one guy around Grizzly Falls who doesn't hunt. He fishes, though. And he runs the cameras."

"Is he sexually involved with the kids?"

"He doesn't do the sex. He makes the movies and sells them."

"Where does he get the kids?"

"Dunno."

"You never spoke to any of 'em."

"If I did, my dad would beat me. He's got a special belt."

She couldn't wait to put Bart Weeks behind bars.

She asked a few more questions, but Phillip had told them everything he knew. When they were done, Tarley told Weeks that he'd be placed in a cell by himself, for his own protection. He'd be allowed to have most of his own belongings in the cell and would be fed separately.

"Almost like a motel," the detective said. "Keeping you safe. You're too valuable to be walking around where somebody might hurt you."

After Weeks had been put away, Tarley walked Regan outside where night had fallen, the sky stretching dark above the illumination of the streetlights.

"I think you got 'em."

God, she hoped.

She checked her watch. Just after ten p.m. Flowers and Johnson would probably be in the woods around Drake's place. Given Phillip Weeks's statement, and the probable imminent arrest of the RV couple, they had enough evidence to raid Drake's place, could easily get a warrant, and probably didn't need anything that Flowers and Johnson might turn up.

She called them from the front steps of the police station, but there was no answer. She left a message and went to look for a motel where she could wait for them to call back.

•◆•

VIRGIL AND JOHNSON HAD WALKED UP THE ROAD TO DRAKE'S CABIN, staying to the side, where they could step back into the brush if anyone came along. Nobody did, and when they crept up the road across from the cabin, they couldn't see the BMW they'd noticed on their first visit, though the Jeep remained in the open garage.

Virgil whispered, "Garage first. See if the other car's here."

They made a long circle through the forest around Drake's cabin, pausing every minute or so for one of them to tell the other to be more quiet. That was almost impossible. The brush was so dense that they were constantly tangled up in it. Virgil finally took out a flashlight and splashed its beam on the ground at his feet, tilted back enough that Johnson could see where to step. They emerged behind the garage, with the secondary cabin to their left. The garage had a back window and, through it, they could see that the second and third stalls were empty. Nothing inside but some lawn-care machinery and the Jeep.

"Now what?" Johnson whispered.

"Let's take a look at the small cabin."

"Could be alarmed."

"If it is, we run."

Johnson handed Virgil a piece of cloth.

"What's that?"

"Bandanna. Cover your face. Like a cowboy outlaw. In case there are cameras."

"Jesus, Johnson. Just because we're in Montana."

But Virgil did it anyway.

He was carrying Johnson's gun, not because he wanted to, but to keep it away from Johnson. A tire iron was Johnson's weapon because he didn't want to go unarmed. Virgil also had his Nikon, with the 14–24 zoom lens, in a day pack.

At the corner of the garage, they sat and waited, watching the house. There were two lights on inside, one in back, one in front, but none on the second story. A satellite dish sat on the roof, but there was no visible light from an operating TV. The lights never flickered, as they would if somebody walked between them and a window, and after five minutes, Virgil whispered, "Let's go."

They snuck, bent over, to the cabin, and stopped, crouching, by the corner and out of sight from the house, listening again. Nothing but the sounds from crickets and frogs, along with a bit of wind sighing through the trees rimming the property. Not a peep from within the house. After a while, Johnson said, "Weird."

"What?"

"No windows on this side. I didn't see any windows or a door on the back, either. Only windows in this place are on the front."

"Cover me," Virgil said.

"With what? A tire iron?"

He laughed. "Okay. Keep an eye out."

Silently, Virgil crawled past the front of the cabin, staying in shadow, to the first window. He sat still for a moment, then rose up to look through the pane.

Couldn't see anything.

A minute later was back with Johnson.

"What'd you see?"

"Nothing. It's a fake window. It's a board with some curtains painted on it."

Johnson said, "Cover me."

"What?"

But Johnson was already headed for the front of the cabin. A minute later, Virgil heard a crackling sound, like wood splintering and then Johnson saying, low voiced, "C'mon."

Through the still damp weeds and grass Virgil crept the length of a cabin, where he found that Johnson had jimmied the door with the tire iron and had gone inside.

Virgil followed. "What the fuck are you doing?"

"Let me close the door."

With that done, Johnson turned on the flashlight app of his iPhone and panned the illumination around the inside of the cabin. There was a bed in one corner with an end table and a couple of rolled-up carpets next to it. Three rolls of seamless paper lay along one wall, and a fourth roll was mounted on a roller behind the bed. Camera stands with umbrellas and soft boxes were crowded across the room along with their power supplies.

Virgil turned on his own cell-phone light, and said, "I need photos of the bed and the walls."

"The walls. That oughta do it," Johnson said, looking at the knotty pine planks that crawled up the sides of the room. "They're like the world's biggest fingerprints."

Virgil pulled off his pack, took the camera out, mounted the compact flash, set everything for automatic, and started shooting.

Quickly.

Efficiently.

He shot everything twice, then packed up.

Two minutes later they were gone, and twenty minutes after that they were talking with Pescoli.

• ◆ •

THE PHONE RANG JUST AS REGAN WAS GETTING OUT OF THE SHOWER.
She wrapped a towel around herself, picked up her phone, and sat on the
edge of the bed.

"It's Virgil. I've got the photos."

"Send 'em."

"I will. But the connection out here at the ranch, in the bar, is slow.
Wi-Fi's not the latest in technology. We'll see how it goes. I'll be sending
you nine shots."

"I'll move them to the FBI guy."

"Call me in the morning, when you hear back."

"First thing," she said and couldn't wait.

She threw on her pajamas and waited, pumping milk again, of course.
Fortunately, the motel had a minibar fridge.

The last of the photos came in a half hour later. They were, she
thought, some of the most boring photographs she'd ever seen. But they
were sharp, and exactly what the feds had asked for. She sent them on. After
a quick call to Santana explaining that she was staying over and would be
home the next day, she charged her phone, turned in, and thought about
her family, her job, and the balancing act that was her life.

The feds called at seven o'clock the next morning.

Regan was still asleep and for a second was disoriented, fumbling her
phone off the nightstand before answering.

"What time is it?"

Burch, the FBI agent, said, "Nine o'clock."

"Or seven o'clock, Mountain Time," she said around a yawn.

She needed coffee.

Then remembered she was still on decaf.

"I've got a lot to tell you," she said into her cell. "Did you see those
photographs?"

"I saw them two hours ago, at seven o'clock Eastern Time, because I
get up at dawn."

"Good for you. What do you think?"

"It's not what I think. It's what I know. This is large. We got an ID on the two people in Vegas. We're not sure we've got their real names, but we know them as Carla and Allen Dickerson."

"I got those names last night from the Weeks kid."

"We've had warrants for the Dickersons for years but haven't been able to nail them down. We thought they were somewhere in Central America. Anyway, we got their address from the Vegas guys, we'll be hitting that apartment—it's a condo, really—in a couple of hours. These are bad, bad people. In fact, the only worse guy I can think of is probably this Drake guy you say you've got up there. We've got flashes of those knotty pine walls in twenty-three films so far, the worst kind of porn you can imagine, which means he's probably made a couple hundred of them. We had no idea who was shooting it. We need this guy. Can the Weeks kid identify him?"

"Not only identify him, he's actually worked for him in a porn film when he was a kid."

"Ah, shit. There's a kid who's going to need some help."

"Yeah. We got him safe for the time being."

"So we're flying in a heavy SWAT team from Denver, but they probably won't get there until early afternoon," Burch said. "I'll be there at the same time; I'm on my way to National right now. The director actually got me a Justice Department jet. We'd like you to wait for us in Butte. That's as close as we can get to your target, and then guide us up there. We don't want to spook this Drake guy, but it'd be good if Flowers could check on him. You know, cruise the place. The thing is, we've got nobody named Michael Drake on file. We've looked at the county clerk's records up there, and they go back to a post office box with a fake name. If we lose him, we might be losing him for good."

"Alternatively, I could go up there right now and bust his ass," she suggested.

"I appreciate that, but one-on-one, too much could go wrong. Like I said, we really don't want to lose this guy. He's a genuine, no-shit monster."

"I'll call Flowers and tell him."

"One other thing. I'm sending you an encrypted link to a file here at the bureau. In another e-mail you'll find a code number to open it. You won't be able to download it. It's read only. A selection of clips from the knotty pine films. You ought to know what we're talking about."

"I'll take a look," she said. Then added, "Maybe."

"If you want to get in touch with me, it'll have to be in the next half hour," Burch said. "After that, I'll be up in the air and the connections to this phone won't be good. I'll have other com equipment, though, and I'll call *you* if anything changes."

Regan didn't really want to look at the films, but thought she had to. She sat staring at the iPad for a minute, then finally opened the mail from Burch, found the code number, copied it, went to the other e-mail from him, and pasted the number in the small square of the encrypted link.

Six links.

Six minutes.

Children.

She didn't even want to speculate on their ages.

Mostly little girls, with an occasional weeping little boy.

"Oh, Jesus, Jesus, Jesus," she whispered, tears in her eyes.

She didn't know if she was praying or cursing. Her stomach turned over and something ugly took hold of her heart and twisted.

"You sick, sick bastard," she whispered thinking of the man she'd never met, the man who went by Michael Drake. When she was done, she clicked away and received a warning that said, *When you leave this link, you will not be able to reenter without obtaining a new authorization and a new password.*

Thank God.

She closed the link.

That was something no one should ever see.

The feds were late, as usual.

Burch had called from the plane in early afternoon.

"Had a problem."

"Tell me."

"We hit the condo, the Dickerson-Foley-whoever condo in Riverdale. The Foleys are retirees, eighty-four and eighty-two, respectively. Never had the Visa account the RV was charged to. That account was active, but was paid online, no paperwork, so they never knew. The driver's license data goes to Clark Foley, but he hasn't had a license for four years."

"What, they pulled these old people at random?"

Damn, damn, and double damn.

Her fist clenched the cell phone in a death grip.

"Worse than that. We showed the Foleys the Dickerson photos, and they identified them as a couple named Smith who live in the same building, directly below the Foleys. We got a new warrant and hit that place. But it was empty, except for one of those cheap cell-phone-linked security systems. As soon as our guys cracked the door, a silent alarm went to a cell-phone number. So the Dickersons, whoever they are, could look at full-color moving pictures of our guys coming in. We didn't find it for three or four minutes after kicking the door."

"Shit," she muttered.

"One good thing. We got a quick fix on the cell phone, which was in Green Valley, Arizona, about forty-five miles north of the border. It looks like they're making tracks for Mexico. We were on to the border guys in ten minutes, and they had pictures five minutes after that. I think we got a good shot at them."

Burch told her that he'd be arriving after four o'clock.

"My plane didn't have quite the speed or the range that I thought. I kinda got shuffled off to a cheaper machine. We had to stop in Minneapolis to refuel and it took forever."

"What about your SWAT team?"

"They should be there before me, but not much."

•◆•

VIRGIL GOT THE CALL.

The Dickersons, who were really Ned and Jennifer Boniface, last known address Bakersfield, California, had been picked up, without incident just before reaching the border. The kids with them were safe and being identified, each with a story to tell. No word yet on if they were part of a bigger ring, but the feds were checking. He and Johnson set up across the river from Drake's house at midafternoon. The BMW was still parked in the yard, but the Jeep was missing.

He called Pescoli to tell her.

"We've got the plates, we'll find them. Problem is, about everybody who doesn't drive a pickup out here drives a Jeep."

"You exaggerate."

But then she drove one. Fairly new, with lots of power, fastest model available.

"Maybe so, but not much," he said.

"I'll tell you something, Virgil. I saw some of the film that Drake apparently shot, stuff that was filmed for sure in that back cabin. It's sick. The worst." She hesitated, felt that same terrible feeling she had when she'd viewed the porn. "I've dealt with a lot in my career as a cop, but this is worse than murder. Drake is worse than a killer."

"Let's not lose sight of the fact that he probably did murder somebody in cold blood."

"Don't worry, I won't," Pescoli said. "It's the homicide that will get him the needle."

"When was the last time someone was executed by the State of Montana?" he said. "I wouldn't count on that. But we can put him away for life."

"Not good enough," she said.

•◆•

REGAN MET THE SWAT TEAM ON THE TARMAC AT BERT MOONEY airport. Burch arrived forty-five minutes later. They all shook hands, went to a prearranged conference room where Burch reviewed the action with the SWAT team, which had been briefed before leaving Denver, and then they moved off to three waiting Chevy Tahoes, rented from the local car agencies, loaded the team's gear, and found the road to Grizzly Falls. She led the way in her own Jeep with Burch in the passenger seat.

He was a slender, tough-looking man who, it turned out, had spent six years with the Navy SEALs before joining the FBI. He skillfully extracted a brief autobiography from her and told her a little about himself. He was smart and engaging, but she got the impression that he badly wanted to be in on the raid for bureaucratic reasons. Taking down the knotty pine filmmaker would be a major coup, a step toward promotion.

Nothing wrong with that, she thought.

Except it annoyed her.

She and the SWAT team would have pulled off the raid in broad daylight, if they'd left without waiting for Burch.

Her cell phone rang.

"Got a break," Flowers said as she answered and negotiated a curve as they headed west. "Drake just got back. He's around behind the house where we can't see him, but I got a good look at him when he came in. He's there. Where the hell are you guys?"

"We're still about an hour out," she said.

"We could take him right now," Flowers said. "You could get the sheriff to deputize me."

"Let me check on that," she said, though it galled her to think Blackwater would be in on the takedown.

She passed Flowers's suggestion on to Burch, who shook his head. "No way. I spent some more time reading Flowers's file on the way here, and he has a way of making simple things complicated. Let me talk to him."

She handed the phone to Burch. "We appreciate what you're doing, but we mostly need intel. Eyes on the place. You were an army guy, right? So you know what we need."

She thought she heard a protest from Flowers, but Burch clicked off and she kept driving, her jaw set, her fingers tight on the wheel, the Montana countryside flying past, the sun sinking lower in the sky.

Flowers called back forty minutes later and said, "Drake just went up to Weeks's place in the Jeep. We could see him turn in, but we can't see what's going on."

"Call us back if anything changes," she said and Burch nodded.

As the miles had passed he'd grown more silent, his eyes steady on the road, he, like she, getting ready.

Twenty minutes later, another call. "Drake's gone back to his place. I don't know, Johnson and I are talking it over, I think he might be packing up or something. We can see him moving around inside the house, but we can't tell what he's doing."

"We're coming," she said. "We're five minutes out. Hold on." She glanced at Burch, then hit the gas.

"Stay on the line," she said to Flowers and punched the phone to speaker, so both she and Burch could hear.

Then she drove like hell.

Nothing changed during the last few minutes of the drive. According to Flowers, Drake was still at his house when she, leading the caravan, drove past the dude ranch. The sun was now down below the mountains, but the sky was still bright.

She pulled over when she was certain the vehicles could no longer be seen from the ranch, and the SWAT team armored up and went through a preraid routine, checking weapons, communications, and armor.

Burch, now out of his sport coat and slacks and into jeans, boots, and armor, told her to stay back. "I know you want to go in, but we don't know you. I don't mean to be offensive, but we've all trained for this and we've got communications and lights and there's lots of firepower out there. We don't want an accident."

She was pissed. "No way. That bastard is mine. I've been right on top of this."

Burch put a finger to his lips. "We really need you to wait here. Believe me, you're going to get a lot of credit in our reports. You wait here, talk to Flowers on your cell phone. If anything critical comes up, we'll leave a radio. You call me."

"I don't give a flying fuck about credit," she said, her lips barely moving, rage burning through her. In her mind's eye, she saw the porn films again, the scared children, the predatory adults. "I want in."

But Burch wasn't having any of it. "We're doing this military style. You know the area, so you call me. Any communication you get from your office, even from Flowers goes through you. I'm not taking any other calls. Only from you. You got that? Pass it on to Flowers. We have to run this tight. He calls you. You pass on the important information. Same with any calls from your sheriff. We do this my way."

Five minutes after they pulled over, and five hundred yards down the road from Drake's house, the SWAT team, with Burch at the point, slouched up the shoulder of the road, looking more like a squad of SEALs in Afghanistan than a bunch of cops in Montana.

And she was stuck back here.

Her teeth ground together and she had trouble reminding herself that being a cop was being a part of a team. Maybe Santana was right, maybe she should quit. She didn't need this shit.

But she loved it.

Flowers called again. "Where in the fuck are you guys? Something's going on. You gotta get up here. Drake is ready to move."

She reined in her frustration and tried to be rational. The important thing was to take down Drake.

"The troops are on the way in, on foot," she said into the phone. "They're five hundred yards down the road. They'll be there in five minutes."

"Can you call them?"

"I can."

Virgil said, "Tell them that. Hey, what the hell is he doing, Johnson? What? Sorry, talking to Johnson. What? Fuck. Look, Drake is up to something. He's loading up the Jeep, if a Jeep comes down the road, that'll be him."

"I'll pass it on," Regan said. "Hang tight, they're coming."

●◆●

VIRGIL AND JOHNSON WERE ON THE FAR SIDE OF THE SHALLOW RIVER, up on the bluff, looking down at Drake's cabin. They saw him throw what looked like a couple of large duffel bags into the Jeep, along with a rifle. Dusk crept through the trees and crawled across the land.

Drake was moving fast, jogging from the house to the studio cabin, where he spent a minute or two, then back to the house and then to the garage. He was carrying something bulky, but they didn't have binoculars and couldn't really tell what it was.

"He's carrying it like suitcases, but they look too small to be suitcases," Virgil said to Johnson. "I think we've got to work in closer."

"He could see us. The slope's mostly rock, not much cover. The feds are just down the road. I kinda like this cop shit, as long as I don't have to look at bodies. Maybe I oughta get deputized when I get back home."

"You have no qualifications, except possibly some insight into the criminal mind," he said.

"Don't need any qualifications to get deputized," Johnson said. "I'd say about two hundred dollars ought to get me a badge."

"Where in the fuck are the feds?" Virgil asked, getting a bad feeling about this.

Drake jogged back to the house from the garage, no longer carrying the suitcases. They could see him through the front windows of the houses, apparently waving another set of the squatty suitcases around.

"Ah, Jesus," he said squinting. "Those aren't suitcases. Those are gas cans. He's getting ready to torch the place."

"And the feds don't know it."

He speed-dialed Pescoli.

She picked up on the first ring.

"He's gonna torch the place," he warned. "You got no time, tell the feds, they got no time. He's gonna torch the place right now."

"I'm calling them."

And she was gone.

Down below, Drake hurried out of the house with a handful of what might be paper or rags, ran to the garage, lit whatever it was with a lighter, then threw the flaming ball into the garage. With a whoosh, the building exploded into flames.

"Damn," Virgil whispered as the building was engulfed.

Drake had apparently doused the BMW, which began burning with enthusiasm. The conflagration crackled to the sky, smoke and flames spiraling upward.

"Where the hell are they?" He searched beyond the inferno, looking for the SWAT team. "Where the fuck are they? I gotta do something."

"You heard Burch," Johnson reminded him.

Drake's next stop was the studio.

Johnson said to Virgil, "Gimme my gun. Maybe I can make him dodge around until the cops get here."

He didn't stop to think about it and handed the gun over. The range was ridiculous for Johnson's concealed-carry, short-nosed nine. But Johnson opened fire, and Drake froze for a moment, then threw a handful of burning whatever into the studio. The building exploded just as the garage had, flames twisting and hissing. Johnson fired fifteen times, but Drake ignored it, ran to the house, threw in the last ball of fire, and the house, obviously doused in gasoline as the other buildings went up quick, flames reaching skyward, lighting the area.

Virgil hit speed dial to Pescoli. "He's on the move."

"Where?" she asked, her own voice rising. "What the hell is happening?"

"He did it, he burned the place. Where is the team?"

"It's there. It should be there."

"Oh, crap. Drake's gone for the Jeep," he said, watching as Drake hopped into the rig and tore out, spraying gravel and speeding away, not toward the main road and into the SWAT team.

"He's in the Jeep, heading away from the main road. Driving toward the dead end. Where is he going?"

He watched the vehicle stop at the Weekses' place, though with the coming darkness and trees, his sight line wasn't clear. He heard shouting and within seconds flames shot skyward.

"He just blew up the Weekses' mobile home."

"Where is he? Still there?" she asked, her voice tense.

"I can't see. Call Burch. Tell him."

She hung up and Virgil said to Johnson, "Bet we find a body in Weekses' place."

"No bet," Johnson said.

Below them, they spied the headlights of what had to be Drake's Jeep, heading due west, away from the main road, toward the dead end.

"Where the fuck is he going?"

Virgil had a sinking feeling. He called Pescoli and when she picked up, said, "Is there some kind of timber road at the end of the dead end? A logging or mining road? Something that no one uses?"

He heard the yelling of the SWAT team now.

"I don't know. Maybe." There was dread in her voice. "Yes. The Long Mining company had some access road here, been closed for years."

"Why else take off in the Jeep? Why torch the BMW? The faster vehicle."

"I'll call Burch."

Again she rang off.

"You're probably right," Johnson, who'd overheard his part of the conversation, said.

"Here come the feds."

Below them the SWAT team streamed up the road toward the burning buildings, in good military order.

One minute too late.

•—◆—•

REGAN WAS WAITING IN HER JEEP WHEN FLOWERS CALLED AGAIN. HE gave it to her in a nutshell. The burning buildings, the stranded SWAT team, his belief that there might be a back way out.

"And he's got a rifle. I think he couldn't let the rifle burn, because we'd still be able to check it, and he doesn't know we never found a slug when Cain was shot."

"I'm going," she said. "No way is he getting out of here."

"Careful," Flowers said. He made no effort to talk her out of it, though she'd be one-on-one with Drake. "Don't forget the rifle. He's armed."

She didn't know of a back road out but knew if there was one, Drake couldn't go east because of the river and the bluff on the far side. He'd have to go west, sooner or later, to cut the highway, and it probably wouldn't be far.

She cranked up the Jeep and wrestled it around onto the road, tromped on the accelerator, and sped off. By the time she burned past the dude ranch she was doing sixty. She hit the highway and turned right, skidding around the corner, not caring, then rolled to the top of the nearest ridge, and waited.

She thought about the implications of all that fire. No fingerprints, no DNA, no knotty pine. Thoughts swirled. Adrenaline pumped.

To hell with the feds.

Again, she thought of the innocent kids, of the pictures she'd seen, the images she could never erase from her mind. Then her own kids, the older two when they were in elementary school, the baby.

Her back teeth ground together and she heard a rushing in her ears, her own blood pumping through her veins. For a second, everything went dark with the insidiousness of it all.

She blinked again. Focused. Amped up.

No way would she let that sick fuck get away.

She had her window down, listening for the sound of an engine. She squinted and smelled smoke. Although the sky was bright, the woods were getting darker, and Drake had to turn on his headlights to plow out of the timber road. She saw him coming when he was still fifty feet back, and then he bounced out of the trees, down through the roadside ditch and up on the highway. He turned right, as she had, and sped away from her. She followed, staying back for a minute, then hit her flashers and dropped the hammer. She knew these roads, that was her advantage, that and a bigger engine in her Jeep.

Drake made a run for it.

Speeding through the ever-closing night, his taillights burning bright.

She drove faster, feeling the tires hum and her heart pound as images of those innocent kids played through her mind.

On a straightaway, heading to a sharp corner, she roared up behind the older, overmatched Jeep until she was no more than six feet behind him. At the corner he swung wide, hit gravel on the far shoulder, a tire catching on the edge of the asphalt. As she slowed she watched his Jeep spin back across the road, headlights arcing, cutting through the night.

"Die, you bastard," she said, hitting the brakes.

Drake's Jeep slid off the side of the road, the front-right headlight smashing against a pine, the hood crumpling with a groan, an axle breaking.

Her vehicle slid to a stop on the shoulder.

Service weapon in her hand, she stepped onto the asphalt and screamed at his vehicle.

"Get out. I want to see your hands, and I want you out."

He didn't move.

"Now! Get out."

She advanced, crouching, wishing she was wearing a vest.

He kicked open his door, then slowly, hands over his head, he emerged from the Jeep. He was dressed in black from head to toe. Black dress shirt, black slacks, black shoes.

"What's this about?" he called out. "You nearly killed me. You some kind of psycho cop?"

"It's about all those children," she said, her throat raw. "Keep your hands over your head, and back away. I want you out in the headlights, or, I swear to God, I'll shoot you."

"I don't know anything about any children," he called to her, but did as he was instructed, and backed away. "I got a bad fire up there, my phone doesn't work, I was going to get the volunteer fire department. Could you call them for me?"

"Shut up," she said.

She was at the back of his Jeep and saw through the plastic window the rifle stacked up between the two front seats, ready to use.

"You were going to shoot your way out, if you didn't get clear, weren't you?"

So why hadn't he tried to shoot her? Something wasn't computing.

"I wasn't going to shoot anybody," Drake said, hands still over his head. "I've never committed a crime in my life. The worst thing I've ever done is let that fire get out of control, and I don't even have insurance. I think that goddamn Weeks started it, I found out he was doing something in my cabin while I wasn't here."

"That's not what Phillip Weeks told me," she said.

She pushed the Jeep's door open, switched hands on her pistol, and used her right hand to fish the rifle out of the Jeep.

"Phillip Weeks is a crazy, drug-addled boy," Drake shouted. "His old man has fed him opiates since he was ten years old. Nobody's going to believe a doper like him."

She looked at him and said, "You've almost got me convinced. You might walk."

"Might, bullshit. I've got the best attorneys in California. You're going to be lucky to have your job when they're finished with you. The best thing you could do right now is forget all this."

She looked down at the rifle.

Large-caliber bolt action, like the gun that had killed Cain. She pulled the bolt back an inch, then shut it, seeing the brassy flash of the cartridge going back into the chamber.

"You know, you killed the wrong guy down in the river. The guy who saw the girl in the RV. He's still back there."

In a split second Drake reached behind his back and pulled out a pistol. She fired.

He went down, his handgun flying from his grasp.

The rush in her ears was overpowering, the anger flooding through her veins nearly blinding her. Without thinking, she turned and using one hand, brought the rifle up and fired a single shot through the windshield of her Jeep.

Glass shattered.

"What are you—" Drake began, sputtering as he watched, white-faced, bleeding. "No. Wait. I didn't do anything."

She wiped down the stock and trigger with the bottom of her shirt.

"Wait," Drake said as the sound of sirens cut through the night. "Those kids. They were better off with me. They wanted to do it. I gave them a place to live and food and made them movie stars. They lived like kings and queens."

Rage swelled.

Blackness pulled at her vision.

Her finger curled over the trigger of her service weapon.

"For Christ's sake." Drake scrambled for his gun.

She shot him twice in the chest.

•◆•

VIRGIL SHOUTED DOWN AT THE FEDS, "HE'S GONE UP THE GRAVEL road, away from the county road."

The SWAT team, in the light of the fires, started jogging up the road toward Weeks's cabin.

"He's not there anymore," Johnson muttered.

He and Johnson crashed through the brush on the bluff, waded the shallow river, and ran down the road to the dude ranch, where everybody staying at the ranch, Katy, her siblings, and her parents, were all standing on the edge of the golf course, looking at the fire in the sky.

Jim Waller called to them as they passed, "Is that the Drake place? What's going on up there?"

They didn't bother to answer, but piled into Johnson's Cadillac and headed out to the highway.

"Gotta be a right turn," Johnson said.

A mile up the road, they found Pescoli sitting next to the right front wheel of her Jeep. She was holding a tissue next to her eye, showing a little blood. Up the road, they could see Drake, spread-eagled in the headlights of his Jeep.

He and Johnson jumped out of the Cadillac and they hurried up to her. She was white faced, her eyes a little glassy, but she answered.

"I'm not bad. I shot him twice, maybe three times. He thought we had him. He had nothing to lose by trying to take me out."

Her hand was shaking a little.

"He was right about that," Virgil said and saw the smashed-up Jeep and the body lying in the grass near the shoulder. "You check him?"

"Enough to know we don't need an ambulance," she said, chalk white, her voice distant, almost disembodied. She cleared her throat and focused on Virgil, as if seeing him for the first time. "I wish we could have taken him alive. I wish we could have gotten him in court."

"Probably better this way," Johnson said, avoiding looking at the corpse. "What if he'd gotten off? If what everybody says is true, the cocksucker deserves to be dead."

He and Regan both gave Johnson a look, and he muttered, "Okay. Sorry about that 'cocksucker.'"

Virgil stood up from checking the body and looked at Regan and Johnson.

"But you're right. He deserves to be dead. And now he is."

LARA ADRIAN AND CHRISTOPHER RICE

THRILLERS COME IN ALL FORMS. THE NUMBER OF SUBGENRES IS staggering, and this story is representative of one of the most popular.

Paranormal.

Lara Adrian has made a name for herself in this world where her books are huge bestsellers. True to his namesake (as the son of Anne Rice), Christopher Rice cut his teeth on dark suspense, before shifting to romance. Teaming these two together seemed like an exciting idea, but it also posed a few challenges. The timeline of Lara's long-running Midnight Breed series spans twenty-five years in the future. Chris sets his stories and characters in the present. So, right away, the clock had to be turned back to a time when Lara's vampires were unknown inside her imagined world.

But that played right into their hands.

Chris's initial idea was to have his Desire Exchange series character, Lilliane, attacked by someone on her home turf of New Orleans where Lara's character, Lucan Thorne, could witness both the altercation and Lilliane's extraordinary powers.

From there, everything fell right into place.

Lara wrote the first draft, then Chris rewrote and edited. The title is a bit of an inside thing. *Midnight* from Lara's long-running series. *Flame* from the candles that symbolically form a huge part of Chris's fictional world.

The result is a gem.

Midnight Flame.

MIDNIGHT FLAME

THUNDER SHOOK THE TINY FRENCH QUARTER BOOKSHOP AS LUCAN Thorne handed his cash to the young woman behind the register. Rain had been hammering New Orleans since he arrived from Boston a couple of days ago. As the evening crept toward midnight, the deluge showed no signs of letting up anytime soon either. He didn't mind getting wet. Besides, this last-minute stop for a special gift before returning home would be worth the trouble and then some.

The perky blond clerk made change for him and handed it over along with his purchase. "You sure picked a bad night to be out shopping. The city's a lot more fun when the weather's nice and everyone's out having a good time." When he reached for the paper gift bag, she brushed her fingers over his. "You gonna be in town for a while? I'd love to show you what I mean."

Under the fall of his damp black hair, Lucan smiled, baring just the tips of his fangs. "I'm not really a people person."

The human sucked in a sharp breath.

She let go of the bag as if it burned her fingers, blinking fast, her mortal brain no doubt struggling to process what she imagined she'd just seen.

"Thanks for your help, Krystal," he said, his fangs now retracted as he slipped the bag into a large inside pocket under his black trench coat.

"Uh, sure."

She gave him a befuddled wave as he left the store.

As he stepped out to the wet street, he heard the locks on the shop door tumble closed behind him. Revealing himself, or his kind's, existence to the humans living alongside the Breed wasn't something Lucan chanced often. As one of the eldest members of his kind, he knew better than anyone how critical it was for the vampire nation to maintain its secret from mankind.

As commander of the Order, a cadre of Breed warriors who'd pledged their arms and their lives to protecting the fragile peace with their mortal neighbors, there was nothing Lucan wouldn't do to ensure the security of both man and Breed alike. And if he thought for one second that the clerk inside the bookstore was any kind of threat to those goals, he'd have mind-scrubbed her on the spot.

Right now, all he wanted to do was get back to the Order's headquarters in Boston, where the rest of his team, and his new Breedmate, Gabrielle, awaited his return. After two days in New Orleans, smoothing the ruffled feathers of Breed civilian leaders worried that recent problems in Boston might spill over into other major cities unless the Order got them under control, he was eager to be done with his diplomatic duties. He itched to be back in combat with his warriors. More than that, he couldn't wait to be back in bed with his sweet Gabrielle.

The book he'd bought was a present for her. A signed first-edition novel by one of her favorite authors whose bestselling books had proclaimed New Orleans the vampire capital of the world and ignited a global obsession. Hell, decades later, women were still swooning over that certain French bloodsucker who was as sinister as he was sophisticated and seductive.

Personally, Lucan didn't understand the appeal.

And, yeah, maybe he didn't particularly appreciate competing with that fictional fantasy where Gabrielle was concerned either. But if the book made his mate happy, who was he to disagree?

Still, his ego needed some reassurance that his fangs were the only ones his Breedmate wanted at her neck.

Not to mention elsewhere.

Smiling as he pictured all the ways he and Gabrielle would celebrate his homecoming, he set out to find a lingerie shop to buy her something skimpy. Maybe something with tiny buttons he could bite off one by one as he undressed her.

Tilting his head down against the sluicing rain, he pushed deeper into the Quarter. He didn't have much company tonight. The storm had driven all but the most stalwart or inebriated tourists indoors. The restaurants and bars were packed and lively, but the streets outside were practically empty. Only a few shops remained open. Lucan walked past half a dozen T-shirt stalls and several more boutiques hawking everything from gourmet foods to sex toys. He wandered without a plan, trusting he'd eventually spot a window full of the frilly lace things Gabrielle liked.

How he ended up near a small, tucked-away courtyard filled with banana trees and a babbling fountain at its center he had no idea. Inside the courtyard, a coffee shop employee was just closing up for the night, dodging past the tarp-covered cast-iron tables and chairs outside. Of the handful of businesses that called the courtyard home, only one appeared to be open. Through the relentless curtain of pelting rain, Lucan's acute Breed vision caught the hand-painted wooden sign above the door.

FEU DE COEUR.

A candle shop, he guessed, noting the small gold flame etched above the logo on the weathered wood. Even through the rain he could smell flame-warmed wax. His keen nose seemed to detect something more, but it was impossibly delicate.

Elusive.

And now that he was staring closer at the small shop, even the storefront seemed hard to define. It wobbled in a peculiar way, seeming to fade in and out of his sight as if it wasn't completely solid.

Or not quite real?

Curious, Lucan started toward the shop.

He didn't get far.

Before he could cross the small courtyard, he heard the sound of rushing footsteps somewhere on the street outside.

"There she is. Let's get her."

A male voice, issuing orders in a low tone that only one of Lucan's kind could pick up from such a sizable distance.

"You knock the bitch down, Danny. I'll grab the case."

The two pairs of footsteps sped up now, heavy boots running hard through the downpour and coming his way.

Lucan didn't like any of it. In a blink, he was out of the courtyard and back on the street, just in time to see a pair of rangy human males beating feet behind a tall, full-figured, and elegantly dressed black woman who was making her way up the street toward the courtyard.

She toted a briefcase in her right hand.

The case her pair of fast-approaching attackers were intent on taking unless he stopped them.

Hadn't he just been thinking how ready he was to be back on patrol?

Dispatching a couple of idiot mortal thieves was child's play, but he'd gladly take it.

Except he didn't get the chance.

No sooner had he moved to take action, intending to leapfrog the woman and position himself between her and the two assailants, than she pivoted on her heels and faced off against the pair.

Was she crazy?

One of the two rushed her.

She tossed him aside with a sweep of her free hand. She was superstrong. Inhumanly so. A spray of gold dust shot out of her fingertips, trailing after her dispatched attacker like an arc of delicate glitter.

Who, or what, the hell was she?

Still, there were two assailants and only one of her. And despite the fact that she was something Lucan had never seen before, she was still a woman and he wasn't about to stand by and let her take on these hoods alone. Calling upon his Breed genetics, he moved in front of her faster than any human eye could track. Combat instinct raged through his veins. His fangs punched out of his gums, firing his dark-gray irises to coal-bright amber behind his narrowing, cat's-eye pupils. He grabbed the second attacker by the collar and held the man aloft, his boots several inches off the ground. The man screamed when he saw Lucan's face, making a frantic, but futile, attempt to scramble loose from his hold. Across the street, his buddy staggered to his feet and stared slack-jawed. Then he bolted, leaving his comrade to face the music alone.

"Let me go. Please. I don't wanna die."

Lucan ignored his struggling, whimpering quarry and turned his head to look at the woman behind him. She was beautiful, with an ageless face and deep brown eyes that seemed fathomless in the darkness.

"You okay?"

She nodded, studying him in guarded silence.

"Please, let me go," the human whined. "I's only doin' a job, that's all. Me and my friend were hired to jump the lady and see what happened. I swear, we weren't gonna hurt her."

The woman scowled.

Her lovely face held an unearthly, dangerous rage. "Who told you to do this? Who wanted to see what would happen?"

The answer came a moment later, though not from the hired thug swinging at the end of Lucan's grasp.

Headlights blinked on from down an alley across the street.

The twin high beams cut through the rain as a dark van rocketed out of the side street and swung past them in a scream of burning rubber.

The lone driver held a video camera in his hand, its tiny red recording light trained on Lucan's face as the vehicle sped away.

• ◆ •

LILLIANE'S FAMOUS TEMPER SMOLDERED AS SHE WATCHED THE VAN disappear into the rain-filled night, its taillights swallowed up by the darkness. She cut a glance at the vampire standing next to her.

"Where did you come from?"

He grunted, sounding as displeased as she was. "I might ask you the same thing. What's your name? How did you end up on the radar of this fool and his friend with the camera?"

Her would-be assailant had since fainted dead away and now hung limp in the big vampire's grasp. She pursed her lips, her fingers curling tighter around the jeweled handle of her briefcase.

"Only a few people know about the kind of business I do around here and this guy's not one of 'em. Trust me."

"Trust is earned."

He released the unconscious human, letting the man slump to the wet pavement. Gray eyes, shot with amber sparks, met her gaze through the relentless deluge. As she watched, his pupils transformed from narrow vertical slits to rounded pools of black. Behind his lips the points of the big male's fangs gleamed diamond-bright.

"Your name," he said again, more demand than inquiry.

"Lilliane."

"Your last name?" he asked, bearing his fangs slightly.

"Smith," she lied, summoning a swell of emotion she knew would fill her eyes with a brief shimmer of gold.

He seemed dazed by this display for a second, then he introduced himself.

"Lucan Thorne."

She smirked. "Your kind isn't the only thing that goes bump in the night, Mr. Thorne."

He frowned, clearly taken aback. "You're not Breed."

"No."

"But you *are* immortal."

"That remains to be seen."

In truth, she was uncertain just how to classify what she and the twenty-three other Radiants like her actually were. On some days she felt special. Blessed by her ability to leap several stories into the air, to send would-be attackers flying backward with just a flick of her wrist. She didn't age. She didn't get sick. All wonderful things, right?

But on other days, she felt cursed by the fact that a decision she'd made decades before had robbed her of the ability to feel anything close to romantic love for another being, mortal or immortal. She wasn't alone in this struggle. There were twenty-three others just like her, extraordinary creatures with extraordinary powers. She served as their mentor and mother, even though she played no role in their creation. But none of them could agree on what to call their condition, just that the exact same chain of events had made each one of them what they were now.

Lucan stared at her in silent contemplation before glancing down at the unconscious human at his feet. "Lilliane Smith, whoever or whatever you are, it's obvious that you and I have a big problem here. We need to talk."

As much as she wanted to deny it, the Breed warrior was right. "Come with me. Let's get out of the rain."

She stepped into the small courtyard, Lucan Thorne walking behind her, carrying the fainted human over his shoulder.

"This way," she said, leading him to the candle shop nestled in the corner of the square.

The vampire cleared his throat. "I'd rather we go somewhere a bit more discreet, Lilliane. Someplace secure."

"We won't find anywhere more discreet or secure in all the city," she assured him. "Or all the world, probably."

She'd been coming to this place when the pair of men assaulted her. And while the shop's enigmatic proprietor, Bastian Drake, wasn't likely to welcome this late-night intrusion, the fact that the store's light was still burning in the window, the fact that the shop itself hadn't disappeared from sight altogether by way of his powerful magic, was signal enough that she and her unwanted new acquaintance could take shelter inside for a while.

She opened the door and led Lucan Thorne inside. Shrugging out of her soaked raincoat, she indicated an empty wooden chair and watched as the vampire dumped the human onto the seat.

"Are we alone here?" he asked.

"Alone enough."

She noticed how his shrewd gaze surveyed the cramped space with its rug-covered, old wood floors and the dozens of thick candles on display in unusual burnt-umber glass containers. "I know the owner of this shop. We won't be disturbed."

"Considering how the rest of this evening's gone already, you'd better be damned sure of that."

She laid down her briefcase. "Suffice to say, the proprietor isn't exactly what you'd call a people person."

The remark earned a cryptic smirk from the massive Breed male.

"Strange place," he said, strolling over to a collection of candles shelved on the far wall. He brought one to his nose and sniffed shallowly. Then he jerked his head away, as if his preternatural senses told him he wasn't merely smelling poured wax and some added fragrance, but something else.

Something primal, raw. Otherworldly.

"Smells terrible, doesn't it?" she asked.

"That and then some." He returned the candle to its shelf. "The presentation had me fooled."

"That's because it's not for you."

"What do you mean?"

"The candle. It's not meant for you. So to your nose it probably smells like pond water or something worse."

"And the one it's meant for? What will it smell like to them?"

Her eyes glazed over but held their natural color. "Ever been in love?"

"I am now."

"Ah, you're sweet."

"I'm not talking about you."

"And I wasn't remotely serious, so sheathe those fangs, big boy. Is the love of your life a he or a she?"

"She."

"She's got a smell, right? A special smell. Not just the smell of her skin, but the way her skin smells when she's flushed and ready for you, beckoning to you. It's a smell that makes you feel like you're in her arms no matter where you are when you smell it."

"I suppose so."

"If that candle was meant for you, that's what it would smell like to you. Only none of these candles are meant for you, because you're already with the love of your life. Or at least it sounds like it. But if you weren't, and the love of your life was in your life, but you weren't man enough to step up and try to make a move, or you had a hundred excuses why it wasn't going to work and you shouldn't even try, eventually, you might find yourself here, smelling her smell in one of those candles."

"I see."

"Do you? Or are you just humoring me? I'm not really sure how to handle skepticism from a vampire, so you'll have to bear with me for a second."

"I've got a question. If there isn't a candle for me here, why'd this place appear to me at all?"

"I don't know."

"Maybe the guy who runs it wanted me to help you. Maybe that's why I wound up in this courtyard right as you were attacked."

His words gave a tense set to her jaw. "Let's stop speculating and get back to the business at hand."

"Fine. You going to tell me what's in that fancy case of yours, or am I going to have to open it and see for myself?"

She saw no reason to lie. After all, as he'd pointed out, they shared a common problem tonight. Namely, both of them being revealed to the world as something other than human. She lifted the glossy leather briefcase and flipped the jeweled locks open. Holding the open case in her arms, she presented the contents to him.

He strode over to look at the half-dozen glowing jars, nestled safe in their cushioned sleeves inside the case. Their illumination seemed to startle the large warrior. He drew back, as wary as any solar-allergic being should be.

"Is that light captured inside them?"

"In a manner of speaking." She glanced at the soft hues that burned like colored embers in the jars. "They hold the pure essence of true desire. That's a force even more powerful than light. More powerful than most anything in this world, or the next."

He swiveled his head and took in the scores of candles that surrounded them. "And your friend who runs this shop. How does he fit into the equation?"

"He's not my friend." Her jaw stiffened. "As for what he does, that's a long story. And one best saved for another time."

The unconscious man slouched in the chair across the room was beginning to rouse.

"I'll just say this. I've got a little business I run that supplies him with what he needs to run his place. All my customers walk away happy. Most of his do too."

"Most, huh?"

"Like I said, long story."

Lucan cursed under his breath. "Long story or not, before this is all over tonight, you will tell me."

She inclined her head, observing as he stalked toward the unconscious human and hoisted the man upright in the wooden chair. The man's head lolled before finally facing Lucan. As soon as his bleary eyes opened, the human sucked in air and practically leapt off his seat in terror.

"Oh, God, no. I thought it was a nightmare."

"That's all it is," Lucan said, placing his palm against the man's sweaty brow. "A bad dream. Relax now."

The human complied immediately.

His trembling ceased, along with his panicked stammering.

"What are you doing?" she asked, setting her briefcase down to draw up beside the vampire.

"I tranced him. He'll tell us everything we ask." Lucan turned his attention back on the calmed human. "You can start with your name."

"Danny Boudreaux."

Lucan glanced her way and she shrugged, signaling that the name meant nothing to her.

"What about your friend in the van, Danny? What's his name?"

"I dunno. My friend Ricky—he knows him, not me."

"Ricky is the other guy you were with tonight?"

Danny nodded.

"And what did Ricky tell you about the man with the camera?"

"He said the dude was offerin' us fifty bucks to come with him and jump this lady he's been watchin' for a couple of months. Said he wanted to see what would happen if we got her good and pissed off."

"You succeeded," she muttered.

"There was supposed to be an extra hundred in it for us if we could grab the bitch's briefcase away from her."

"A lousy hundred dollars," she said. "You don't have the first idea what's in these jars or what to do with it. And you'd spend the rest of your miserable life trying to figure it out."

Lucan slanted her a look. "I don't think it mattered to anyone what was inside it. The man with the camera knew the briefcase was important to you. He only wanted to test your reaction to the theft. He's been watching you long enough to know your habits, where to find you."

"What for? Just to make a feeble attempt to mug me?"

His face turned grim. "So he could capture the altercation on video. More specifically, your reaction."

She arched a brow as a cold understanding settled on her. "Because whoever's been watching me knew my reaction would be something more than human."

He nodded. "And now he has both of us on video during the attack."

"We need to get that camera."

"The man who hired you, Danny. Do you know where we can find him?"

The human shook his head, his eyes closed, his mind still caught in the web of the trance. "I don't know anything else. Ricky set it all up."

Danny slumped and a cell phone screeched with a heavy metal ringtone. The grating noise filled the shop, although it didn't seem to register with the dazed human at all. Lucan rifled through Danny's pockets and found the bleating phone.

"Jackpot."

He held the phone up, showing her the name on the screen.

Ricky.

He pushed the call to voice mail, silencing the racket. "We have everything we need now. I've got a plan."

She pointed at Danny. "What are you going to do with him?"

He smirked. "Mind-scrub the little fuck, then toss him back in the gutter. When he comes to again in the morning, he'll have one wicked hangover, but he won't remember a thing that happened."

"Nothing at all?"

"Not a thing."

She walked over and punched the human in the face.

"Feel better?" he asked.

"Much. Let's hear your plan, vampire."

•◆•

AFTER DUMPING DANNY IN A SIDE ALLEY A FEW BLOCKS AWAY FROM the candle shop, Lucan and Lilliane hailed a taxi and headed to the Bywater to find one Richard "Ricky" Dubois.

A quick call to Gideon, the Order's resident computer genius at the Boston headquarters, had been all it took to gather a full dossier on Danny's erstwhile partner in crime. The GPS tracer Gideon placed on Ricky's cell-phone signal now led them straight to the small-time thief's location outside a seedy bar down at the river. The place was packed, never mind that it was also dank and dilapidated, a squat redbrick eyesore sitting about as far off the tourist maps as you could get.

Lucan didn't have to guess which of the huddled, drowned rats smoking blunts under the tattered awning at the bar's entrance across the street was the human he needed to find. He could still picture Ricky's slack-jawed stare from earlier tonight. Judging from the way he weaved and swayed on his feet, Ricky had been trying to take the edge off his tattered nerves. Better that he ended up here instead of running to the police station with his eyewitness account of paranormal happenings. Although, given Ricky Dubois's rap sheet, Lucan doubted he would ever approach the authorities on a voluntary basis.

He paid the cab fare, then looked at Lilliane beside him. "You sure you're ready to do this?"

"I've never been ready for most of the things that have happened to me, and yet here I am. Hunting lowlifes with a vampire. Next stop, Disneyland."

"Yeah. You could be one of the attractions."

"I feel like I should be offended by that."

"I'll let you make jokes about me stopping off at the blood bank for a snack if it makes you feel better. In the meantime, we've got work to do."

He wasn't used to bringing civilians along on patrols with him, least of all an unarmed woman of questionable powers who might slow him down. As one of the Breed he could traverse miles in mere minutes. He would have done so on this mission, but Lilliane had made it clear before they left the candle shop that this was her problem as much as his and she wasn't about to sit on the sidelines. So, like it or not, and for the record he didn't, he was saddled with a partner.

"I repeat," he said. "Are you ready?"

"Do it."

They stepped out and the taxi rolled away.

He'd hoped to have the element of surprise on their side, but as they crossed the street, Ricky Dubois glanced over and spotted the incoming threat. His face paled to a ghostly shade of white.

Then he bolted.

Straight into the crowded bar.

"You take the front entrance," he told Lilliane. "Flush him out toward the back. I'll cover the rear of the building and make sure our little rat doesn't slip his trap."

She nodded and they split up.

He knew he didn't have to wait and make sure she made it inside. The woman was strong and capable of handling herself. He only hoped she'd stick with the plan to collar Ricky so they could interrogate him, not cold-cock the idiot into next week the way she'd done to Danny.

Not that he blamed her.

It wasn't so long ago that his famous temper had ruled him too. He'd been angry at the world. Angry with himself for all the ways he'd failed in life, and for all the things he couldn't change. Meeting Gabrielle had changed that. She changed him. He couldn't help wondering if some of Lilliane's fury might be from self-inflicted wounds as well.

In another place, another time, he might be interested to find out.

Right now, all he wanted to do was fix this situation, then get home to his mate and team.

Lilliane Smith's problems were her own to solve.

Calling on his Breed genetics, he flashed past the crowd near the front entrance like nothing more than a chilled breeze. He was waiting at the bar's back door when Ricky crashed through from inside and stumbled onto the rough gravel.

Lilliane emerged right behind him.

Her eyes glowed with that same unearthly fire she'd shown him when he first bared his fangs. For a moment the effect was so jarring, Lucan might have mistaken her for Breed.

But she was something else.

And this time she was truly pissed.

Lilliane pushed the human several feet in the air with a sweep of her hand. Screaming as he sailed high in the air, Ricky came down hard on a rickety old dock at the river's edge. The rotting wood groaned from the crash, some of the boards cracking as they heaved and rocked over the dark water. Her hands fisted at her sides, she stalked forward onto the dock. Ricky's wide eyes were locked on her in terror. Beneath him, the old dock swayed as he frantically crab-scrambled for the farthest edge. The wood started to break. The dock pitched violently to the side. Ricky lost his hold. The platform gave way, dumping him into the murky drink.

Only then did she pause.

No. More froze.

Watching, stock-still, as their quarry started swimming away.

Lucan plowed past her and dove in.

●━◆━●

"YOU WANT TO TELL ME WHAT THAT WAS ABOUT BACK THERE AT THE dock?" Lucan asked, shrugging out of his soaked black leather trench coat.

To avoid attracting any more attention, after fishing Ricky Dubois from the Mississippi they'd immediately brought the human to an abandoned house a few blocks away. Inside the neglected ruin that likely hadn't seen inhabitants since Katrina, they'd conducted a tranced interrogation. He'd given them the name and address of the local private investigator who hired them tonight, but like his pal Danny, Ricky didn't know how or why Lilliane had ended up on the PI's radar.

Now, with Ricky mind-scrubbed and unconscious following his questioning, she watched as Lucan set his coat aside then pulled off his shirt and squeezed the foul water from his clothing. She couldn't help noticing the complicated pattern of skin markings that danced and swirled over the Breed male's torso and muscled arms. They weren't tattoos, not the way their colors changed and moved.

There was a lot she didn't know about his kind.

And vice versa.

Yet here they were, forced to work together to protect the secrets of both their people.

"I don't swim," she said, belatedly answering his question as to why she froze.

"All that power and badassery, but you don't know how to swim?"

"I know how to swim. I said I don't swim. Not anymore. Not since . . ." Her words trailed off.

"Not since when?"

"Since I became what I am."

"Which is?"

"I'm called a Radiant. Fifty-odd years ago I was just a woman. Mortal."

"What happened?"

She shrugged nonchalantly, but the taste of regret hung bitter in her throat. "I made a terrible mistake. One I cannot correct."

"Does your mistake have something to do with that strange candle shop back in the Quarter?"

She nodded, seeing no need to hide the facts from him. "One of those candles, the one meant for me. It found me. The shop. The man who runs it. The *ghost* who runs it. They all found me. Light this flame at the scene of your greatest passion and your heart's desire will be yours."

"Did you?"

"My heart's desire was the white son of the family I cleaned house for. It was 1959. What do you think our chance of success would have been?"

"That's not what I asked."

"I lit it. And something came out of it I had no words for. I thought they were ghosts at first. But they weren't. They were more like a force, a force from the spirit world itself. I was supposed to give myself over to it. It filled me, literally. It filled me with a desire to go to him, to make my feelings known. Feelings I knew he shared. But I was one of the few people strong enough to resist. As a result, I was changed forever. Changed into this."

With a flick of her wrist she caused the remains of the nearest rotting door to slam shut on its weak hinges. For added effect she flicked her index finger against the ball of her thumb and sent a little trail of gold dust shimmering through the humid air.

"It's like the force that came out of the candle that night is trapped in me forever. But it's more than that. I was offered a chance at true love, and I denied it. I was afraid. I wasn't ready to risk everything. This," she said, gesturing to herself, "is my punishment. Alive, but loveless. My powers, my gifts, if you can call them that, I use them to help others find their true desire. But as for me I can't love anymore. Not like that anyway. Not like I loved him."

"What was his name?"

"Doesn't matter."

His hard gray eyes softened as he listened to her pitiful history. "No wonder you're mad at yourself and the world. If I didn't have Gabrielle, if I had lost the chance to have her in my life as my mate." He blew out a sharp curse and shook his head. "I'm sorry, Lilliane. For everything you've been through. It doesn't seem fair. It doesn't seem right. To have your entire existence shaped by one choice like that."

She wasn't accustomed to compassion. Lord, it was so rare she hardly knew what to do with it anymore. She spent most of her time caring for the other Radiants. Bossing them around. Cautioning them against leaping seven-story buildings in broad daylight or getting their aliases confused. To suddenly have her needs addressed by this inhuman predator whose reputation for cold justice and a general lack of mercy was legend, even among her kind, left her at a total loss for words.

She watched in awkward silence as he pulled something out of his trench coat, his dark brow furrowed, his broad mouth flattened in a dismayed line. From out of a sodden paper bag, he withdrew a waterlogged book.

His eyes were filled with disappointment.

"A souvenir for your lady?" she asked.

"A novel by one of her favorite authors. A signed first edition. Now it's only fit for the trash."

She caught the author's name on the jacket and smiled. "I know some people who might be able to help. The business I run, we've made a lot of contacts in the city over the years. Maybe when this is over tonight, I can arrange to procure you another copy."

He stared at her for a long moment, the hint of a smile playing at the corner of his lips. "You're a good person, Lilliane Smith. Better than you seem to believe."

Reluctantly, she allowed a rare smile to curve her mouth too. "I have a feeling the same could be said of you, Lucan Thorne."

He chuckled as he donned his wrung-out shirt, then tossed his wet trench coat and the ruined book onto a pile of rubbish in the corner of the decrepit house.

"What do you say, partner? Ready to go conduct a breaking and entering on Ricky's friend with the camera?"

She nodded. "Let's get out of here. Oh, and Lucan?"

He stared at her.

"It's Williams. Lilliane Williams."

•—◆—•

ALTHOUGH THE PEELING, STENCILED SIGNAGE ON THE DOOR OF Harold T. Grainger's office in the Ninth Ward proclaimed him a private investigator, Lucan was willing to bet the man collected just as many fees for skip tracing and bounty hunting than he did legitimate investigative work.

Sitting alone in his dingy office, Grainger yammered on the phone at his desk with his back to the door, oblivious, as Lucan silently tripped the lock and he and Lilliane entered.

"I'm telling you, this footage is the real deal, Bart. The woman threw a grown man halfway across the street with one hand and the big dude in black leather who came to her rescue had a mouth full of fangs and eyes like a pair of glowing coals. What? No, I'm not smoking something, wiseass. I saw the whole thing with my own eyes and I've got the damned footage to prove it right here in front of me." He leaned back in his brown leather swivel chair and chuckled, pausing to munch on a half-eaten Slim Jim. "Look, the point is there've been rumors about this Desire Exchange place for years and I'm willing to bet the house this woman's part of it." He paused, listening. "Who cares if I don't own a house? Goddammit.

Listen. Never mind how I managed to get the video. You want a piece of this action, or not?"

Lucan barely contained his growl as he stole farther into the office. Beside him, Lilliane radiated anger too, all of it focused on the sleazy opportunist seated a few paces in front of them.

Under the glare of the fluorescent ceiling lights, Grainger's pale, balding head gleamed like a sweaty cue ball as he rocked in his creaky chair.

"So, what do you say, Bart? I called you first because we're friends. Wanted to give you first dibs, but I gotta tell ya. This video is not gonna come cheap. Soon as I can link this woman to one of those rich bitches who head out into the swamp to have their deepest fantasies realized, or some such shit, this whole thing's gonna blow up. But for now, I'll be generous. I'm looking for twenty grand, no less." A pause. "What do you mean you want a clip to prove it's legit? I wouldn't shit you, Bart. Yeah, yeah. Okay, sure. I can send you a couple of frames. Tell you what. I'll e-mail—"

Some instinct must have finally clued Grainger into the fact that he wasn't alone in the dank little office. With the skinny tube of processed meat clenched between his molars like a cigar, he swiveled slowly in his chair.

All the color drained from his jowly face.

Lucan gave him a flash of fangs. "You have something that belongs to us."

Grainger's mouth opened in mute shock, his eyes bulging in their sockets. The gnawed stick of salted meat tumbled into his lap, along with his cell phone. Lucan severed the connection to the man on the other end of the line with a sharp mental command. Grainger fumbled with the center drawer of his desk, pulling out a revolver, barely holding onto the weapon in his shaking hands.

"What do you think you're going to do with that?" Lucan asked, confident that the terrified human wouldn't be able to squeeze off an accurate shot, much less one that could stop a member of the Breed.

Grainger's fearful, bug-eyed gaze bounced between Lucan and Lilliane. "What the hell are you two?"

Lilliane's answering smile was cold. "We're your worst nightmare."

Lucan nodded. "If you're lucky, when you wake up tomorrow, that's all this will be."

"Fuck both of you," Grainger shouted, overcome with a sudden burst of bravado and stupidity.

The barrel of the gun wobbled, his finger tightening on the trigger.

With his mind, Lucan whisked the weapon from the human's hands and sent it clattering away. Grainger let out a high-pitched scream and threw himself out of his chair, frantically crawling for the door. Lilliane planted the heel of her boot in the center of the mortal's back, pinning him to the floor.

"You're not going anywhere," she said. "We need to have a little talk about why you've been following me."

"It wasn't like that. It wasn't you I was following," Grainger sputtered, his cheek mashed into the filthy commercial tile. "Not at first, that is."

They exchanged looks.

"Explain," Lucan growled.

"I was on a job. Tailing a cheating husband around the Quarter." His terrified eyes rolled up to look at Lilliane. "That's when I noticed you and that fancy briefcase you always carried with you. I saw you going into a candle shop with it one day. And while I was watching you, I swear to God I saw the place just disappear."

"What else did you see?" Lilliane asked.

The investigator squirmed under her foot, but she gave him no room to break loose.

"What else did you see?" Lucan demanded.

Grainger wheezed beneath her boot heel. "I started following you after that. Shadowed you for a couple of weeks. And I saw you go into that same shop again. Feu de Coeur. Except the shop was in a different place than before. An entirely different part of the city. And then I knew I wasn't imagining things. Something odd was going on. I knew there was something odd about you. And I figured it had—"

"You figured it had what?" she asked.

"Look, we've all heard the rumors. Some place out in the swamp where rich folks go to get their jollies on. Either it's some club or some weird cult. But they do all sorts of crazy stuff. Some folks come back saying it's the drugs they were given. Others, they say it's some crazy shit. People who can lay their hands on them and make their fantasies come true. Almost like they're transporting them to another world. Look, I didn't make this stuff up, I'm just saying that is a great story. We're talking Pulitzer quality."

Lucan grunted. "Since when do third-rate PIs give a damn about winning Pulitzers?"

"Fame is fame, my friend," Grainger said.

"And so you decided to hire a couple of stooges to knock the lady over because you didn't have the balls to get your own hands dirty?"

"I needed to know what would happen."

"You needed to see if you could profit from it," she said. "Who were you planning to sell your tape to?"

"You," Grainger said. "I figured I could sell it to you, to protect whatever secrets you were keeping."

Lilliane's eyes narrowed in fury. "You weren't out to expose the Desire Exchange. And you couldn't have cared less about fame. All you cared about was blackmail?"

"I never expected to see everything I did tonight," Grainger said. "I never expected to see a vampire."

Lucan reached down and freed the man from under Lilliane's heel. Holding him by the throat, he made sure Grainger got up close and personal with his razor-sharp canines and smoldering amber eyes. "Take a good look, because my fangs are going to be the last thing you see tonight. Right before they shred your carotid."

"Oh, God, no. I'm begging you."

"Then you'd better give us every bit of video you took tonight. And if I find out you already sold it to anyone or made a bunch of copies—"

"I swear, I didn't."

"I don't believe him," she said. "I vote you sever his artery anyway."

Grainger's eyes popped in horror. "I'm telling you the truth. You've got to believe me. The only footage is what's on the card in my camera. Please, don't kill me."

Lucan wouldn't murder a civilian in cold blood, no matter how tempted he might be.

He glanced at Lilliane and she arched a knowing brow. "Oh, come on, vampire. Can't we just play with the mortal for a little while?"

He knew her well enough now to realize she was only kidding, but Grainger didn't know that. He'd already pissed on himself once, but from the way he trembled now, Lucan wouldn't be surprised if Grainger wet his pants all over again. Before his grin could betray him, Lucan reached out and pressed his palm to the human's forehead.

The touch put the man into a deep trance.

"You're no fun," she grumbled.

"Remind me never to piss you off, Radiant." He nodded to the video camera lying on Grainger's desk. "You grab the memory card out of that camera and I'll make sure we're not leaving anything else behind here in the office."

As she moved to carry out his instructions, Lucan called Gideon at the Order's headquarters and explained what happened. "Grainger swears he didn't make copies, but that's not good enough for me. Can you wipe out all the video files he has on his computers?"

"You seriously did not just ask me that. I can do this blindfolded and with one hand tied behind my back."

"Just do it," Lucan said. "I'll give you five minutes to make it happen. I'm overdue at home and I've got a plane to catch before sunrise."

THANKFULLY, GIDEON ONLY NEEDED THREE MINUTES.

With the video camera memory card confiscated and Grainger's hard drives infested with a virus that no one without a PhD in advanced computer science could untangle, Lucan and Lilliane stepped out of the private investigator's office and locked up behind them as stealthily as they'd arrived.

"Mission accomplished," she said as they paused together on the darkened street. She held the small video card between her thumb and forefinger. "To think this little piece of circuitry could've proven a disaster for us both."

He arched a brow. "Not to mention for your candle maker and his unusual shop. And this Desire Exchange place."

"You heard the man. The Desire Exchange is just about people getting together to have a little fun. It's just about sex."

"And whatever you do out there with your rich clients, that's where the jars come from? And then you take them to this Bastian Drake guy so he can make more candles out of them. Even though it's one of his candles that made you what you are."

"I didn't say it was a perfect arrangement. But what can I say?" She threw him a warm smile. "Extraordinary people have to find ways to work together. Right, vampire?"

"You're working for the man who made you what you are. You're working for the man who stole your ability to love."

"Twelve hundred," she whispered.

"What?"

"Twelve hundred people. That's how many have accepted his little gift of candles. That's how many people followed the instructions on the card and suddenly found the courage to embrace their heart's desire. Do you want to know how many there are like me?"

He nodded.

"Twenty-three. Twelve hundred people find true love thanks to Bastian Drake and his shop. Twenty-three end up never aging another day in their lives and leaping seven-story buildings in a single bound. Whatever magic governs that shop, whatever Bastian Drake is, maybe it's a fair trade-off in the end."

"You really believe that?"

"Today I do. 'Cause I got my tape, thanks to you."

She snapped her fingers and suddenly a light rain of gold dust showered down on his head and shoulders. He smiled despite himself, but by the time he went to brush it away, it seemed to be evaporating already.

"You must be eager to return home to your Gabrielle."

"I am," he admitted. "Two days is the longest I've been away from her since we mated."

"Then you should go to her. Our work is done."

"So it is." He cleared his throat, holding out his hand. "Not that I don't trust you with it, but I'll take that video card now."

"Of course. I have no use for it." She dropped it into his open palm. "Consider it a memento of your visit to my city."

He chuckled. "I hope you'll understand if I'd rather burn it than watch it. I don't need any reminders of the fact that both of us were nearly outed tonight."

Her mouth quirked as she stared at him in the postmidnight darkness. "You know, I never thought I'd say this, but it's been a pleasure meeting you, Lucan Thorne."

"Likewise," he said as he slipped the video card into his pocket. He extended his hand and smiled when she clasped his fingers in a firm grasp. "I hope you get it back, Lilliane."

"Get what?"

"Your ability to fall in love."

Her smile faded, but the light in her solemn, dark eyes seemed warm with acknowledgment. "Even if it means losing this?"

She vanished from view.

Then he saw her standing on the rooftop of the old house two stories overhead.

"Godspeed and a good life to you, Lucan Thorne," she called down.

"To you as well, Lilliane Williams."

She turned as if she were about to walk the length of the roof.

Instead, she took to the air and disappeared from view.

●◆●

LUCAN HAD BEEN HOME FOR JUST OVER TWENTY-FOUR HOURS, TOO many of them spent in the Order's war room with his comrades, reviewing the fire he'd put out in New Orleans and gearing up to fight the even bigger problems taking shape in Boston. As critical as his work was with his fellow warriors, the only place he wanted to be was in bed with his lovely Breedmate.

As the meeting wore on, Lucan found his thoughts straying repeatedly to Gabrielle. He'd even go so far as to say his distraction these past few hours bordered on obsession. Every breath he drew into his lungs seemed wreathed with the scent of her. The elusive cinnamon-sweet fragrance tickled his nostrils and made his pulse hammer heavily, his veins drumming with the need to be as close as he could get.

"What do you think, Lucan? Do we take out the Rogue nest down in Southie first or chase down the lead on those skin traders over in Chinatown and ash the Rogues another night?"

The abrupt question from one of his comrades seated around the conference room table snapped him out of his sensory haze. He blinked at Tegan and the other Breed warriors, feeling embarrassed to have been caught daydreaming in the middle of the patrol review he was leading.

He cleared his throat.

"I want those skin traders stopped first. The Rogues are a nuisance, but we can flush them out anytime." He stood, effectively adjourning the meeting. "I have something I need to take care of right now. Tegan, Dante, you two come up with a plan for the raid on the Chinatown location. You can run it by me later."

With his orders dispersed, he stalked out of the war room and headed through the Boston compound with a purpose, all his thoughts and senses homed in on Gabrielle. Just thinking about her made his mouth water and his fangs punch out of his gums.

He sought her out like a man possessed, oblivious to everything except the thought of closing the distance between himself and his mate. And the strange perfume that seemed to beckon to him for the past hours only intensified now that he was on the path to Gabrielle's side.

He found her in their living quarters.

Fresh out of her bath, she was sitting in their massive bed wearing just a frilly little bit of black lace.

God, she looked delectable.

He was so swept up in the sight and scent of her that he hardly noticed she held a book in her lap, which she held up as he approached the bed.

"Your package arrived from New Orleans a while ago," she said, smiling. "A signed first edition of *Interview with the Vampire*? I have the best mate in the world."

He frowned. "I didn't send that book. The one I bought for you got ruined."

Gabrielle's auburn brows rose. "So this must be from your new friend, Lilliane?"

"Apparently so."

"Does that mean she sent the candle too?"

"Candle?" A twinge of uncertainty arrowed through him. "What kind of candle?"

"That one."

She pointed to the flickering flame.

For a second, he expected to see one of the burnt umber glass jars he'd spotted in that mysterious shop. But the candle resting on the bureau across the room came from some other, more ordinary store. The label said *Cassidy's Corner* and the name of the fragrance was Orleans. He inhaled the air above its flickering flame and smelled vetiver, sweet olive, and a dozen other scents that reminded him of one of the most magical cities in the world.

"This came with the candle," she said, pulling a delicate white card from between the pages of her book.

He took it from her and read the calligraphic script written on the back of the Feu de Coeur calling card.

Light this flame for your greatest passion and be grateful that your heart's desire is already yours.

A slightly modified version of the card Lilliane had described to him, the one that had changed her life.

A custom-made version just for him.

And Gabrielle.

She was smiling when he looked at her. "I followed the instructions." She patted the bed where they'd so often made love. "It works. I've never been so grateful to have you back."

"Grateful," he said, tossing the card aside to climb onto the mattress. "Gratitude is just the beginning of what I feel when I'm with you."

And he found himself grateful for something else as well.

He'd lost many things in his immortal life, but never the ability to rest in the arms of a lover, to cherish the smell and feel of the one for whom he felt destined.

And he had Lilliane to thank for that realization.

LISA SCOTTOLINE AND NELSON DeMILLE

WHEN LISA SCOTTOLINE WAS ASKED IF SHE WOULD BE A PART of this anthology she said yes, but with a condition.

"I want to write with Nelson DeMille."

Aiming to please, we contacted Nelson who said, absolutely, since he was a huge Lisa Scottoline fan.

And the team was born.

Both Lisa and Nelson are seasoned pros. They each have tens of millions of books in print worldwide, and they've each created a memorable character. Lisa's Bennie Rosato is a tough-as-nails Philadelphia lawyer with a big heart, while John Corey is a former NYPD homicide detective, who still carries a gun and seems to have trouble keeping a job.

For Lisa, animals are a huge part of her life as she shares her home with a variety of dogs, cats, and chickens. So it's not unexpected that animals are involved in this story. The challenge came with Lisa having to deal head-on with Nelson's alpha-male protagonist, and Nelson having to work firsthand with an alpha-female hero.

Right off, they both agreed to help the other get the opposite sex right.

How this story was physically produced could be a tale in and of itself. By his own admission Nelson writes all his novels in longhand, on a yellow legal pad with a number one pencil. Lisa utilizes modern technology with a word processor. But though their techniques differ, their skills as writers are similar and the result is an entertaining and humorous encounter between two people who could not be more different.

The title itself is even prophetic.

Getaway.

GETAWAY

JOHN COREY, FORMER NYPD HOMICIDE DETECTIVE, AND FORMER Federal Anti-Terrorist Task Force agent, sat in an Adirondack chair with his fingers wrapped around a glass of Dewar's, contemplating the possible end of his third career—with the Diplomatic Surveillance Group—and his second marriage. Was it possible, he wondered, that his career and marital problems were of his own making? No. Shit just happens. He took a sip of scotch and stared into the gathering twilight toward Lake Whackamole. That wasn't the name of the lake, he knew, but it was some gibberish Indian name. P.C. correction. Some melodious Native American name.

Whackyweed?

No, that's marijuana.

Anyway, it was a lake. A small one in upstate New York, in the middle of nowhere, and the closest town was Nowheresville, about forty miles away.

It had taken him nearly ten hours from Manhattan to get to this godforsaken place in what was called the North Country, sometimes called God's Country, and he wondered why he was there. He was a city boy and nature made him nervous. So maybe this wasn't a good place to relax. It sounded good in theory but he should have known better. He sipped more scotch. The familiar smell and taste of it made him relax, even before the alcohol hit his brain.

He looked again at the darkly mirrored lake and the woods around it. He could make out a few other cabins set back from the opposite shore but they were dark. The only lit one, aside from his own, was the one he could see through the trees about two hundred yards to his left. He wondered who his neighbor might be. With any luck, he'd never find out. But maybe it was a hot babe on the lam from city problems, as he was. Or maybe it was a local girl, single or divorced, no kids, great cook, and looking for a drinking buddy.

And she drank scotch.

Most likely, though, it was some backwoods *Deliverance* psycho who had a collection of chain saws that he wanted to show his new neighbor.

Dick Kearns, Corey's former police buddy who'd loaned the cabin, had assured him that no one would be at the lake in late October, and if anyone was, they'd keep to themselves.

Good.

So he sat back and stared at the trees.

There were a lot of them. More than in Central Park. In fact, he was actually in a park—Adirondack State Park, a sparsely populated stretch of land bigger than Vermont—and much of it was designated as Forever Wild, meaning he'd have a hard time finding a pub.

He'd been in this neck of the woods a few years before on a case involving a guy named Bain Madox who owned a lodge called the Custer Hill Club. Madox was a billionaire nut job who tried to start a nuclear war with the world of Islam, and the Custer Hill Club was his secret headquarters. In fact, this nearly uninhabited land seemed to be visited by a number of weirdos and bad guys—survivalists, antigovernment wing nuts, mobsters, Irish Republican Army guys in the old days, and more recently Islamic extremists who needed to test their weapons in private. The FBI and the Anti-Terrorist Task Force, as well as the State Police and park rangers, had long taken a special interest in the Adirondack State Park.

On a happier note, the aforementioned unwelcome park visitors were relatively rare and kept an understandably low profile, and he didn't expect to bump into any of them while he was here. It was more likely that he'd run into a bear. He hated bears. And with good reason. Bears were dangerous. They ate people.

He saw something moving in the brush near the lake, about two hundred feet from his deck. He focused on the spot, but it was getting darker and he couldn't see anything. It may have just been a breeze off the lake stirring the brush.

Or it could have been a deer.

Or a bear.

He'd left his 9 mm Glock in the cabin, a stupid thing to do when you're alone in the wilderness. He'd looked death in the eye more than once, and feared no man. But he did have two fears—nuclear weapons, which was rational based on a few of his cases, and bears, which he knew was not totally rational.

He kept staring at the brush, thinking about going inside for the Glock. But he was comfortable in the deep chair, and the scotch made him lazy.

It was mid-October and the trees were already shedding here in the North Country. And it was chilly. He took another sip of scotch. This place was okay in the summer, but after Labor Day most of the tourists and fishermen were gone and the North Country became eerily deserted until ski season began. So even if this wasn't a good place to relax, it was a good place to disappear for a while. His last case, on his new job with the Diplomatic Surveillance Group, had left him in career limbo, known officially as administrative leave.

He thought back to that case.

He'd been on a routine surveillance of a Russian UN diplomat, Colonel Vasily Petrov, who was actually an SVR intelligence officer and a dangerous man. But the routine surveillance had turned into something that was anything but routine. More politically sensitive. Long story short, he'd broken some rules—or, to be more positive, he'd shown extraordinary initiative—and gotten himself into major trouble.

As usual.

But he'd brought the case to a successful conclusion.

As usual.

So while Washington was trying to decide if he should get a

commendation or a pink slip, he was told to stay home and keep his mouth shut.

Feds were such assholes.

On top of all this, his FBI wife, Supervisory Special Agent Kate May-field, had accepted a transfer to D.C., and they were now what was called estranged.

Meaning what?

Barely speaking and definitely not fucking.

And to further complicate his life he was involved with a young lady named Tess Faraday who'd been assigned to him as a DSG trainee. Turned out she was an undercover State Department intelligence officer, tasked with keeping an eye on him.

Life was full of surprises.

Some pleasant, some not.

Bottom line, he needed a break from his professional and personal problems and Dick had offered him a cabin on Lake Whatchamacallit. *No one will bother you there. No one can find you and, best of all, cell-phone service is pretty bad.* That's what his friend had said. To complete the isolation Dick had no landline phone in the cabin or Internet service. He was reach-able, as per the requirements of his admin leave. But how do you know if you're reachable before you get to where you're not?

Right?

Anyway, it was good to get away. All he had to do now was figure out what to do with his time. The problem with doing nothing, as he always said, is not knowing when you're finished.

He yawned and finished his scotch, which had found its way to his brain. Dick had a few fishing poles in the cabin so tomorrow he'd go fish-ing. And the next day, too. He wasn't sure what to do with a fish if he caught it. Shoot it? Maybe he'd also take a hike in the woods. Could a 9 mm Glock drop a bear?

He heard more rustling in the undergrowth, coming from the trees to his left. He sat up, listening hard. It was deathly quiet here except for the birds, and sound traveled far in the cool air. He heard the sound again and focused on the nearby tree line. Something was there and he could hear it moving. He assumed it was a deer, foraging for leaves at dusk.

A flock of birds rose from the trees and flew off.

He laid his glass on the flat armrest of the Adirondack chair and stood.

The sound got closer.

Fight or flight?

If he was a bird, he would have taken flight. But he wasn't, so he took a step toward the edge of the deck. Then, remembering that his gun lay on the kitchen table, he retreated back toward the door. It was not inconceivable that someone had been sent here to whack him. He had lots of enemies. Russians, Islamic terrorists, and criminals he'd sent to jail, not to mention the CIA who had actually tried to kill him in Yemen. But none of those potential assassins were stupid enough to make that much noise.

He relaxed.

It had to be a deer.

He stood focused on the tree line that ended about twenty feet from the cabin, expecting to see an animal emerge from the woods.

But it wasn't a deer that charged out of the tree line and ran directly toward him.

•◆•

BENNIE ROSATO HELD HER CELL PHONE TO HER EAR, BECOMING angrier by the minute. She couldn't believe what she was hearing, though she only caught every fourth word because the cell reception was terrible. She had driven all the way up to this lake to spend a romantic weekend with her boyfriend, Declan, who was on depositions in Pittsburgh. He was supposed to meet her here tonight but was canceling on her.

And she wasn't hearing near enough of a good enough excuse.

"Bennie, I'm sorry. But it can't be helped," he was saying.

"What can't be helped? What are you talking about? I'm here alone in this stupid cabin."

"You know how depositions go. You're a lawyer, too. There's just too much material to cover in one day. We couldn't get it done."

"It's the weekend. Do it Monday."

"I can't. The witness has to go back on Monday and they're refusing to produce him. I think it's going to take both Saturday and Sunday. I'm sorry. I'll make it up to you."

She should've guessed that this would all go south. Declan had placed the winning bid on the Woodsy Weekend Getaway at the silent auction to benefit the Equal Justice Center at the University of Pennsylvania Law School, her alma mater. She'd said they should just write a check. But no, Declan thought they should get something for their money.

She should've known better.

Those silent auction items were a scam. You didn't "win" if you had to pay, plus they were always for vacations she didn't have time to take and to places she didn't want to go. They were always in the off-season, like now. A chilly October night by a lake in the middle of nowhere. God's Country, the auction catalog had said. No, godforsaken.

With mosquitoes and probably bears.

Maybe even wolves.

She plopped onto the old plaid couch, which smelled of mildew. Everything up here smelled horrible.

"I have to go," he said. "I'm really sorry."

"What am I supposed to do now?" she demanded, and even she didn't like her tone.

She was never one of those women who nagged, until she was. She had so much work to do back in Philly, a caseload that would keep two associates busy, and an entire law firm to run. Plus she'd been counting on vacation sex, and lots of it. After all, a girl had needs.

"You should just take the weekend. Enjoy yourself."

"How can I enjoy myself? I didn't bring any work."

He chuckled. "That's the point. Don't work. Enjoy yourself."

"I didn't even bring a book."

"So download one."

"There's no Internet. There's almost no cell reception. There's not even a telephone, a television, or a radio." She couldn't remember the last time she'd listened to the radio, but still. "It's hell on earth. With bears."

"Did you see a bear?" His tone turned serious. "Are there bears?"

"Probably. I bet the bears get lousy reception, too."

"But it looks beautiful in the pictures. Is it beautiful?"

"It's dark." She threw up her hands, resigned. "I should just go home."

"I think you should stay and relax."

"The only place I feel relaxed is a courtroom."

"Really?"

"Have we met?"

He paused. "Maybe you need to think about that, babe."

"Oh, I do?" she shot back, then, on impulse, hung up the call and tossed the phone on the couch. She'd be damned if she'd be lectured by the man who was standing her up.

This sucked, there were no two ways about it.

She and Declan were crazy about each other, but the problem was their schedules, and the lives of two trial lawyers didn't leave time for much frolic and detour.

She folded her arms, fuming. Then glanced at the phone, waiting for Declan to call back. If he did, she'd hang up on him again. She certainly did not need him telling her that she needed to relax, work less, and not stress. She'd heard it all before, and he was just as much of a workaholic as she was. Maybe not quite as much, but still, he worked hard too. And they both owned their own law firms, so he was no more mellow than she was.

Maybe a little.

She glanced at the phone but it didn't ring, and she found her gaze flitting restlessly around the room. There was a living room/kitchen combination with mismatched plaid furniture and a battered coffee table that held an old book of crossword puzzles, but otherwise no reading matter. The wood floors looked splintery, and the walls were paneled with grooved knotty pine, like somebody's basement from the 1960s. The kitchen cabinets had been painted pukey yellow, and the kitchen was stocked with only the barest essentials. She'd arrived in the daytime and sat on the back deck, sipping a Diet Coke, enjoying the scenery and waiting for Declan's call announcing his imminent arrival. Now, as the sunlight faded, the cabin and the woods began to feel sinister.

She glanced again at the silent phone.

Maybe he couldn't get a call through. She thought about calling him back, but decided against it. He should call her back, if anybody should call anybody. She stewed, arms still folded. It wasn't that she didn't know how to relax. It was just that if she were going to take the weekend off, she wanted to have fun.

She stood and walked to the sliders that faced the deck to lock up for the night. She glanced outside and noticed lights in the cabin through the woods to her right. So at least there was one other person in the world. She wondered who else was stupid enough to come here. Probably another silent auction winner.

Then suddenly, she realized she'd forgotten something.

Her dog, Max, was gone.

•◆•

IT WAS HARD TO SEE IN THE DARK, BUT COREY WAS CERTAIN IT WAS A ravenous wolf running toward him. Or his wife's lawyer with a subpoena. Hard to tell the difference—even in broad daylight. Actually, it was a dog, specifically a golden retriever who scampered onto the deck, his bushy tail wagging frantically, his wet nose to the deck as if he'd gotten the scent of some animal.

Maybe a bear.

He felt a bit silly for thinking a wild animal or an assassin had been stalking him. But better to imagine the worst than to experience it. A little paranoia is a good thing. Keeps you from relaxing too much.

Keeps you alive.

He dropped to one knee and called out, "Come here, buddy."

The retriever trotted over, his pink tongue lolling out of a broad smile. The dog was panting heavily, obviously overexerted, and the next thing he knew the dog stuck his muzzle between Corey's knees, slobbering all over his baggy cargo pants.

He buried his fingers in the dog's thick scruff, warm with sweat. "You chasing rabbits?"

A bark answered.

"You need a drink?"

More barking.

"Dewar's and water?" He thought the retriever's ears perked up, so he commanded, "Sit."

The retriever instantly plopped his butt on the deck, his tail still wagging like a windshield wiper.

"Good dog."

He wouldn't have minded the companionship for the week, but he guessed that the obedient retriever belonged to somebody. He felt around the dog's neck, finding a collar. He took his cell phone from his pocket, navigated to flashlight function and shined it on the nylon collar, locating the tag, which he read.

"Max."

The dog barked in recognition.

"Last name?"

Nothing.

"Date of birth?"

A curious look.

"Any prior arrests?"

More silence.

"Don't lie to me, Max."

The dog barked.

So it had come to this.

Talking to a dog.

He looked closely at the tag and saw the owner's name. Bennie Rosato. There was no address, but there was a phone number with a 215 area code, which was Philadelphia. The dog certainly had not walked here from Philly, so the owner had to be in the area.

He sat cross-legged on the deck, looking into Max's big liquid eyes. The dog stared back as if to say, *You're a nice human, but I'm lost and looking for my owner.*

He punched Bennie Rosato's number into his phone and petted the dog while it rang in his ear. There was static on the line, which meant that cell reception was weak. The call went to voice mail and a default computer voice said, "You have reached the cell phone of Bennie Rosato. Please leave a message at the beep."

He waited for the signal, then said, "Mister Rosato, my name is John Corey and I think I found your golden retriever, Max, at Lake Wha . . . the lake. He's safe and sound. Call me at this number."

He hung up and said to Max, "That should do it."

It was possible that Max would run off again. Then when Mr. Rosato called, he'd have to say, *Sorry, pal, your dog skipped out.* So he went inside the cabin and found a ball of twine in a junk drawer. He returned to the deck and tied the twine around Max's collar and started to tie it to the rail. Then he had another thought.

"Maybe you could find your owner. You're a retriever. Right?"

A bark seemed to agree with the observation.

"Okay, let's take a walk while we're waiting for the phone call."

With Max at the end of the makeshift leash, he stepped from the deck and allowed the dog to lead him toward the lake. Then they turned left toward the other lit cabin a few hundred yards away. The shoreline was rocky and strewn with glacial boulders, and Max seemed easily distracted by any scent that he picked up, so they weren't making much progress.

"Not much of a bloodhound, are you?"

Max seemed insulted.

"Sorry."

He started to realize this was not a good idea. The dog was more interested in nature than in finding his owner, plus it was getting dark and cold and he was wearing only a sweatshirt. Also, he'd left his Glock on the kitchen table. Max was pulling at the leash, trying to ferret out something between two boulders.

"We're going back," he said.

But Max had become disobedient and pulled at his twine leash, which might snap.

"Come on. I'll find you a dead squirrel for dinner."

But Max wasn't listening and he found himself out in the cold, dark night, unarmed and alone except for a hyper dog. This was how small bad decisions lead to big bad consequences. He pictured the headline in the *New York Post*.

"Bear Eats Fed."

His instinct was to let the animal go and head back to his cabin. But he'd called Rosato, so he at least had to keep Max with him. The dog was lapping water from the lake, then he raised his hind leg and pissed.

He noticed that Max was now looking up the slope at the lighted cabin in the distance. "Is that where you live, boy? Where's Bennie, Max? Let's go find Bennie."

The dog barked and began trotting along the shore toward the cabin.

"Good boy. Go to Bennie."

Max tugged at his leash and Corey trotted along behind him toward the lit cabin.

He redialed Rosato's number as he walked, but it went to voice mail again and he ended the call without leaving another message.

It was getting colder, and he was tired from the long drive, and he was feeling naked without his gun.

A thought popped into his head.

No good deed goes unpunished.

•◆•

"MAX," BENNIE CALLED OUT, AS SHE TORE THROUGH THE WOODS, frantic.

She waved her flashlight back and forth but didn't see him in the thick brush. Max had been with her on the back deck, but she'd forgotten about him when Declan had called.

Tree branches tore at her bare skin since she was clad only in a T-shirt, shorts, and sandals. A wave of guilt washed over her and she was afraid for Max's life. She'd only had the golden retriever a few months, but she loved him and so did Declan. They'd rescued him together, and she couldn't lose him up here in the middle of nowhere.

"Max."

But heard no barking or panting anywhere.

The woods surrounding her were dense, dark, and cold, and she kept her hands out in front, clearing the branches with her hands. She wondered if Max had gone to the other house, the only lighted one on the lake, so she headed toward it in the distance. She kept going, threading her way through the pines and fall foliage. She felt her forearms getting scratched and cut, and she almost tripped on some tree roots, but she kept going, deeper and deeper. The lights of the cabin slowly became brighter and bigger, and she knew she was getting closer.

She called the dog's name again and again, feeling tears come to her eyes. Anything could happen to him in these woods. Max was just a goofball, like most golden retrievers. They trusted everybody and loved everything. Plus he was a city dog and he had no idea what was going on in the country. She'd had him on a leash earlier because he'd been so distracted by all the different smells, and he'd gone nuts when he'd seen a squirrel.

She tripped, almost falling to the ground, which was when she realized something. The light was closer but she didn't see the lake anymore. Somehow, when she'd teared up, she'd become turned around in the woods, drifting away from the lake, which was a mistake.

She whirled around in the darkness, casting the jittery cone of light around her in a circle. Which only confirmed her fear. The lake was nowhere in sight and she was surrounded on all sides by woods. If she wasn't headed toward the lighted lake house anymore, where was she going? But there were lights ahead, and maybe Max was there.

She took a few steps through the trees, heading toward whatever lights they were, but something made her slow her step and proceed with caution. She found herself lowering the flashlight, then switching it off, because whatever she had reached in the middle of nowhere was putting out a lot of electricity.

But it wasn't a house at all.

She remained motionless, peering out at the scene from behind a tree. The light was coming from a pole-mounted floodlight, which cast a harsh brightness on a clearing. All the trees had been cut down and the land leveled around a large modular building, like a windowless storage shed, but the strangest thing was that the building was covered with camouflage netting. A black pickup was parked outside the shed, and she thought it was running, but then she realized she was hearing the hum of a generator.

She'd been a criminal lawyer long enough to know when she was seeing trouble. The shed was in the middle of a thick forest, it had its own generator, and was camouflaged. She wondered if this was drug related, a meth lab, or maybe stolen goods. It was some kind of clandestine operation, and for a moment she wasn't sure what to do. She didn't want to call 911 until she was safely out of the area. And she didn't want to get out of the area until she was sure Max wasn't near the building.

Or inside it.

She ducked down as the woods were suddenly swept with bright high beams, and she watched as another black pickup pulled into view from a dirt road on the other side of the camouflaged shed. She realized she was wearing a white T-shirt and flattened herself on the ground so she wouldn't be easy to spot.

Two men climbed out of the truck, but it was too dark to see anything more than their silhouettes, though she heard their voices. They were speaking a foreign language. It wasn't French, Spanish, Italian, or German, and it didn't have the soft squishy sounds of Polish or Eastern Europe. She didn't want to be politically incorrect or paranoid, but it sounded Arabic.

One man began unloading a large box and the other man helped him, and the two of them inched along with the box, stutter-stepping on the way to the shed. They passed through a pool of light, and she could see that the box was a wooden crate, long and narrow. She took one look at its shape and thought instantly rifles or armaments.

Her mouth went dry.

She was a lawyer, not a cop.

And she was no terrorism expert, but she watched CNN. The idea was, if you see something, say something. She didn't know what she was seeing, but she knew she was going to say something. But first she had to get out of there without them seeing her.

Suddenly her cell phone rang.

The men turned to the sound.

She fumbled in her pocket for her phone and hit the button with trembling fingers, silencing it.

But the men stood looking in her direction, then lowered the box.

The floodlights went dark.

So she ran.

•◆•

COREY AND MAX CLIMBED THE DARK SLOPE TOWARD THE LIGHTED cabin, and he saw a white BMW parked in the gravel driveway with Pennsylvania plates, which was a good clue that Mr. Rosato of Philadelphia lived here.

Max was pulling at the leash, so he let him go.

The dog ran onto the back deck and he followed and saw that the sliding glass door was partly open. Max beelined into the cabin, so obviously this was where his owner was.

Case closed.

He didn't necessarily want to meet Mr. Rosato and he didn't want Mr. Rosato to thank him or offer him a drink or ask him to stay for a spaghetti dinner, so he decided to just slide the door shut and head back to his cabin.

But what if this was not Rosato's cabin?

Then whoever lived here would have a new dog.

And Rosato would still be calling about his.

No good deed, indeed.

He resigned himself to some human interaction and called in through the half-open slider, "Mr. Rosato."

No reply.

He stuck his head into the cabin. Max was curled up on the couch. He noted that this living room was almost as grungy as the one in his cabin. Whoever owned or had rented this place would be better off living in the BMW. He called out again, "Mr. Rosato."

Max barked.

But no one seemed to be home, which was odd, considering the car outside. Maybe there was a second car. Or maybe a bear had gotten in through the open sliders and eaten Mr. Rosato. Served him right for losing his dog and leaving the door open.

Then it occurred to him that Rosato might have gone off on foot to find his dog. But this could still not be Rosato's cabin. He could make a call and run the Pennsylvania license plate number, but that was a lot of effort.

He looked at Max on the couch.

Dogs don't have to make decisions.

They eat, sleep, play, and screw.

In his next life?

Maybe.

All great detectives—as he was—came to conclusions based on clues, evidence, and information. Not on assumptions, speculation, or lazy thinking. So, reluctantly, he entered the cabin. Nothing in the living room or kitchen provided a clue as to who lived here, or if they were still here.

He called up the staircase, then climbed the steep creaky steps to the second-floor bedrooms. He realized he was technically trespassing, and he hoped Bennie Rosato—or whoever lived here—didn't pick this moment to return. The story of Goldilocks and the three bears popped into his head.

At the top of the stairs was an open bathroom door and two closed doors. He knocked on the door to his left, hoping he wasn't waking someone from a postcoital slumber.

He opened the bedroom door and peeked inside. Empty.

The other bedroom door was slightly ajar and he looked inside. There was a small unpacked suitcase on the bed, but no evidence that a bear had eaten the occupant.

He stepped into the bedroom and read the tag on the suitcase. Bennie Rosato. A Philly address and the same phone number that was on Max's collar.

Now the case was closed.

He went downstairs and filled a bowl with water and left it for Max who was still curled up on the couch.

"There's more water in the toilet bowl. Don't pee on the floor. See ya around, pal."

Max looked up at him and seemed to say thanks with a bark.

He left the cabin and slid the door shut, happy that he'd fulfilled his duty as a good citizen. He started back toward the lake rather than take the shortcut to his cabin through the dark woods. As he headed downhill toward the lake he redialed Rosato to tell him, or leave a message, that his dog was in his cabin. The number rang as he continued toward the lake, and he waited for voice mail to kick in.

The phone stopped ringing.

Then a breathless voice said, "Help."

The fuck?

●◆●

BENNIE TORE THROUGH THE WOODS, NOT KNOWING WHERE SHE was going. She didn't know if the men had seen her, but she wasn't taking any chances. She kept the flashlight off but clutched it in case she had to use it as a weapon. She hurried as fast and as quietly as she could, away from the light. She held her phone, pressing 911 on the run, but she could tell it wasn't connecting. She knew she had her GPS function on, and she prayed that dispatch would find her call and pick up her signal.

Suddenly the phone vibrated in her hand.

Her heart leapt to her throat. Maybe it was 911 calling back. Or Declan. But she didn't recognize the number.

She answered on the run, whispering, "Help. Please, come quickly, I'm lost in the woods near the lake. My name is Bennie Rosato. Please, hurry. I think I saw—"

"You're Bennie?" a man's voice asked.

"Yes. Is this 911?"

"No. I'm John Corey. Did you get my message that I found your dog. Max. He's back in your cabin. Are you a woman?"

She used her arms to whack branches out of her path. She didn't hear anyone behind her so either they were being quiet or she'd lost them. "Listen, I think I saw some terrorists in the woods. I'm trying to call 911."

"Where are you?"

"In the woods. They might be following me. They were loading a box of guns into a shed that's camouflaged with netting. They spoke Arabic."

"You sure?"

"I watch *Homeland*."

"That makes me feel better."

A smart-ass? Just what she needed at the moment.

"Can you describe where you are?" he asked. "Look around. What do you see?"

The man's tone was calm, oddly businesslike, which comforted her in a strange way. "I see woods. It's dark."

"Are you moving uphill or down?"

"Down."

Actually, she was practically stumbling forward.

"Keep moving downhill. The lake sits at the bottom of a bowl. Understand? I'm at the water's edge, about a hundred yards from your cabin. Stay on the line."

"Okay."

She kept running through the woods. Branches swatted her bare arms, legs, and face, and she stumbled a few times, but kept going, making sure she was headed downhill. She still didn't hear anyone behind her, but she didn't slow her pace though she was becoming out of breath.

"Are you okay?"

"I'm getting there."

"As soon as I see you, I'll call 911."

"Hang up and call now."

"I don't want to lose you. Do you see the lake?"

"Not yet."

"Have you crossed the gravel drive that runs around the lake?"

"I don't know. It's dark."

"Can you hear anyone behind you?"

"I don't know."

"Stay on the phone and keep moving."

●◆●

COREY STOOD ON A BOULDER NEAR THE LAKE, SCANNING THE WOODS at the top of the slope. A half-moon was rising and he hoped Bennie Rosato would see him silhouetted against the water. She could be right about someone chasing her, but he didn't think she'd stumbled onto a terrorist camp.

Those things didn't happen in real life.

A sign of the times, though, as everyone liked to play cop.

He'd learned never to form a conclusion without evidence. For instance, Bennie Rosato had turned out to be a woman.

He said into his phone, "Listen, my cabin is the lighted one a few hundred yards to the right of yours, as you face the lake. Understand?"

"I got it."

"Go there. I'm heading there now to get my gun."

"What?"

"I'm a federal agent. I have a gun."

"Thank God. But why aren't you carrying it?"

That, he thought, was what an FBI postmortem inquiry would ask. So he came up with a good excuse. "Your dog distracted me."

"You're blaming a dog?"

"Just head for my cabin."

He started jogging that way, glancing at the woods as he moved.

●◆●

BENNIE NOTICED THE TREES THINNING OUT AROUND HER, THEN SHE crossed the narrow gravel road that circled the lake and picked up her pace. The forest vanished around her and she was on a bare rocky slope close to the lake. To her left was her cabin and to the right was the other lit one.

John Corey's.

In fact, she saw a man running along the shoreline toward the cabin. She wanted to yell out to him but didn't want to risk it if she was being followed.

She added a burst of speed and ran down the slope on a course that would intersect with Corey. She waved her arms to attract his attention, but he didn't see her, though he was glancing at the woods as he ran. She whispered into her phone, "I can see you. Look to your right."

But he wasn't listening to his phone.

She looked back over her shoulder, relieved to see that no one was on the slope behind her. She turned on her flashlight and waved it around.

Finally, the man on the shore saw her, stopped, and turned toward her. He called out, "Bennie?"

They ran toward each other in the moonlight, like lovers in a three-hankie movie. As they got closer, she saw that Corey was a good-looking man, tall and with the unmistakable air of a lifetime spent in law enforcement, but this wasn't the time for biographical details. She slowed her pace, caught her breath, and began to stand down. As he approached, she saw that he was wearing a gray sweatshirt, baggy cargo pants, and old running shoes. Most federal agents dressed more buttoned up, but he seemed relaxed. She shut off the flashlight, reached him, and put out her hand.

"Bennie Rosato."

He took her hand and said, "John Corey."

Then he added, "At your service."

•◆•

COREY STUDIED BENNIE ROSATO IN THE MOONLIGHT.

She was either wearing elevator sandals or she was as tall as he was, about six feet. Her bare arms and legs were extremely well toned, like an athlete's. Whoever had been chasing her was lucky they didn't catch up. He thought her blond hair looked like it had been combed with an egg-beater, but maybe her sprint through the woods had messed up the coif.

He focused on her face.

Her eyes sparkled in the moonlight and were the color of her lips. Blue. She must be cold. She had good cheekbones, a slightly jutting chin, and an aquiline nose. She wore little makeup and probably didn't need much. And finally, he noticed that she filled out her T-shirt.

Actually, he noticed that first.

All in all, an attractive woman with a striking presence.

"Are you okay?"

She was sweating and still breathing hard.

"I think so."

He glanced back up at the slope. "Were you followed?"

"I don't know."

"The woods are deceiving at night."

"I know what I saw, Mr. Corey."

"Right. Please call me John."

"Are you really a federal agent?"

"I am."

"I'm a lawyer."

"What else could go wrong tonight?"

She frowned. "What's *that* supposed to mean?"

"Just joking." He further explained, "My ex-wife is a lawyer. And my estranged wife is also a lawyer, and an FBI agent."

"You're a lucky man."

She tossed him a half smile.

He wanted to tell her his joke about him marrying lawyers so he could screw a lawyer rather than vice versa, but he didn't know her well enough. Maybe later. Instead, he said, "Let's go to my place."

"Why?"

"So I can get my gun."

She hesitated. "Do you have any ID? A badge?"

"My creds and badge are with my gun. You can see them all in my cabin. We shouldn't be standing here in the open."

"I think we should call 911. We're not going to cowboy this out alone."

"I already called. No connection."

She hit the 911 feature on her phone, but it didn't connect.

He tried 911 again too, but couldn't get a connection. "Service sucks. By the way, you left the slider open in your cabin."

"It's not my cabin. I won a Woodsy Weekend Getaway."

"Congratulations."

"I should have stayed in Philadelphia."

"Right. A weekend in Philadelphia seems like a month."

"Not funny."

"Sorry."

"Are you from Washington?"

"New York."

"Figures."

He couldn't resist and said, "So second prize is two weeks in Philadelphia, and third prize is four weeks in Phila—"

"I'm going to my cabin, getting my dog, and going home."

"You're leaving me alone with terrorists?"

She shot him a look.

"I know," he said. "I'm a wiseass."

She started to walk away, then hesitated. "Look, I don't like to admit I need help, but this is the life-or-death exception. Walk with me, would you?"

"My gun is in my cabin."

"Why do you need a gun, if you don't believe me about the terrorists?"

"Why do I think I can outtalk a lawyer?"

"Are we having a power struggle?"

"No, a divorce."

She shook her head.

He said, "Look, Bennie, I think you saw something. I don't know what you saw and neither do you. But I'd like you to come to my cabin and you can tell me what you saw and we'll keep trying 911, and if we can't get through, we'll go to the nearest police station. Okay?"

She didn't appear like someone who surrendered control easily, but she also was scared.

That was clear.

"All right."

They scrambled down the edge of the slope to the lake and began walking quickly along the rocky shore toward his cabin.

Not exactly hand in hand.

But shoulder to shoulder.

He crossed his back deck, slid open the glass door, and without waiting for Bennie went inside the cabin and made straight for the kitchen. His Glock was still on the table where he'd left it, stuck inside his pancake holster. Only an idiot or a rookie would have left the gun out in plain sight. What was he thinking? Then he remembered. It was the dog's fault. Or maybe the scotch.

He was aware that Bennie was behind him and knew she was looking at the gun. So, as casually as he could, he picked up the holster, lifted his sweatshirt, and clipped it onto his belt in the small of his back. Then he said to his houseguest, "My mother told me that a gentleman should never pull a gun on his date."

"This isn't a date."

"It could be."

"No, it couldn't."

He reached inside a suede jacket hanging on a chair and pulled out his credential case, which he handed to her.

She let the case fall open, revealing his FBI photo ID and badge. She handed the case back to him. "This seems to be my lucky day."

"The day's not over yet. You want a drink?"

"Water."

He smiled, plucked two glasses from the cupboard and made one water and one scotch and water. "Sorry, no ice."

"I don't need ice."

"Did anyone ever tell you you're kind of uptight?"

She smiled. "Did anyone ever tell you you're not uptight enough?"

He smiled back.

They clinked glasses and she said, "*Cent'anni.*"

"Cheers."

They drank, then he led her into the living room and indicated an armchair. He locked the sliding doors, then sat in a creaky rocker.

She looked around. "This is worse than my place. Did you win a Woodsy Weekend too?"

"I lost a bet."

They both laughed.

She asked, "Do you have a landline phone here?"

"I don't even have ice."

"Let's try 911 again."

They both tried on their cells, but neither could get a connection.

He pointed out, "It could take an hour for a local cop or the State Police to get here anyway."

"Then let's get out of here."

"First tell me what you saw in the woods."

"We can do that on the way to the police station."

He looked at Bennie Rosato. She'd gone from lady in distress to ball-busting lawyer in ten minutes. "We're going to take separate cars out of here. In case we're not coming back. So tell me what you saw."

She sipped on her water and told him. He listened. As with most attorneys her narrative was clear and concise, though he suspected she hadn't been as cool and collected when she was lost in the woods, finding what she thought was a terrorist facility.

When she finished, he said, "Something was going on there. Maybe criminal activity. Maybe some poachers. Maybe a meth lab or maybe park workers or environmental scientists doing something good for humanity."

"They were speaking Arabic."

"Other than from watching *Homeland,* would you know what Arabic sounded like?"

"I think so. And don't forget the camouflage netting."

"Right. What were these guys wearing?"

"Black pants and dark jackets."

"Beards?"

"No."

"Age?"

"Young."

"Describe the crate."

"Long and narrow."

"Heavy?"

"Both men had to carry it."

"Were there other crates in the truck?"

"I don't know."

"How big was this shed?"

"Are you taking my deposition?" She set down her water. "This is crazy. Let's just go to the police."

"I think I have enough for us to file a report." Then he let her know, "You're a good witness."

"I grill witnesses for a living."

"Me too."

"So we have that in common."

"That makes it a date."

"No, it doesn't."

"It's datelike."

"Whatever that means."

She smiled, and he found himself admiring her crossed legs.

"You a runner?" he asked.

"Rower." She headed for the door. "If we're not coming back here, I need to get Max."

He stood. "I'll get my stuff. We'll drive to your place, collect your dog, and you'll follow me in your car. There's a State Police barracks in Ray Brook, about an hour from here. I worked with those guys once. They're good."

"We should try to call them from the car. They can meet us halfway. I don't want these men to get away."

"They're already gone."

She frowned, disappointed. "What makes you say that?"

"Bitter experience. Are you willing to go with the State Police and try to find this place?"

"If you come with me."

He figured it was that life-or-death exception, striking again. "You'll need better hiking clothes."

"Look who's talking."

He smiled again. He liked her. "So are you enjoying your Woodsy Weekend Getaway?"

"No. Are you?"

"Actually, I am."

"You weren't chased by terrorists."

"There's still hope."

"Mister Macho."

"My middle name. Let's move out."

He grabbed his small duffel bag, and she shut off the lights, then they went out to his Jeep Cherokee. She got into the passenger seat as he set his bag in the back, opened it, took out four loaded magazines, and shoved them into his cargo pockets. He slammed the hatch shut and jumped behind the wheel, starting the engine and engaging the four-wheel drive. He used only his parking lights to navigate the dirt driveway. His driveway ended and he turned onto the one-lane gravel road that connected the cabins around the lake.

"Did you cross this road when you were lost?" he asked her.

"I think so. Why?"

"I'm trying to determine where this place was that you saw."

"I think I did cross this road."

"Did it occur to you that you were heading uphill, away from the lake and away from my cabin?"

"I was upset about Max. I was just following the lights."

"Follow your senses."

"You forgot your gun."

"Your dog distracted me."

"Again with the dog blaming."

He liked women who didn't take his crap. That was why he'd liked Robin, his first wife, and Kate, his future ex-wife. But maybe he should lay off lady lawyers for a while. "Do you think you could find this place again?"

"Maybe. Maybe they can find us. You should go faster."

"We're almost there."

He looked at the thick forest that hugged the narrow road and listened to the sound of the tires crunching over the gravel. He saw the lights of her cabin off to his right and slowed down.

She said, "The driveway is between those big pines."

He found the entrance and turned into it. The dirt drive continued downhill for a few hundred feet into the clearing around her cabin and he stopped the Jeep behind her BMW.

He shut off the engine. "I'll check it out, just in case. Stay here."

"Are you serious?"

She opened her door, climbed out, and headed around to the back deck.

He followed and said to her, "Stand back." Inside he saw Max, still on the couch, looking at him. He didn't think he needed to draw his gun, so he slid the door open with Bennie right behind him. Max jumped off the couch and ran directly to Bennie.

He locked the sliders as a standard precaution, then said, "I'll go upstairs and get your bag. You haven't unpacked anything, right?"

She shook her head. "I'll get my purse and some stuff in the cabinets." Then she did a double take. "How do you know where my bag is or that it's still packed?"

"I was searching for clues."

"To what? And where's the probable cause?"

He grinned. "It's not like I went looking for undies."

Max was wagging his tail at a bag of dog food on the counter. He felt his own stomach rumbling. "Did you bring any people food?"

"There's yogurt in the fridge. Help yourself."

"I'd rather eat the dog food."

She grabbed Max by the collar. "Let me get him in the car before he runs away again." She left with the dog through the sliders, leaving them open, and he headed upstairs, lifted her small suitcase off the bed, then returned downstairs.

Two men in ski masks held Bennie at gunpoint in the living room.

"Put your hands up," one said to him.

He stood looking at the two men.

The taller man was pointing a Glock at him, holding it in a two-hand grip. The other guy had his gun at the port arms position, his head and eyes darting around the room.

They were professionals.

But professional what?

They both wore black pants, black running shoes, dark, quilted jackets, and gloves. Along with black ski masks. So he couldn't tell their ages or their ethnic origins or read their faces. But he had the impression that they were both young. He didn't know if they were drug dealers, mobsters, terrorists, or some other variety of assholes, but he'd find out soon enough.

Or maybe not.

"Hands up," one of them ordered.

He knew from experience that if these guys wanted him dead, they'd have just blasted away and left. So they wanted something else. Not that this meant they wouldn't kill him later.

"Hands up, asshole. Now."

He didn't detect an accent, and he noted the proper grammatical use of the word asshole, so they weren't from Sandland. But they could be homegrown extremists, or whatever Washington was calling them this week. "What do I do with this overnight bag?"

"Shove it up your ass."

Not a bad idea. That's where his gun was. Near his ass.

The shorter guy yelled, "Put it down."

He crouched and placed the bag on the floor.

The taller guy, who seemed in charge, said to Corey, "Stay down. Hands on your head."

He remained in the crouched position and placed his hands on his head. The couch, which sat in the middle of the floor, was to his right. He could dive behind it as he drew his own Glock and get off two rounds.

The smaller guy asked, "You got a gun?"

He shook his head. His mind raced. Dive behind the couch, pop up, and fire? Or maybe shoulder roll left, draw, and fire? Or just draw and fire? The big guy was taking no chances, keeping his head and eyes locked, holding his gun in a steady two-hand grip.

"Get down. Face on the floor. Hands behind your back."

He lay facedown on the floor, otherwise known as the prone firing position. This could work. As his right hand moved behind his back, the smaller guy kicked his hand away, and quickly snatched the Glock from his holster.

Close, but no cigar.

He replayed the last five minutes in his mind. "You guys on the job?"

The small guy asked, "Who the hell are you?"

"John Corey, NYPD, retired."

"Yeah, and I'm Billy the Kid."

"Really? I thought you were dead."

The big guy produced a pair of handcuffs and cuffed Bennie's hands behind her back. "Cuff him. I'll cover."

He felt the cuffs snap shut around his wrists.

So that's what it feels like.

The big guy said, "Stand up. Both of you on the couch."

He came to his feet and made eye contact with Bennie. "It's okay."

"No, it isn't," she shot back, tense. The bigger guy directed her to one end of the couch and the small guy holstered his Glock and pushed Corey onto the other end.

He turned to the men. "I really am John Corey."

The two men exchanged glances. The smaller guy asked, "You got ID?"

"In my jacket. Right-side pocket."

The guy plucked the cred case from his pocket, opened and looked at it. He passed the creds to the other guy who also studied it.

Just then, the big guy's cell phone chimed and he glanced at it. He said to the other guy, "BMW is registered to a Benedetta Rosato, Philadelphia." He looked at Bennie. "That you?"

She nodded.

The big guy continued, "Jeep belongs to John Corey."

"Until my wife gets it in court."

Both men looked at Corey, and the bigger man said, "Holy shit, you're *the* John Corey."

Bennie looked at the two men, then at Corey. He imagined what she was thinking. The menfolk were measuring their egos. But women knew that size there didn't matter. In fact, with respect to egos, every woman preferred the inverse relationship.

The bigger guy asked, "What are you doing here?"

"Relaxing."

Both men laughed.

So he asked them, "Who you working for?"

The big guy replied, "ATTF. Out of Albany."

"FBI?"

"Don't insult us."

He smiled. "PD?"

"SP."

Bennie frowned. "What the hell are you guys talking about?"

He explained, "These gentlemen are New York State Police, working with the Federal Anti-Terrorist Task Force."

The big guy said to Bennie, "Sorry if we frightened you, Ms. Rosato. We didn't know who you were."

"I'm a lawyer. I prosecute excessive-force cases, among other things."

"You shouldn't have said that," Corey noted. "Now they'll kill us."

The two guys laughed again.

She jangled her handcuffs. "Take these off, please. Along with those masks."

Both men removed their ski masks. Corey looked at their faces. The bigger guy was about thirty and sort of Irish-looking. The smaller guy was younger and looked maybe Hispanic or Mediterranean.

Bennie stood with her back to them and the big guy unlocked her cuffs. The smaller guy uncuffed Corey.

The big guy said, "I'm Kevin." He put out his hand to Corey and they shook. "This is an honor.'

Bennie rubbed her wrists. "And to think, I actually shook John Corey's hand."

The other guy returned Corey's credentials and handed him his Glock, butt first, and Corey slid it back into his holster, telling him, "You're good."

The man introduced himself and said, "I'm Ahmed, the token Arab. I know, I looked better with the ski mask."

Cops had a wonderfully warped sense of humor.

"Officers, aren't you supposed to identify yourselves when confronting civilians?" Bennie asked, staying on lawyer mode.

Kevin replied, "We're deep undercover."

Bennie said, "You should have run our plates earlier."

"Yes, ma'am," Kevin said. "But we thought we had a situation of hot pursuit. Your friend here is a legend. Detective Corey was one of the best and most successful and respected agents in the Anti-Terrorist Task Force."

She glanced at Corey with a smile. "So he's smarter than he looks?"

"Bingo."

He recalculated his odds of getting laid, which remained slim to none.

"We're all still talking about that case you had up here with that nut job at the Custer Hill Club," Kevin said.

"Just another day of preventing nuclear Armageddon."

Ahmed and Kevin laughed.

Then he said to Bennie, "Forget you heard that."

She rolled her eyes.

Kevin asked, "Didn't you work for the DSG for a while?"

"Still with them." He added, "On leave."

Kevin let him know, "You came to the right place to relax. Great fishing. And it's bow season now."

"Can't wait to get mine out."

"So, Officers, can you fill us in on what's going on?" Bennie asked.

Kevin and Ahmed exchanged glances, then Ahmed said, "We were setting up a training facility in the woods. That's all I can say. Please keep this to yourself—in the interest of national security."

She gestured to Corey. "But do me a favor, Ahmed. Please tell the Legend here that it was Arabic I heard."

Before Ahmed could reply, Kevin said something in what Corey recognized as Arabic.

Funny, coming from an Irishman.

Kevin said, "I'm learning the language. It's just a training exercise. There are no terrorists in the woods. You can relax."

Corey didn't think he was getting the whole truth, and there was no reason why he should. But if he had to guess, this was more of a sting operation than a training exercise. In a week, or a month, or a year, there would be terrorists at that site, lured there by Ahmed or other Arab-Americans on the Task Force. He had a sudden nostalgia for the ATTF. He disliked the bureaucracy, the political correctness, and working with the FBI, but he missed the excitement. And the satisfaction of doing something important for the country.

But that train had left the station.

Bennie said to Kevin and Ahmed, "Well, thank you, Officers. But even if I'm safe, I'm going back to Philly tonight."

Kevin assured her, "You're safer here than in Philadelphia."

Which was true.

Thousands of people died in Philly every year from boredom. But Corey kept that wisecrack to himself.

Kevin and Ahmed said good night and left.

He gestured to the sliders. "If you'd locked them when you got back in the house, we wouldn't have been terrorized by terrorists."

"They weren't terrorists."

"But they were terrifying."

She smiled. "And apparently you're a big deal."

"No apparently about it."

"I like a modest man."

"Some men have a lot to be modest about. I don't." He looked at his watch. "You're really going back tonight?"

"I wouldn't sleep tonight anyway, after all that." He sensed that they'd reached their good-byes sooner than either of them had wanted. He thought about offering to stay in touch, exchanging numbers and e-mails but decided to only stick out his hand, which she shook.

"Thank you," she said. "And I'm seeing someone."

"Figures. Nice meeting you, and have a good trip back to Philly. Tell Max I said good-bye."

"Will do."

"And lock the door after I leave."

"Will do that, too."

"Good night, Benedetta."

He left the cabin.

He wished they could've gotten to know each other better, and he thought she felt the same way. He liked strong women, and she was one of the strongest yet.

They'd have made a good match.

He climbed into his Jeep and drove away.

Not a total loss, though.

He had her cell-phone number in his phone and she had his. So maybe one day he'd get a call or a text.

Or maybe someday he'd need a Philadelphia lawyer.

But, if not, they'd always have Lake Whatever.

J.A. JANCE AND
ERIC VAN LUSTBADER

OF ALL THE TEAMS, THIS ONE MAY HAVE HAD THE MOST difficulty. Eric's character, Braverman "Bravo" Shaw is an accomplished medieval scholar and cryptanalyst, a solid East Coast kind of guy. Judith's character is all western, born one afternoon while she was watching the news in Tucson. Her favorite female newscaster was not on that day. She later learned that the new thirtysomething news director had decided that, at age fifty-three, the woman had to go. That's when ex-newscaster, Ali Reynolds, was born.

Like their characters, both writers live and breathe from different sides of the country. Further complicating things was the fact that collaboration was foreign to both of them. Neither had much worked with someone else on a story.

They're both loners.

Their styles are quite different.

Eventually, though, they realized that those differences were actually strengths. Eric wrote a first draft, then Judith took it from there. In the end, despite all the hurdles, these two were the first, among the eleven teams, to finish their story, five months ahead of the deadline.

Not bad for a couple of loners.

You're going to enjoy learning about—

Taking the Veil.

TAKING THE VEIL

BLACK HILLS, ARIZONA
1601

FRA IGNACIO WAS TIRED—EXHAUSTED, REALLY. HE AND HIS FIVE fellow Jesuits had been on the run for the better part of a year. They had started in the Holy Land, where they had been sent on a secret mission by Pope Clement VIII to bring back to Rome the fabled *Sudarium*—the Veil of Saint Veronica—the cloth used to wipe the blood and sweat from the brow of Jesus on his way to the Crucifixion, imprinting his face on the fabric. He had been told that it had been unearthed in the Sinai by tomb raiders who had no idea of its significance to the Holy See, to the church itself.

Clement VIII had bought the holy relic from a merchant in the Levant. Fra Ignacio and his group had been dispatched from Rome to fetch it since the Holy Father trusted no one other than his beloved Jesuits to ensure that this Veronica, as it was sometimes called, was the genuine article as, over the years, any number of fakes had been foisted upon the Vatican.

He made contact with the merchant and the judicious biblical scholar, who had authenticated the Veronica for Clement VIII. He never saw the veil itself, for it was already housed in a quiverlike cylinder made of zinc, clad in three layers of copper, with a watertight seal at one end. Twelve days after arriving in the Levant, they made their way back to the ship Clement VIII had provided for them.

But luck was not with them.

Before they could board their ship with the treasure, they were ambushed and attacked by a band of thieves who had stolen the veil and boarded a waiting pirate ship. Fra Ignacio's ship had pursued the pirate vessel across the full length of the Mediterranean, out into the Atlantic through the Straits of Gibraltar, and all the way to the pirates' base in Honduras where his crew had retrieved the veil in a daring nighttime raid. With the veil in hand and their ship resupplied they had set off for home, only to be blown off course by a hurricane and left shipwrecked off the coast of Texas.

Stranded off the coast of the vast New World, he took the veil along with the few surviving members of his crew and headed north through the Rio Grande Valley. Turned away by the priests at the mission in Albuquerque but now reprovisioned and with horses and pack mules, they turned westward toward California.

Days later, after crossing through a red-rock-lined valley and in the face of an early winter storm, they had holed up for several days in a limestone cavern under a thick canopy of ponderosa pines. Late in the day, they said their prayers, then ate a meager dinner. Afterward, Fra Ignacio left the others, moving deeper into the cavern where he had buried the Veronica case upon arriving. It took all his strength to move aside the protective boulder he had used to conceal the treasure. Then, as he did every evening at this time, he placed his trembling hands around the cool copper protecting the relic.

It was at that precise moment he heard screams and pleas for mercy coming from the men he had left behind near the cavern's mouth. He heard the soft whir of shot arrows, the clink of obsidian against rock, and knew a band of marauding Apaches had found them.

Returning the veil to its hiding place and rolling the boulder back into position, he kissed the rock before retreating deeper into the cavern. His torch guttered, and the way grew dim. Eventually utter blackness engulfed him. He slowed his pace and paused, waiting for his eyes to adjust.

Suddenly, without warning, he was grabbed from behind. His throat was slit with the blade of a hunting knife.

BLACK HILLS, ARIZONA
PRESENT DAY

MARTIN PRICE LOVED AMERICAN INDIAN ARROWHEADS. OVER THE years he'd amassed an impressive collection. None were more beautiful than the Apache obsidian arrowheads, masterfully chipped and honed to razor sharpness. So it was no surprise when he saw the glint of chipped obsidian on the floor of the limestone cavern adjacent to an abandoned glory hole. The hopeful miners from years past who'd dug the test hole must have left the place empty-handed and disappointed.

Not Martin.

Seeing the almost perfect arrowhead and slipping it into his pants pocket lifted his spirits. They needed lifting because he and his two fellow Gnostic Observatines had been up here in the wilds of the Black Hills, high above Sedona and Jerome, for over a week now without finding what had purportedly been hidden here since the beginning of the seventeenth century.

The Veil of Saint Veronica.

So many fakes had surfaced over the centuries that the Vatican had given up all hope that the Veronica still existed. But Bravo Shaw, the head of the Gnostic Observatines, a lay splinter sect of the Franciscan Observatines, had received information from one of his many worldwide sources not only that the Veronica existed, but that it was hidden in a limestone cave somewhere in Arizona's high desert country. A diary entry found in the Vatican, purportedly written by the sole survivor of Fra Ignacio's doomed expedition verified that fact. But the story of the Veronica ending up in Arizona had seemed far too preposterous to be believed.

By everyone, but Bravo.

He'd dispatched Price and his companions to go in search of both the cave and the veil. It was early November, about the same time of year when, according to the diary, Fra Ignacio and his men had been slaughtered. It was cold, and after weeks of rough living and of finding nothing, Price's companions were growing restless, itching to get back to the warmth and comfort of their San Francisco headquarters.

But Price's luck had changed when he had asked a group of elk hunters about the existence of a limestone cavern, and they'd directed them here. There were plenty of signs of human presence. Empty beer cans, tobacco cans, paper wrappers, a fire pit. And yet that arrow had somehow escaped everyone else's notice.

Was it a sign that had been meant for him alone?

Thoughtfully, Price stood where he was and used his Maglite to examine his surroundings, looking for something to speak to him, but there was nothing. If the solid limestone walls around him held a secret, they weren't telling. Moving deeper in the cavern, he heard the steady drip of water and saw the ghostly forms of looming stalactites and stalagmites. Looking at them rather than watching his feet, he stumbled over a boulder. As he struggled to regain his balance, the boulder moved. The movement was minuscule, but it was enough to tell him that the rock wasn't a natural part of the cavern itself.

It seemed separate.

Had it been put there deliberately and for a reason?

Was that even possible?

With his heart rate climbing, he dropped to his knees and shoved against the rock with all his strength. With that much pressure exerted the boulder moved with surprising ease, revealing a hand-dug depression below. The beam of his flashlight illuminated the verdigrised surface of a metallic curved object. He had been told that the Veronica was preserved in a copper-clad cylinder. On the ground next to the cylinder lay a pile of beads and an ivory crucifix. He scooped up the crucifix and slid it in his pocket.

Two screams resounded through the cavern.

The Gnostic Observatines, declared anathema by Clement VIII for their belief that truth went beyond traditional church canon, were well trained. Price, one of the best of Bravo's men, understood his priorities. The veil came first, his life and the lives of the others second.

Quickly now, for he had little time, he typed a message into his phone.

UNDER ATTACK.

Then he dropped the phone into the depression next to the cylinder and the scatter of beads. Shoving the boulder back in place, he loped deeper into the cavern and away from the spot where the veil lay buried, dousing his flashlight as he went and hearing the sound of pounding feet behind him. Light from some other source temporarily blinded him. He'd already drawn his .45, but before he could take cover behind the nearest looming stalactite, something whirred behind him and a stabbing pain shot through the space between his shoulder blades.

He fell facedown onto the cold damp rock.

Before he could regain his footing, hands he couldn't see grabbed his arms and hauled him upward. A heavy blow shattered his cheekbone, then another punch in the pit of his stomach doubled him over. He gasped, trying and failing to suck air into his lungs. Whoever was holding him let go of his arms, and he crashed facedown on the cavern floor in an explosion of pain.

That pain, however, was nothing compared to what was to come.

•◆•

SISTER ANSELM BECKER WAS STILL SLEEPING PEACEFULLY IN HER solitary cot at St. Bernadette's Convent in Jerome, Arizona, when the jangling ringing of her cell phone awakened her. It was a distinctive ringtone, one that belonged to her benefactor, Bishop Francis Gillespie, calling from his residence at the archdiocese in Phoenix.

Glancing at her bedside clock, Sister Anselm read 4:45 a.m.—well before her normal waking time for morning prayers. A nighttime call like this could only mean one thing. Somewhere in Arizona a badly injured patient was in desperate need of a patient advocate. That was Bishop Gillespie's self-appointed mission—to care for badly injured patients, often solo travelers or undocumented immigrants—who found themselves suddenly thrust into the world of hospital care and unable to cope. Sister Anselm, an eightysomething Sister of Providence, was the bishop's main tool in that regard. Not only was she a skilled nurse, she was conversant in any number of languages and was able to translate health-care jargon into something understandable.

"Good morning, Father," she said. "What seems to be the problem?"

"Two hours ago, a pair of elk hunters camped out in the Prescott National Forest came upon a badly injured, naked man lying in the roadway. There was an arrow in his back. I'm told he'd also been tortured and is suffering from severe hypothermia. The hunters were out in the middle of nowhere. They wrapped the guy up as best they could and drove him to St. Jerome's Hospital in Flagstaff. I'm told he's in serious condition."

"Why did they call you?" she asked.

"They believe the victim may be a priest. The only thing he had in his possession was a bloodied crucifix. So far he hasn't regained consciousness, and he's likely to go into surgery soon. I'd like you to be there as soon as you can."

"Absolutely," she said. "I'm on my way."

It took more than an hour for Sister Anselm to arrive at St. Jerome's Hospital in Flagstaff. Once there, she paused outside the ER to read through what little information there was on John Doe's chart. He had indeed been struck in the back by an arrow. After stabilizing the patient, ER personnel had used ultrasound imagery to thread the arrow through the chest cavity and out through his rib cage without damaging any additional internal organs. His next stop would be an operating room where surgeons would address other pressing internal injuries.

Squaring her shoulders, she entered the ER and approached the proper cubicle only to find that another visitor—a distinguished-looking and fit young man—had preceded her.

"Who are you?" he demanded, barring her way. "And what business do you have with Martin Price?"

"That's his name?" she asked, making a notation on the iPad. She carried it with her. "Martin Price?"

The man nodded.

"I'm Sister Anselm Becker, a Sister of Providence," she said. "I've been asked to serve as Mr. Price's patient advocate. Who might you be, and how do you know this man? Are you a relative?"

"My name is Bravo Shaw," he said. "I'm the director of the order of Gnostic Observatines. Martin Price is a member of our order."

A pair of nurses hurried past Sister Anselm and Bravo Shaw and disappeared into the cubicle. They appeared moments later, wheeling Price and his IV tree out of the ER and toward the operating wing. While Shaw watched Price, Sister Anselm studied him. He didn't look like any priest she'd ever seen, and if he and the patient were members of an order, why would Shaw refer to himself and the patient by their given names?

"Father Shaw, I've been a Sister of Providence for more than sixty years," she said. "I've never heard of an order called the Gnostic Observatines inside or outside the church."

"Bravo, please, rather than Father," he said, smiling at her in a way she didn't much care for. "We're Franciscans, adhering to St. Francis's original dicta. The order was cast out by Pope Clement VIII because we refused to go against St. Francis's edict and remain Conventuals. Over the years, my predecessors developed an interest in religious relics and have conducted explorations outside the strict boundaries of the church."

Father Shaw had a way of speaking that she found both intimidating as well as annoying. She also didn't like the fact that he obviously knew far more than he was willing to share.

"I suppose you called the Vatican for support," she said dryly.

A slow smile spread across Bravo's face, a smile she found unsettling, even a bit wicked, and a little shiver traveled down her spine.

"The Vatican and the Gnostic Observatines are not in contact," he said. "As I indicated, we haven't been since the era of Clement VIII. When it comes to church doctrine, and methods, we don't see eye to eye."

"And just what is the Observatines' mission, Father?"

Bravo gave a small laugh. "I see I have come up against an immovable object."

She lifted one eyebrow. "And are you declaring yourself an unstoppable force?"

"I suppose," he said, "you'll have to judge for yourself."

Sister Anselm allowed herself the ghost of a smile, the smallest treat. "Your mission, Father."

"In a nutshell, Sister, we're humanists. We are locked in an eternal battle against evil for the souls of mankind."

"As is the church."

"Method, Sister. I told you our methods differ."

Having been put in a thoughtful mode, she made another note.

"Returning to facts," she said, looking up from her iPad. "Father Price's date of birth? Next of kin? Place of residence?"

Bravo continued to be amused by her use of the word *Father* but had said all he was going to on the subject. "All that information is confidential, I'm afraid. Because of the nature of what we do and the dangers involved to ourselves and potentially to our loved ones, that information is never divulged."

"Then tell me what Father Price and his team were doing up in the mountains."

"I'm afraid I can't do that, either."

"Can't or won't?" she asked, irritated. "I'm quite sure they were looking for something, and if you are who you say you are, the odds are you sent them to find it."

Bravo remained silent.

"Very well then," she said, slipping her iPad into the generous pocket of her jacket. "In that case, we're even."

"What do you mean?"

"Have you ever heard of HIPAA?"

Shaw frowned. "Of course."

"It's now officially invoked. Father Price was the victim of a vicious attack. He's been tortured, was unconscious when he was brought to the ER, and remains unable to communicate. You claim to be concerned about him. Perhaps you are, but for all I know, you may have been responsible for what happened to him in the first place. What if you're here masquerading as his friend, but really came here for the express purpose of finishing the job? Until I have a clearer idea of whether or not you pose a threat, you won't be allowed anywhere near him."

"Are you kidding?" Bravo demanded. "You're trying to kick me out?"

"I will kick you out," she declared without a hint of smile. "That's not a threat. It's a promise. Since you won't tell me what Father Price was searching for, I won't allow you to have access to my patient, simple as that. In fact, I could most likely have you thrown out of the hospital altogether. Once the police get here."

"The cops aren't coming," Bravo said.

She appeared to be genuinely startled. "What do you mean they're not coming?"

"The hunters who found Martin didn't report the incident to the authorities at the time they brought him to the hospital, and I've been assured that they won't be doing so in the future. Neither will the hospital. Once he leaves here, all trace of his having been here will be erased."

"You're impeding an official investigation into the commission of a crime," she said. "Why would you do such a thing?"

"Because the presence of law enforcement would instantly alert our enemies to the fact that Martin is still alive, in which case, the first thing they would do is send someone here to finish the job. Once Martin is out of danger and declared fit to travel, I intend to have him transported back to our U.S. headquarters where he'll be able to recover in relative safety."

"You believe he's still in danger?"

"Absolutely."

"If I'm caring for him, doesn't that mean I'm in danger, as well?" she asked.

Looking uncomfortable, Bravo nodded. "I suppose it does."

She fell silent for a moment. "As long as Martin Price is a patient in this hospital, Bishop Francis Gillespie has charged me with protecting him. I fully intend to do so, against all comers."

"But, Sister," Bravo said, "you have no idea what you're up against."

"I'm up against it?" she asked. "It sounds as though we're both up against it, so why don't you explain it to me? If I'm expected to defend the man, it's only fair that I know from what. It also seems reasonable that I should have some understanding of what Father Price was doing or some idea of who his attacker or attackers might be. Now, if you'll excuse me."

Turning her back on Bravo, she walked into Martin Price's empty cubicle. She returned a moment later carrying two small clear plastic bags, which she handed to Bravo. Inside one was a wooden crucifix, black with dried blood. In the other was the bloodied tip of a hunting arrow.

"The crucifix was found on his person, clutched in Father Price's hand. The arrow was in his back," she said. "By giving these to you, I'm now guilty of concealing evidence of a crime. So how about we declare a peace treaty? What if we decide right now that Father Price is both our responsibilities? In which case I need you to be straight with me, but first let's go out into the lobby and find somewhere to sit. They're ready to clean this cubicle, and we're in the way."

•◆•

IT WASN'T LIKE BRAVO SHAW TO CONCEDE DEFEAT TO ANYONE, especially to an elderly nun, but there was something fearless about this woman that he could not help but respect. Obligingly he followed her out into the hospital's main lobby where she led him to a quiet corner seating area.

"Tell me," she said, once they were both seated.

But he was busy examining the crucifix, which he'd removed from the plastic bag. As he turned it over and over in his hands, Sister Anselm said, "What is it?"

"This is old. Perhaps from the time." He looked up at her. "It seems possible now that Martin found what he and his team had been sent to find."

She cocked her head. "And that would be?"

He sighed. "We're a lay order. Part of our mission is locating lost artifacts dating from the earliest days of the Christian church. Once those priceless relics are found and authenticated, we see to it that they are returned to their rightful place. Unfortunately, there are powerful forces both inside and outside the church who would prefer to keep those treasures for their own benefit and profit. Those people have always allied themselves with an organization called the Knights of Saint Clement, named for the pope who branded us heretics."

"So you're supposedly the good guys and the so-called Knights are the bad guys?" she asked. "But if you're returning the artifacts to the church, what's the problem?"

"Unfortunately, not everyone inside the church or even inside the Vatican is trustworthy."

"And if the Knights and their friends lay hands on those relics before you do, what happens then?"

"They usually auction them off to the highest bidder, which is often someone among the most rich and powerful people in the world. And dangerous."

"It sounds to me as though you must consider Bishop Gillespie to be on the right side of this conflict, on the side of the angels, as it were."

He couldn't help smiling. "I don't know the man, but since people I trust in turn trust him, you could say that. At this point, however, it's important that the good bishop not be drawn into this incident any more than he has been already. He could be in mortal danger, as could you."

"I'm perfectly capable of taking care of myself," Anselm bristled, "but you still haven't told me what Martin Price and his cohorts were searching for. And speaking of his teammates, what about them. Are they even still alive?"

He shook his head. "I doubt it. The Gnostic Observatines operate either individually or in teams. The same is true for the Knights of Saint Clement. Their teams refer to themselves as extramuros. Believe me, they are utterly ruthless. I can't imagine how Martin managed to escape their clutches. As for his teammates? I would hazard a guess that they're both dead and their bodies will never be found."

"Which now means we're interfering with the investigation into three crimes rather than just one?"

He nodded.

"And what exactly was Father Price's team searching for?"

Knowing he was going all in, he sighed. "What do you know about the Veil of Saint Veronica?"

The nun's eyes widened. "The cloth used to wipe the blood and sweat from Jesus's brow along the Via Dolorosa?"

"We had reason to believe that centuries ago it was hidden somewhere here in the Arizona high country. Martin and his team were dispatched to search for it. Two weeks into the hunt, Martin texted me that he thought they were getting closer, but he gave me no further details. His last text to me said they were being attacked. After that, he didn't answer repeated texts and calls."

"The phone wasn't found with him?"

"No, the elk hunters who brought him to the hospital said he was stark naked when they found him. The only thing he had in his possession was this crucifix."

"It sounds to me as if you . . . and I," she said, "have some serious opponents."

He agreed. "The Knights of Saint Clement want the veil as much as we do. In fact, given what's happened, they may already have it. If not, once Martin awakens, I have no doubt that they'll stop at nothing in trying to gain its possession. Centuries ago, their original purpose was to eradicate our order, and that is still high on their list. These days, however, their agenda has shifted. They take our operatives out when they can—as they did here, but they are far more focused on grabbing power, which they do through a cabal of corrupt cardinals inside the Vatican."

"Then we'll have to stop them at once, won't we," she said, sitting bolt upright. "And I happen to know of someone who could help."

"Please," Bravo said. "No help. I must insist on absolute secrecy. I simply can't afford to involve anyone else."

"Tell me about Father Price's phone," she said. "You said that he left you a message just before he was attacked. But you don't know exactly where he was at the time."

"I have the names of the two hunters who brought him to the hospital. I'm hoping that if I speak to them, they'll be able to give me the general location. The clerk in the ER said something about a place called Mingus Mountain, although I have no idea where that is."

"But it may be close to where the attack took place."

He nodded. "A good place to start the search."

"Except it's November," she said. "Did you happen to notice the snow on the ground outside? There'll be snow on Mingus Mountain, too, and I've heard it's likely that a storm is blowing in from the west. We can't risk going out searching blind. We need help, but you have to agree to let someone else into our little circle."

He was intrigued. "And who might that be?"

"Ali Reynolds, a close friend I trust absolutely. She and her husband live in Sedona and run a cybersecurity company called High Noon Enterprises that operates out of Cottonwood. If you'd give me Father Price's phone number, I wouldn't be surprised that they'd be able to give you the exact coordinates on the phone when it was last in use."

"But the phone's battery is probably dead."

"That doesn't necessarily matter. If it pinged somewhere, they'll be able to find it. In addition, Ali grew up in this area. Her father was an avid outdoorsman in his day, and Ali tagged along with him wherever he went. She knows the backwoods around here like the back of her hand. I'm sure she'd be able to help."

This nun knew a lot about things that nuns don't usually deal with. But still he had to object.

"Sister," he began.

"Ali has had police training. She's quite resourceful. And she has Bishop Gillespie's stamp of approval."

"That may well be," he said. "But, as I said before, I don't want to endanger anyone else in this endeavor."

An audible ding on her iPad announced the arrival of an e-mail. "I'm afraid it's too late for that."

"What do you mean?"

"Did you happen to look at the arrow tip I gave you?"

He shook his head.

"If you had, you might have noticed that it's stamped with a serial number of some kind. Before I bagged it, I took a photo and sent it to Ali. Turns out it's from a high-end hunting arrow sold at only a few outlets in the area. The one you're holding in your hand was sold a week ago at a specialty hunting store in Phoenix that caters specifically to bow hunters. Does this person look like anyone you know?"

She passed him her iPad. Bravo studied the photo. He said nothing, but the slight stiffening of his jaw spoke volumes.

"One of those Knights?" she asked.

"How did you get this?" he asked.

"As I said before, Ali Reynolds is resourceful. Her people were able to trace the serial number on the arrow tip, the manufacturer came up with the batch number that went to a specific retailer, and the retailer remembered the woman. The way she talked, the arrows she requested, he assumed that she was an expert bow hunter. The owner located the security footage, Ali's team enhanced it, and there you are. Who is she?"

"Her name is Maria Elena Donahue. She works with an extramuros team leader named Anson Stone, sometimes referred to as the Archer. She's one of the only females inside the Knights. She wasn't worried about being seen purchasing the arrow. It was never supposed to be found."

"But Father Price escaped," Sister Anselm said thoughtfully.

"Martin is probably one of the best team leaders I've ever trained."

He stood abruptly.

"Where are you going?" she asked.

"I need to go back to the beginning and find the place where the attack took place. If Martin really did find the Veronica, there's a chance it's still there."

"He was tortured," she said.

"Doesn't matter. He wouldn't give up the veil no matter what."

She frowned. "You're suggesting that perhaps the veil is still there, but what if the phone is, too? You said that Father Price texted you that he and his team were under attack, and that was the last communication you had from him. What if there was a struggle and the phone somehow disappeared in the course of that? Maybe the Knights didn't know he had a phone with him and they didn't bother to look for it."

"I know cell-phone companies can track the pings on phones, but getting them to do it is a complicated, time-consuming process, even for cops. And as I said before, we're not involving cops."

"I understand," she said. "But as I told you earlier, Ali's company, High Noon Enterprises, is a cybersecurity company. In order to do what they do, they deal in a lot of cyber insecurity. I have every reason to believe that Ali's people will be able to track Father Price's phone regardless of where it may be at the moment."

He thought about that, but not for long.

"If Ali Reynolds and her people can find Martin's phone, she sounds like someone I should have met yesterday."

•◆•

BRAVO DISCOVERED THAT ALI REYNOLDS AND HER HUSBAND, B. SIMP-
son, lived in a large midcentury modern house in Sedona. As he stepped
up onto the wisteria-shaded front porch, a tall, fit woman somewhere in
her fifties opened the door to welcome and beckon him inside.

"You must be Father Shaw. I'm Ali," she said as she escorted him into
the house. "My office is this way. I've asked the butler to serve coffee."

He followed her through a spacious living room and a pair of French
doors into a cozy office. The desk in front of the window was littered
with files. She motioned him into one of a pair of wingback chairs set in
front of a burning gas-log fireplace. He had no more than sat down when
a miniature long-haired dachshund leaped into his lap.

"That's Bella," she said with a smile. "That's also a good sign. She's
pretty picky when it comes to making friends with strangers."

"I'm assuming Sister Anselm told you why I'm here?"

"She did. The *Reader's Digest* condensed version, but now that you're
here, maybe you'd like to tell me more."

Before he could reply, an older gentleman wearing a suit and tie
stepped through the French doors bearing a tray laden with coffee, cups
and saucers, sugar and cream, and a plate of gingerbread cookies.

"Fresh out of the oven," he said, placing the tray on the coffee table
between them.

"Thank you, Leland." Reaching toward the carafe, she asked, "Coffee,
Father Shaw?"

"Call me Bravo, please. And yes, coffee is perfect."

While Ali poured, he examined his surroundings. The house was impressive in an understated yet elegant way, and the fact that a manservant
had delivered the coffee spoke of a certain amount of money. As for the
woman seated across from him? Even in jeans and with her hair pulled
back in a ponytail, she had a classy, no-nonsense way about her.

She passed him a brimming cup and saucer, then settled back in her
chair. "Sister Anselm filled me in as best she could with the information
you provided. Finding your injured associate's cell phone is something my
people can do. However, to be honest, Sister Anselm seems to think it is

highly unlikely that the actual veil exists. She says that according to Bishop Gillespie, several items alleged to be the veil have shown up at the Vatican over the centuries and that each in turn has been proven to be a fake."

"I don't believe this one is a fake. Martin sent me a text to that effect just as they came under attack."

"You call it an attack, but it was more than that," she observed. "It was an assault with intent. Martin Price was severely injured and two of his teammates are missing and presumed dead. Sister Anselm mentioned your reasoning against involving local law enforcement." She hesitated for a beat. "So your contention is that you're above the rule of law?"

"Not so much above, as outside. If a local law enforcement agency were to try to lay hands on Anson Stone or one of his team members, they'd forfeit their lives. Believe me, Ms. Reynolds, this is not something you've encountered before. And, other than helping locate Martin Price's cell phone, you'd be well advised to stay out of it now."

She set down her coffee. "One thing puzzles me. If you're a priest, I'm a bit confused about why I'm supposed to address you by your given name."

"The Gnostic Observatines are a lay order. Addressing our members as 'Father' is unnecessary." He tossed her a wry smile. "A distinction your Sister Anselm refuses to acknowledge."

She nodded, slightly amused. "Yes, that certainly sounds like her."

Her phone rang.

"Excuse me," she said. "It's Sister Anselm." She listened for a moment. "Good," she said, before turning to Bravo. "She says Martin Price is out of surgery. They've removed his spleen and one of his kidneys. He's in critical condition and has been moved to the ICU."

"Please thank her for me. I'm sure Martin will appreciate her tender mercies."

She relayed the message. "Yes," she answered, apparently a question from Sister Anselm. "Stuart has the hospital surveillance in place. And yes, we'll have eyes and facial rec on all exits and entrances. And yes, if push comes to shove, that's probably a good plan."

She ended the call.

"What's a good plan?" he asked.

"We've created a backup security plan at the hospital."

"I have additional personnel flying in to Flagstaff even as we speak."

"Who may or may not arrive," she said, "since by all accounts there's a blizzard on its way. And if you have people showing up to help out, we need to have photos of them. Otherwise, our facial recognition program will have no way to tell good guys from bad guys. Neither will Sister Anselm."

He pulled out his phone. "Where should I send them?"

She gave him an e-mail address for Stuart Ramey. She waited until he'd pressed Send before adding, "If you want us to try locating that phone, you'll need to send along both Martin's number and yours."

He keyed in more information and sent that off too.

"Do you really think any of this is going to work?" he asked, pocketing his phone. "I only came here at Sister Anselm's insistence, but the idea of your getting a good result doesn't seem likely. I'm quite sure Martin would have been using a burner phone for the purposes of this expedition, and all our in-house communications systems are encrypted and supposedly secure."

"But what if they're not?" she asked. "What if your encryption program has somehow been penetrated? Suppose someone managed to gain access to your phone. In that case, the Knights may have learned that Martin had found the veil at the same time you did."

Looking troubled, he made as if to rise. "I should go back to the hospital. That way, when Martin comes around, maybe he'll be able to tell me exactly what happened and where I should look."

"My understanding is that the hunters who rescued Martin Price found him on the back side of Mingus Mountain. Going there from here will be a shorter trip than it will be starting from Flagstaff. Besides, if and when Martin recovers enough to speak, Sister Anselm will pass along that information."

The words were barely out of her mouth when her phone rang again. "It's Sister Anselm again."

She answered and switched the phone to speaker.

"I just spoke to him," Sister Anselm said. "He was able to tell me his name. When I asked if he knew Bravo, he nodded and said something about a boulder. I couldn't make out any more than that, but I suspect it has something to do with the location of the veil."

"But no indication of the location of said boulder?"

"None."

"Keep us posted."

The call ended.

Ali turned back to him. "At the time Martin was delivered to the hospital, no one knew who he was. How did you know he was there?"

"All Gnostic Observatines are outfitted with medical alert chips that can be scanned if one of us is hospitalized. It gives hospital personnel access to our medical records, but it also notifies us so we can come in and do damage control."

"So you can make sure your so-called war casualties don't end up in any official police or hospital records?"

He smiled and nodded. "Exactly. But it would seem I wasn't the only one who had that information. I'm not sure about his sources, but Sister Anselm's friend, Bishop Gillespie, must have known something about it as well. Is he trustworthy enough?"

"He always has been, as far as I can tell."

"But what about those above him, the people he answers to?" he said. "Can you vouch for all of them?"

She sat forward. "You think some of the people inside the church might be members of the Knights?"

"It's entirely possible. That's why the possibility that the veil might be found here in Arizona has been handled with such strict secrecy."

Just then her cell dinged and she looked at the incoming text message. "We now have the last coordinates of Martin's cell phone before the battery died. They're being sent to us along with both topo maps and satellite imagery of the area.

He was impressed. "That was fast."

Ali smiled. "You'd be surprised how fast Stu can do things when he isn't hampered by having to wait around for properly drawn warrants."

They were seated side by side at a dining room table peering at the two sets of images Stu had sent along, both of them with a pin indicating the location of Martin's missing phone.

"Wait a minute," Ali said, after studying the expanded images for some time. "I remember this place."

"You've been there?" he asked.

"A long time ago when I was a kid. My dad was into prospecting back then. We went up and explored some old glory holes, looking for gold and silver."

"What's a glory hole?"

"Test holes dug, mostly by hand, by early explorers looking to strike it big. Some of them date from the time your Fra Ignacio was wandering in these parts. But what really impressed me about that trip was the cavern. Complete with stalagmites and stalactites. I'd never seen one like that. It seemed to go on forever."

"Can you take me there?" he asked.

"Now?"

"Please. Because that's what the fragment we found in the Vatican said. That the veil was hidden in a cavern. We'll need backup, though. I'll call and see if my people are on the ground in Flagstaff."

She glanced out the window where fat snowflakes were already starting to fall. "That cavern is a lot higher than we are here in Sedona. By the time your people get here from Flagstaff, if they're even in Flagstaff, the road into the mountains may be impassable. Besides, you'll have backup. You'll have me and Mr. Leland Brooks."

"The old guy who was here a little while ago?" he asked with no attempt to conceal his disbelief. "The one who brought our coffee?"

She nodded.

"Please, Ms. Reynolds. This might be terribly dangerous for everyone concerned, and the idea of involving a frail old man is out of the question. Tell me how to get there and I'll do it alone."

"I saw your rental. A front-wheel-drive sedan. Where we're going, that will never do. As for Mr. Brooks? You'd be surprised. He came of age as a Royal Marine, and you know what they say, 'Once a marine, always a marine.'"

The butler appeared at the French doors.

"You called, madame?"

"I did," Ali said. "Stuart Ramey has located the spot where one of

Mr. Shaw's associates, Martin Price, was viciously attacked. He and I are about to set off on a mission to retrieve an item of Mr. Price's property. Would you care to join us?"

"What kind of mission?"

"Most likely a dangerous and snowy one."

"So winter gear then," Leland said without so much as a pause. "What about weaponry?"

"We're hoping there won't be any law enforcement involvement. But just to be on the safe side, nothing that can be traced back to you," she noted.

"So batons then, rather than handguns?"

"Probably a good idea." She turned to Bravo. "What kind of hiking gear do you have along?"

"I came prepared. Everything I need is out in the car."

She nodded. "Leland can show you to the guest room so you can change, and I'll go do the same. Wheels up in ten."

•◆•

LEFT IN A GUEST ROOM TO CHANGE OUT OF BUSINESS CLOTHING AND into something more suitable for wintertime hand-to-hand combat, Bravo did more stewing than changing. He wasn't accustomed to working with people outside the order, and yet, in this case, shorthanded as he was, there didn't seem to be a choice. If the veil really was within reach, he didn't want to lose it to the Knights of Saint Clement.

That meant speed was of the essence.

Ali knew how to get to the location where they needed to be. He did not. In the meantime, the weather outside the guest room window was deteriorating by the minute. He supposed, if nothing else, the old man could serve as a lookout while he and Ali searched for the veil. It was possible that Anson Stone was no longer anywhere nearby, but if things came down to taking out Anson Stone?

He himself would handle that task.

Once dressed, he called his sister back in New York. Emma was in charge of research for the inner circle of Gnostic Observatines.

"How's Martin?" she asked.

"He's out of surgery, but still iffy. It's unknown if he'll make it. I'm working with a woman named Ali Reynolds from a company called High Noon Enterprises. They located an image of the woman who bought the arrow used on Martin. Maria Elena Donahue."

"The Archer's sidekick?"

"None other," he said. "Ali's people have also locked in on the location where the veil is still hidden. We're about to go there now."

"You and who else?"

"The three of us. Ali, an elderly gentleman named Leland Brooks who's supposedly a former Royal Marine, and yours truly."

"Three people, including a woman and an old man, up against Ansor Stone? That's nuts."

"If it goes bad, sis, I want you to know where we are and who's involved. In the meantime, I want you to find everything there is to find on the Archer."

"Will do," she said. "But I don't like this. I don't like any of it. Can't you wait for reinforcements?"

"The more we delay, the better the chance that we lose the veil."

"Be careful," she said with a sigh. "Please be careful."

He left the guest room just as Ali was leaving a room at the end of the hall. She was dressed in a pair of sturdy hiking boots along with jeans topped by what looked like several layers of flannel shirts.

"Ready?" she asked.

He nodded.

"In case this takes longer than just in and out, Leland is in the kitchen putting together a few supplies."

Minutes later, he found himself in the front passenger seat of a silver Porsche Cayenne. As far as he was concerned this was a life-and-death mission. He shook his head as Leland Brooks loaded a woven picnic hamper into the back of the SUV. Seeming to read Bravo's disapproval, the old man winked.

"Eat when you can," he said with a grin as he closed the luggage gate, "but carry a big stick." And Leland pulled what was clearly a weighted baton from the vest pocket of a down-filled jacket.

Ali immediately connected her phone to the Cayenne's Bluetooth. They had yet to reach the bottom of the driveway when the phone rang.

"Push just came to shove," Sister Anselm said over the car's speaker system. "Stu and Cami spotted the woman from the hunting video and a man walking through the hospital parking lot. By the time they made it to the entrance, we had Father Price on the maternity ward."

Bravo was concerned.

"It's the only part of St. Jerome's that can go on complete lockdown on a moment's notice," Ali explained. "It's also the least likely place for a critically injured patient to be taken for treatment." To Sister Anselm, Ali said, "What happened?"

"They came inside and went up to the desk where they were told no one by the name of Martin Price was being treated in the hospital. They tried arguing with the desk clerk. She and a security guard ended up sending them packing. They left the hospital under protest, but Stu tells me that as they drove out of the lot, they were being followed by another vehicle. Facial rec of the driver of the car following matches one of the ones provided by Father Shaw earlier."

"That means they're handled then," he said quietly. "If Stone is on his own, that makes our odds a little better."

"I didn't quite get that," Sister Anselm said.

"Doesn't matter," Ali said. "Are you and Martin staying on the maternity floor for now?"

"They've lifted the lockdown, but since we're already here, it can be reinstated at a moment's notice."

"Has Martin said anything more?" Bravo asked, speaking loudly enough so Sister Anselm could hear.

"Not so far. His doctors are keeping him heavily sedated for the time being."

"Keep us posted," Ali said, ending the call. "What will happen to the man and the woman?"

"An eye for an eye," he responded quietly. "That's the way it works in our world. May God have mercy on their souls. As for Anson Stone? My sister just sent me a file. The Archer is exceptionally dangerous on every level. He's ex–Special Forces, and that was before he took to the bow and arrow."

"Can I read it?" Leland asked from the backseat. "It's always a good idea to know thy enemy."

Bravo nodded and handed over his cell.

Leland scanned the file, nodding to himself, then returned the phone to Bravo. "Invaluable. Thank you."

They drove in silence for more than an hour, through darkening clouds and thickening snow. Steering with confidence, Ali guided the nimble-footed vehicle up one trackless road after another, with each branch narrower than the one before. Even though they were under a thick canopy of pine, enough snow had filtered down that there was at least four inches on the ground when Ali finally stopped and cut the engine.

"We're here," she said. "As close as we can get, anyway. The cavern is going to be another mile or so in that direction. From here on, we walk." She pulled out a compass. "The snow canopy is playing havoc with the GPS. But I've been in snowstorms before."

They left the Cayenne and headed north, straight into the teeth of a rising wind that galloped over the mountains to the north and west. It bore down on them with a gathering ferocity, cutting visibility to nothing more than a few feet.

Ali pressed forward with confidence.

Bravo followed on her heels with Leland Brooks behind him. Despite the sharply steepening and narrowing path, he noted that the spry old man had no difficulty keeping up.

"There were mines up here?" he asked, huffing with exertion at the unaccustomed elevation.

"Not this far up," she replied. "The really big strike was back down at Jerome. Even though people had known the ore was there for centuries, it couldn't be profitably extracted until someone finally invented the narrow gauge railroad. Men, horses, mules all died attempting to bring the riches from up here down to market."

A rumble of thunder rolled around overhead, accompanied by a sudden flash of lightning. The flash illuminated their way in bizarre and lurid colors.

"Lightning in a snowstorm," she said. "Highly unusual, and bad luck for us. This one's about to become a doozy."

The snow fell in diagonal sheets, driven so hard by the wind that it stung their faces, forcing them to continue half blinded. Their progress slowed. The snow piled up at an alarming rate. It was already above their ankles. Drifts had formed in some spots, driven against the rock face calf high.

"Let's keep going," she advised. "We'll be able to shelter inside the cavern and wait it out."

They reached a particularly hairy stretch where both Ali and Bravo slid back twice. Looking behind him, he noticed that Leland had fallen behind.

"Are you all right?" he called.

"You go on," Leland yelled. "I'll just rest here a minute and then catch up."

He and Ali plodded on.

She stopped time and again to check the compass, and each time he was convinced they were hopelessly lost. He'd fallen behind by a few steps when she suddenly disappeared completely, melting into a gash in the cliff wall that had been entirely invisible in the swirling snow.

He followed.

Inside, he removed a Maglite from his pack and used it to examine the interior of the cave. Dark stains on the floor testified to what had happened here. It shook him beyond measure to know that this was where his people had made their last stand against the Knights. Here and there he caught sight of bloodied bits of cartilage that told him this had also been the scene of Martin's appalling torture.

He said nothing to Ali.

"If the veil is here," she said, "where do we start looking?"

A sound broke the silence.

The soft skitter of a pebble or boot heel against rock.

●◆●

SISTER ANLEM WATCHED AS MARTIN PRICE, IN HIS BED OF DRUG-blunted pain, stirred briefly, opened his eyes, and stared upward into her face.

"Welcome back," she said, squeezing his hand. "My name is Sister Anselm. You're in St. Jerome's Hospital in Flagstaff, Arizona. You've been gravely injured, but an excellent surgeon has taken care of all that. Your job now is to rest and let your body heal."

Instead of calmness a look of urgent dread flashed across his face. "Bravo Shaw. I must speak with him at once."

His voice came out thin and reedy. Some words dropped to little more than whispers, others disappeared altogether, forcing her to piece them together like a patchwork quilt.

"Not to worry," she said. "Father Shaw has been here already. He's discovered where you were when you sent that last text, and he's probably there by now."

"In the cavern? Oh, no."

"Please be still," she begged. "It's okay."

"It's not okay. You don't understand. It's a trap," he whispered, and she bent closer to hear his words. "I hid the veil. I didn't tell the Archer."

He stopped, panting.

Monitors indicated that his pulse raced.

"The Archer will be there waiting for him. You . . . must . . . warn him."

"I will," she said. "You mentioned a boulder earlier. Something about a boulder."

"Inside the cavern," he said. "On the floor . . . a boulder that moves."

His eyelids fluttered.

His heart rate spiked and he slid back into unconsciousness.

She reached for her iPad. The day before, Martin Price had been able to send a text message from somewhere inside that cavern. Now, falling to her knees, she prayed that the reverse would also be true.

•◆•

ALI FULLY EXPECTED LELAND TO STEP INTO THE CAVERN. BUT HE WAS nowhere to be seen. Instead, an arriving text dinged on her phone. She glanced down at the message.

ARCHER'S THERE. TRAP.

Before she could pass the warning along to Bravo, the figure of a woman materialized in the entrance of the cave behind them. She was dressed all in black. Assuming a bowman's stance, she sent an arrow whirring into the cavern. Bravo ducked to the ground, shoving Ali down with him an instant before the arrow ricocheted off the cavern wall an inch from her right cheek.

Their attacker reached for another arrow.

•—◆—•

BRAVO LAUNCHED HIMSELF FORWARD AND SLAMMED HIS LEFT FOREarm into the woman's head, then raced past into the snowy void at the cavern's mouth, hoping to engage the Archer.

To his surprise, the woman didn't give chase.

Behind him, though, he could hear the sounds of a one-on-one battle as Ali engaged the Knight he'd thrown off-balance. He hoped he'd given her enough of an opening.

Another vague outline, far larger than the first, appeared out of the snow. He shifted right at Anson Stone, striking him before his adversary had time to notch an arrow.

The Archer tumbled over backward, arms and legs flying.

He struck three or four times with his closed fist, driving the Archer back beneath the thickening carpet of snow. The Archer's right arm arced upward and slammed a rock into Bravo's temple.

He collapsed.

The Archer grabbed the front of his coat, jerked it hard to the left. Bravo tried to clear the fog the blow had caused. The Archer reversed their positions, now on top, trying to pound the back of Bravo's skull against the ground.

But the snow acted like a cushion.

The Archer pressed one hand onto Bravo's face, trying to force his head under the snow. But the chill only served to revive Bravo, and he emerged from his stupor with the alacrity of someone fleeing an ice bath.

Still, his breathing was being stifled.

Full understanding of his dire situation flooded him.

He forced his body to go limp.

The Archer, sensing that his prey was either unconscious or dead, heaved Bravo's head upward to find out which. He intended to deliver a closed-fingered blow straight to the Archer's windpipe.

But never had a chance.

He heard the dull thud of Leland Brooks's weighted baton smash into the back of Anson Stone's head.

The Archer landed dead weight on Bravo's back, forcing what little breath he still had out of his lungs. Seconds later, the still body was rolled away and Leland helped Bravo to his feet.

The two men then raced into the cavern.

They could hear breathing in the pitch dark. Bravo had lost his Maglite during the struggle. Fortunately Leland still had his, which was switched on. In the beam's glare they saw Ali leaning against the side of the cavern, gasping for breath, her opponent on the rocky floor, out cold.

Bravo dug into his backpack and came out with a fistful of tie wraps. "We need to secure them." He looked at Ali. "Are you all right?"

She nodded. "You?"

"I wouldn't be if it weren't for Leland."

Who was busy fastening the prisoner's arms behind her.

"He thumped Anson Stone a good one on the head with that baton of his. I don't think Anson's dead, but it's going to be a while before he comes around."

"Let's get him tied up before that happens," Leland said.

Bravo nodded. "And bring him inside."

"Do you think there are any others?" Ali asked.

"I hope not."

•◆•

WHILE THE TWO MEN STEPPED BACK OUTSIDE, ALI STRUGGLED TO locate her phone. She found the unit and sent Sister Anselm a text created with trembling fingers.

THANKS FOR THE WARNING. IT WAS A TRAP. WE'RE ALL OKAY.

A few moments later a reply text came.

FATHER PRICE SAYS TO LOOK FOR A LOOSE BOULDER INSIDE THE CAVERN. IT'S THERE, SOMEWHERE. I THINK IT MAY BE ON THE RIGHT HAND SIDE.

Anson Stone was still unconscious when Leland and Bravo carried him inside the cave, then dropped him to the ground.

"I heard from Sister Anselm. Martin tried to warn us that it might be a trap. But he said to look for a boulder inside the cavern."

"What exactly are we looking for?" Leland asked.

"A copper tube, probably green with verdigris," Bravo said. "It contains the Veil of Saint Veronica."

• ◆ •

LELAND MANAGED TO BUILD A FIRE JUST OUTSIDE THE ENTRANCE TO the cave, leaving their prisoners next to it for warmth while Bravo and Ali searched for the boulder. When they finally found it, they were surprised at how readily it moved, revealing the treasures hidden underneath—a dead, no-brand flip phone, a pile of loose beads, and the copper tube.

"The Veronica," Bravo said in a reverential tone. "The cloth used to wipe Christ's brow on his way to the Crucifixion. A holy relic from the earliest days of Christianity."

"An ancient holy relic," Ali agreed. "Along with a modern burner phone."

"Kind of emblematic of how the world works nowadays." Bravo rolled the tube, examining it closely. "Amazing craftsmanship. It had to be to ensure the veil's survival over the centuries."

"Are you going to open it here?" she asked.

"Absolutely not."

He shoved the quiverlike tube into his backpack. "The veil is more than two thousand years old. It will need to be opened by a professional, under the most controlled of circumstances."

"Inside the Vatican?" she asked.

He shook his head. "Not until we've established what it is."

"And your prisoners?"

"They'll be handled."

"Murdered, you mean?"

"No. We'll give them a chance to tell us what they know."

"Tortured then?"

He smiled. "We're the good guys, remember?"

"Sometimes it's hard to tell. But still no cops?"

"Not our style."

"What about the two men you lost?"

"If the Knights tells us where they are, we'll arrange for a proper burial."

"If not?"

He shrugged and said nothing.

He'd earlier sent a text to the men he'd brought to Flagstaff as backup, the ones last seen following the part of the extramuros team that had come to the hospital. With the backup agents on their way, and before Ali and Bravo had launched their search, Leland had offered to hike back down to the end of the road to guide the new arrivals back to the cavern. By the time Leland returned, the snow had stopped falling. Bravo and Ali were sitting outside the cave, huddled next to the fire, keeping it going.

His men dealt with the prisoners, who were starting to come around.

Leland deposited the picnic hamper in a spot near the fire and then settled down next to it. "Since I went to the trouble of preparing this food, we're going to sit here and eat it before we hike back down the mountain. Now, would anyone care for a Cornish pasty?"

•◆•

SIX WEEKS LATER, SISTER ANSELM BECKER SAT BY THE GAS-BURNING log fire at the newly remodeled St. Bernadette's Convent in Jerome while another fierce snowstorm, the third of the season, swirled outside.

It was almost Christmas.

She was glad to be home and warm on this cold and windy night.

When her phone rang with Bishop Gillespie's distinctive ring, she was sure she was about to be summoned to some poor soul's bedside.

"No," the bishop said. "No call-out tonight. At least not so far, but I've just had a fascinating conversation with Bravo Shaw."

Sister Anselm had never taken to the man she still insisted on referring to as Father Shaw. He claimed to be a Franciscan, and she was determined to have him live by those words.

"What did he have to say for himself?" she asked, not bothering to conceal the disapproval in her voice.

"They opened the sealed quiver earlier this afternoon. What they found inside wasn't the Veil of Saint Veronica."

"I knew it," she declared. "The whole thing was a fake from beginning to end, just like all the others."

"It's not exactly a fake," the bishop said. "It's cloth all right—fragments of cloth—but it turns out the fragments are from something even more valuable than the veil. It contains seven tiny words written in Phoenician glyphs."

"What difference does that make?"

"It means," he said, "rather than coming from the time of Christ, it may be much older than that. In addition to the glyphs there appears to be the seal of King Solomon inconspicuously woven into one corner."

She was nothing short of astonished.

"In this instance," the bishop said, with a smile she could hear in his voice, "it seems we've encountered something that is both fake and real at the same time. I also believe that Bravo Shaw and his associates will see to it that those fragments end up where they belong."

"You're saying I misjudged the man?"

"I believe so."

He chuckled.

"Sister Anselm wrong? I'm marking that down on the calendar. As far as I know this is a singular occurrence."

AUTHOR BIOGRAPHIES

LARA ADRIAN is the author of more than twenty-five novels, including the Midnight Breed vampire romance series, with nearly four million books in print worldwide. She also writes as Tina St. John, where her historical romances have won numerous awards including the National Readers Choice, the *Romantic Times Magazine* Reviewer's Choice, and the Booksellers Best. All her novels regularly appear in the top spots of all the major bestseller lists. She lives in Florida. To learn more, visit laradrian.com.

STEVE BERRY is the *New York Times* and #1 internationally bestselling author of twelve Cotton Malone adventures and four stand-alone thrillers. His books have been translated into forty languages with more than twenty-one million copies in fifty-one countries. He's a member of the Smithsonian Institution Libraries Advisory Board and a founding member of International Thriller Writers—a group of more than thirty-eight hundred thriller writers from around the world—serving three years as its copresident. Find out more at steveberry.org.

C. J. BOX is the #1 *New York Times* bestselling author of twenty-three novels including the Joe Pickett series. He won the Edgar Allan Poe Award for

Best Novel in 2009, as well as the Anthony Award, Prix Calibre 38 (France), the Macavity Award, the Gumshoe Award, Barry Award, and the Western Heritage Award for Literature. His novels have been translated into twenty-seven languages. Four have been optioned for film and television. He's an avid outdoorsman and lives with his wife, Laurie, on a ranch in Wyoming. His website is cjbox.net.

SANDRA BROWN is the author of sixty-seven *New York Times* best sellers. She has upward of eighty million copies of her books in print worldwide. She holds an honorary doctorate of humane letters from Texas Christian University, where she and her husband Michael Brown, have instituted an annual scholarship. She has served as president of Mystery Writers of America, and in 2008 was named a Thrillermaster, the top award given by International Thriller Writers. In 2011, she participated in a USO tour of thriller writers to Afghanistan. Lots more can be found at sandrabrown.net.

LEE CHILD was born in Coventry, England, but spent his formative years in the nearby city of Birmingham. In 1995, at the age of forty, as a result of being fired during a corporate restructuring, he decided to see an opportunity where others might have seen a crisis. So he bought six dollars' worth of paper and pencils and sat down to write *Killing Floor,* the first in the Jack Reacher series. Now there are tens of millions of Reacher novels across the globe in too many languages to count, and two major motion pictures involving the character. He divides his time between Manhattan, France, and England. Check him out at leechild.com.

NELSON DeMILLE spent three years at Hofstra University, then joined the army and saw action as an infantry platoon leader in Vietnam, where he earned the Air Medal, Bronze Star, and the Vietnamese Cross of Gallantry. His first major novel was *By the Rivers of Babylon,* published in 1978. There have been many more since, most #1 *New York Times* best sellers. He is a past president of Mystery Writers of America and was named Thrillermaster by International Thriller Writers in 2015. He holds three honorary degrees: doctor of humane letters from Hofstra University, doctor of literature from Long Island University, and doctor of humane letters from Dowling College. He lives on Long Island, New York, with his wife and son. For more, visit nelsondemille.net.

DIANA GABALDON holds degrees in zoology, marine biology, a PhD in quantitative behavioral ecology, and an honorary doctorate in humane letters. She spent a dozen years as a university professor before venturing into novel writing, creating the phenomenally successful Outlander series, which is published in forty-two countries and thirty-eight languages. It is also a hugely popular television series on the Starz network. She lives in Scottsdale, Arizona, with her husband. Her website is dianagabaldon .com.

ANDREW GROSS majored in English at Middlebury College. After earning an MBA from Columbia University, he first worked at the Leslie Fay Companies, a women's clothing firm started by his grandfather, then went into the sports apparel field. Eventually, he followed his dream and started writing. Ultimately, he became the author of fourteen *New York Times* bestselling thrillers, five cowriting with James Patterson and nine on his own. His books are now sold in over twenty-five countries. His latest, *One Man,* is a World War II thriller built on his own family's history. He lives in Westchester County, New York, with his wife. Find out more at andrew grossbooks.com.

CHARLAINE HARRIS was born and raised in the Mississippi River Delta. First published in 1981, she was firmly embedded in the mystery genre before branching out into new territory. Starting with the premise of a young woman with a disability who wants to try interspecies dating, she created the Sookie Stackhouse urban fantasy series. The first book in the series, *Dead Until Dark,* won the Anthony Award for Best Paperback Mystery in 2001. The series, which ended in 2013, ultimately found readers in over thirty languages and became the HBO series *True Blood.* She lives in central Texas with her husband and, when not writing, takes care of a house full of rescue dogs. Learn more at charlaineharris.com.

LISA JACKSON is the #1 *New York Times* bestselling author of more than eighty-five thrillers. Before being published Lisa was a mother struggling to keep food on the table by writing novels, hoping that somebody would pay her for one of them. Eventually, that hope became a wonderful reality. Today, she's neck deep in murder with over twenty million copies of her books worldwide. Learn more about her at lisajackson.com.

PETER JAMES is a bit of a rebel. In 1994, Penguin published his book *Host* on two floppy disks. Those disks are now in a London museum as the world's first electronic novel. He is the author of twenty-eight novels with over seventeen million books worldwide. His list of awards is staggering. He's also a self-confessed "petrol head," at one time or another owning four Aston Martins, an AMG, a Brabus Mercedes, a Bentley Continental GT Speed, and two classic Jaguar E-Types. He still maintains an international racing license and divides his time between a country home near Brighton, Sussex, and his apartment in Notting Hill, London. To learn more, check out peterjames.com.

J.A. JANCE was introduced to Frank Baum's Oz books as a second-grader. After reading the first book she was hooked, knowing from that moment on she wanted to be a writer. She published the first Detective J. P. Beaumont adventure, *Until Proven Guilty*, in 1985. Since then there have been twenty-one more Beaumont books. Two other series have joined the Beaumont collection, one with Arizona County Sheriff Joanna Brady and the other with a former Los Angeles news anchor turned mystery solver, Ali Reynolds. She divides her time between Bellevue, Washington, and Arizona. All things about her can be learned at jajance.com.

MICHAEL KORYTA is the author of eleven *New York Times* bestselling thrillers. Before turning to writing, he worked as a private investigator and a newspaper reporter, then taught at the Indiana University School of Journalism. His first novel, the Edgar-nominated *Tonight I Said Goodbye,* was accepted for publication when he was only twenty years old. He wrote his first two novels before graduating from college and was published in nearly ten languages before he fulfilled the "writing requirement" classes required for his diploma. He lives in Indiana with his wife, Christine, a cranky cat named Marlowe, an emotionally disturbed cat named John Pryor, and an exceedingly athletic dog of unknown heritage named Lola. For more check out michaelkoryta.com.

ERIC VAN LUSTBADER published his first international best seller, *The Ninja,* in 1980. Since then he's written more than twenty-five bestselling books, which include not only his own works, but, a continuation of the famed Jason Bourne series. His work has been translated into over twenty languages. Before turning to writing full-time, he enjoyed highly successful careers in the New York City public school system, where he still holds licenses in both elementary and early childhood education, and in the music business, where he worked for Elektra Records and CBS Records. He lives in both New York City and Long Island. Find out more at ericvanlustbader.com.

GAYLE LYNDS is the *New York Times* bestselling, award-winning author of ten espionage novels, including *The Assassins, The Book of Spies,* and *The Last Spymaster.* Her career began oddly—with short stories published in literary journals while at the same time writing male pulp fiction. After that, her first novel, *Masquerade,* was listed by *Publishers Weekly* among the top ten spy novels of all time. Still focusing on suspense and geopolitics today, she's hailed by *Library Journal* as "the reigning queen of espionage fiction." With Robert Ludlum, she created the Covert-One series. A member of the Association of Former Intelligence Officers, she cofounded International Thriller Writers with David Morrell in 2004. She lives with her husband in Maine. Get all the details at www.GayleLynds.com.

VAL McDERMID didn't have the practical skills to make a success of writing stage drama, and her first agent did nothing to help her acquire them. Instead, he fired her as a client. That's when she turned to crime writing (thrillers, on this side of the pond), a genre she'd always enjoyed reading. She started writing *Report for Murder* in 1984, but the book wasn't published until 1987. Thirty-five more novels have followed (look who got the last laugh on that inconsiderate agent). She splits her year between writing and promoting, living in South Manchester and Edinburgh. To learn more visit valmcdermid.com.

DAVID MORRELL was a mild-mannered college professor when he wrote a novel called *First Blood* (1972), a story about a Vietnam veteran suffering from posttraumatic stress disorder who comes into conflict with a small-town police chief, the two fighting their own version of the Vietnam War. That troubled veteran was named Rambo. He went on to write many more *New York Times* bestselling thrillers, including the classic spy trilogy *The Brotherhood of the Rose, The Fraternity of the Stone,* and *The League of Night and Fog.* Lately, he's been exploring 1850s Victorian London in his Thomas De Quincey series. With Gayle Lynds, in 2005, he cofounded International Thriller Writers. He lives with his wife in New Mexico. To explore more, visit davidmorrell.net.

KATHY REICHS is actually Dr. Kathy Reichs, one of only eighty-two forensic anthropologists ever certified by the American Board of Forensic Anthropology. For years she consulted to the Office of the Chief Medical Examiner in North Carolina, and she continues to do so for the Laboratoire de Sciences Judiciaires et de Médecine Légale in the province of Québec. Her first novel, *Déjà Dead,* became a *New York Times* best seller. There have been twenty-three Temperance Brennan novels since, most #1 *New York Times* best sellers. The hit Fox TV series *Bones* is based on her books. She divides her time between Charlotte, North Carolina, and Montreal, Québec. All things Kathy Reichs can be learned at kathyreichs.com.

CHRISTOPHER RICE wrote four *New York Times* bestselling thrillers, received a Lambda Literary Award, and was declared one of *People* magazine's Sexiest Men Alive—and all before he was thirty years old. His debut novel, *A Density of Souls,* was published when he was but twenty-two. It became both a controversial and overnight best seller, greeted with a landslide of media attention, much of it devoted to the fact that he is the son of famed vampire chronicler, Anne Rice. Nowadays, with his best friend, *New York Times* bestselling novelist Eric Shaw Quinn, he has his own Internet radio show. You can download, or stream, every episode at TheDinnerParty Show.com. For more on Chris visit christopherricebooks.com.

JOHN SANDFORD is the pseudonym of John Roswell Camp, who won the Pulitzer Prize for journalism in 1986. He is the author of forty published novels, all of which have appeared on the *New York Times* bestseller lists, most in the #1 slot. He is also the coauthor of three young adult books with his wife, Michele Cook, and coauthor of the science fiction thriller *Saturn Run* with Ctein. The past is one of his passions, and he is the principal financial backer of the Beth-Shean Valley Archaeological Project in the Jordan River Valley of Israel (with a website at rehov.org.). He has homes in Santa Fe, New Mexico, and in the countryside near Hayward, Wisconsin. Learn more at johnsandford.org.

LISA SCOTTOLINE is an Edgar Award winner and *New York Times* bestselling author of suspense fiction. She also writes a humorous nonfiction series with her daughter Francesca Serritella, which began with *Why My Third Husband Will Be a Dog*. She has served as president of Mystery Writers of America and has over thirty million copies of her books in print, published in over thirty-five countries. She lives in the Philadelphia area with an array of disobedient pets. Get better acquainted with her at scottoline .com.

KARIN SLAUGHTER is the New York Times and #1 internationally bestselling author of sixteen novels and countless short stories (they could actually be counted, but she's too lazy). Her work has been translated into thirty-five languages and has sold nearly forty million copies. She enjoys running and not running. She once swam with sharks in Australia, went weightless in the zero-g Vomit Comet, jumped naked into the Baltic after a bracing sauna in Finland, and plans to enter the suborbital space program once stuff reliably stops blowing up. She lives in Atlanta, Georgia, and divides her time between the kitchen and the living room. Learn more at karinslaughter.com.

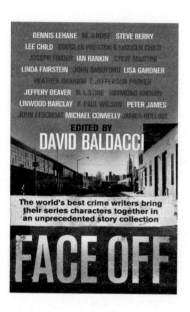

The first collaborative ITW anthology, *Face Off*
includes the meeting of Ian Rankin's Rebus and Peter
James' Roy Grace; a case for Dennis Lehane's Patrick
Kenzie and Michael Connelly's Harry Bosch, and a page-
turning mystery starring Lee Child's Jack Reacher
and Joseph Finder's Nick Heller.

Edited by international bestseller David Baldacci,
this page-turning collection is a must for crime fans
and a brilliant companion to *Match Up*.